W9-BYF-500

BRITANNIA'S FIST

OTHER BOOKS BY PETER G. TSOURAS

Alexander the Great: Invincible King of Macedonia
*The Anvil of War: German Generalship in the Defense on
the Eastern Front* (editor)
Battle of the Bulge: Hitler's Alternate Strategies (editor/contributor)
The Book of Military Quotations (editor)
Changing Orders: The Evolution of the World's Armies, 1945 to Present
Cold War Hot: Alternate Histories of the Cold War (editor/contributor)
The Daily Telegraph Book of Military Quotations (editor)
Disaster at D-Day: The Germans Defeat the Allies, June 1944
Dixie Victorious: An Alternate History of the Civil War
(editor/contributor)
Encyclopedia of the U.S. Army (co-editor with Bruce W. Watson)
Fighting in Hell: The German Ordeal on the Eastern Front (editor)
Gettysburg: An Alternate History
The Great Patriotic War
The Greenhill Dictionary of Military Quotations (editor)
Hitler Triumphant: Alternate Strategies of World War II
(editor/contributor)
Military Lessons of the Gulf War
(co-editor with Bruce W. Watson/contributor)
*Military Quotations from the Civil War: In the Words of
the Commanders* (editor)
Montezuma: Warlord of the Aztecs
Operation Just Cause: The Invasion of Panama
(co-editor with Bruce W. Watson)
*Panzer Operations on the Eastern Front: General Erhard Raus and
his Panzer Divisions in Russia* (editor/contributor)
Rising Sun Victorious: How Japan Won the Pacific War
(editor/contributor)
Third Reich Victorious: How Germany Won the War
(editor/contributor)
Warlords of the Ancient Americas: Mesoamerica
Warriors' Words: A Quotation Book (editor)

BRITANNIA'S FIST

From Civil War to World War

AN ALTERNATE HISTORY

PETER G. TSOURAS

THE BRITANNIA'S FIST TRILOGY
VOLUME 1

POTOMAC BOOKS, INC.
WASHINGTON, D.C.

Published in the United States by Potomac Books, Inc. All rights reserved.
No part of this book may be reproduced in any manner whatsoever without
written permission from the publisher, except in the case of brief quotations
embodied in critical articles and reviews.

Library of Congress Cataloging-in-Publication Data

Tsouras, Peter.
  Britannia's fist : from Civil War to World War — an alternate history / by Peter
G. Tsouras. — 1st ed.
     v. cm. — (The Britannia's fist trilogy ; v. 1)
  Includes bibliographical references.
  ISBN 978-1-57488-823-2 (hardcover : alk. paper)
  1. United States — History — Civil War, 1861–1865. 2. United States — History —
1865–1921. 3. United States — Foreign relations — Great Britain. 4. Great Britain —
Foreign relations — United States. 5. Imaginary histories. I. Title. II. Title: From
Civil War to World War — an alternate history.
  E661.T83 2008
  973.7 — dc22

                                             2008021576

Printed in the United States of America on acid-free paper that meets
the American National Standards Institute Z39-48 Standard.

Potomac Books, Inc.
22841 Quicksilver Drive
Dulles, Virginia 20166

First Edition

10 9 8 7 6 5 4 3 2

To the honored memory of Maj. Gen. George H. Sharpe,

the Civil War founder of

American All-Source Intelligence

CONTENTS

INTRODUCTION

The Anglo-American War of 1863 that ignited the Great War, which, in turn, dragged in all the great powers and nearly ruined Western civilization is a tale never before told—for the simple fact that it never happened. The Four Horsemen paused at that crossroads, and War leaned forward over his black charger and looked longingly in that direction. But history pulled the dreaded four in another direction, and this path not taken still shimmers like a mirage of what might have been.

ALTERNATE HISTORY

For many historians, their field of study moves under the pressure of great causes and betrays the taint of too close an affection for the idiocies of Karl Marx and his disciples. History all too often pivots on great or petty men, mixed signals, lost letters, spite, nobility, greed, and sacrifice, as much as it does on the great transformations produced by sharp bronze, the industrial age, democracy, and the sublime message of a Galilean rabbi. Two centuries ago, Samuel Johnson had already put his finger on it.

> It seems to be almost the universal error of historians to suppose it politically, as it is physically true, that every effort has proportionate cause. In the inanimate action of matter upon matter, the motion produced can be but equal to the force of the moving power; but the operations of life, whether private or publick, admit no such laws. The caprices of voluntary agents laugh at calculations. It is not always that there is a strong reason for a great event. Obstinacy and flexibility, malignity and kindness, give place alternately to each other,

and the reason of these vicissitudes, however important may
be the consequences, often escapes the mind in which the
changes are made.[1]

The British Empire and the United States were not fated to go to
war. Almost no one in positions of responsibility on both sides of the
ocean wanted war, and if you had polled each country, the vote against a
third cousin's war would have been overwhelming, but "the caprices of
voluntary agents" came very close to making just that happen. This then
is an alternate history of just such a cataclysmic war.

BACKGROUND

Before going down this tale of a path not taken, it is important to review
the path that history actually took. Great Britain and the United States
came alarmingly close to war twice during the American Civil War. In
both cases, war with the British Empire, like the Angel of Death, passed
the embattled Union by. In each case, the French jackal, Napoleon III,
was eager to follow the British lion into war. The first case, the Trent
Affair, set the stage for the second pass at war—the Laird rams. In both
cases, cooler heads eventually prevailed, and the crises were resolved.
However, the margin was paper-thin.

On November 8, 1861, Capt. Charles Wilkes of the USS *San Jacinto*
stopped the British mail steamer, RMS *Trent*, which had just departed
Havana. Wilkes seized two Confederate diplomats, John Slidell, minister to Great Britain, and James Mason, minister to France, over the protest of the *Trent*'s captain. The British prime minister, Lord Palmerston,
stated upon hearing the news, "I don't know whether you are going to
stand this, but I'll be damned if I do." The cabinet was fully prepared to
go to war over this affront to British honor and what they saw as a clear
violation of international law. The Royal Navy and British Army quickly
developed war plans that as a member of the cabinet stated would iron
the smile off the American face. The object was to inflict enough damage on the United States to serve as a salutary lesson. That such a lesson
would also ensure the independence of the Southern Confederacy was
something that the British government, "society," and business circles
looked forward to with undisguised glee. The American experiment in
participatory democracy and the American character, especially that of
the Northern people, were equally detested. The aristocratic society of
the South was far more congenial and sympathetic to the British estab-

lishment. That establishment found itself, on this issue, on the horns of a dilemma. All of British society was united in its distaste for slavery. A crippling blow against the North would perpetuate that institution in the South. The cabinet attempted to finesse the problem by splitting the issues. While going to war with the United States, it would not cooperate with the Confederacy in that war. It was a fine point that did not impress the rest of British society, the lower and middle classes, whose opposition to slavery and support for increased democracy at home saw the Union not as an enemy but as an example. Over time, the success of the American Union was seen as a mighty impetus to domestic British reforms to increase the franchise. Nevertheless, the Trent Affair blew so hot that these considerations had no time to become politically important.

The war plan called for the Royal Navy's North American and West Indies Station to be heavily reinforced. Its commander, Adm. Alexander Milne, proposed to break the blockade at Charleston, decisively engage the U.S. Navy, blockade the North, dominate the Chesapeake Bay, and strike at Washington by coming up the Potomac River.

The Army's plan concentrated on the defense of British North America, which at that time consisted of the Maritime Provinces, Lower Canada (Quebec), and Upper Canada (Ontario). A spoiling attack down the Hudson Valley was developed to protect Kingston, Montreal, and Quebec from an American attack along this traditional invasion route. A more aggressive element was the seizure of the state of Maine. Geographically, Maine juts between the Maritimes and Quebec. Because of that, rail communications between the Maritimes and the Canadas ran from Hailfax in Nova Scotia through New Brunswick to Portland, Maine, and then up to Sherbrooke in Quebec and beyond. This Grand Trunk Railway was the first international rail system, and the control of it was vital to the survival of British North America. Without it, reinforcements and supplies could not reach the Canadas. In addition, some genius at the British War Office concluded that the people of Maine, to whom making money was the primary consideration, were so disillusioned with the war that they would gladly leave the Union and just as gladly join the British Empire. To implement these plans, more than ten thousand reinforcements were immediately dispatched with several times that number planned to follow. Among the arrivals was Lt. Col. Garnet Wolseley, who would eventually become Field Marshal Viscount Wolseley, the most celebrated of all British generals of the Victorian Age.

With all this in mind Palmerston wrote a blistering ultimatum. Fortunately, the prince consort, Alfred Albert, toned it down. At the same time, despite the immensely popularity of Wilkes's deed in the North, President Abraham Lincoln and Secretary of State William Seward knew they had to give in. A major financial crisis had struck the Northern states. At this point, the imperial Russian government stepped in to offer invaluable diplomatic advice. It clearly stated that Wilkes's action had, indeed, been a violation of international law. Lincoln and Seward fully appreciated the Russians' goodwill and diplomatic experience. The United States and the Russian Empire had been on the friendliest terms since the American Revolution when Catherine the Great refused the British request to hire mercenaries by saying, "My subjects are not for sale." She then formed the League of Armed Neutrality to defy British attempts to close down American trade with the rest of the world. Since then Russia and America had had no strategic conflicts and found much in common in the development and peopling of vast open continents. The Russians had a deeper motive, however, in supporting the United States. They had been so badly drubbed in the Crimean War by British strategic reach and power that they had come to fear British world hegemony. They saw the survival of the American Union as the only real counter to that eventuality.

Lincoln swallowed his pride and gave in to the British ultimatum to release the diplomats but ignored the other demand to offer an apology. He had no other choice but to back down. The North was in the throes of a painful mobilization and was suffering repeated reverses at Southern hands. If it could not subdue the South with less than one-third of its population and barely 10 percent of the country's industrial base, it was a reasonable question to ask how it could hope to prevail against the immense power of the British Empire, which had so frightened the Russian bear.

Twenty-one months were to pass until war nearly boiled over again in September 1863. The casus belli for the Union was the construction and delivery of one commerce raider after another to the Confederacy from British shipyards. These ships were lethal to the American merchant marine. American-owned and operated merchant shipping was competing with the British everywhere around the world for the vast market of the international carrying trade. The Confederate commerce raiders destroyed more than six hundred ships and drove far more to take foreign flags or to be sold outright to foreign, usually British, interests. The level of anger in the North over these depredations stoked white hot at the British, whose Foreign Enlistment Act seemed useless in enforcing the Queen's neutrality. Worse than the abundant loopholes in the act was the outright connivance of British officials and courts in giving it the most liberal interpretation that always seemed to be in the interests of the Confederacy.

In 1862 the issue was already serious enough for the U.S. government through its able ambassador, Charles Francis Adams, to put enough pressure on the British government to stop the construction of the commerce raider Number 292 being built by the Laird Brothers in Birkenhead across the Mersey River from Liverpool. But a Confederate sympathizer in the Foreign Office warned the Confederate agent in Britain, James Bulloch. Recent speculation as to the source of this warning has centered on Austin David Layard, member of Parliament and undersecretary to Lord John Russell at the Foreign Office.[2] As a result, Number 292 was taken out of port on a trial run for which it did not need the permission of the customs officer of the port. Number 292 just kept on going. It was renamed the CSS *Alabama* and married up in the Azores with its guns, stores, and crew, most of whom were former Royal Navy seamen. The names CSS *Alabama, Florida*, and *Shenandoah* struck terror to any ship that carried the merchant ensign of the United States.

Twinned with what the Northern people saw as British collusion to attack American shipping, British free trade policies encouraged British shippers to make immense profits running war supplies and luxuries to the Confederacy through the Union blockade of Southern ports. Despite an increasingly effective blockade, huge amounts of British-made war materials continued to reach Confederate armies. Gen. Ulysses S. Grant was particularly incensed. He noted in his memoirs that the Confederate Army that surrendered at Vicksburg was uniformly armed with superior British Enfield rifles compared to the antiquated firearms his own men were using. During the siege of Petersburg in late 1864, he forwarded to the War Department shells bearing the stamps of royal arsenals. It was natural, then, for Northern public opinion to see a malevolent hand in British actions.

What neither public opinion, Ambassador Adams, nor Secretary of State Seward realized was that the British Foreign Secretary, Lord Russell, was the major advocate in the cabinet for military intervention in the American Civil War to force an armistice. Such an armistice would result in de facto Southern independence. The Americans were convinced that Lord Palmerston was the one beating the drum for war, but, in fact, he was the calming hand on Russell. Russia also consistently opposed efforts by Palmerston to enlist it and other European powers in imposing mediation by force.[3]

All through the winter, spring, and summer of 1863 American interest focused on the two new hulls, Number 294 and Number 295, being built for the Confederacy by the Laird Brothers. They were double-turreted armored iron ships, the first such built in British yards. Heretofore, all British armored ships had been broadside ironclads. What made these hulls even more unique was that they were fitted with rams, much like ancient triremes, to smash a hole in another warship. The ships' overall powers were advertised as being able to outfight anything in the U.S. Navy and being capable of raiding at will Northern ports. That threat was taken with the greatest seriousness, and the tension rose month by month in Washington as the U.S. consul in Liverpool, Thomas Haines Dudley, reported the progress of their building. That tension became even more excruciating as Lord Russell turned down every representation of overwhelming evidence as being insufficient proof necessary to halt the delivery of the ships. Secretary of State Seward recommended that a warship be dispatched to British waters to intercept the rams once they left port. Secretary of the Navy Gideon Welles turned him down, stating that every ship was needed to maintain the blockade.

Ever since the Trent Affair, Lincoln had strictly followed a policy of "one war at a time," in full knowledge that the Union had its hands full with the Confederacy.[4] That is why it could do no more than offer moral support to the deposed government of Mexico in the face of a blatant French conquest. But even this policy had to be set aside as the losses to American commerce on the high seas became intolerable as did the threat of the Laird rams.

Finally, Lincoln instructed Adams to draw a red line for the British beyond which was war. On September 5, a desperate Adams penned one last remonstration to Russell and ended it with the statement that if the rams escaped, "it would be superfluous in me to point out to your Lordship that this is war." It is arguably the most famous line in the history of American diplomacy.[5] Adams was unaware that Lord Russell had finally come around to the danger of taking no action and had informed Palmerston of his decision to detain the rams on September 4. The weight of evidence had finally brought Russell around. However, Adams was not informed of this decision until September 8, due in part to the Layard's inexplicable delays in the notification of critical parties.

Layard did act with considerable dispatch, though only after the receipt of Adams's last notes, by notifying the British embassy in Washington that instructions had been given to detain the rams.[6]

Interestingly, Russian and American interests crossed paths again at this time. In January of that year the Poles had risen in revolt against Czar Alexander II. His armies crushed the revolt with a typical heavy hand. He then abolished the kingdom of Poland whose crown he held. The crown had come to the Romanovs as part of the Treaty of Vienna in 1815, which re-created the Polish state. Britain and France were the guarantors of the treaty and Poland's status. Now they threatened war. Alexander was determined that the Royal Navy would not trap his fleet in its bases as it had been in the Crimean War. He dispatched a strong squadron of the Baltic Fleet to New York and the Pacific Squadron to San Francisco, so that in case of war they could issue from neutral ports to savage British and French commerce on the high seas.

The Laird rams affair was a close-run thing. But this time, unlike the Trent Affair, the United States was in a much better position if war came. The Confederacy had suffered twin catastrophes at Vicksburg and Gettysburg in July of that year. The Union armies were no longer armed mobs but veterans commanded by increasingly talented leaders. The Union Navy won no comparable dramatic victories but was slowly strangling the South with the blockade. More important, the Navy was riding a technological wave with the development and commissioning of its turreted armored warships of the monitor type. Of equal importance was the Navy's powerful armament, the various calibers of the Dahlgren gun, developed by Adm. John A. Dahlgren, the father of American naval ordnance. Although they were muzzle-loading weapons at the dawn of the breech-loading age, they were the finest and more destructive guns in the world and outclassed anything the British had in reliability and destructiveness.

The U.S. Army's efforts at similar innovation, however, were much less successful, despite the Civil War's reputation as being the nursery of military technology. The Army's story, unfortunately, was one of repeated lost opportunities. The Army simply did not have the structure to field new technology, develop doctrine, devise tactics, and integrate these with the armies in the field. Worse was the outright sabotage of the Army's Chief of the Ordnance Bureau, Col. James Ripley, who had a determined phobia of "newfangled gimcracks," such as breech-loading and repeating firearms, not to mention the first machine guns.

Lincoln was as open minded and visionary as Ripley was close minded and reactionary. It was because of Lincoln that the Balloon Corps entered the Army of the Potomac, where, by the battle of Chancellorsville, it was providing real-time intelligence to the Union commander. Lincoln was behind another innovation, the coffee mill gun, the first machine gun, which he personally ordered, bypassing Ripley. But Lincoln could not be everywhere and do everything. The Balloon Corps simply withered away when its founding genius, Prof. Thaddeus Lowe, was driven out of the Army by an officious captain set over him by senior officers jealous of his civilian pay. Ripley similarly sidelined the coffee mill guns and made sure those that were ordered ended up carefully stored and forgotten in the Washington Arsenal. Despite repeated remonstrations and indications of presidential approval, Ripley simply refused to order repeating weapons despite overwhelming evidence in the field of their effectiveness. If he was finally pressed by a presidential order, he made sure the fine print negated Lincoln's intent. Secretary of War Edwin Stanton finally fired Ripley in September. By then, the production of the standard muzzle-loading firearms was meeting the demands of the huge Army.

Although repeating weapons were subsequently bought in large numbers for several mounted infantry brigades and proved dramatically successful in combat, there never was an attempt to reequip any of the armies in the field. Thus, the opportunity to go into battle with a seven-to-one fire superiority in the clash of field armies was never attempted. Not even legendary Southern valor could withstand the storm that would have ensured that there was no second round.

Nevertheless, at a time when the armies of the Confederacy had fought the Union to a standstill, war with the British Empire and France would have been a momentous step. A betting man would not have given the United States decent odds. The population of the United Kingdom was equal to that of the Northern states while that of France was 50 percent larger. British industrial production outweighed the Americans' considerably, and the Royal Navy was significantly larger and stronger than the U.S. Navy. In a war, the United States could count on being isolated from the rest of the world and losing access to imports and money markets. Falling on the scales to balance these weaknesses was the vulnerability of British North America, a factor that obsessed the British and prompted the hurried reinforcement during the Trent Affair. American invasions of 1776 and 1812 had been with weak forces.

This time that would not be a problem as the Union armies now numbered in the many hundreds of thousands.

This alternate history pivots on the failure of the British Foreign Office to take seriously the protests of the United States over the Laird rams, which leads to war. Besides playing out the clash of armies and fleets, a significant element is the story of the acceleration of stymied military technology under the intense pressure of what will become for the Union total war.

THE PROTAGONISTS

The story is told largely through two characters—Brig. Gen. George H. Sharpe and Lt. Col. Garnet Wolseley. Their real lives were remarkable enough. Sharpe was the intelligence officer for the Army of the Potomac and would later rise to fill that function for Grant. Sharpe was a natural intelligence officer. He had probably received the finest education in North America, had trained the logic of his mind at Yale Law School, had traveled widely, served as the chargé at the embassy in Vienna, and was fluent in French. He was a sophisticated, thoughtful, and wily man. His contributions at Gettysburg and beyond gave the Union the vital edge in winning the war in the Eastern Theater. By the second night of the battle at Gettysburg he was able to report to Maj. Gen. George Meade that his staff had identified every regiment of the Army of Northern Virginia having been committed except those in Gen. George Pickett's division. It was a priceless piece of intelligence that helped steel Meade's resolve to fight it out. The raid he instigated to seize Jefferson Davis's dispatches to Gen. Robert E. Lee added additional priceless operational and strategic intelligence. Sharpe had created the first all-source intelligence organization in military history, but tragically in its postwar penury the Army failed to institutionalize that achievement. All-source intelligence would only be reborn in World War I on the French model.

Wolseley was a rising star of the British Army who had lost an eye in Burma and won renown in the Crimea, in the suppression of the Great Mutiny in India, and in the punitive expedition against China in 1859. He had been sent out to Canada as part of the reinforcement triggered by the Trent Affair. He would later rise to be the greatest of Victoria's generals, aided in no small part by the talent of surrounding himself with talented subordinates. In a famous escapade in 1862 he took leave to the United States, slipped through Union lines, and introduced himself to Robert E. Lee, for whom he developed a lifelong case of hero worship.

He had an intense dislike for Americans of the Yankee type, almost as virulent as his contempt for the Irish. He was in favor of war with the United States to ensure Southern independence in order to cripple America's future potential to contest British power. For all that he was a man of rare military insight and organizational ability. Luckily for everyone, he would spend the rest of his tour in Canada, fishing, hunting, and chasing pretty Canadian girls.

All the rest of the crowded cast of characters, save a handful of fictionalized individuals, are real people who walked the stage of history.

ACKNOWLEDGMENTS

I would like to thank Professor Wade Dudley, East Carolina University, for his meticulous review of the manuscript of this book, and Professor Steven Badsey, formerly of the Royal Military Academy Sandhurst, for his advice in the development of this story. Not least, I would like to acknowledge Thomas Bilbao for serving as a sounding board with his exhaustive knowledge of military history.

MAPS

DRAMATIS PERSONAE

Adams, Charles Francis, Jr. Captain, U.S. Volunteers, 5th Massachusetts Cavalry, and son of Ambassador Charles Francis Adams.

Adams, Charles Francis, Sr., U.S. Ambassador to the Court of St. James, son of President John Quincy Adams and grandson of President John Adams.

Adams, Henry. Private secretary to and son of Ambassador Charles Francis Adams.

Alfred Ernest Albert, His Royal Highness. Lieutenant, Royal Navy (RN), aboard HMS *Racoon*, the 19-year-old second son of Queen Victoria and Prince Albert.

Babcock, John C. Civilian order-of-battle analyst and Assistant Director, Bureau of Military Information (BMI), Headquarters, Army of the Potomac.

Baker, Lafayette. Director of the Secret Service of the War Department.

Bazaine, François Achille. Major General, French Imperial Army, Commander, French Forces in Mexico and of the Texas Expedition in support of the Confederacy.

Bazalgette, George. Captain, Royal Marine Light Infantry.

Beauregard, Pierre Gustave Toutant de. General, C.S. Army, commander of the coastal defenses of South Carolina and Georgia.

Berdan, Hiram. Colonel, U.S. Volunteers, Commander, Rifle Regiment.

Bowles, Dr. William. A leader of the Copperhead conspiracy in Indiana.

Bragg, Braxton. General, C.S. Army, Commander, Army of Tennessee.

Bright, John. Member of Parliament and advocate of the Union, derisively referred to as the "Member for America."

Bulloch, James Dunwoody. Captain, C.S. Navy, and chief Confederate agent in the United Kingdom.

Callaway, James E. Major, U.S. Volunteers, 21st Illinois Volunteer Infantry, assigned to the Army of the Cumberland.

Carnegie, Andrew. Railroad executive, entrepreneur, and organizer of the first train to rush troops to the defense of Washington at the outbreak of the Civil War.

Carrington, Henry B. Colonel, U.S. Volunteers, chief anti-Copperhead intelligence officer in Indiana.

Chamberlain, William Charles. Captain, RN, Commander of HMS *Resistance.*

Chamberlain, Joshua Lawrence. Colonel, U.S. Volunteers, Commander, 1st Brigade, First Battle of Portland.

Clay, Cassius Marcellus. Fiery Kentucky abolitionist and U.S. Ambassador to the Imperial Russian government in St. Petersburg.

Cline, Milton. Major, U.S. Volunteers, 3rd Indiana Cavalry, and senior scout of the Central Information Bureau (CIB).

Cochrane, Hon. Arthur. Captain, RN, flag captain to Rear Admiral Seymour.

Cromwell, J. B. Lieutenant, USN, Commander of USS *Atlanta.*

Dahlgren, John A. Rear Admiral, USN, Commander of the South Atlantic Blockading Squadron.

Dahlgren, Ulric. Colonel, U.S. Volunteers, hero of Gettysburg and son of Admiral Dahlgren.

Dana, Charles. Publisher, U.S. Assistant Secretary of War.

Davis, Jefferson. President of the Confederate States of America.

Dennis, George. Lieutenant Colonel, Canadian Militia, Commander of the Royal Guides.

Dow, Neal. Brigadier General, U.S. Volunteers, the Colonel of 13th Maine Regiment of the Army of the Potomac; sent home on recruiting duty.

Doyle, Sir Hastings. Major General, British Army, commanding Imperial Forces in the Maritime Provinces of British North America.

Dudley, Thomas Haines. U.S. Consul in Liverpool, England.

Fox, Gustavus "Gus." U.S. Assistant Secretary of the Navy, essentially in modern terms, Chief of Naval Operations.

Gorchakov, Aleksandr. Russian Foreign Minister.

Hall, Basil. Lieutenant, Royal Navy, and flag lieutenant to Admiral Milne.

Halleck, Henry Wager. Major General, U.S. Volunteers, General-in-Chief of the Armies.

Hancock, George. Captain, RN, Commander of HMS *Immortalité*, temporarily detached as naval attaché to Lord Lyons, Ambassador to the United States.

Hines, Henry Thomas. Captain, C.S. Army, Morgan's Cavalry Brigade, Army of Tennessee.

Hogan, Martin. Private, U.S. Volunteers, recently arrived young Irish immigrant and scout for the Bureau of Military Information (BMI), Army of the Hudson.

Hooker, Joseph. Major General, U.S. Army, Commander, Army of the Hudson.

Ingraham, Duncan. Captain, C.S. Navy, Commander of the Charleston Naval Station.

Lambert, Rowley. Captain, RN, Commander, HMS *Liverpool*.

Lamson, Roswell Hawks. Lieutenant, USN, Commander, U.S.S. *Nansemond* and *Gettysburg*.

Langely, Charles. Lieutenant Colonel, British Army, Commander of the 1/16th Foot.

Layard, Austin David. Member of Parliament and Undersecretary to Lord Russell at the Foreign Office.

Lee, Robert E. General, C.S. Army, Commander, Army of Northern Virginia.

Lincoln, Abraham. Sixteenth President of the United States.

Lindsay, Hon. James. Major General, British Army, Commander, Brigade of Guards at the battle of Claverack.

Lisovsky, Stefan S. Rear Admiral, Russian Imperial Navy, and Commander of the Baltic Squadron sent to New York City.

Longstreet, James. Lieutenant General, C.S. Army, Commander, First Corps, Army of Northern Virginia.

Lowe, Thaddeus. Scientist, Colonel, U.S. Volunteers, founder and commander of the Balloon Corps.

Lyons, Lord. British Ambassador to the United States.

McCarter, Michael William. Former Sergeant of the Irish Brigade discharged for wounds after Chancellorsville.

McEntee, John. Captain, U.S. Volunteers, Chief, Bureau of Military Information (BMI), Army of the Hudson.

McPhail, James L. Civilian, Provost Marshal of Maryland and later Deputy Chief, Central Information Bureau (CIB).

Meade, George Gordon. Major General, U.S. Volunteers, Commander, Army of the Potomac.

Meagher, Thomas Francis. Major General, U.S. Volunteers, Commander, XI Corps, Army of the Hudson.

Mercier, Edouard-Henri. Imperial French Ambassador to the United States.

Milne, Sir Alexander. Vice Admiral, RN, Commander of the North American and West Indies Station.

*Morgan, George "The Contraband." Body slave to John Hunt Morgan.

Morgan, John Hunt. Colonel, C.S. Army, Commander, Morgan's Cavalry Brigade, Army of Tennessee.

Morton, Oliver. Republican Governor of Indiana.

Paulet, Lord Frederick. Major General, British Army, Commander of the Hudson Field Force in the invasion of New York.

Porter, Benjamin H. Lieutenant, USN, Executive Officer, U.S.S. *Nansemond* and *Gettysburg*.

Rimsky-Korsakov, Nikolai Andreyevich. Ensign, Imperial Russian Navy.

Ripley, James W. Colonel, U.S. Army, Chief, Ordnance Bureau.

Rivers, Pitt. Lieutenant Colonel, British Army, late Assistant Quartermaster of the garrison of Ireland and on detached duty to British North America.

Rosecrans, William "Old Rosy." Major General, U.S. Volunteers, Commander, Army of the Cumberland.

Russell, Lord John. British Foreign Minister.

Scott, Thomas. U.S. Assistant Secretary of War.

Sedgwick, John. Major General, U.S. Volunteers, Commander, VI Corps, Army of the Potomac, and in independent command of the relief of Portland.

Semmes, Raphael. Captain, C.S. Navy, Commander of the C.S.S. *Alabama,* the greatest of the Confederate commerce raiders.

Seward, William H. U.S. Secretary of State.

Seymour, Sir Michael. Rear Admiral, RN, Commander of the squadron sent to destroy the U.S. Navy's South Atlantic Blockading Squadron at Charleston.

Sharpe, George H. Brig. Gen., U.S. Volunteers, Director of the Central Information Bureau (CIB) and Commander of the 120th Regiment, NY Volunteers.

*Smoke, James R. "Big Jim." Chief agent for the Copperhead movement in Indiana.

---

* An asterisk before a name denotes a fictional character.

Stanton, Edwin McMasters. U.S. Secretary of War.

Stidger, Felix. Agent of the War Department among the Copperheads.

St. Ledger, George Grenfell. British military adventurer, late of the C.S. Army.

Stoekel, Baron. Russian ambassador to the United States.

Thomas, George "The Rock of Chickamauga." Major General, U.S. Volunteers, who succeeded Rosecrans as Commander, Army of the Cumberland.

Trenholm, George. Owner of Trenholm, Fraser & Company, the chief financial backer of the Confederacy in the United Kingdom.

Vallandingham, Klement. Former U.S. Congressman and head of the Copperhead movement in the North.

Wainwright, James Francis Ballard. Captain, RN, Commander of HMS *Black Prince*.

*Washington, Willie. Old handyman for the Orphan Asylum for Colored Children in New York City.

Welles, Gideon. U.S. Secretary of the Navy.

Wetherall, E. R. Colonel, British Army, Chief of Staff to Lt. Gen. William Fenwick Williams.

Williams, William Fenwick. Lieutenant General, British Army, Commander, Imperial forces in British North America.

*Wilmoth, Michael D. First Lieutenant, U.S. Volunteers, senior order-of-battle analyst, Central Information Bureau (CIB).

Windham, Sir Charles Ashe. Major General, British Army, Commander of the Portland Field Force.

Winslow, John. Captain, USN, Commander of the USS *Kearsarge*.

Wolseley, Garnet J. Lieutenant Colonel, British Army, Assistant Quartermaster, Imperial forces in British North America.

Wright, Charlie. Contraband who had revealed vital information about the Army of Northern Virginia in its invasion of the North in the Gettysburg Campaign.

1.

Cossacks, Copperheads, and Corsairs

KAMERINSKI WOODS, OUTSIDE LODZ, POLAND, JULY 12, 1863

The sweat ran down his face as he lay hidden in the cool Polish forest. Jan Szmanda's heart pounded as he aimed his musket at the cavalry patrol wending its way along the narrow woodworkers' road. There were fifteen Cossacks, their lances bobbing with the canter, and an officer who rode at their head, his whip dangling from its loop around his wrist. He was the same one who had "pacified" the three surrounding villages and left them filled with corpses dangling from the trees. "God save Poland," Jan prayed.

"Wait . . .wait . . .wait," he told himself. He chose the officer as his target and waited, waited. The seconds seemed like hours, then CRACK, the first shot broke the silence of the woods. The officer lurched in his saddle, and Jan's finger pulled the trigger as did twenty other Poles. Unfortunately, almost everyone had aimed at the officer, the result of amateurs at war. Man and horse sprayed blood as they thrashed into the trees.

The Cossack sergeant had seen this twenty years before in the forests of Chechnya and had not forgotten its lessons. "Into the woods, my children!" he shouted as they lowered their lances, and he spurred his horse into the trees still shrouded by the black powder smoke. They had practiced this often, these men who fought the border wars of the empire. Their nimble horses dashed through the spaced trees of this well-tended estate forest. Jan saw them come as he frantically tried to reload, but it was too late. The beast was upon him as he cast away the rifle and fled. He dodged among the trees with the quickness of his seventeen years, but the Cossack's pony was swifter as it followed. The sergeant could see his prey glancing back wide-eyed with terror as the distance closed. Then with a move he had practiced a thousand times and executed for real too many times to count, he picked the spot on the boy's back just below the left shoulder blade, low enough to miss it and high enough to avoid the ribs. He leaned forward in the saddle, his boots pressing into the stirrups to cushion the blow and channel the shock through the horse to the ground. Jan looked back one last time and shrieked. Just then the Cossack struck, driving the lance's point through the boy's back and into his heart. He choked on a scream as his body ran forward a pace or two on its own momentum, and the Cossack jerked out the point in a deft move. He passed the corpse as it went tumbling head over heels into the leaves.

It was over in ten minutes. Thirteen dead Poles and against one Cossack officer—a bad trade, the sergeant thought, if one didn't take into account what a prick Lieutenant Golitsyn had been, but he was thankful it was not Chechens that had sprung the ambush. Those bastards knew what they were about. No Chechen would have flinched from a one-on-one fight with even a mounted Cossack—not like these Polish amateurs in revolt against their God-anointed ruler, the Czar Emperor Alexander II.

Yes, God save Poland, save it from its geography and its pride. It was the pride of this people that kept them hung on this Russian cross. Had they given up their pride and settled for assimilation and Russianization, boys like Jan would still be alive, albeit with a cringe in his bearing.

As the blood of the Napoleonic Wars dried thirty-five years before, the victors apportioned the thrones of Europe. Napoleon III had toyed with the re-creation of the Polish state as an ally. The victors did him better. They re-created the kingdom of Poland and then threw it to the wolf in the Kremlin, awarding its crown to the Russian Czar to add to his collection of crowns. The heavy Russian hand finally provoked a widespread revolt in January that by July was in its failed last stage.

ORPHAN ASYLUM FOR COLORED CHILDREN, FIFTH AVENUE AND FORTY-THIRD STREET, NEW YORK, JULY 13, 1863

Bricks shattered the ground-floor windows, and the large double door thudded with the blows of clubs. Outside the mob howled like a blood-drunk beast. "Burn the nigger nest!" was the shout that turned into a chant, a chant with a distinct Celtic lilt, at that. Inside the asylum the white matron coolly organized the evacuation out the back doors of her 237 young wards, all younger than the age of twelve. Her Negro handyman, old gray-haired Willie Washington, stood back from the doors, a fire ax at the ready.

The city was in the grip of a riot. The reading of the draft draw had been a match thrown into kerosene. It was hugely unpopular among the working classes of New York, especially the mass of Irish immigrants who competed with free blacks for the bottom rung of the economic ladder. A hot, sticky July had settled on the city, feeding the discontent. Gangs appeared on the streets in the morning. A single pistol shot was fired in the crowded offices of the District Draft Office on Third Avenue and Forty-Sixth Street. The police guard was barely able to get the draft officials out of the building before it went up in flames.

Rushing to the scene, Police Commissioner John Kennedy was set upon by the rioters and clubbed to the ground. He staggered to his feet and tried to run, but the mob brought him down for another beating. The mobs grew like a fire racing through dry tinder and came across a detachment of soldiers from the Invalid Corps, men too incapacitated by their wounds to serve in the field. Surprised, the troops got off a ragged volley that only enraged the rioters who surged over the soldiers, killing two and wounding fifteen.

Guided by more than instinct, the mob surged to the Armory at Second Avenue and Twenty-First Street. The police defense collapsed after an hour and a half. Now the mob was armed as it left the Armory also in flames. Leaders appeared who sported the cutout of the Indian head of a penny on their lapels, egging the rioters on and pointing out new targets for their wrath. The mobs were spreading like a cancer throughout the city now, aiming a special wrath at Negroes. As fire licked the Armory roof, the Orphan Asylum drew another mob.[1]

As the last of her wards disappeared through the back gate, the matron went back into the building to tell Willie he could abandon his post. Too late, she saw the door splinter apart and its fragments swing back on their hinges. The old man had straightened his bent back and flew into the crowd as it burst in, his ax arched over his head to sink into the face of the first man through. Blood gushed over the crowd as Willie wrenched the ax free. He did not get a second swing as the pack fell on him.[2]

OUTSKIRTS OF CINCINNATI, OHIO, NIGHT OF JULY 13-14, 1863
Utter exhaustion gripped the remnants of the brigade as it staggered forward into the night, its way lit by torches wrapped with looted calico. So bone weary were man and beast that the cavalrymen sought out in the torchlight the path of those gone before from the spattered lather that dripped from their horses' mouths.

No Confederate force had ever penetrated so far into Yankeedom as the cavalry rode around the Ohio metropolis, too tired now to think of taking it. Col. John Hunt Morgan's foray into the north had been his own initiative. He had not bothered to inform his commander, Lt. Gen. Braxton Bragg, commanding the Army of Tennessee. Morgan's fame had grown from his raider's instincts and flair for leadership, qualities that chaffed under Bragg's limp hand.

Morgan had left a trail of burned railroad bridges and factories, looted homes and stores, plundered payrolls, and roused state governments in Indiana and Ohio. Morgan's leadership talents had not extended to the discipline of his men, who went on an uncontrollable rampage as they rode through southeastern Indiana. Capt. Henry Thomas Hines, one of his most intrepid company commanders, was beside himself in anger at this thoughtless display. Lithe and dark-haired, barely 130 pounds, the daring young Hines had more than once been likened to the rising star of the famous Booth family of actors, John Wilkes Booth. Looks aside, Hines had far better control of his emotions than the tempestuous actor. He had to swallow his dismay that Morgan was casting away the very allies he had sought to find among the disloyal elements in these states. He had returned from a June foray in the region and sought out the leaders of this movement and been promised their willing support.

These were the Copperheads, men who called themselves the Sons of Liberty or Knights of the Golden Circle. They wore the Indian head on their lapels. Others were less charitable in their political sentiments, and for them the word "Copperhead" meant the serpent that hid in the grass and struck without warning. The North in this ever-bleeding war was rife with such men for whom nothing was worth all the bloodshed, and yet they were willing to shed more blood to stop it.

Mostly they were Democrats who could not abide the war for the Union and emancipation, close cousins to the Southern branch of their party, and so disaffected that they made common cause with those same rebels. They obstructed the war effort and made a special attempt to stop the Army's recruiting. Their political agitation was intense as their rage against "King Lincoln" swelled with bile. President Abraham Lincoln could be sure of a kinder reception in Richmond than in some parts of the Midwest. He had had the temerity to suspend the writ of habeas corpus and round up a few hundred such agitators. But he had only skimmed the indiscreet surface of where the Copperheads seethed and plotted. Whatever they called themselves, they were united in their determination to seize power and overthrow the Lincoln administration.

Their leader was the fiery Ohio orator and politician, Klement Vallandingham, who Lincoln had convicted of treason and exiled to the Confederacy in May in an act of executive common sense that had the civil libertarians up in arms. That hardly bothered Lincoln, who saw a danger that these critics did not when he explained that he was willing to bend the Constitution here and there to save the entire document. On his Fourth of July address to Congress in 1862 he had asked "whether all the laws but one were to go unexecuted . . . and the government itself go to pieces, lest that one be violated?" There in a nutshell was the common sense of the matter.[3]

Once cast into the Confederacy, Vallandingham had gone straight to Bragg's headquarters and then to Richmond. He argued with great effect to Confederate president Jefferson Davis that the Copperheads of the Northwest would rise in revolt when the famous Gen. John Hunt Morgan led his men into their states. Captain Hines had been sent ahead in his June raid to test Vallandingham's assurances. Specifically, he was to search out Dr. William Bowles, an acknowledged Copperhead leader in southern Indiana who had not hesitated to defy both state and federal authority. Hines found him at French Lick in command of a gang known as "Bowles's Army"—deserters and escaped Confederate prisoners of war—armed with fine Henry rifles and Colt revolvers. Bowles was described by a historian of the movement as "about fifty-five, . . . a slight man with a prominent nose, glaring eyes and tufts of white hair which gave him the appearance of an outraged old eagle. Bowles had served as colonel in the Second Indiana Volunteers during the Mexican War. To him was attributed the disgraceful retreat at Buena Vista." He promised Hines he "could command ten thousand men in twenty-four hours."[4]

Captain Hines's report had been the trigger that set General Morgan in motion. So secret was the mission that Jefferson Davis gave the orders directly to Morgan, pointedly bypassing Bragg. As brilliant a raider as Morgan was, he could not plan beyond the raid. Accounts of the depredations of his brigade flew ahead on the telegraph wires to every town in three states during his three-week raid on Indiana and Ohio. The many homes that displayed the single star flag of the Knights of the Golden Circle were looted just as thoroughly as those of their pro-Union neighbors. Adding insult to outrage, Morgan's men seemed to key on such homes, laughing that the occupants should "give for the cause you love so well!"[5]

The Copperheads stayed home, while the loyal men of Indiana and Ohio rushed to join their militia and home guard units reinforced by Union Army cavalry and infantry. Now Morgan was the hunted. They harried him from place to place, closing in tighter and tighter until they trapped him on the banks of the Ohio. On July 26, he was captured along with seven hundred of his men.

Fragments of his command eluded the disaster. The captain of an Ohio River tugboat, tied up at small wharf, was startled out of his sleep by the click of a Colt Dragoon pistol being cocked by his head. Captain Hines apologized for his lack of manners but would appreciate if the good captain could get his boat away to the Kentucky shore. An hour later Hines and twenty-three men stepped back onto a friendlier territory.

KRONSTADT NAVAL BASE, ST. PETERSBURG, RUSSIA, 9:20 AM, JULY 15, 1863

Midshipman Nikolai Andreyevich Rimsky-Korsakov was excited about the possibilities of this new cruise aboard the frigate *Aleksandr Nevsky*, as the flagship of both the Baltic Squadron and the Russian Imperial Navy swung out of the naval base harbor. The excitement even took his mind away from the symphony he was composing in his head. This nineteen-year-old from Novgorod had just graduated from the Naval Academy eager to serve Czar and empire. The ships of the squadron were slipping out under the cover of an elaborate deception of an extended cruise in the Mediterranean. Maximum stores were taken aboard, and the captains were issued funds and warrants to obtain fresh provisions, coal, and repairs in neutral ports. Six ships would leave Kronstadt in staggered succession. A similar expedition was leaving from the Pacific Fleet's base at Vladivostock. These were new ships, all steam and propeller driven, the products of the post–Crimean War shipbuilding program, all launched between 1859 and 1861.[6]

The midshipman's berth had learned the real destination easily enough; rumor floated through the ship — New York! America! The reason was not hard to guess for any reasonably astute person. War with Britain and France over control of Poland was expected any day now. The two powers had been the guarantors of the kingdom of Poland in the 1815 Treaty of Vienna. The Russian Czar had just abolished the kingdom as a response to the Polish rising and incorporated it as a mere province into the empire. Now the powers Britain and France threatened war to rescue Poland. Nikolai stood on deck, wondering why anyone would fight over a pledge to Poland.

If war came, the Russian Navy was determined not be caught in its bases again by the Royal Navy. That had happened in the Crimean War and resulted in the fleet's shameful impotence in that war. It would not happen again. The Czar wanted the fleet to be at sea when the war came, able to savage British and French commerce around the world. But unless it was going to be a one-way suicide mission, the Russian ships would need a secure and friendly base. There were few ports that British threats would not make untenable.

The choice of a neutral country willing to offer a base and willing to thumb its nose at Britain in the process was obvious – the United States. Russian and American strategic priorities were rapidly converging. The two countries had been on the friendliest terms since Catherine the Great formed her League of Armed Neutrality during the American Revolution to protect neutral trade with the new country from British interdiction. Since then, they had found natural attraction in the similar problems and opportunities of developing vast continents. They also shared a healthy fear of British world hegemony. For the Russians, it had been the sting of their defeat in the Crimean War that had reinforced the danger facing them. For the Americans, it had been the undisguised British desire for a Southern victory and its huge and blatant support of the rebel war effort.

Czar Alexander II and his foreign minister, Aleksandr Gorchakov, supported the survival of the Union, and their diplomatic assistance and advice in the first two years of the war had been critical. Russian advice had led to defusing the Trent Affair's slide toward war between the United States and Great Britain in late 1861. Lincoln's appointment of Cassius Marcellus Clay as ambassador to the imperial court had been a brilliant stroke in cementing the natural alliance between the two countries. Clay was a Southerner famous for his pro-Union and antislavery views, and he was a man not to be trifled with. He had fought and won more than one duel with his bowie knife. In Russia, he lectured on the necessity of industrializing the empire and weaning it away from its thrall to Great

Britain's manufactures. His speeches were met with thunderous applause by Russian audiences.

Yet the thought of an open-ocean voyage and the excitement of New York pushed thoughts of geopolitics from Midshipman Rimsky-Korsakov's mind. He was intrigued by the squadron commander, whom he watched walking the bridge of the *Nevsky*. Adm. Stefan S. Lisovsky was a seaman to be reckoned with by all accounts. He was notorious for his irascible and ungovernable temper. Nikolai remembered a lieutenant telling the boys as Lisovsky's appointment was announced, "Do you know what they say of him? In his last command, in a fit of wrath, he had rushed up to a sailor, guilty of some offense, and bitten off his nose!" The lieutenant crossed himself, "Dear God, it will be an interesting voyage. At least, you will be comforted, my boys, to know that the admiral felt badly enough about the nose-biting to get the poor man a pension."[7]

Nikolai rubbed his own nose.

WAR DEPARTMENT, WASHINGTON, D.C., 3:43 PM, JULY 15, 1863

He was an impatient man, Thomas Francis Meagher "Meagher of the Sword," hero of the Young Ireland Movement, the gallant Gael who had led the Irish Brigade into the teeth of hell through the cornfields of Antietam and up the cold slopes of Marye's Heights above Fredericksburg. Now an impatient man in civilian clothes, his resignation had been moldering for four months in some War Department file. He wanted it back. Hat in hand he had come from New York to retrieve his commission as brigadier general with a promise to raise three thousand Irish to fight for the Stars and Stripes and for the green flag of Ireland — the mystic golden harp on the emerald green field.

President Lincoln had shown interest in his offer, and Meagher had come to Washington to see it through. Now he cooled his heels in the lobby of the War Department building as officers and clerks scurried about, stirred by the bloody riots in New York. Meagher was heartsick that his own people had raised their hands against their new country. He had argued again and again that the road to a new life in this country was to share its battles. And many had flocked to the colors. His own Irish Brigade, now death-shrunk through too many battles, had marched off full of enthusiasm a year ago. So much had soured since then. The Copperheads and the Democrats had seduced too many of his people to turn their backs on this country in its hour of peril. Too many had swallowed the lie that it was a nigger war to set the black man up above them.

The Irish were not about to compete for last place. To many of them, coming to America had not been the choice of a new beginning, a bright future — it had been the simple choice to flee blighted Ireland or starve.

Churning this pool of bile were the Fenians, the secret society bent on the independence of Ireland and possessed of a primal hatred of England. They saw the war for the Union as a distraction from their goal of Irish independence. Some did see a value in military service — to train the exiled Irish to form an army and filibuster the conquest of Canada from an American base. As far-fetched as it seemed, the thought was to trade Canada for Ireland's independence. Meagher had fashioned an argument that would allow a man to serve both the land of his birth and the land of his refuge. Freedom was his cause, suckled on Ireland's green, but he was a generous friend to it everywhere else. He saw it as a duty for every liberty-loving man to fight for the preservation of the Union and freedom. The Irish would do best to fight alongside each other. "I hold that if only one in ten of us come back when this war is over, the military experience gained by that one will be of more service in a fight for Ireland's freedom than would that of the entire ten as they are now."[8]

No man had greater credentials and greater respect as an Irish patriot. He was cast in the mold of an Irish prince — proud, brave, gifted with the magic of words, and fey marked. He was also a gracious gentleman, with that extra touch of bearing that the Irish so admired in their leaders. In his bid for Ireland's freedom, they had called him "Meagher of the Sword," a title he treasured above all others. Ireland had made him a hero when his conspiracy to free Ireland was betrayed and he mocked the judge who held his life in his hand. Fame and exile to Australia followed. Greater fame fell on him in his daring escape that brought him to America.

However, he was also a man who could not see an endeavor through, and his soaring spirit all too often fell into a bottle when the heat of battle had cooled. His drunkenness had become more than a whisper. His resignation after Chancellorsville had been accepted with an all too obvious alacrity.

A clerk now interrupted his pacing. "I'm sorry, sir, but the Secretary is so pressed by business that he finds it impossible to set an appointment at this time."

"But I have a letter from the President authorizing me to . . ."

"Yes, sir, many people have such letters, but Secretary Stanton has only so much time."

Meagher's hand tightened on his cane but relaxed when he recognized Charles Dana entering the lobby. Dana was Edwin Stanton's assistant secretary of war. Meagher walked briskly to him, "Dana, so good to see you again."

Dana was used to office seekers and politicians swarming around him, but Meagher was more than an annoyance. He was a presence, tall and thickset but graceful, with a shock of fine brown hair, penetrating green eyes, and the coiled power of a wolfhound. "Well, hello, Meagher. What brings you to Washington?" It was a question he instantly regretted.

Meagher poured out his distress. Dana took him by the arm into his office. "I'll not hide it from you, Meagher, but the Irish are in a bad odor at this time. The government wonders if the Irish can be trusted now."

"Trusted? By God, sir, that question was not asked on all the blood-soaked fields my brigade fought upon."

"The riots in New York were Irish-led; we can deal with only one rebellion at a time. If you want to be of service, wean your people away from the disloyal elements that have them in such thrall. Then we can talk of another Irish brigade. Right now Stanton will not hear of it."

Stanton was trying to make sure Lincoln heard no more of it either, but later the President brought the subject up again and asked how Meagher was doing. Stanton huffed that the Irishman had lost interest. Lincoln was surprised and replied, "Did you ever know an Irishman who would decline an office, or refuse a pair of epaulets, or do anything but fight gallantly after them?"[9]

USS *NANSEMOND* AT SEA OFF WILMINGTON, NORTH CAROLINA, 10:15 AM, AUGUST 1, 1863

The lookout in the crow's nest shouted out, "Ahoy! Black smoke to the southwest!" Battle stations sounded, scattering men to their posts. The engines pulsed with heaps of coal-fired energy as the *Nansemond* turned after its prey.

She had been built just the year before as a side-wheel steamer of four hundred tons and named the *James Freeborn* and taken into service as a blockade ship. Her speed of almost fifteen knots was enormous but necessary if the Navy was to intercept the even fleeter blockade-runners being built in Britain. She had taken the name of *Nansemond*, the James River tributary of that name, to honor the intrepid successes her new commander had won on that river. This twenty-five-year-old naval prodigy, Lt. Roswell Hawks Lamson, had been second in the Annapolis class of 1862. Under his hands, she raced through the waves.

It was a rare navy that would allow one so young to trod his own quarterdeck as captain, but national crisis brought out talent, and Lamson's hard fighting on the Virginia rivers had delighted the old admirals. They could not reward him fast enough for the qualities that were a premium in this grinding war against a resourceful and valiant foe. They called his skill "Lamson's Luck," though "luck" was not the half of it.

He was commanding a gunboat squadron on the Nansemond River in late April during the Suffolk campaign. Lt. Gen. James Longstreet and his 1st Corps of the Army of Northern Virginia had been sent there to counter an expected Union offensive fueled by reinforcements. When the reinforcements were sent elsewhere, he converted his defensive mission to an offensive one to cut the communications of the twenty thousand Union troops in the Suffolk area. He had to cross the Nansemond to do it. On the morning of April 14, Lamson was taking the USS *Mount Washington* down the river to Suffolk when he was engaged by a Confederate battery at Norleet's Point. The first enemy salvo blew up his boilers, and the ship began to drift ashore under heavy fire. Another of his vessels pulled him off the shore, only to ground the *Mount Washington* in crossing the bar. Another ten pieces of enemy artillery and hundreds of riflemen opened up at 11:00 AM. He fought them from his stationary position on the bar until 6:00 PM. He reported later that

> her boilers, cylinders, and steel drums pierced and ten shells went through the smoke pipe, and the rest of the machinery much damaged. Her pilot house riddled, wheelropes shot away, and her decks and bulwarks completely splintered, everyone who has seen her says there has not been another vessel so shot to pieces during the war. The flag-staff was shot away, and when the flag fell into the water, the rebs cheered exultingly; but they did not enjoy it for long before we had the dear old stars and stripes waving over us again, with everyone more determined than ever to fight them to the last timber of the vessel.[10]

Followed by a master's mate and seaman, Lamson climbed through the wreckage to the upper deck. They hauled up the flagstaff by the ensign halyards, raised and lashed it to the stump. He considered it a miracle that they all survived unscathed, only one of many miracles that seemed to fall on that ship amid the rebel shot and shell. "After the action was over, the sailors gathered around me on the deck, took hold of my hands and arms, threw their arms around me, and I saw tears starting from eyes that had looked the rebel battery in the face unflinchingly."[11]

The enemy had fared far worse. Ten of its guns had been smashed, and hundreds of the sharpshooters had been killed or wounded by the guns of the *Mount Washington*. More important, because of Lamson, Longstreet did not cross the Nansemond to fall like a wolf among the second-rate Union generals who cowered in fear of him. Lamson's courage had stopped his plan dead in its tracks. With men like Lamson on the river, Longstreet would not chance the move.

The Secretary of the Navy wrote that the Service "is proud to see in the younger members of the corps such evidence of energy and gallantry, and execution and ability as scarcely surpassed by those of more age and experience."[12] The *Nansemond* was Lamson's reward. He fitted her out himself at the Baltimore Navy Yard but was only able to find a small part of his needed crew, though they were the pick. When he reached the flagship of the North Atlantic Blockading Squadron, the large frigate *Minnesota*, he asked the captain for permission to recruit the men who had served with him on the *Mount Washington*. When he went to fetch them, half the frigate's crew begged to be included. He took fifty, "as true blue jacket as ever walked a deck, and ten officers." A hundred officers had applied for his ship. His executive, Benjamin Porter, was a treasure.

The *Nansemond* was as trim and well run as any ship that flew the Stars and Stripes, all shipshape and Bristol fashion, as the petty officers said. The old salts had already taken the measure of this young man and threw the weight of their goodwill on his side and set the tone for the ship. They whispered that he was Davy Farragut all over again and for good reason—he was Navy through and through. Lamson knew his job and everyone else's. He was a teacher, vital in a navy that had ballooned from five thousand to fifty thousand men in two years. It did not take long for the word to spread that the *Nansemond* was a hale ship with a lucky captain who plucked fat prizes off the sea.

A good-looking but not striking young man, with his carefully combed and slicked-down black hair, Lamson looked younger than his years—something he did not appreciate when a captain's maturity was a given attribute of his ability. He grew a mustache and a goatee to make him appear older. Officers and men did not seem to care. There was something about him that compelled a willing obedience, something hard to put your finger on. It went beyond his considerable competence. His presence seemed to generate a certain excitement in others who wanted to be around him. He was like an electric current that caused others to glow. He was also a fighter, and men follow such a man.

He was also lovesick. Every mail packet would carry a handful of his letters to his cousin and fiancée, Kate Buckingham. The ahoy had found him at his writing desk, where he had just had time to write, "Dear Kate, Again the *Nansemond* is dashing through the water, and

> Again on the deck I stand
> Of *my own swift gliding craft*"[13]

before leaping through his cabin door and racing up the gangway to his quarterdeck.

Porter handed him the eyeglass. "The vessel is running offshore, a blockade-runner for sure."

"Let's give chase, Mr. Porter. Stand to intercept. We shall see what our new engines can do."

The *Nansemond* leaped through the sea like a hunting dog on the scent. By noon, she had gained so much on the vessel that Lamson opened fire on the chase, and the shots fell just short. The sextant reading told him they were gaining, when a strong breeze from the southwest came up to whip the sea into heavy swells. The *Nansemond* slowed as the waves struck under her low guards, but the quarry suffered the same handicap as well. Lamson pressed on, straining his engines to close the distance. The next two hours saw him gain. The pursued began to throw cargo overboard to lighten its load, but the *Nansemond* continued to close until 3:50 PM when a shot from her bow gun shattered the vessel's figurehead. The vessel came about to signal her surrender.

She was the *Margaret and Jesse*, seven hundred tons, registered in Charleston and bound for Wilmington from Nassau. Lamson sent two officers aboard to hoist the American flag. With a prize crew in control of the captured vessel, Lamson cut a course for the North Atlantic Blockading Squadron off Wilmington, and when everything was secure and under way, he returned to his cabin and picked up his pen to finish his letter to the fair Kate.

The next morning in the early light the ships swung in among the squadron. Lamson, at his breakfast, was interrupted by a knock on the cabin door. "Enter," he said.

A tiny cabin boy, all of eleven years old, stood owl-eyed for few seconds until he blurted out, "Mr. Porter's compliments, sir. Flagship signaling."

Lamson put his breakfast aside and went topside, nodding at Mr. Porter as he scanned the squadron bobbing in the sea. Most were converted merchantships like the *Nansemond*, meant to run down blockade-runners. There was also a handful of the purpose-built, pre-war, steam-driven warships. As powerful as the squadron was, Lamson knew its strength paled compared to that assembled under Adm. John Dahlgren's South Atlantic Blockading Squadron off Charleston. Admiral Dahlgren had command of the Navy's new iron fist, all eight of the new iron monitors. Riding low in the water with their great double-gunned turrets, the *Passaic* class monitors were a marvel rushed to production after last year's great duel on in Hampton Roads between the USS *Monitor* and the CSS *Virginia*, but not a one of these wonders bobbed here off Wilmington.

"What is the signal, Mr. Henderson?" Lamson asked the acting ensign. He had been lagging in his signal recognition skills, and Lamson had had him at practice in every spare moment.

Henderson blinked, read the signal flags, and then said quickly, "'Captain *Nansemond* report squadron commander immediately,' sir."

"Very good, Mr. Henderson."

INDIANAPOLIS RAIL YARDS, INDIANA, 3:22 AM, AUGUST 3, 1863

"Traitor!" The speaker spat out the word, a letter clutched in his hand. But it was his eyes that glowed with hate. Big Jim Smoke was a hater by nature, but now he had a cause.

The Copperhead rebellion could not succeed by merely hamstringing the war effort — it must succeed by an act as overt as the rebels firing on Fort Sumter, and for that they needed arms. Tens of thousands of small arms and tons of ammunition were siphoned off the open market to fill secret arsenals, but even that was not enough. Raids on federal arms warehouses followed.

Such as the one on this warm summer's night.

Their target was the arms warehouse, one of many that fed the rail yards of Indianapolis, which poured arms and supplies south to the armies that had finally starved out proud and obdurate Vicksburg. Thirty men slid through the shadows. Wagons waited deeper in the gloom. Two o'clock in the morning is a dangerous time for sentries and in particular for these men who were members of the Invalid Corps, the light duty men released from the charnel house hospitals as unfit for field duty but able to do some valuable service. In these early hours a man could be seduced into the sleepy arms of Orpheus. It was burden enough to nurse a limping leg from a minié ball at Chancellorsville or Champion Hill without struggling also against leaden sleep.

The man with the letter had tucked it and his anger away. He had work to do but had to wait while others did their own work. He stepped around a corner to be out of sight and lit a match to his cigar. The guards did not stir from their sleep as shadowy forms scurried through the lamplight. A few practiced motions, and the guards slumped to the ground, cut throats gushing black blood in the pale light. The wide double doors swung open with a creak, and the gang rushed in. A lamp waved back and forth down the street to summon the wagons.

"You see," Big Jim Smoke said to the young man who had joined him, "how easy it is." Felix Stidger's handsome, pale face had not even twitched when the guards were killed. Calm, self-control was the shield and buckler of a good spy, and Stidger was among the best. An ardent Unionist, Stidger had enlisted and served in the office of the Provost Marshal General of Tennessee. He had volunteered to infiltrate the Copperhead organization in Indiana and had succeeded beyond his wildest hopes. With great charm he had ingratiated himself so well with Dr. Bowles that he had been appointed the group's corresponding secretary, and the information flowed to Washington. Now, though, beneath that placid exterior he was worried. Big Jim and his gang should have been caught in a trap.

Big Jim instead reached into his pocket and pulled out the letter. "Looking for this?" he sneered. Stidger's eyes widened only a bit as he heard Smoke's pistol cock and felt the muzzle stab into his belly. "You, of all people, should have known that we are everywhere, even the post office. And you mailing so many letters, and the Army making so many raids on our hidden weapons and making so many arrests." He pressed the muzzle deeper into Stidger's belly. "And now, if you please, we find this one, telling about this little raid of ours." He grinned, his incisors gleaming in the lamplight, wet and wolf-like through his beard. He gave the muzzle another shove. "What gets me is how you got Bowles to trust you. But then he is too much the trusting fool. From the first, you weren't right by me."

"Come to your senses, Big Jim." Stidger's voice was about as even as Smoke had ever heard. "Of course, I wrote it. They think I work for them, and I give them just enough truth to make me believable. I am working under Vallandingham's instructions." Smoke was listening, he could tell. He had captured his attention by dropping the biggest name in the Copperhead movement. Now he had only to play it out and make him doubt. "Look at the date, man. I wrote that the raid would be on the twelfth not the second. Check it." Stidger was counting on the split second distraction for Big Jim to look at the letter again in which to draw his own pistol. Instead, Big Jim pulled his trigger. The bullet's sound muffled in the young man's middle. It severed his spine as it spewed blood and bone out behind him in fiery tongue, and he fell like a rag doll.

"Good try, traitor. But if you had meant the twelfth, you should not have written the second." The light had not entirely gone out of Stidger's eyes when Big Jim kicked him in the face. He paused long enough to wipe his bloody shoes on the corpse and then crossed the street. By then, most of the five thousand new Springfield rifles had been loaded into the waiting wagons and were disappearing into the gloom.

OFF CAPE TOWN, SOUTH AFRICA, 2:15 PM, AUGUST 5, 1863

The greatest of the great white sharks made the cold waters off the Cape of Good Hope their home. These primal killing machines now had competition from an even deadlier killing machine, man. The CSS *Alabama* was an iron-hulled steamer, 220 feet long and 32 feet across her beam, three-masted, and bark-rigged with powerful engines that sent her sleek hull through the water at thirteen knots. Six gun ports pierced each side. She was circling her helpless forty-fifth victim, a small Yankee bark, *Sea Bride*, close inshore. The entire population of Cape Town had decamped to the shore to watch the spectacle of death on the water. A reporter for the *Cape Argus* described the hunt.

> The Yankee came around from the southeast, and about five miles from the Bay, the steamer came down upon her. The Yankee was evidently taken by surprise.
>
> Like a cat, watching and playing with a victimized mouse, Captain Semmes permitted his prize to draw off a few yards, and then he upped steam again and pounced upon her. She first sailed around the Yankee from stem to stern, and stern to stem again. The way that fine, saucy, rakish craft was handled

was worth riding a hundred miles to see. She went around the bark like a toy, making a complete circle, and leaving an even margin of water between herself and her prize.[14]

There was more than a little glee mixed in with the excitement. The sentiment in this colony of the British Empire, on which the sun never set, reflected the mother country's political prejudices as closely as they parroted the latest fashions — contempt for the Yankees and admiration for the Confederates. Cape Town's elite was already in competition to invite the *Alabama's* captain, the famous Capt. Raphael Semmes, into their homes. To the rage of the U.S. consul, the city prepared to fete the captain and his officers even before the *Alabama* had made its kill.

The Confederate commerce raider finished toying with its prey and sent over a boat to fetch its captain and his sailing papers. The defeated captain climbed aboard stone-faced, his life in ruins. He owned his ship; it was his home as well as his livelihood. Semmes greeted him cordially before reviewing his papers. The *Sea Bride's* captain observed him as he read. Semmes was a thin, wiry man, all sinew and determination. His already famous waxed mustache protruded at right angles for three inches from either side of his face.

Semmes looked up. "I declare the *Sea Bride* a prize of war, Captain. I will send a prize crew to take her. You and your crew I will land in Cape Town." The man held no hope of escape; his manifest clearly declared his cargo of machinery to be the property of American merchants. What sickened him though was the thought that Semmes might burn her, his home of so many years, as the captain of the *Alabama* had done to so many whalers. Their oil-soaked timbers had created vertical infernos floating on the sea, visible for great distances, and had become a specter haunting every American ship's captain. The *Alabama* had hunted for less than a year, and already she had spread terror through the American shipping world, driving insurance rates skyward and giving owners no alternative but to reflag, sell their ships to foreign owners, or face ruin at sea. Bit by bit, Semmes was breaking Yankee commerce on the high seas.

The world was already putting the praise of the *Alabama* to song in a dozen languages. As Semmes sailed into Cape Town Harbor, the locals were already singing in Afrikaans, "Daar kom die *Alabama*, die *Alabama* kom oor die see." It would become a local legend that would endure for more than one hundred years.[15]

2.

Russell and the Rams

WASHINGTON NAVY YARD, WASHINGTON, D.C., 10:20 AM, AUGUST 6, 1863

Gus Fox was not the sort of man to wait on events much less on other men. The assistant secretary of the Navy was a burly, powerful man, with a bushy mustache-goatee that bristled with power. He bent events to his will as the foundries did that shaped the great flat slabs of armor plate into the rounded turrets of his beloved Monitors. On this day he was waiting for one man as he paced the Navy Yard's Anacostia River dock, and a naval lieutenant at that.

Whenever Fox appeared at the Yard, a primal energy was unleashed. Adm. John Dahlgren, during his time as superintendent of the Yard, had had the self-confidence and connections with Lincoln to withstand and guide Fox's enthusiasm. But his successor, Capt. Andrew Harwood, was not as well connected and knew it. He would pay Fox the courtesies his dignity allowed and then get back to his own work and leave the Assistant Secretary to whatever had brought him to the Yard. Fox understood the game and played it well. Being the brother-in-law of the Postmaster General and the son-in-law of a major figure in the Republican Party had been the trick that landed him the job. That he was uniquely qualified for it was not something that American patronage politics encouraged, but this time it had hit a bull's-eye.

Everyone knew that Gideon Welles was the Secretary of the Navy. Everyone also knew that Fox *was* the Navy. Secretary Welles stuck to policy and left the conduct of actual operations to Fox, who had the complete confidence of the officer corps. He was, after all, one of their own. A former naval officer, he resigned during the service doldrums of the 1850s, but the war had drawn him back like a magnet.

In late 1860, as the issue of war or peace had hung in the balance and the new President and his cabinet struggled with whether to relieve Fort Sumter, Fox had figured out the how and threw the plan into Lincoln's lap. It was hardly his fault that the relief expedition he accompanied had arrived in Charleston Harbor just as the Confederates began the bombardment of the fort. Fox had the dubious honor of escorting the surrendered garrison home. That experience only fueled his aggressive and energetic nature. He had suggested and organized the first important naval success of the war by seizing Port Royal in South Carolina and turning it into the Navy's forward operating base without which the blockade could not have been maintained so far south.

Lincoln had been overjoyed that the Navy had pulled such a beautiful rabbit out the hat when most news had reeked of bitter frustration and failure. If Dahlgren was close to Lincoln, now so was Fox. He had piled high his credit with the President with his enthusiastic support of John Ericcson's famous *Monitor* and especially of the follow-on class, the *Passaics*. Those ships formed the fighting core of Dahlgren's force off Charleston. Another larger class of shallow-draft monitors, the *Casco* class, was now abuilding along the Atlantic coast and along the Ohio.

Fox was not one to hoard his credit. He wagered it freely on new games as they came up. He was ruthless and arrogant, but admirals had more to fear from those features than lieutenants did. He was also an instinctive fighter, seized new ideas and opportunities, and could size up good men in a snap.

One such man was on the bridge of the *Nansemond* gliding up to the dock. Fox liked such men and gave them bigger and bolder commands. There were plenty of commands to go around in a navy that had mushroomed so quickly in size — and not nearly enough bold and lucky men to take them. The evidence of that lucky boldness was the prize trailing behind Lamson's *Nansemond*. She was the British blockade-runner, the *Margaret and Jesse*. Lamson had caught her off Wilmington, where his luck had blossomed. He had come across her low in the water with a heavy cargo of lead — those deadly accurate Whitworth breach-loading rifled guns and enough ammunition to keep them firing for years. The weight of her cargo had been her undoing. Built as a British mail packet, the iron-hulled, side-wheeler *Margaret and Jesse* was the only ship afloat able to do sixteen knots, but slowed by the greed of her cargo, *Nansemond* had fallen on her like a hawk.

Lieutenant Lamson knew Fox by sight. Any aggressive officer among the blockading and river fighting squadrons along the Atlantic coast was sure to have met Fox. As the ship came alongside the dock, Fox took the time to examine the sleek ship coming up to dock outboard of *Nansemond.* Then his eyes moved to the bridge and locked on Lamson's.

"Captain, come ashore immediately. I must speak with you," Fox's voice boomed. Lamson bounded down the gangplank as soon as it hit the dock. He took Fox's extended hand and found the older man was trying to crush it as he grinned at him. Lamson smiled back and met grip with grip until Fox let go. "Good to see you again, young man. A fine prize." He looked thoughtful for a moment and said, "You may not have seen the last of her." He motioned to the carriage nearby. "We must hurry. You are wanted at the White House.

BALTIMORE AND OHIO RAILROAD STATION, WASHINGTON, D.C., 10:30 AM, AUGUST 6, 1863

The lieutenant saluted. "Colonel Sharpe?" he asked the officer who had just stepped off the train car. George H. Sharpe was on the short side of medium height, round shouldered, and with a walrus mustache, a plain, even homely looking thirty-five-year-old man and not a very martial figure by any means. He was a man you could easily miss—until he spoke, that is.

"Lieutenant, I am Colonel Sharpe." The young man was taken aback at the transformation. Sharpe's face had brightened with a disarming smile and his blue-gray eyes sparkled with good humor.

"I am to take you to the White House, sir, by direction of the Secretary of War."

Sharpe reflected that life was getting more and more interesting as the carriage clattered down Pennsylvania Avenue. He had been summoned by the iron-willed Secretary to Washington with no explanation from his staff position at the headquarters of the Army of the Potomac at Brandy Station in Virginia, the furthest point of the Army's advance after Gettysburg. He had met the formidable Edwin McMasters Stanton before. His duties had taken him to Washington repeatedly before Gettysburg, and he had briefed Stanton any number of times. He knew that the Secretary of War was a force of nature, single-minded will personified. Stanton had come to national prominence shortly before the war when he had defended Dan Sickles for shooting his wife's lover dead right outside the White House and won the case by advancing the insanity defense for the first time in American legal history. Because of those briefings, Stanton had acquired a taste for what Sharpe had to say.

Sharpe, a slope-shouldered man from Kingston, New York, was unique in any number of ways. He was a Hudson Valley aristocrat, sophisticated and cosmopolitan. He was one of the best-educated men in the country, with degrees from Rutgers and Yale Law School. He had been the chargé at the Vienna legation and was something of a linguist, fluent in Latin and French. His mousy exterior gave no indication that he liked to have good time. A connoisseur of fine food and wine, he was not above staggering back from the Irish Brigade's St. Patrick's Day celebration tight as a tick. He also had a mind as sharp as an obsidian razor.

When Joseph Hooker had blown into the command of the Army like a cleansing wind, Sharpe had been his inspired choice for something new. Hooker had been that transformational man who had leapt out of an old paradigm into the new. With a taste for the value of military intelligence, he had experimented with various collection means as a division and corps commander. When he became Army commander, he did something unique. Heretofore, commanding generals had been their own intelligence officers, a role that had worked for great commanders like Washington when armies were small. Hooker saw that the scale and complexity of modern war had made it impossible for any single man to both command an army and control its intelligence operation as well.

For the latter task he chose Sharpe. At Fredericksburg, he had seen Sharpe decisively sort out a muddle on the field. A regiment of French immigrants had milled about in confusion, unable to understand the order of their non-French-speaking colonel. Sharpe rode over from his own 120th New York (NY) Volunteers, gave the orders in parade ground–loud perfect French, and the regiment moved smartly into line. Hooker had called Sharpe in for an interview and showed him a French book on how to create a secret service. He asked if he could translate it and how fast. Sharpe replied, "As fast as I can read it." When he did, the job was his.

Sharpe had taken this new ball and run with it. He created a fully functioning intelligence operation—the Bureau of Military Information (BMI)—practically from scratch. He assembled a contingent of hardy and clever scouts, developed a spy network, and established interrogation, document exploitation, and order-of-battle operations. Hooker had given him carte blanche, which he used to coordinate the other intelligence collection means of the cavalry, Balloon Corps, and Signal Corps. He also established contacts throughout the Eastern Theater of operations that often took him to Washington and Baltimore. His efforts had presented Robert E. Lee "the Incomparable" to Hooker on a silver platter in April, the most magnificent gift of intelligence in the war. However, at Chancellorsville early the next month Joe Hooker had lost faith in Joe Hooker, and all of Sharpe's efforts went for naught.

Hooker's successor, Maj. Gen. George G. Meade, had listened to Sharpe at Gettysburg and not flinched. It was Sharpe's report on the night of July 2 that had convinced Meade to stay and fight it out on the third day of the battle. It was also Sharpe's special operation raid the morning of the same day that had snatched dispatches to Lee from Jefferson Davis that laid bare the Confederacy's defensive strategy and force deployment in the East. Stanton was so elated that he poured gold into the hands of Sharpe's chief of scouts, the sandy-haired Sgt. Milton Cline, who had personally seized the dispatches. Yes, Stanton knew Sharpe.

Now Sharpe was pondering the reason for his cryptic summons. He considered the possible sources in the reports he had forwarded to Washington. Almost everything had been a running account of Lee's movements, strength, logistics, and possible intentions. There was nothing really special or earthshaking there, just patient building of a picture of the enemy and the daily effort to keep it current. Although Stanton absorbed everything like a sponge, his interest had shown no special emphasis in the month since Gettysburg except for the case of a contraband named George.

George, a Confederate officer's servant, had come through the lines only last week. He bore a strange tale, one that normally was outside Sharpe's area of responsibility. Cline had come to see him, "Colonel, you should talk to this boy, yourself." And he did.

The boy was obviously intelligent. His astute observations confirmed much of what Sharpe's office already knew, a vital cross-checking feature of intelligence. It was the normal order-of-battle information, but George had more to say when Cline nudged him and said, "George, tell him about the white folks up north." He then told a tale that made even Sharpe's eyes widen.

As Sharpe mused in his carriage, Fox's and Lamson's carriage was also moving down Pennsylvania Avenue toward the White House. Fox chewed on his cigar briefly between sentences. He was too active a man to endure long silences. "These Confederate commerce raiders are gutting our merchant navy, ruining our international commerce, and driving people whose livelihoods have been destroyed into the arms of the people who want this war stopped."

Lamson watched the man's body language radiate hostility. Fox went on, "They're as serious a threat as the blockade-runners that keep the rebels alive with the bounty of Her Majesty's foundries and arsenals." He looked at the ruin of his cigar with disgust and tossed it out the window. "And, I'll tell you straight out, Lamson, that we are on the losing end of the fight at both ends. We are just not catching enough blockade-runners, and even when we catch one, Semmes and his infernal *Alabama* seize two of our ships. A losing game, a losing game."

Lamson had not been discouraged by Fox's venting. Rather his interest had been piqued. It was not every day that a junior naval officer received an invitation to the White House. Within Fox's lament, Lamson could smell opportunity for something grand. It was with a delicious sense of anticipation that he followed Fox into the White House.

Charles Dana, the assistant secretary of war and Fox's counterpart, was already in the anteroom chatting with an Army colonel. He saw Fox and said, "Gus, let me introduce Col. George Sharpe. Colonel, this is Gus Fox whom I'm sure you've heard of."

Fox sized up Sharpe and was not impressed as they shook hands. "Dana here speaks highly of you, Colonel, don't you, Charlie?" Sharpe's handshake was firm, not what Fox expected from such a nondescript-looking man. Then Fox was as taken aback as the lieutenant at the railroad station had been by the transformation of Sharpe's face. There was power there. He remembered to introduce Lamson, who found some comfort in the presence of another officer in this otherwise intimidating setting of the Executive Mansion, even if it was an Army officer three grades his senior. Fox and Dana drifted off to a corner to talk, leaving the colonel and the lieutenant to their thoughts.

Upstairs the cabinet was meeting with the President. The room in which they regularly met was austere, the only decorations being a large series of maps on one wall and on the other an old engraving of Andrew Jackson and a small framed photographic portrait of John Bright, a man Lincoln admired immensely. Bright was a member of the British Parliament whose impassioned support of the United States in its struggle had earned him the derisive title of "Member from the United States." At times he seemed to be the only member of the British establishment who took up the cause of the Union. His powerful antislavery message resonated more with working- and middle-class Britons than with the ruling and business classes whose palpable disdain for the Union was returned

with a bitter resentment by the Americans. Establishment Britain anticipated a Southern victory with undisguised glee. That was not lost on the
men sitting at the table. A recent centerpiece for the table, a jagged piece
of shell, had been presented by Meade after Gettysburg. It had been fired
by a Whitworth breech-loading rifled cannon presented as a gift to the
Confederacy by the London Chamber of Commerce.[1]

Lincoln's Secretary of State, William H. Seward, held the floor. He
was the man who informed opinion acknowledged should have been
president and was probably the most distinguished man in the country
before the war. He had been governor of New York and a senator thereafter. The 1860 nomination of the new Republican Party seemed his for
the taking, until the Log Splitter from Illinois carried off the prize from
under Seward's enormous Roman nose. That was not the first time he
had underestimated Lincoln. When the new president sought the best
men for his cabinet, he turned to Seward to be his senior cabinet officer.
Seward thought at first that that position gave him license to determine
policy for the unsophisticated lawyer from the West. When he got over
his shock that Lincoln would be his own man and was quite capable of it,
their relationship settled into one of mutual respect and even friendship.
Seward was a man without political rancor and served to the best of his
considerable ability. For that reason, he did not object when Lincoln made
Thomas Haines Dudley the U.S. consul in Liverpool. Dudley was the
Connecticut politician whose support had swung the Republican nomination away from Seward to Lincoln. The appointment was more than a
political reward; Lincoln had placed an able man in a sensitive post, which
Seward did not fail to recognize.[2]

Still, Seward was an enormous presence in any room. A slight
man, thin-faced with a mop of tousled hair that no comb dared approach,
he was the master of his own domain of foreign policy, subject only to
Lincoln's broad policy guidance. William Russell, the famous British
journalist, described him in 1861 as "a subtle, quick man, rejoicing in
power, given to perorate and to oracular utterances, fond of badinage,
bursting with the importance of state mysteries, and with the dignity of
directing foreign policy of the greatest country — as all Americans think —
in the world."[3] He had not hesitated to use that power in the dangerous
first months of Lincoln's presidency. He had recommended and executed
the policy to suspend the writ of habeas corpus to arrest thousands of
Southern sympathizers and collaborators. He had pressured the British
diplomatically by putting on an aggressive, anti-British front to warn
them off from supporting the South too much. That and every other

measure to curb British support for the Confederacy had failed. That failure was the subject of today's cabinet meeting and Seward's briefing. It would be laced with the Secretary's widely acknowledge gift for swearing, something Lincoln took enormous amusement in.

"We are approaching a damned crisis we do not seem able to control. Ambassador Adams reports that the work on the two infernal rams at the Laird Brothers' shipbuilding works in Birkenhead near Liverpool continues at an accelerated pace. Adams writes as of the 11th of last month, 'All the appliances of British skill to the arts of destruction appear to be resorted to for the purpose of doing injury to the people of the United States. . . . It is not unnatural that such proceedings should be regarded by the government and people of the United States with the greatest alarm, virtually as tantamount to a participation in the war by the government of Great Britain.'"[4]

Seward continued, "I do not need to remind you that Laird built the infamous *Alabama*. Her construction number was 292; that of the rams, 294 and 295. Laird Brothers is so damned confident that they mock us with the very ship's construction numbers. Our consul in Liverpool, Thomas Dudley, has reported in minute detail the progress of construction and proof that they are intended for delivery to Confederate agents." He brought a letter out his portfolio. "This is from Dudley on the 21st of last month, describing the construction of even another ram up in Glasgow. 'On Thursday of last week I went to Glasgow and took with me one of my men. I obtained a good view of the Ram building for the Confederates by George Thompson from the river, which is very narrow. She is up high and so much exposed that I could see her as if in the yard. Only a part of the armour plates are on as yet, and from appearances I should judge she could not be ready for launching for two months at least.' He also writes they intend to name this ram the *Virginia*."[5]

Seward went on, the steam almost rising from his collar. "Adams presents these proofs to the British Foreign Minister, and Sir John Russell, in turn, replied with a straight face that they constitute no real proofs, that they are based on 'hearsay rumor.' I am convinced he is only following the direction of the Prime Minister. Lord Palmerston is no friend of the United States and sets the tone for the entire cabinet. He is set upon the success of the rebellion. I am convinced that otherwise the English Ministry are our friends with the exception of the chief. His course and conduct are execrable." He handed the papers to Lincoln.[6]

"Seward," began Lincoln with such a hard edge that the Secretary of State straightened in his chair, "I would not so easily assume Russell's good will. He has expressed the opinion that the South should be and will be independent. I still haven't forgotten his comments on the Emancipation Proclamation." His hand grasped the papers so tightly that they crumpled as his jaw set hard. "That man is no friend of the United States." The cabinet was taken aback. None of them had ever heard him speak so harshly of anyone.

The President picked up another document from the table and went on, "Russell wrote, 'There seems to be no declaration of a principle adverse to slavery in this proclamation. It is a measure of a very questionable kind.'[7] A very questionable kind? How dare he affront this great thing we are about? I have to bring the people along on emancipation step by step. They will not be rushed, but are willing to learn. I cannot beat into them what only time and the evidence of their own common and moral senses tell them." His fist with the crumpled papers pounded the arm of his chair.[8]

"England will live to regret her inimical attitude towards us. After the collapse of the rebellion, John Bull will find that he has injured himself much more seriously than us."[9]

Seward tried to lighten the mood. "I have this description from a fellow countryman of Russell's, Sidney Smith. He said of Russell, 'He would have been willing to have built St. Peter's, commanded the Channel Squadron, or to have operated on a patient for the stone and would not have been deterred by the collapse of the sacred edifice, or the patient's death.'" The corners of a few dour faces rose.

"I've heard that Russell is only 5 foot 4 inches and barely weighs 8 stone. Why, Little Johnny Russell gives small men a bad name. He was once, as Smith said, 'over six foot tall but he has been so constantly kept in hot water that he is boiled down to the proportions in which you now behold him.'" Half smiles broke into laughter.

Lincoln had quickly shed his uncharacteristic anger, and he was not to be outdone in story telling. "That reminds me," he began — for those around Lincoln, those three words — were very familiar "of a barber in Sangamon County. He had just gone to bed, when a stranger came along and said he must be shaved; that he had four days' beard on his face and was going to a ball, and that the beard must come off. Well, the barber reluctantly got up, and dressed, and seated the man in a chair with a back so low that every time he bore down on him he came near dislocating his victim's neck. He began by lathering his face, including his nose, eyes, and ears, stropped his razor on his boot, and then made a drive at the man's countenance as if he had practiced mowing a stubble-field. He made a bold swath across the cheek, carrying away the beard, a pimple, and two warts. The man in the chair ventured the remark, 'You appear to make everything level as you go.' Said the barber, 'Yes, and if this handle don't break, I guess I'll get away with what there is there.' The man's cheeks were so hollow that the barber could not get down into the valleys with the razor, and his ingenious idea occurred to him to stick his finger in the man's mouth and press out the cheeks. Finally he cut clear through the cheek and into his own finger. He pulled the finger out of the man's mouth, snapped the blood off it, glared at him and said, 'There, you lantern-jawed cuss, you've made me cut my finger.'"

Lincoln concluded with a twinkle in his eye, "Now, England will find that she has got the South into a pretty bad scrape by trying to ad-minister to her, and in the end she will find that she has only cut her own finger."[10]

The men burst out laughing. Even Gideon Welles nodded his great bushy beard. If ever there was a flinty New England Yankee, it was Welles. He was a good Navy Secretary and a War Democrat whom Lincoln brought into the cabinet to attract support for the effort to restore the Union. Welles had the wit to use Fox and did so now that Lincoln was in a good mood. "I would like Fox to discuss the potentialities of these ships." Lincoln nodded, and an assistant went to fetch him.

But Lincoln was on a roll and went on. "It makes me think of an Indian chief that we had out West. He was visited by an Englishman once who tried to impress him with the greatness of England. 'Why,' said he to the chief, 'the sun never sets on England.' 'Humph!' said the Indian. 'I suppose it's because God wouldn't trust them in the dark.'"[11]

They were still laughing when Fox entered the room to lay out the facts in stark detail. The two rams were iron hulled, 230 feet in length by 45 feet in the beam. They carried 4.5 inches of armor on the hull, which was designed to be only 6 feet above the waterline. They carried four heavy 9-inch British rifled guns, two each in twin turrets in 10 inches of armor. They had a speed of 10.5 knots and a cruising range of 3,000 miles. Most ominously, though, were the 7-foot steel rams jutting from the prows, an innovation reintroduced from ancient times.

"Those are facts, gentlemen, of the ships themselves. The ships are Numbers 294 and 295, and are being built in the same slip as the *Alabama*. Mr. Dudley's quick fingers have acquired for us the intent of the rebels. Their chief agent in Britain, James Bulloch, has written, 'I designed these ships for something more than harbour or even coast defence, and I confidently believe, if ready for sea now, they could sweep away the entire blockading fleet of the enemy.'"

Lincoln calmly broke the silence that followed that announcement. "Gus, when do we expect the first ship to be finished?"

"Our best estimate is late September, sir."

Lincoln turned to Seward. "Mr. Secretary, have we exhausted every means to persuade the British government to intervene and block the delivery of these ships?"

"Mr. President, we face the subtle but no less malevolent hostility of Palmerston. The Prime Minister works his hostility out like a puppeteer. Russell can do nothing to block him. His Chancellor of the Exchequer, Mr. Gladstone, is his ally. Is there anyone in this room that forgets his open endorsement of British recognition of the Confederacy last October?" Seward snorted in disgust. "He openly stated that the rebels had made a government and an army, and infamously 'what is more than either, they have made a nation.'[12] He publicly announced that the Confederacy would win its independence. The announcement caused a sensation in Europe and a case of delirium in the South."

Lincoln seemed lost in thought once Seward finished speaking, and no one else wanted to break into it. The clicking of the clock filled the room. The President leaned back in his chair, crossed his gangly legs, and put his long hands on the armrests. "Since the early days of this administration, I have done everything in my power to avoid being dragged into a second war, firm in the belief that the Union can bear only one war at a time. That is why during the Trent Affair I chose to suffer the public outrage and return the Confederate commissioners. The British were serious about war, and we were not."[13]

Turning to look at John Bright's picture on the wall, he said, "There are times when a policy simply can no longer be sustained. Our foreign trade is in a shambles, our merchant fleet in ruins or fled to foreign flags, economic ruin spreads along the East Coast. There may come a time when I can no longer ignore these injuries." Looking at Seward, he said, "Mr. Secretary, we must prepare a message for Mr. Adams to present to Lord Russell, a message that his government cannot ignore, that there is a line that cannot be crossed."

Fox saw his opening. "Mr. President," then remembering Welles, he added, "Mr. Secretary," and nodded. Navy Secretary Welles was a man who could be ruffled, if the proprieties were ignored. "May I suggest another measure that could prevent a war even if the British look the other way while the ships escape into international waters?"

Lincoln was intrigued, "Go on, Gus."

"As you know, the Foreign Enlistment Act was passed some years ago ostensibly to prevent British subjects from violating British neutrality by providing overt military assistance to a belligerent. Unfortunately, for us, the law was written so loosely that the Confederates have been able to sail the equivalent of a commerce-raiding fleet through it.

"The law forbids British subjects and firms from supplying ships of war to a belligerent, that is, ships outfitted with guns, ammunition, and military fittings in general. It also forbids the recruitment of British subjects as crews for belligerent warships. Our rebel friends get around this by building what are obviously commerce raiders but without the guns, ammunition, and fittings. Then as with the *Alabama*, they sneaked it out of Liverpool Harbor and sailed it off to the Azores, where it married up with another ship carrying guns, ammunition, fittings, and military stores, as well as a mostly British, former Royal Navy crew. The military cargo was transferred and fitted to the commerce raider in short order."

Seward added, "We have evidence that British officials from the harbor master in Liverpool to the Foreign Ministry itself connived to alert the Confederate agents in the port to take the ship out when our diplomatic pressure became too great." He nodded to Fox to continue.

"Yes, that is just my point. We can expect the British to try this again. If we intercept the rams just outside of British waters in the Irish Sea, we can seize or sink them easily since they will be unarmed and with minimal crew."

Seward thumped the table with a bang. "Excellent. Just what I have been recommending to you, Gideon!"

Welles glowered. "And I have told you, Bill, we simply do not have the warships to pull off blockade duty. Even one purpose-built warship is too much."

Fox had an answer. "Mr. Secretary, we do not need to use such ship. The rams will be unarmed and with only a small transfer crew on its sea trials voyage. What we need is something fast with a bold captain to strike suddenly like a shark."

Lincoln said, "I like what I'm hearing. Go on, Gus. And what will you use if not a purpose-built warship? And who will be our bold captain?"

"I have him downstairs, Mr. President. It is Lt. Roswell Lamson of the *Nanesmond*. I took the liberty of ordering him to the Navy Yard."

"I've heard of this young man. Didn't he bring in quite prize just a few days ago?"

"Yes, sir, the fastest ship on record, the British mail packet the *Margaret and Jesse*. And here is my second point. Such a stroke requires the greatest speed and agility, and that is just what the *Margaret and Jesse* has—sixteen knots to the ten and a half knots for the rams."

"But this ship isn't armed, is it?"

"No, sir, but that can be remedied in ten days at the Navy Yard if I have priority. The guns, fittings, and skilled workmen are there. They've worked wonders before."

"Well, Gus, you've brightened my day considerable. Let's meet this young man."

All this time Sharpe and Lamson had been in the middle of an animated conversation. Lamson found himself pouring out everything he knew about blockade-running prompted by one deft question after another from Sharpe. Lamson was in the middle of his account of running down the *Margaret and Jesse* when a secretary announced that the President would see him. He straightened his uniform; slicked back his straight, dark hair; and followed the secretary as Sharpe sent after him an encouraging, "Good luck, Lieutenant."

When they were alone, Dana leaned over to speak in confidence. "Colonel, your report of the contraband, George, caused quite a stir here coming on the heels of Morgan's raid."

Sharpe had hoped that it would. He asked, "How so?"

"How much do you know about the Copperheads?"

Sharpe knew a great deal. His intelligence duties included, on his initiative, counterintelligence as well. He was aware of the attempts by the Copperheads to attack the morale of the Union soldier through the mails and by visiting agitators. He also knew how they preyed on furloughed soldiers and did everything to discourage recruitment. He went over these issues one by one with Dana, who was impressed with Sharpe's grasp of an issue not directly tied to his duties.

"I must tell you, Sharpe, that the President and Secretary Stanton want to discuss your report with you. It bears on the Copperhead conspiracy centered in the Midwest to launch another rebellion; take Ohio, Indiana, and Illinois out of the Union; and join the Confederacy. They are not just talking, either, or attempting to poison the minds of citizens and soldiers. They have raided military warehouses and depots for small arms and ammunition, and are even making huge purchases on the open market. They've even welcomed rebel officers among them to plan the military operation. We are convinced they plan to overthrow the government and take the Northwest into the Confederacy."[14]

Now it was Sharpe's turn to be impressed. "What is the source of your information?" he asked.

Dana smiled. "We have a remarkable young agent in their midst. Felix Stidger, a clerk for the Tennessee Provost, volunteered for the mission and reports to Col. Henry Carrington. The governor of Indiana requested Carrington by name to get a grip on these damned traitors, and the colonel recruited Stidger. The young man ingratiated himself so well with the conspirators that he was appointed, of all things, their corresponding secretary! Hah! We get all the news faster than some of their own leaders. We've been able to raid many of their arms caches and arrest a number of their leaders, but I'm afraid we're just scratching the surface. That's why Stidger is so important. He is an admirable young man. His country owes well of him."

3.

George the Contraband and One-Eyed Garnet

THE WHITE HOUSE, 4:00 PM, AUGUST 6, 1863

Dana and Sharpe had their heads together when Fox and Lamson passed through the anteroom. "Dana," Fox said, "the President approved my plan." He patted Lamson on the back and grinned. "This is the young man who is going to pull it off."

"Well, congratulations to you, Gus, and better yet, good luck to you, Lieutenant. You're going to need it to pull off any of Fox's schemes." Dana said good-naturedly. Lamson and Fox left deep in conversation.

Dana shook his head. "Sharpe, I want you to know that Gus Fox saved the Navy, and its successes stem from his drive and judgment, but there are times when Gus Fox's grasp exceeds his reach." He sighed. "Well, I have enough to do looking after Mr. Stanton's office without worrying over the Navy." Sharpe would have loved to inquire what Fox had meant about the plan that the President had just approved, but common sense told him to stay silent.

A secretary then announced that the President would see them. They had just stood up when Lincoln himself walked into the room. "Hello, Charlie," he said as he extended his long arm to shake Dana's hand. Sharpe had never met the man, but he had seen him on his visits to the Army as commander in chief. "I have been sitting too long and wanted to stretch my legs, and since they're longer than most, they need more stretching than most."

Lincoln turned to Sharpe, taking his hand as he said, "You must be the shadow man I keep hearing about from the Army of the Potomac. I make it a point to read every one of your reports that General Meade sends to the War Department. They make for lively reading, Colonel, lively reading. Especially one in particular."

Sharpe was studying the man intently. He had rarely been put at such ease so quickly by another man. He had heard sneers about President Lincoln's lack of sophistication and dignity. But there was a warmth and kindliness to his face and a humble self-assurance that was strangely comforting. Sharpe had spent his life in the most exclusive circles in New York and Europe, and their manners, pedigrees, and protocol had become second nature. Yet Sharpe found that Lincoln had not affronted those preconceptions. In his work as a lawyer and as a first-class interrogator, Sharpe had become able to detect the smallest hint of affectation or deception. There was none of that in this man. He was what he presented himself to be. Sharpe was even flattered that the President had heard of him. He realized that in these few short moments, he wanted to please this man more than just duty or personal ambition required.

"Well, gentlemen, let's go into my office and talk," Lincoln winked. "We can't keep Mr. Stanton and Mr. Seward waiting. They are mighty important people." As they walked out, Sharpe noticed that Lincoln was wearing well-worn slippers. Amazing.

Lincoln's office was where he held his most intimate conversations. He had adjourned the full cabinet to confer with his two senior ministers over the implications of Sharpe's report. "You know Colonel Sharpe, don't you, Stanton?"

"Of course," Stanton smiled at seeing Sharpe. "How can I forget Sergeant Cline and those dispatches from President Davis he dropped into our hands? Give my regards to the good sergeant, Sharpe. And tell him there's more gold where that came from."

He began to introduce Sharpe to Seward, but Seward said, "We know each other, Mr. President. His father and I were friends when we were young. I regret that he passed so soon. I was also the one who recommended to the governor of New York that he ask Sharpe to raise a regiment in '62 when you called for three hundred thousand more men. And look how well he's done." Turning to his only rival in the cabinet, he said genially, "You see, he may belong to Mr. Stanton, but I take credit for him." Stanton frowned. A sense of humor at his own expense was not one of Edwin McMasters Stanton's finer points.

However, sticking to business was. "If you've finished patting yourself on the back, Bill, let's get down to what we are here for."

"Yes, Colonel, let us hear more about George the Contraband." Lincoln was leaning back in a cane-backed rocker, one knee draped over the other, his slipper dangling half off.

Sharpe noticed that his sock was darned. It occurred to him that the precariously hanging slipper was not a form of rudeness but a compliment. He was trusted. That was a relief. After Gettysburg, Meade had turned his acid tongue on Sharpe and stripped him of his duties to coordinate all the collection resources of the Army outside those in his own bureau. Meade was a general of the old school in a new war. It was not a happy headquarters. How strange that the commander in chief was capable of spreading trust and calm, where so many generals could not.

"Tell us the story about how you found him."

Sharpe was no mean storyteller himself. This was business, and the facts were what mattered, yet he had to convince, and that was the storyteller's art.

"Mr. President," Sharpe leaned forward. "Before you can understand George, you have to understand what we do in the Bureau of Military Information. Since we were formed in February, thousands of men, white and black, have passed through our hands—prisoners of war, deserters, refugees, and contrabands. My chief interrogator, John Babcock, and I have developed a fine nose for the truth and just as fine a technique to get at it. We are rarely deceived.

"Those who come to us willingly are apt to exaggerate or invent what they think we want to hear. It is a common thing and easily found out, for already we have such a body of information on the organization, strengths, leaders, and problems of the Army of Northern Virginia that a simple comparison will tell if the story rings true or false. We know every regiment in Lee's Army, its commander, and its strength. We know the state of their horses, the rations and forage they receive or not, the arrival of reinforcements or not. We follow them when they move their regiments, brigades, and divisions from one place to another, and issue updated maps and orders of battle to the general commanding on a regular basis."

Lincoln asked, "Do you mean you get all of this from simple interrogations?"

"No, sir, we take our information from any and all sources at our disposal—and that means, in addition to interrogations, reports of my scouts and agents, examination of enemy documents, even personal letters, reports from the Signal Corps, the cavalry, the agents of the Secretary of War, and even the Provost Marshal of Maryland, James McPhail.

I even encourage the pickets to obtain information from their Confederate opposites. They exchange coffee, tobacco, and newspapers often enough, why not information? That reminds me—" and before he could get further, Lincoln smiled as Seward and Stanton rolled their eyes.[1]

Sharpe took it in stride and pressed on, "Of the time one little private from Rhode Island took my admonition with great enthusiasm. As soon as he got onto the picket line, he called out, 'Johnny Reb, what's your regiment?' The Rebel called back, 'The 21st South Carolina. How about you, Yank? What's your regiment?' The little soldier responded proudly, 'The One Hundred and Forty-Seventh Rhode Island!" That seemed to get the South Carolinian in a real twist, as he yelled back, 'You're a damned liar, Yank, there aren't 147 men in that whole measly little state!'"[2]

Lincoln burst out laughing and slapped his knee. "By heavens, Colonel, I will just have to steal that one from you, if you won't stand on copyright."

"Consider it in the public domain, Mr. President."

Lincoln chuckled, "I don't make the stories mine by telling them. I'm only a retail dealer."

Stanton had enjoyed the story as much as everyone else, but thought that one storyteller in the room was more than enough. "Let's get back to George the Contraband, Sharpe. Did he pass your test?"

"Indeed, sir, he did so without a doubt. Mr. Babcock and Sergeant Cline like to chat up the occupants of the Bull Pen, the Provost Marshal's prison pen, to see if they can skim any cream right off the top. Cline came to me. 'I think you should talk to this one. He came through our lines last night, gave himself up to the pickets, and claims to be John Hunt Morgan's body servant.' He had my attention immediately. You will remember that Morgan was rampaging through Indiana at the time before his capture.

"I could tell at once he was no field hand. You could almost say that he carried himself like a gentleman; he was a light-skinned mulatto, about five feet and four inches tall and well dressed. I didn't even get the first word. He told me point blank, 'I have news for you, Colonel.' His English had that Southern lilt, but it was clear and grammatical as any white rebel I have interrogated. He can read and write as well. He had a copy of *Les Misérables* in his pocket. In my line of work, I make it a habit of not interrupting a man who wants to share something. I encouraged him to start.

"'Let me introduce myself, first,' he said. He was a straightfor-
ward man, and his eyes remained fixed on me. There was no telltale of a
lie in his unconscious up and rightward glance. 'I am William George
Morgan, and I was born in General Morgan's household. They call me
George. The general and I received the same education while we were
boys so that I could become his body servant. Mr. Morgan was a generous man, perhaps because I have, by a most strange coincidence, an uncanny resemblance to the old gentleman.'" Sharpe paused with a smile
and commented, "In my journeys south before the war, I gathered that
the chivalry down there acted as if the profusion of mulatto children in
their great houses seemed simply to have fallen out of the sky."

Sharpe continued, "At this point, I asked him the obvious question: 'Why weren't you with Morgan on his raid?'

"'You must understand, sir, that the general knows perfectly well
that I am his brother, and he has done everything he can to recognize that
unwelcome fact, short of acknowledge me in public. I can't blame him;
he's trapped by slavery as much as I was – more so, because I can run
away from it, and he cannot not. I went off to war with him proud to be
a soldier and, strange as it may sound, fight for the South. After all, it is
my home, too.'"[3]

Sharpe interrupted his story to comment again, "This is not as
strange as he makes out. General Lee's Army could not function without
its thousands of Negroes, although they are not officially enlisted in the
Confederate Army except, strangely, as bandsmen. After Gettysburg,
Lee's white troops were so depleted in strength and numbers that he ordered our five thousand prisoners escorted South by armed Negroes from
his Army. And I must say they were punctilious in their duties. There
was more than one white backside poked along to Richmond's Belle Island Prison by a bayonet in black hands. I have learned also that after
Grant took Vicksburg, he offered the 400 slave body servants the opportunity to go North. Everyone went South with their paroled masters."

Stanton asked impatiently, "Then why can we trust what he has to
say if they're so damned loyal? And how do you explain the hundreds of
thousands of contrabands that come into our lines?"

"One thing I have learned, Mr. Secretary, in my years with the old
Negro community in Kingston, New York, and here in Virginia in deal-
ing with thousands of contraband slaves, Negroes are eminently secret
people; they have a system of understanding amounting almost to free
masonry among them; they will trust each other when they will not trust
white men.[4]

"Their actions, however, speak louder than words. I will defy any-one to claim that a Negro, outside a Confederate Army, has ever be-trayed a Union soldier. The lives of my scouts and agents in the heart of Virginia have depended on the active goodwill of Negroes. They have come to the aid of my people to warn them of danger and guide them to safety countless times. Where fear made them dare not give overt assis-tance, they could be depended on to remain silent despite great reward. There is little in their immediate neighborhoods that they do not know, although most slaves' knowledge does not extend beyond five miles of their plantations."

"This George is no field hand," Stanton replied.

"No, he is not, but he shares with his people the same dream."

Lincoln spoke, "It seems you have learned exactly the same lesson that Mr. Douglass has been pressing.[5] How many forget that freedom is the most intoxicating of all the works of man?"

He said this with such a humility that Sharpe was taken aback. Anyone else would have said it with a righteous flourish. Lincoln had said it as if the very idea was a precious marvel that one could only re-vere. The man dangling his slipper had assumed a glow that Sharpe had only seen in an El Greco saint in the Prado in Madrid.

The room was silent for a long moment before Lincoln leaned over and said, "Now tell us, Colonel, how Jeff Davis has his fingers all over this."[6]

Sharpe picked up his narrative. "Davis himself unwittingly pro-voked George's escape. Morgan relied on George to act as his clerk, to do much of his paperwork and file his papers. In turn, Morgan's adjutant depended upon George and was happy to pass paper to him. Carelessly, he passed the deciphered message to George. That is not as strange as it may seem. The chivalry are uniformly careless around their body ser-vants and speak of the most secret matters around them. They are like the furniture to them. I have it on good authority that even Lee discounts them as useful sources of intelligence for us because of their simple na-tures. My experience is that they are often astute observers.

"Why, it was the contraband Charlie Wright, an officer's body ser-vant, who came into our lines and gave us the information that two of Lee's corps were passing through Culpeper Court House into the Shenandoah Valley for the invasion of Pennsylvania last June. He had an almost encyclopedic knowledge of a good part of the Army of Northern Virginia, one in which Mr. Babcock could not find a single error. It was on this intelligence that General Hooker began to move the Army of the Potomac north to counter Lee. We actually crossed the Potomac before Lee did. Charlie Wright's warning may well have been the deciding factor in our ability to meet Lee at Gettysburg rather than to our disadvantage on the outskirts of Baltimore or Washington.[7]

"It was Davis's deciphered telegram that made George realize what was at stake. His memory was quite good, and he told us that the object of Morgan's raid was to raise the Copperheads in the Northwest and assist them in the overthrow of the state governments and the destruction of the authority of the federal government. Furthermore, Morgan was to liberate the prisoner of war camps within reach, especially the six thousand men held in the camp at Indianapolis and the eight thousand in Chicago. The Copperheads were to assist in this and bring sufficient arms to completely equip them. Morgan would have had the equivalent of several rebel infantry divisions at his disposal along with thousands of Copperheads in the heart to the Northwest. The message also stated that the strategic goal was more than overthrowing the authority of the government but to bring the Northwest—at least Illinois, Indiana, and Ohio—into the Confederacy."[8]

"Thank God, the rebels failed miserably," Stanton said. "We have Morgan locked up tight as a tick."

"Morgan is not the end of this, Edwin." Seward added, "As I understand it, Morgan's men behaved so badly that the damned disloyal fuse did not light. I can tell you, from the political end of this business, the Copperheads are in no way discouraged. They are biding their time. We nearly had an open revolt when that son-of-a-bitch Vallandingham was convicted of treason. I would not discount the rebels and Copperheads trying this again."[9]

Dana commented, "Morgan's capture did not prevent them raiding an arms warehouse on the second and murdering the guards. We lost five thousand new Springfield rifles. That would be almost enough to equip all the prisoners in the Indianapolis camp."

"Well, Sharpe," Stanton added with a rare smile, "if Colonel Carrington's man, Stidger, wasn't doing such a splendid job for us, your Sergeant Cline would seem to be the perfect man to spy upon the Copperheads. And he's a Hoosier, too, if I remember, 3rd Indiana Cavalry."

Sharpe's Excelsior College pride promoted him to throw in, "Actually, sir, he's New York born and raised and has only recently made his home in Indiana."

"It seems you New Yorkers are a thick lot," Lincoln winked at Seward. "Why Seward here just recently hosted a dinner for the star of the New York stage, Edwin Booth. Have you seen him perform?"

"Many times in the city, sir. My wife adores him."

"He was here at Ford's Theater doing his Shylock in "'The Merchant of Venice.'" Lincoln's voice had gone sad and soft. "A good performance, but I'd a thousand times rather read it at home if it were not for Booth's playing." [10]

Stanton spoke. "The President often goes to the theater and without any bodyguard at all. They let him quietly in the back." Then assuming his official frown, he said, "Mr. President, I must again beg you to be not so careless of your personal safety. There are many who would do you harm."

"Oh, Stanton, the fact is, I am a great coward. I have moral courage enough, I think, but I am such a coward physically that if I were to shoulder a gun and go into action, I am dead sure that I should turn and run at the first fire. I know I should." [11]

There was an awkward silence.

Lincoln smiled and said, "That reminds me."

An hour later, as Sharpe and the others were leaving the White House, Stanton took him by the arm. "Colonel, I want you to stay in Washington for a few days; I think we haven't heard the end of this." Turning to Dana, he said, "Charlie, wire Meade to tell him we have kept him here on my orders." Without waiting for a reply, he rushed off.

Dana said to Sharpe, "You should be able to find a room at the Willard. Washington empties out in August, even in wartime. This vile summer heat drives out all but the most hardy. Can I give you a ride? It's not far, but no one should have to walk in this heat."

Sharpe replied, "Well, my wife certainly would agree. At her insistence I took a house for the family here in Washington, but she fled to the Hudson Valley in June. I'm afraid I will have it all to myself. At least I don't have to go far; it's right here on Lafayette Square." Sharpe pointed to it just beyond the rearing bronze equestrian statue of Andrew Jackson in the middle of the square. He was about to take his leave when he noticed two men walking up the path to the main door. One was a spare cavalry captain and the other a short, stocky, white-haired civilian. Dana smiled as they approached. On closer examination, Sharpe could tell the white-haired man was young, not old.

As they came up Dana said, "Charles, Andy, how the hell are you?" Turning to Sharpe he said, "Let me introduce you to two friends." He

nodded to the captain who saluted Sharpe. "Capt. Charles Francis Adams,
Jr., 5th Massachusetts Cavalry." Adams bore the natural self-possession
of a man who knew who he was. Dana did not have to explain that he
was the son and grandson of presidents. He only referred to it obliquely.
"Charles's father is our ambassador in London and a very busy man, as
we have been saying, trying to get our British friends from building more
commerce raiders for the rebels."

The white-haired man broke in and said in a brogue so thick it
could have been spread with a trowel, "British friends, indeed. Our only
British friends are those who work for a living. And it is a thankless job in
that royalty-ridden island, it is."

Dana laughed. "I don't want you to think that this sour-faced Yankee is all work and no play. He is quite the politician, though luckily not
a very good one." He winked at Charles, who forced a smile. "Charles
was Seward's campaign manager for the presidency, which is why Mr.
Seward is now Secretary of State.

"And this," he said, taking the white-haired man by the arm, "is
Andy Carnegie or, as he is affectionately known, 'that little white-haired
Scotch devil.'"

Dana affectionately clapped a hand on Carnegie's shoulder. "Andy
here single-handedly opened the rail line between Baltimore and Washington in early '61 as it looked like Maryland would secede along with
the rest of the South. He organized the train that brought Ben Butler and
his troops to Washington in time to save the city. Rode on the cow catcher,
he did, to see that the tracks and telegraph were not broken up. See that
scar on his cheek. He got it by trying to free some wires that had been
sabotaged. They sprang back and sliced him good. Why, he is so modest, I must be the one to tell you he was the first man to bleed for his
country."

He turned serious. "All fooling aside, young Andy here organized
the military telegraph and railroad for us early in the war, and they've
been one of our great advantages. He rushed the trains to rescue thousands of our men wounded at First Bull Run. It's just a pity he didn't ask
for a brigadier general's commission; he would have had one at the drop
of a hat, but he could not resist the money piling up in the Pennsylvania
Railroad business. I tell you, Sharpe, if ever you need a keen organizer,
call on young Andy here."[12]

Carnegie had waited patiently to get a word in. "Achh, noo, Charlie,
you think you can dangle stars before the eyes of a poor Scottish weaver's

son. Shame on yea. I tell you I do more for the Union by running a railroad well than I would as a major general. Oh, and it's a pleasure to meet you, Colonel Sharpe."

"And did I tell you how modest he was," Dana added. Carnegie blushed a bright red, quite a contrast to his light blue eyes and white hair. Dana was not through getting a rise out of him and added, "And how much reverence he has for the British crown?"

Carnegie's entire demeanor changed instantly. The color drained from his face, and his eyes glinted like ice. "I came to this country to see the last of crowns. The sooner Britain is a republic, the better for the whole world."[13]

Dana pulled him by the arm. "Come on, Andy, you can damn the monarchy later. We have business." Adams saluted and excused himself as well to deliver dispatches to the White House. Sharpe wished them all good evening and headed for home. He had walked as far as Jackson's statue, when a White House secretary chased him down.

"Colonel Sharpe," he said breathlessly, "the President requests that you attend him in the morning on his visit to the Navy Yard."[14]

EBBITT GRILL, WASHINGTON, D.C., 8:00 PM, AUGUST 6, 1863

Without his family, Sharpe's big house echoed with silence. The servants had been let off for the summer, and there was no food. After washing, Sharpe sought out dinner. The Ebbitt Grill was close and among the best eating establishments in the city. He was lucky to find a table near the door and an open window; the city may have emptied out, but that left hundreds of officers tied to their duties who liked to relax over a good meal as the evening cooled.

He had just been given the menu when he noticed the maître d' telling a British naval officer and another man with an eye patch that it would be at least an hour before they could be seated. Sharpe walked over, "Gentlemen, you are welcome to share my table." Interesting company would compensate a bit for the cheerless house.

"Most handsome of you, sir. I am Capt. George Hancock, of Her Majesty's Ship *Immortalité*, attached to our embassy as a temporary observer of this unfortunate war.[15] May I present Mr. Garnet Wolseley, a visitor from our country." The one-eyed man was about thirty years old, with a weak chin and a thin mustache. His single blue eye, however, was hawk sharp and intelligent. The man's military bearing was unmistakable. Sharpe introduced himself as the commander of the 120th NY Volunteers. This was more than just company to pass the time, thought

Sharpe. The one-eyed man was too interesting. "Mr. Wolseley" indeed. The captain's skills at concealment were, to say the least, lacking.

The waiter recommended an excellent French wine and the roast quail stuffed with wild rice and creamed carrots. The wine instantly reminded Sharpe of the two delightful years he spent in Paris, where he perfected his French and refined his palate. In his mind, he upped the already generous tip he normally would have given.

As much as he looked forward to the wine, he was far more interested in his civilian dinner party guest. The one-eyed man was no other than Lt. Col. Garnet Wolseley, the Assistant Quartermaster General for the British forces in Canada. That alone made him a person of interest for Sharpe. During the crisis of the Trent Affair, the British had reinforced their garrison in Canada to more than eighteen thousand men, including a Guards Brigade of two battalions. Wolseley had not come by the position as reward for good breeding, but as a protégé of Lt. Gen. Sir Hope Grant, the hero of the Sepoy Revolt and the best general the British had. Wolseley had been one of Grant's brilliant subordinates in the campaigns that had broken the Sepoys in India in 1857–58 and sacked the imperial summer palace outside Peking in 1860. He had ridden the glory path with Grant and was in Canada, considered with Corfu to be the best duty station in the British Army, as a reward for gallant service. He came from a military family and had lost his eye as a subaltern in the Crimean War. He was very much a man on the way up.

Of equal interest and the obvious reason for Captain Hancock's flimsy cover story was Wolseley's notoriety. Out of boredom apparently, he and another officer had taken leave to see the war among the Americans. They had drawn straws to see which side each would visit. Wolseley had drawn the South. He had slipped through the Union pickets and across the Rappahannock River to Fredericksburg and on to Richmond, where he was received at the highest levels and given handsome letters of introduction to Lee. The visit developed into an unabashed case of outright hero worship. For the rest of his life, he would hold Lee as the absolute paragon and say in his later years, "I have met two men whom I prized above all the world I have ever known, and the greater of these two was General Lee." The other was the British general Charles "Chinese" Gordon, who would perish gloriously at Khartoum a generation later.[16]

Wolseley's visit to Lee might have gone unnoticed save for the article he wrote for *Blackwood's Magazine* that received much notice not only in Britain but also in the States. It had given astute professional insight into the Army of Northern Virginia. His opinion was that he never saw an army composed of men who "looked more like work" than this one.[17] The contrast with their ragged condition could not have been starker in the eyes of an officer from an army of sartorial splendor. In a review held of Hood's Texas Division for his benefit, Wolseley was shocked to see so many trousers worn out at the bottom as the ranks passed. Noticing his surprise, Lee remarked, "Never mind the raggedness, Colonel. The enemy never sees the back of my Texas Brigade." Sharpe could appreciate that because he had helped the Army of the Potomac prove Lee wrong at Gettysburg.

Wolseley's escapade might have created less controversy had he not offered good reasons for a British alliance in order to safeguard Her Majesty's possessions in North America. His statement that a defeated North could not attack Canada if threatened by Britain's Confederate ally won him no thanks in the Union.

With all this in mind, Sharpe was most interested in what Wolseley was doing back in the United States. Wolseley seemed most interested in Sharpe's experience at Gettysburg and his opinion of the battle. It was a safe subject to draw him out on, and Sharpe steered the discussion to the conduct of the battle in general. Wolseley's disappointment in the outcome of the battle was clear. He could not believe Lee had blundered and kept quizzing Sharpe to discover some explanation that would exculpate his hero. Nonetheless, Sharpe had to admit that his questions were penetrating and his comments insightful. This was a man who knew the business of soldiering.

Wolseley snorted in contempt when Sharpe described the moving scene of the Irish Brigade kneeling to receive the benediction of Father William Corby, who blessed their heroic charge. He evidently assumed that Sharpe's name put his ancestors on the Anglo-Saxon side of the Irish Sea. Wolseley asked, "Are you by chance related to Col. Richard Sharpe of the 95th Rifles?"

Sharpe saw no reason to tell him that it was the Anglicized form of the German Sherfe. "Not that I know of. My people have been in this country for almost two hundred years. I'm afraid I am not familiar with that officer."

Woolsey was clearly disappointed. "Why, Richard Sharpe was one of Wellington's favorite officers, risen from the ranks for gallantry, and a very prolific killer of Frenchmen, I might add." It was evident that the latter quality was high on Wolseley's list of martial virtues.[18] But the subject of the Sharpe family name had only diverted him from this Gaelic distaste. "And as for the Irish, my dear Colonel, they are an ugly race with noses so cut away that you can see the place where their brains should be."[19]

Sharpe had to control himself as he thought of all the Irish boys in his regiment from Kingston who had fallen on that field as well as the daring and courage of his scouts, the Carney brothers, and young Martin Hogan just three years off the boat. Instead, he smiled blandly, "Well, sir, they don't always present themselves to best effect. But I would think that a country that has made such use of the Irish in the building of its empire could be a bit more charitable."

Wolseley brushed off the olive branch and went on, "They are a strange, illogical, inaccurate race, with the most amiable qualities, garnished with the dirt and squalor which they seem to love as dearly as their religion. I tell you, the Irishman soon takes his hat off when he finds a master who is not afraid of him and who is always ready to tackle him."[20]

When Wolseley had decided that he had chewed on that scrap of bile long enough, he asked, "Well, Colonel, what is the feeling in the Army now that the South has been set back on both heels—Gettysburg and Vicksburg?"

Sharpe considered that an honest answer would actually be the most useful. "It is only a matter of time. The South is exhausted and devouring itself to supply its armies just as the Union's strength is redoubling. If it weren't for blockade-runners bringing in British weapons and munitions, they would collapse in a month or two. All your country is doing is to prolong the struggle. Who knows what unforeseen incident could provoke another Trent Affair? Everyone knows that we came too close to war that time. It would serve no one's interest to come that close again. I do not even mention the mutual catastrophe that a war would entail. British entry on the side of the Confederacy would only earn it the undying enmity of the United States but fail in the long run to secure independence for the South. Do you really want to create an enemy that for the next one hundred years searches out every enemy of the British Empire to make common cause?"

Wolseley fixed him with that single, hard, blue eye as the waiter cleared the table, "But you can hardly hold the support of your own population to continue the war. I understand there is extremely powerful, popular opposition. How then could you add the burden of a war with a great power," he paused to add, "such as France? Forgive me for my bluntness, but you would go to pieces at the first blow."

Sharpe just smiled, "A war with a," he paused to emphasize the object of this preposition, "*major foreign power such as France* would kindle a fire that would weld our people into an implacable unity. Make no mistake of it."

Sharpe let his message sink in. He had not been empowered by the government to speak at this level, but there was no time to ask, and he did not think that Seward would mind. He would report to Dana tomorrow on their interesting conversation. The silence continued until the waiter returned with a box of cigars and brandy, which immediately deflected the conversation. The Ebbitt offered an excellent array of cigars. Sharpe did not remark on how such fine Southern tobacco was so readily available in the Union's capital. It was an embarrassment how badly the blockade leaked, not to mention overland trade, something his companions were no doubt aware of.

Sharpe coolly blew a ring across the table. "I must apologize for my bluntness, gentlemen. Please, forgive a simple colonel of infantry for a lack of subtly." Perhaps that was laying it on too thick. Time to change the subject. "Tell me, Captain, what of the French? What does your government think of the French adventure in Mexico?"

Hancock had taken little part in the conversation concerning Army matters, but now he had something to say. "I would say that the British government considers Napoleon's ambitions to be a measure of Gallic excess. Mexico is no place to stay. You Americans were clever to win quickly, take what you wanted, and get out. Your example was lost on the French, I'm afraid."

"And you are not worried about the expansion of the French Navy?" That was fresh meat thrown to Hancock.

"By God, sir, afraid of the French? You do have a strange, Yankee sense of humor."

"But the French *Gloire* class ironclads did steal a march on the Royal Navy in '59, did it not?" Sharpe spoke in French. Hancock, not to be outdone, also switched, showing a remarkable grasp of French military terminology.

"Yes, I'm afraid the French were the first to build a serious ironclad, but they were following the example of the British ironclad batteries in the Russian War of the last decade. But our *Warrior* class put the

French right where they belong—in second place. The HMS *Warrior* and her sister-ship, *Black Prince*, were designed and built in record time. They are so superior to the French ships that there is no comparison. The *Warriors* are completely iron ships while the *Gloires* are wooden hulls with only ironclad casements. *Warriors* are almost 65 percent larger and are meant for open-ocean sailing whereas the Frenchies would have a hard go of it anywhere but the Channel and the Mediterranean. Our armament is clearly superior as well with twenty-six 68-pounders, four 70-pounders, and eleven breech-loading rifled 110-pounders of Mr. Armstrong's manufacture against the French thirty-six 6.4-inch rifled guns. All the British guns are superior as is our powder, the best the world."[21]

Sharpe thought that Admiral Dahlgren might disagree. He was not known as "the father of American naval ordnance" for nothing. His series of Dahlgren guns at IX, X, XI, and XV inches were considered by us to be the best in the world. The Royal Navy had tried to buy Dalgreen guns in large numbers, but the United States had declined to share such an advantage.

Hancock continued, "There is another area in which we completely outclass the French—no private French foundry can roll the armor necessary for such a ship; a number of British establishments can do that with ease. The French simply do not have the iron industry to support Napoleon's ambitions of an ironclad fleet."

Hancock's tail was up as he listed every point of British naval superiority over the French, which had the unspoken message that that superiority applied to the United States as well. "Why, sir, if these facts do not impress you, perhaps the words of Mr. Dickens might give a more poetic impression. He said after a recent visit to the *Warrior* that she was, and I quote, 'A black vicious ugly customer as ever I saw, whale-like in size, and with as terrible a row of incisor teeth as ever closed on a French frigate.' Another gentleman described her as 'a black snake among rabbits.' Having seen her myself, I can attest that the Mr. Dickens has caught its menace most properly."

Sharpe was enjoying the class on British naval technology, all grist for his intelligence mill. He had concentrated so much on the Confederate Army that it was refreshing to learn about the service of another country. He had scrupulously forwarded every bit of naval intelligence that came his way to the Navy and had learned something by way of it. He prodded Hancock further. "And our ironclads?"

"Why, sir, they are interesting designs, to be sure, but are dwarfed by the *Warriors*. Your *Passaic* class monitors have, indeed, proved to be a gallant, hard-fighting class but weigh in at 1,335 tons to the *Warrior*'s 9,210, and only two guns to forty. I wager that none of them would fare well in an open-ocean voyage either."

"I'm afraid you have me, Captain. I'm just a soldier and no naval expert."

Wolseley had been following all this carefully. His good eye widened a bit.[22]

4.

Gallantry on Crutches

WASHINGTON NAVY YARD, WASHINGTON, D.C., 8:00 AM, AUGUST 7, 1863

The President's carriage clattered through the Navy Yard's brick gates to the precision salute of the Marine guards. Superintendent Hardwood was aware of Lincoln's fascination for all things mechanical, and the Yard drew him like a magnet. It was an opportunity to polish the Navy's reputation with a smart military display. He never did figure out that Lincoln simply didn't care about that aspect.

What Lincoln cared about was winning the war. He may have been a lawyer from the Prairie State, but he had an instinctive appreciation for the budding technologies of the new and vigorous industrial age. He found the Army and Navy departments hopelessly mired in their own red tape at the expense of innovation. It was as if both services had missed the business revolution that had accompanied the Industrial Revolution. Once he was presented with a committee report on a new naval gun. He glanced at the report that had consumed an entire tree's worth of paper and exclaimed, "I should want a new lease of life to read this through." He hurled it on the table. "Why can't a committee of this kind occasionally exhibit a grain of common sense? If I send a man to buy a horse for me, I expect him to tell me his *points* – not how many *hairs* there are in his tail."[1]

The man with the common sense Lincoln had been seeking had been Capt. John A. Dahlgren, Yard superintendent at the beginning of his administration. He was an officer with an international reputation for technological innovation in naval gunnery and for deft management, and Lincoln had come to depend on him for advice in such matters and naval and military affairs in general. Finally in June he had reluctantly agreed to release now Rear Admiral Dahlgren to command the South Atlantic Blockading Squadron off Charleston.

When Sharpe stepped out of his door that morning to walk across the square to the White House, he was surprised to be greeted by a familiar voice from the carriage parked outside. He looked up to see a stove-pipe hat nodding down at him. "Good morning, Sharpe. Jump in." It was not every day that a President picked up a colonel. "If you were expecting us to wait on ceremony, my apologies, but we need an early start thing morning."

As they drove away, Lincoln said, "I thought your stay in Washington might be put to good use by broadening your horizons. The Navy Yard is just such a place. It is the most fun I have. I feel like a little boy who has escaped from some evil chore whenever I can sneak away from the White House. That reminds me."

By the time they were riding through the Navy Yard gate Lincoln had finished his fourth story, and Sharpe was laughing. Only later would he consider how much of his policy Lincoln had passed to him through his wit. He only regained his composure after they had passed the smoking cannon foundries and stopped near the towering and cavernous wooden dry dock into which the seven hundred–ton *Margaret and Jesse* was being drawn. Gus Fox had driven straight to the Yard after leaving the White House to put things in motion. The skilled workers and masters of the Yard were paid overtime to work through the night. But the ship was a trim and graceful thing at seven hundred tons and slipped easily into the dry dock.

Sharpe and Lincoln saw Gus Fox and young Lamson standing nearby, watching the ship's progress. It was a grand sight, Sharpe thought. He could tell the President was enjoying himself as much as a boy in a toy shop watching the latest windup gadget. When Fox and Lamson saw the President, they hurried over to pay their respects. "Good to see you boys at work so early. So, Gus, what are you planning to do to this leviathan?"

She did look a bit petite in the dry dock meant for a ship at least four times her size. "If you don't mind, sir, I'll let the ship's new captain explain," Fox said, turning the floor over to Lamson.

The young man was not shy at all but rather bursting with such enthusiasm that he was eager to share his delight in his new command.

"Sir, the first thing we are going to do is inspect her engines and weight-bearing structures, then reinforce the decks and ribbing to take the guns. We decided on three Dahlgren XI-inch guns per side and a seventh as the forward pivot gun. We'll round it out with an 8-inch Dahlgren rifle on the aft pivot."

Lincoln whistled softly. "That's a huge weight of metal. Are you sure she can bear it?"

"Yes, sir. The Yard shipwrights have been all over her, and she is a remarkably strong ship. We are reinforcing her decks and hull with more iron bracing just to make sure. I've never had such firepower on the *Nansemond*, sir. These XI-inchers have an enormous advantage over British armament. Why, one XI-inch shell has more destructive power than three 32-pounder shot, even if they all hit close together. And it does twice the damage of two 8-inch shells with even more explosive power. It also means that I can fight the ship with fewer men.[2] I won't mind getting into a fight with these guns on the *Margaret and Jesse*."

"Now that name, *Margaret and Jesse* is an awkward mouthful and none too martial either. This ship needs a new name, an American name," Lincoln suggested.

Everyone paused in thought, until Sharpe said simply, "Gettysburg. Let her be named after Gettysburg."

Lincoln slapped Sharpe on the shoulder. "Capital idea! USS *Gettysburg,* it is!" Fox and Lamson took a minute to digest that their prize would be named after the Army's greatest battle. But with the President having pronounced, they accepted Sharpe's fait accompli gracefully.

Lincoln turned to Fox, "Gus, I haven't heard much about the new shallow-draft monitors from the Navy Department. How are they doing? I've heard rumors that Stimers is having problems. Does this mean another delay?"

Alban Crocker Stimers was Fox's protégé and project manager for this ambitious twenty-ship *Casco* class of follow-on monitors to the *Passaic* class. They were designed for operations in the shallow coastal waters and harbors where the Navy was doing most of its fighting. Immense resources in materials and skilled labor had been devoted to the project. These resources were tight and much was expected of Stimers, who had successfully pushed the *Passaic* class, also based on Ericsson's design, to completion. The shallow-draft monitors were also originally an Ericsson design, but other priorities had pushed the genius Swedish designer on to new projects, leaving the project completely in Stimers's control.

Unfortunately, Stimers had been trying to outdesign Ericsson, and the scale and complexity of ambitious redesigns had overwhelmed the project. It had experienced delay after delay, and this had come to Lincoln's attention. Fox himself had begun to worry, but every inquiry had drawn the same responses from Stimers — that the ships would meet the new deadlines and that Ericsson had fully approved the changes. Fox was unaware that Stimers had merely assured Ericsson that things were under control. Welles was also on his back, suspicious of Stimers, whom he described as "intoxicated, overloaded with vanity," and "more weak than wicked."[3] Making things even worse, the larger *Tippecanoe* class was also late. Before Fox could answer, Lincoln said, "Gus, I think it would be a good idea to take a good look yourself."

Lincoln began to walk along the length of the dry dock to take a better look at the ship. Lamson followed. Sharpe and a chagrined Fox stayed behind. Fox looked after Lincoln as he walked along the dry dock. "He loves anything mechanical, you know. He has a surprisingly good nose for what works and doesn't." Fox said.[4] "And if it weren't for him, I don't know how I could have blown the cobwebs out of the Navy Department's old-fashioned bureaus. My God, they would still be happy to be accounting for every cannonball fired in the War of 1812 if we hadn't shaken them up enough to make the teeth rattle. Luckily, Dahlgren left the Yard in superb shape and gave us a model to bludgeon the rest of the departments with. We'd be in desperate shape if it were not for Dahlgren and the guns he's developed over the years. I tell you, the British are jealous of his guns."

Sharpe said, "Captain Hancock thinks not."

"Hancock? How do you know Hancock?"

"We had dinner last night at the Ebbitt Grill. He arrived late. I had just taken the last table, and invited Hancock and his guest to join me. It was a very interesting evening."

"The hell you say. That Limey bastard is like a Mississippi catfish — a magnificent bottom feeder. He sucks up every bit of information he can about the Navy and especially our monitors. So, tell me what he had to say."

Fox listened intently to Sharpe's recounting of the evening's conversation and said, "Dwarfed by the *Warriors*, did he say? Well, it's lucky for HMS *Warrior* that she has not met USS *Passaic*. Let me tell you something, Sharpe, about the new naval warfare. A broadside ship like *Warrior* has to go to great effort to maneuver itself to fire on its opponent. The entire ship has to be positioned for the shot. A monitor's revolving turret aims the guns in any direction regardless of the position of the ship. We can wrap a turret in 10 inches of good American steel while a broadside ironclad so far has rarely been able to mount more than 4.5 inches because that armor belt must run most of the length of the ship and form a casemate as on the *Warrior* and on our *New Ironsides*. The latter is the only such broadside ironclad that we built and that was in the initial competition for designs that included the *Monitor*. The fact that we have built no more broadside ironclads is a good indication of which we think is the more successful design. The monitors also have a low freeboard, making it difficult for a broadside ship to hit the hull at all. The broadside ship, on the other hand, is nothing but a big target."

Both looked down the dry dock at the sound of laughter from a crowd. Lincoln stood in the middle of a hundred Yard workers and had them in stitches. Fox smiled, "The working people and the sailors love him. He's not afraid to talk to them and what he says makes sense. Not only that, they know he cares for them."

"Yes, the feeling among the troops is largely one of affection, despite the die-hard McClellan worshippers. A thousand stories of his kindnesses circulate throughout the Army. He talks to the men when he visits the Army, too. I've heard them laugh just like this."

Fox added, "He's just the same with the seamen of the fleet. The stories of him are legion. One I can vouch for. I got it from the chief of hospitals here in Washington. After Gettysburg, he insisted on visiting every hospital in the city and Alexandria, and they were overflowing with the wounded. Not just ours but rebels, too. He said he wanted to shake every man's hand. The surgeon protested that there were thousands of men. Lincoln said to point the way, and so help me, the surgeon stated flatly he shook every hand, even visited the rebels. Afterward, to get the feeling back in his hand he chopped a small pile of cordwood outside one hospital ward. The orderly picked up every single chip to keep as a souvenir. Now, here's the truly remarkable thing. The surgeon swore that after he was done, Lincoln raised the ax straight out by the end of the haft and balanced it there for the longest time. His arm did not shake a bit. Never saw anything so remarkable."[5]

They could see Lincoln tip his hat and move back down the dry dock toward them.

"Gus, I think I will take the good captain of the *Gettysburg* away from you for a few hours. I want him and the good colonel to see someone."

BRITISH EMBASSY, WASHINGTON, D.C.,
11:00 AM, AUGUST 7, 1863

Hancock walked with Wolseley through the embassy's valiant attempt at a rose garden. He plucked a fungus-ruined bud and waved it at the one-eyed man. "Dreadful climate. We are rated a tropical post, you know? Such a country for weeds and blights. Makes you pine for the rose gardens of England. Well, the climate and blights seem to match these rude people, I must say. Perhaps it is what draws the Irish."

Wolseley had zero interest in roses or gardens. "I'm used to it after Burma and India. I prefer the cool Canadian summers, though, but I tell you I would much rather be campaigning in an Indian summer than bored to tears in cool Canada."

Hancock tossed the bud away and brushed his hands off. "I take it your opinion of the Yankees has changed since your last visit."

"Well, they are not a lovable people, to be sure. I like the Southerners, I must admit, though not enough to care about their Confederacy for itself. The source, indeed, of most of my good wishes arise from my dislike of the people of the United States, taking them generally, and my delight at seeing their swagger and bunkum rudely kicked out of them."[6]

"What did you think of our simple colonel of infantry at dinner last night, Wosleley? Damned well-informed if you ask me."

Wolseley had also been thinking about last night's dinner companion. "Did you notice, Hancock, that he did not let slip anything of importance? His account of the battle did nothing but add to the impression that their Army has put itself in good order. Did you also notice that when you had delivered your talking points, his questions put a finger on critical points of imperial policy toward the United States."

"Well, I must admit, it was as if I had been speaking to Mr. Fox at their Navy Department or Mr. Dana at their War Department. His question about their monitors was too close to the bone." Hancock may have been outclassed by Sharpe, but he knew his business.

"The Navy does not like to publicly admit that we are worried about the American monitors. Yes, we have *Warrior* and *Black Prince* and the two smaller 6,000-ton broadside ironclads *Defence* and *Resistance*, but the Americans already have eight of their *Passaic* class monitors, with more building, and two large broadside ironclads similar to our *Defence* class. Their building program is enormous at every major port on the East Coast and on the Ohio River as well. They have twenty hulls of a powerful shallow-draft monitor, the *Casco* class, which should be completed this autumn. There is a *Canonicus* class monitor with seven ships, and a *Milwaukee* class with five ships, all due next year. The point is that the Americans do not have to have an open-ocean Navy; their mission will be to defend the ports, waterways, and coasts, and their smaller size and shallower drafts will be ideal for these waters.[7]

"And what is abuilding in England? Three ships of the *Prince Consort* class and three more of the *Royal Oak* and *Hector* classes. All of them are broadside ironclads. None of them are the low-silhouette, turreted monitor types. And the *Royal Oak* is just a converted wooden ship with iron armor. We have only two turret ironclads building now, *Royal Sovereign* and *Prince Albert*. Do you realize the Americans have 10 inches of good armor on those turrets? All of our ships have armor belts only of 3 to 4.5 inches.[8] We have learned from our Confederate contacts and from the American press that in the battles in Charleston Harbor, the turrets have been well nigh invulnerable."

This was all news to Wolseley. The British services had had an excellent record of cooperation compared to any other country, but knowledge of the other service was not something an officer concerned himself with. "You don't mean the Americans have the advantage over the Royal Navy?"

"It is not as simple as that. Our purpose-built wooden and iron-hulled ships outnumber and outclass most of their American counterparts. We would have no trouble sweeping the American Navy from the seas. But, you must understand, that in a war with the Americans we cannot simply control the seas in order to win. They could easily be self-sufficient. No, we would need to break the blockade of the Southern ports and then go after them in their own harbors. And there is where we found these swarms of turreted monitors armed with Admiral Dahlgren's fearsome XV-inch guns."

"I seem to recall that the Dahlgren guns on the *Monitor* failed to breach the armor of the broadside ironclad *Virginia*," Wolseley said.

"True, but the *Monitor* carried only Dahlgren's XI-inch guns, not the XV-inch guns being fitted now on every new ship. The monitors at Charleston now each have one of their two guns a XV-inch. Moreover, at Hampton Roads, the *Monitor* only used 50 percent of the proof charge, meaning the maximum powder charge the guns were rated as being able to take. According to our sources, that deficiency has been corrected. In combat the Americans will use nearly 100 percent of the proof charge.

American tests on armor similar to the *Virginia*'s found that not only the XV- but the XI-inch projectiles would go right through her plate."

Hancock led him into the shade of the garden pergola and motioned him to the bench. "Damned tricky equation a war with the Americans, trickier than they think back home. I wonder if anyone in London reads my reports."

Wolseley was trying to sort out the implications of Hancock's review. "I understood that we were absolutely convinced during the Trent Affair that we could have crushed the Americans. Have the monitors upset that assumption so completely?"

"You must remember that in December 1861, the Americans had just embarked on this ruinous war. Their Navy was small — barely ninety ships, or one-tenth the size of the Royal Navy. Their admittedly fine harbor forts were in many cases unmanned and ungunned. We would have crushed them in one blow, I believe.

"But with the declaration of the blockade, the American Navy began to grow like Jack's magic beans. In four months, they had doubled the number of ships; in ten months they had grown sixfold. Mr. Welles was quoted, in speaking of one of the new ships rushed to completion, that its keel had been growing in a forest three months ago. Many of these new ships were gunboats or were converted merchantmen, but the point is that they did the job. Moreover, their crews have learned their jobs. The Americans have always been good sailors and when given even odds have embarrassed the Royal Navy too many times for me to consider — not at all like fighting the French. It is the American ability to organize and produce that worries me, Wolseley."

It occurred to Wolseley that the Army had had a similar experience with this American talent. During the Crimean War, when the production of the new Enfield rifled musket could not meet the war demand, the British Army had to swallow its pride and send an ordnance delegation to the United States. They toured the War Department's Springfield Arsenal and observed the "American method" of mass production. The Army immediately put in an order for comparable American-made machinery to completely reequip the Royal Small Arms Factory at Enfield. They also hired an American to manage the factory. The Royal Small Arms Factory had been transformed by its American additions into the pride of British manufacturing. The production of the superb Enfield rifle was more than sufficient to completely equip the British Army and its territorial forces as well as sell hundreds of thousands to both the

Confederacy and the Union before the latter's production increase by this time made imports unnecessary.[9]

"There's more, Wolseley. Are you aware that Adm. Sir Alexander Milne developed a war plan against the United States during the Trent Affair? He proposed to break the Union blockade at two points. Charleston, of course, would be the main effort, with a secondary effort to open a port such as Galveston, Texas. He also proposed to counterblockade the ports of the North and to sail up the Chesapeake Bay and attack Washington itself. At that time, we could have easily done it. I understand Admiral Milne says that today he would find such a plan most risky."[10]

"But, Hancock, given the neutrality of Her Majesty's government, the risk of war seems highly unlikely, does it not?"

"Not as unlikely as you think. London does not understand the deep anger the North feels toward Great Britain. British commerce keeps the Confederacy alive through our blockade-runners. Our Foreign Enlistment Act is so flimsy that British shipyards have produced a squadron of commerce raiders that is ruining the American merchant navy and whaling fleet with disastrous effects in the ports and businesses of the North. The press feeds the public's anger. Too many Americans already feel that we are secretly at war with them now. Adding constant insult to injury is our open partiality for the South. Such articles as yours in *Blackwood's*, I must say, Wolseley, are exactly what feeds anti-British sentiment. I cannot count the number of Americans of consequence who have angrily asked me to explain the advocacy of Her Majesty's Assistant Quartermaster General of Canada for British alliance with the Confederacy."

Before Wolseley had time to come to his own defense, Hancock exclaimed, "It's frightfully hot even here in the shade. Let's go indoors. Besides, I have something to show you that may be of interest."

4½ STREET, S.E., WASHINGTON, D.C., 11:15 PM, AUGUST 7, 1863

The carriage had only a few blocks to go as it trundled out of the Navy Yard gate. Lincoln explained that the object of their visit was a gallant young soldier—Col. Ulric Dahlgren, son of the admiral, who was recuperating at his father's home. Ulric had lost his leg while pursuing Lee after Gettysburg. Sharpe looked forward to the visit. Young Dahlgren and he had been appointed on the same order to Hooker's headquarters. It was a small headquarters, and the two were easily drawn to each other. Captain Dahlgren had been a twenty-one-year-old, handsome, lithe, blond *beau sabreur*, with a taste for daring forays into the enemy, and Sharpe had been the homely looking colonel with a master's touch for intelligence. It was this relationship that had led to the incredible raid that captured Jeff Davis's dispatches to Lee on July 2 at Gettysburg. Sergeant Cline had brought the information of the courier's route and timing, and Sharpe had organized the raid with Dahlgren in command. It had been the stuff of legend as Dahlgren led his band of fifteen men into a surprise attack on the courier escort and a passing Confederate wagon train in the middle of Greencastle. It was Cline who had seized the couriers with a cocked pistol at their heads. Dahlgren immediately rode the thirty miles for Meade's headquarters at Gettysburg and arrived at midnight to put the dispatches into Meade's hands. They were wired to Washington the next day; their content exposed the strategic weakness of the Confederacy in detail. Meade asked Dahlgren how he could reward him, and the young man said to give him a hundred men and send him out again. He had his wish. As he harried Lee's rear as it crossed the mountains, a bullet had shattered his foot. The wound went bad, and the leg below the knee had to be taken off.[11]

A look of sadness came across Lincoln's face. "I wanted you both to meet Ulric; in the two years that I have known his father, the boy had become almost like one of my own sons. It distressed me deeply to see the best this country has maimed."

Sharpe knew that Ulric's first visitor had been the President, who sat for hours by his bedside as the young man hovered near death. "Sir, Colonel Dahlgren and I are old friends. The staff of the Army of the Potomac is a small family, and we joined it at the same time last year. He is very much liked and very much missed."

Pleased, Lincoln said, "He seemed to have taken the operation in stride, but he went quickly into such a decline that we thought we would lose him. When Secretary Stanton had come to present him with his commission to colonel, the boy was too sick to even recognize him. Stanton then closed the street to wheeled traffic so as not to disturb his rest. He posted that guard," Lincoln pointed to the soldier lounging by the door of a small house, "to refuse admittance to anyone but doctors."[12] The soldier saw the carriage and grew bug eyed as he recognized the tall man in the stovepipe hat getting out of the carriage. He immediately presented arms.

A maid answered, curtsied, showed them to the parlor, and disappeared. Moments later an elderly gentleman, obviously not in the best of health, came in. Lincoln presented Mr. Lawrence, Ulric's uncle who had come from Connecticut to supervise his care. "How is our boy today?" Lincoln asked.

"Ever so much better, Mr. President. He will be delighted to have company. He is itching to get out of that bed and try that cork leg you had made for him, but I fear he has many weeks more to go."

A clear, strong tenor voice called down from the upstairs. "Uncle, do we have visitors?"

Sharpe saw Lincoln's face brighten as he walked into the hallway and looked up the stairs. Ulric was standing at the top of the landing, teetering on a pair of crutches. His uncle hurried over, clearly distressed. "Ulie, you must stay in bed. The doctors said you are not ready to try the crutches."

"Let the brave lad be, Mr. Lawrence. It is his nature." Then glancing at Sharpe, he said, "My boy Willie would have been like him." A look of grief passed over his face. "Stay there, my boy. We'll come up to see you." He took the steps three at a time to throw his long arms around Dahlgren. Sharpe noticed Dahlgren's look of delight when he recognized Lincoln. This was a mutual affection.[13]

When Sharpe and Lamson reached the top of the stairs, Lincoln had helped Dahlgren to a chair in the small upstairs sitting room and pulled another up close. Dahlgren recognized Sharpe and tried to rise, "Colonel Sharpe, what a surprise!" He reached out his hand, and Sharpe grasped it. Ulric's handshake was as firm as ever.

"Well, *Colonel* Dahlgren," he said emphasizing the rank, "I'm glad to see you doing so well. We were worried about you. I will have to tell everyone that the bold twinkle has not left your eyes." He was telling the truth. Dahlgren was thinner than he remembered; his brush with death had shrunk some of the flesh from his already thin body. He had been a splendid horseman and reputedly the best dancer in Washington. The girls would miss him on the dance floor. But he had lost none of the spirit Sharpe remembered. His fine fair hair was neatly cut and combed, his face shaved, and his small goatee trimmed.

Lincoln introduced Lamson, and while the two were talking, he said in a low voice to Sharpe, "I like to put my thoroughbreds in the same pasture on occasion. It convinces each to run a bit faster." Sharpe could see what Lincoln meant. One fair and one dark, the two were deep in conversation. They had instantly recognized the same thing in each other. Lincoln interrupted to say, "I'll wager you two have no idea what you have in common." They looked at him. "Why, it's Gettysburg! Dahlgren covered himself with glory there, and I've just named Lamson's new ship after that battle, at the suggestion, I might add, of Colonel Sharpe."

Lincoln went on to describe Lamson's mission to intercept the Laird rams, drawing a parallel between Dahlgren and the dispatches and Lamson and the rams. Both required both boldness and brains. He remarked on the importance of luck, though to him the luckiest men were the best prepared. "That reminds me of story about Napoleon. Whenever a man was recommended for promotion, he would always ask, 'But is he lucky?' Seems the little Corsican knew what he was talking about, at least some of the time."

UNITED STATES BOTANICAL GARDEN, MARYLAND AVENUE, WASHINGTON, D.C., 12:30 PM, AUGUST 7, 1863

After dropping Lamson back at the Yard, Lincoln and Sharpe went to the Conservatory, a great glass botanical garden at the base of Capitol Hill on Maryland Avenue. As they walked through the gorgeous plant-filled corridors, each with a different grouping of the most exotic plants and flowers, Lincoln found a bench and motioned for Sharpe to sit. "Sometimes a soul just needs to rest, Colonel. Can you think of a better place?"

"No, sir, there's nothing else like it in this country. Kew Gardens in London is even larger, and the French have wondrous gardens, too, but give us time."

"Yes, dear God, give us time. That is what I am about. To give this country time. Every day I do my best to make sure that we have time for all that the future has in store for us. This war cannot be our end of times. We are a new start, proof that man's history is not confined to an endless rut of tyranny and misery.

"And I come here because my boys loved to play here. I'm afraid they were a trial to the conservators, racing around and plucking their choicest flowers. I had not the heart to stop them. Mary always said I was too indulgent. Now my Willie is gone." His ungainly body slumped in the iron bench as he put his face in his hands and wept.

Sharpe's heart went out to this man who with all the weight of the world on his shoulders suffered that indescribable grief. Lincoln said, "We have words for those who have lost parents and a husband or wife, but we do not have a word for those who have lost a child. There is just no word capable of such a meaning."

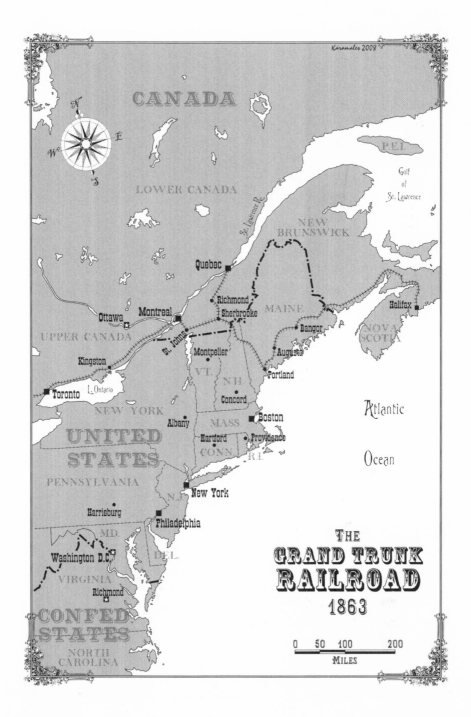

Karamales 2008

CANADA

LOWER CANADA

St. Lawrence R.

Gulf
of
St. Lawrence

P.E.I.

NEW
BRUNSWICK

Quebec

Richmond
Sherbrooke

MAINE

Halifax

NOVA
SCOTIA

Ottawa   Montreal

Bangor

UPPER CANADA

St. Johns

Augusta

Kingston

Montpelier

Portland

VT.

Toronto   L. Ontario

NH

Concord

NEW YORK

Albany

MASS

Boston

UNITED
STATES

Hartford   Providence

CONN

R.I.

Atlantic

Ocean

PENNSYLVANIA

N.J.   New York

Harrisburg

Philadelphia

MD.

Washington D.C.

DEL.

VIRGINIA

Richmond

CONFED.
STATES

NORTH
CAROLINA

THE
GRAND TRUNK
RAILROAD
1863

0   50   100   200

MILES

He paused and looked at Sharpe. "Is there a word for a people who have let their country die or, worse, helped kill it?"

"Copperhead."

"Yes, Sharpe, that is why I keep you in Washington. I can feel a great underground seething in the North, as if this fanged and perverse serpent is uncoiling itself, feeling its strength, readying itself to strike. At least the South is honest in its rebellion — man to man in the open field — but these Copperheads cover themselves with the Constitution while they seek to destroy it. They are abetted by the radical civil libertarians who insist on making the government too weak to defend itself. Thank God Carrington is doing such a good job keeping a finger on their pulse. His man, Stidger, has been a godsend. I truly fear that we would be in far greater danger without his intimate intelligence of their activities."

He paused to reach out and run his long fingers gently over the flowers of a clematis vine. "I know how much you contributed to the victory at Gettysburg, Sharpe. It is not your fault that more was not made of it. I have been thinking that we may need your talents in organization for a secret service here. I'm not talking of what Mr. Baker is doing in chasing spies, but something larger and more comprehensive that gathers together all of the strands of what we must know about not just the rebels but about all of our enemies.

"I'm almost as worried about Louis Napoleon and his ambitions in Mexico as I am about the British and their rams. He conducts his foreign policy simply as a means to strengthen his hold on power in France. As a monarch he feels no affection for our experiment in government by the people. As a monarch of the French, he must consider the affection of the French people for the United States and their decided dislike of slavery. Now he's got himself stuck in Mexico. He thinks that if the South wins, the Monroe Doctrine will be a dead letter, and he will be allowed to keep what he has stolen. He doesn't know our Southron countrymen," he said mimicking the Confederate transformation of the word "Southern." He went on. "It would not take them long to cast covetous eyes on Mexico. But what he thinks is more important than what is. If we win, he knows that we will not let him keep his Mexican Empire. On his own, he will do nothing.[14]

"Adams in London and Drayton in Paris have kept us informed of his attempts to organize the great powers to force an end to our war on terms that would ensure Southern independence. Last year the Russians turned him down, and the British were not eager to be led in anything by the French. So he waits. Mr. Drayton pointedly asked the French foreign minister, Drouyn de Lhuys, what the Emperor's current policy was toward the United States. The Frenchman must have been at his wit's end to actually blurt out the truth. 'He has none. He awaits events.'[15]

"I'm just afraid that in order to keep his Mexican spoils, Louis will get in deeper than he can handle. That reminds me of a story. In early days, a party of men went out hunting for a wild boar. But the game came upon them unawares, and scampering away they all climbed the trees save one, who, seizing the animal by the ears, undertook to hold him, but despairing of success cried out to his companions in the trees, 'For God's sake, boys, come down and help me let go.' So far John Bull and the Czar are still up in those trees."[16]

Sharpe smiled. "Mr. President, the French are eminently an idealistic people. They will fight more for ideas than interests, and if the Emperor can convince them that France has been grossly insulted by an affront to French glory — glory simply does not translate fully into that concept the French feel for themselves as expressed by their word 'gloire' — if he can tie Mexico to *gloire*, then the leash on his action is slipped. But I don't think he will act without Britain, and Britain will not be pushed into it."

Lincoln leaned forward intently, "Exactly why I told you of our plan to stop the Laird rams from getting out to sea. I have taken you into my confidence on this matter, Sharpe, because we may well have need of the sort of intelligence on the great powers that you have been putting together about the rebels."

He leaned back on the bench, one arm draped over the back. "The job is yours, Sharpe. You will report to me alone. I will have a chat with Seward, Stanton, and Welles to make sure they realize that you will not be stepping on any toes."

"Mr. President, I am truly honored," Sharpe said. Yet he hesitated at the enormity of the offer. Although seconded to Meade's staff, he was still the official commander of the 120th NY and took a deep concern in the welfare of the regiment. Every month the men gave him their pay. He traveled to Washington to deposit it in the Rigg's Bank and sent a check to his uncle's bank in Kingston. His uncle then paid the money out to the families of the soldiers. It was the only regiment in the Army that had such an efficient way to care for the families of the men.[17] It was a small consideration compared to the power of the position he was offered, but these men were his neighbors. To come to Washington, he would have to resign his commission and abandon his men. He explained his concern.

Lincoln, rather than seeing an obstruction, was moved by Sharpe's concern for his men. "I'll tell you what, Sharpe. You will not need to resign. I would prefer you kept your commission, and I will see about getting your Kingston boys duty in the garrison of Washington. Some of these big artillery regiments are getting fat in the forts here and could use some exercise with the Army in the field." He offered his hand. "Deal?"

Sharpe took it. "Deal."[18]

BRITISH EMBASSY, WASHINGTON, D.C., 1:10 PM, AUGUST 7, 1863

Captain Hancock shut the door to his office as he motioned Wolseley to a seat. He opened the safe in the corner and drew out some papers that he handed his guest. "The assistant quartermaster general of Canada should find this most interesting. We have a prolific source in the American War Department who copied this for us."

Wolseley's single eye raced across the pages. It was a letter from the governor of Maine, Israel Washburn, to Lincoln and dated October 1861. He realized it was a very important document and nothing less than a shrewd and insightful assessment of the strategic importance of Maine and an appeal for resources to properly defend the state.

> Portland should be made the great naval depot of the United States on the Atlantic Ocean. Its geographical position commands Canada on the north and the lower provinces on the east, if properly fortified, as lines of railway . . . radiate from it to Quebec and Montreal and to Saint John and Halifax.
>
> The harbor is one of the finest on the Atlantic Ocean, or in the world, and can easily be so fortified as to be as impregnable as Gibraltar, and far stronger than Quebec, Sebastopol, or Cherbourg.
>
> Halifax Harbor, the great British naval depot on the American continent, is now occupied by the combined fleets of England and France. Close the outlet of the great gulf lying between Cape Cod and Cape Sable, and unless Portland is defended the whole peninsula east of Lake Champlain is easily subjected to foreign control.
>
> If Great Britain held the harbor of Portland and the line of railway to Montreal and Quebec she would drive American commerce from the ocean and the great lakes.[19]

Wolseley glanced up and shook his head. Hancock said, "I thought you would be impressed. But do read on."

> An enemy in possession of Portland would find it to be the terminus of the longest line of railroad in the world. The Grand Trunk Railway of Canada embraces a line of 1,131 miles . . . It extends from the Atlantic Ocean at Portland to Lake Huron, a distance of 794 miles, with a branch to Detroit of 59 miles, a branch to Quebec of 96 miles, and to the River du Loup of 118 miles.

Wolseley's eye bulged at the next sentence. "This line has the capacity to move 10,000 troops between Portland and Quebec or Toronto and Detroit in a single day."[20] It went on to describe the European and North American Railway, which from its Portland terminus ran through Bangor and Saint John to Halifax over a distance of 576 miles.

> Without it the complete defense of our coast would be impossible, for the British fleet, holding command of the ocean, would prevent any attack on the lower provinces by water. Holding Halifax, the line to Quebec by the Saint John Valley would be kept open, and an overwhelming force would be thrown into New Brunswick, Canada, or Maine at any moment.[21]

Wolseley looked up, "And do you know if the Americans have taken any of this excellent advice to properly fortify Maine? My office has only the most superficial information on these matters. This, of course, is the purpose of my visit."

Hancock responded, "None of the coastal forts in Maine were completed when this war began. There was a flurry of activity initially, but not much substantial improvement. Maine is far away from the fighting. None of the forts have their full complement of guns, and what they have are not all of modern types. There are three forts in Maine of any importance." He brought out a map. "See, the northernmost, Fort Popham, guards the Kennebec River, and the other two, Forts Gorges and Preble, guard the entrance to Portland Harbor. As far as we can ascertain, the garrisons are home guards, frequently rotated."

Wolseley stood up and began to pace up and down the office. "Hancock, when the Trent Affair nearly brought us to war, the government decided to reinforce our weak garrison in Canada with more than ten thousand men. They were sent over late in the year through dreadful weather. They had to travel by sled up the snow-covered trails paralleling the St. Lawrence and from there scatter to a dozen garrisons. It would be impossible to repeat this in wartime. We have eighteen thousand men in Canada now and a growing colonial defense force, but I'm afraid that any American attack would be with numbers that would overwhelm us, and Maine would be the logical starting place. It is the normal port of entry for much of Canada's commerce, and as Governor Washburn has so carefully pointed out, railroads radiate from Portland throughout Canada. Invasion armies could ride the rails and splinter our defenses so rapidly that we would be unable to mass sufficient forces anywhere to successfully defend anything."

Hancock nodded. "I'll have a copy of this sent you in the pouch; wouldn't do for some officious customs officer to find it on you. I think I will inquire into this Colonel Sharpe as well."

Wolseley stopped his pacing and fixed his eye on Hancock. "Railroads can run in two directions, you know, Hancock."[22]

5.

Sergeant Cline Gets a New Job

U.S. ARMY ORDNANCE BUREAU, THE WINDER BUILDING, SEVENTEENTH STREET, N.W., WASHINGTON, D.C., 10:35 AM, AUGUST 8, 1863

Sharpe discovered that Lincoln's offer entailed more attendance on the President in his travels about Washington. Lincoln explained as they alighted in front of the Ordnance Bureau, "If I introduce you about town as someone in my confidence, you will be taken a lot more seriously. I don't intend to do this thing by halves."

On the drive from the Navy Yard, Lincoln had vented his frustration in working with the chief of the Ordnance Bureau, Col. James W. Ripley. The essence of that problem was found in the nickname he had acquired within his own bureau as "Ripley van Winkle." Ripley rejected any new innovation in firearms technology as "new-fangled gimcracks" and a nefarious plot to slow down the production of the tried-and-true basic weapons determined by the Ordnance Bureau to be the proper and sufficient arms for the Army.[1]

"I swear, Sharpe, the man defines stubborn and single minded. Every time I want a new idea tried, I must undergo the labors of Hercules to get him to do it. He reminds me of a story. During the Creek War a requisition was made on a certain lieutenant of ordnance, stationed at the South, which he refused to comply with, on the ground that it had not reached him through the channel pointed out by the regulations. He soon after received a message from Gen. Andy Jackson, the substance of which was that if he did not make the issue immediately he would send a guard to arrest him and bring him into camp, and there hang him from the first tree. The requisition was, of course, promptly complied with.[2]

"What makes it so painful, Sharpe, is that it was Ripley who told this story about himself! As I said, I only retail my stories, and some of them come with thorns. I'm constantly suggesting he order some of these new breech-loading or repeating weapons, but he always argues against it, like a dog defending his last bone. I tell you, I envy Old Hickory's willingness to hang a man to be taken seriously. We wouldn't have had this war if a man like Jackson had been in office instead of Buchanan, who simply sold off the store before I took office. When South Carolina made its first threat to secede, Jackson announced if they dared, he would march the Army into the state and hang the first traitor from the first tree with the first rope. You never saw the chivalry come to heel so fast.

"But no one takes me seriously on that. The nearest I can come is to personally go to this office and give him a direct order to buy so many of these weapons. That is about as close as I can come to threaten to hang him. And it works but not as well as the specter of a tree and rope. He issues the contracts, but then in the fine print he stipulates that if the order is delivered even one day late, the contract is canceled."

"Why don't you simply dismiss and replace him?"

"Hah! Easier said than done. There were few truly qualified men in the Army when this war started. The people and Congress had been happy to keep the Army small and penurious. A pinched purse is no friend to a new idea. We planted lieutenants in a bed of punctilious forms and now have harvested colonels who cannot think beyond what has been done before. The motto of the Ordnance Corps might as well be the one coined by Voltaire—'Learned Nothing and Forgotten Nothing.' Do you know that he refused to purchase breech-loading weapons for [Hiram] Berdan's rifles, the finest sharpshooters in the Army? Let me tell you how I finally got the 1859 Sharps rifle into the hands of his sharpshooters.

"The sharpshooters were barely settled into their camp when their prowess began to cause quite a stir among folks. Visitors buzzed around them like flies on molasses. So not to miss the fun, I showed up trailing Generals McClellan, [Irvin] McDowell, and [Joseph] Mansfield and a lot more stars, the Prince de Joinville and his considerable French entourage, and three cabinet officers. Quite a party.

"I reviewed the men, and then we went down to the rifle pits, where they had been practicing. Everybody got to fire at targets at six hundred yards. Well, all of these important people could only get about one in four rounds into the targets. They wouldn't have made it on the frontier, that's for sure. Then Tom Scott, the assistant secretary of war

back then, and a friend of Ripley, sneered something powerful at Colonel Berdan, asking him how he could compare his knowledge of ordnance with the phalanx of 'experts' in the government. I knew what he
was up to right off. You see, Berdan had hoped to get on the good side of
Ripley by agreeing to the muzzle-loaders, but then changed his mind
and ended up on Ripley's bad side. I guess his boys gave him an earful.
But he only earned Ripley's ill will. Well, now, Berdan did not rise to
Scott's bait, so Scott challenged him to try a shot at the target himself.
Poor Scott—he and bad judgment went together. A target of a man was
set up at six hundred yards and they wrote the name of Jeff Davis on it."
Lincoln laughed. "Now Berdan said that he was a bit reluctant to take a
shot at a chief executive in the presence of another, and I said, 'Oh, Colo-
nel, if you make a good shot it will serve him right.'

"Berdan borrowed his sergeant major's personal breechloader.
Then Scott, like the Serpent in the Tree, said, 'Now, you must fire standing, for officers should not dirty their uniforms by getting into rifle pits.'

"Berdan answered as coolly as could be, 'You are right, Colonel
Scott. I always fire from the shoulder.' It was a huge, heavy gun, too.

"'What point are you going to fire at?' Scott asked.

"'The head.'

"Scott added, 'Fire at the right eye!'

"Scott gloated as the target was brought in, thinking he had run a
log through his spokes. Then, I swear, his face fell to his boots as everyone could see Jeff Davis's right pupil had been cleanly shot through! Now
Berdan is an uncommonly good shot, but even Davy Crockett or Dan'l
Boone would have trouble with that shot. Who cared? I don't know when
I had laughed so hard, but I did control myself long enough to call back
from my carriage, 'Colonel, come down tomorrow, and I will give you
an order for your breechloaders!'[3]

"And you might think that was the end of that. Ripley simply refused to fill the order, and Scott backed him up." Sharpe's eyebrows rose
in incredulity. "Yes, I thought so, too. And so did General McClellan,
who tried to compromise the issue by requesting the Colt repeating rifle,
but if Ripley could scorn the President, who was the general in chief of
our armies? Ripley did not report to him. The matter rested as the boys in
Berdan's regiment stewed and fumed. They even offered to buy the Sharps
and pay the difference between that and the Springfield, but Ripley had
the same answer for that, too—no.

"About this time, I met this young feller from Connecticut named
Chris Spencer. He was about as inventive as it is possible to be with this

repeating rifle.[4] Dahlgren gave it a test and couldn't have been happier. Five hundred cartridges fired and one misfire — and that due to bad fulminate. Dahlgren didn't hesitate and ordered seven hundred Spencers for the Navy. It was from Dahlgren that I heard about this marvel, and I went down to the Navy Yard to see it and meet the inventor. Then McClellan sets up a board to test it. The members of the board practically beat it to pieces; it still fired as well at the end as the beginning.[5] Again McClellan recommended it enthusiastically. But Ripley whined that it was too heavy and too expensive and needed special ammunition, and insisted that the Army's weapons must be standardized. He also, and I must say slyly, said that seventy-three thousand breechloaders had already been ordered, but these were only for the cavalry. I guess even he did not have the face to insist that mounted men carry muzzle-loaders.

"Spencer came to see me and laid it all out. There was nothing for it. I sent him an order — buy those weapons. And you know Ripley even staved that off. And still Berdan's men had no decent weapons. Those boys finally did what I could not. They threatened to mutiny in January '62, and it came close to a fight right in the shadow of the Capitol. God knows he did not fear me, but I guess that scared Ripley. Ripley signed the order for the Sharps, probably with smoke billowing out of his ears.

"Replace him? Would that I could! But who would I find to replace him? There is no one else with his qualifications. Then even should I be able to find a replacement, the law requires a formal retiring board, and that would be drawn out and public. In fairness, I must admit that I owe to Ripley the fact that we are able to get a fine Springfield musket into the hands of every soldier by now, and the man has the uncanny ability to squeeze a penny until it screams, but we could have done so much better.

"Let me give you another example. I saw it early in the war in the loft of Hall's Carriage Shop across from the Willard Hotel." An observer would later describe Lincoln's delight with the weapon.

> Mounted on a two-wheeled slight artillery carriage, the Union Repeating Gun consisted of a single rifle barrel with an ingenious breech mechanism. On top was a hopper which Mills had filled with steel cartridge cases, designed to hold regular .58-caliber paper cartridges. Lincoln turned a crank on the side of the gun and delightedly watched the cartridge cases drop

one by one into the grooves of a revolving cylinder, while the mechanism automatically tripped the firing pin, extracted the cylinders and dropped them into a receptacle for reloading. Seeing the level of the cases sink lower in the hopper while others were spewed into the receiving tray.[6]

"Yes, right then and there I saw its resemblance to a coffee mill with the hopper and all. That's just what I called it, the 'coffee mill gun,' and the name kind of just stuck. The inventor, a fellow named J. D. Mills, called it the 'Union Repeating Gun.' Said it was 'an army in six feet square.' Why, he never got over the name change. Hurt his feelings something powerful."

Lincoln interrupted himself to order the driver to stop next to a construction site. He got out of the carriage and walked over to a wood-pile. He picked up an ax as the workmen recognized him and crowded around. "Sharpe," he said, "you may talk about your 'Raphael repeaters' and 'XI-inch Dahlgrens,' but here is an institution that I understand better than any of the generals or weapons makers." He held the ax out at arm's length by the end of the handle. His arm did not betray the slightest tremble.[7]

So, thought Sharpe, Fox's story was true. The man's strength is phenomenal. He said, "No, sir, I think you understand a great deal more."

Lincoln winked. "Care to try, Sharpe?"

"No, sir, not on my best day."

Lincoln laughed and slowly lowered the ax to the ground without a tremble. The workmen crowded around to shake his hand until he waved good-bye and climbed back into the carriage. Still, he could not shake his unhappiness with the chief of ordnance.

"Ripley was badgered into a field test at the Washington Arsenal, and I made sure a good crowd was there—three cabinet officers, five generals, and the governor of Connecticut, too. Everybody but Ripley was impressed. I even sent him a note telling him it was worth the attention of the government. Still nothing happened. Finally, I bought ten of them on my own on the spot. I pushed McClellan into ordering another fifty. I put them in the hands of the generals, and do you know what happened? Nothing. Good ideas are laying around like chestnuts in the fall, Sharpe, and no one has the wit to pick them up." Lincoln slumped back in his seat, "I just can't do it all."

Then he straightened up again. "There was small fight in Middleburg, Virginia, last October where the gun was actually used. It was turned on a squadron of cavalry and cut them up so badly that they fled the field."

Sharpe commented, "It is a common problem. These weapons arrive, and no one has any idea how to use them, and more importantly, no one has the sole responsibility of seeing that they are used and used properly. Let me give you an example, sir. You godfathered the Balloon Corps and when Hooker was with the Army, Dr. Thaddeus Lowe's balloons did great work. They were a vital source of intelligence, which I found most useful in supplementing the work of my bureau." Sharpe referred to the hydrogen gas balloons invented by Dr. Thadeaus Lowe. It was only a demonstration with Lincoln himself that had resulted in their introduction into the Army. Hooker had been the first general ever to go up in a balloon. They proved critical in the survival of McClellan's Army in the Peninsular Campaign. And so ubiquitous were they hovering over the Union lines, peering into the enemy's depth, that the Confederates developed a healthy fear of them and went to great lengths to hide from their searching telescopes. Reports flashed from telegraphers in the balloons whose wires ran down the heavy tethering cables and directly across the battlefields to Army headquarters. "I tell you, sir, I have no other words than to describe their reports as 'near-time' intelligence. Nothing else at our disposal for the collection and transmission of intelligence was almost instantaneous.

"The corps just died of neglect, sir, *neglect*, and petty-minded spite. The officer appointed to supervise the Balloon Corps, since Mr. Lowe remained a civilian contractor, was as officious as he was small minded and rank conscious. He drove Lowe to resign by reducing his pay and refusing to seek funds to repair or replace the worn-out balloons. When Lowe left, the Balloon Corps died."[8]

Lincoln's jaw set. "I will tell you, Ripley is only a pale shadow to John Dahlgren when he was chief of naval ordnance. He was rich in invention, open minded, and with the knowledge of technical things that I found in almost no one else. Is it any wonder that I looked to him for shrewd advice and friendship? I must look after his poor boy now. But I don't think we have heard the last of young Colonel Dahlgren, one leg or no."

As they rode along, Lincoln said, "You know, Sharpe, Lowe told me the story of his first flight when he was a cobbler's apprentice in Portland. That was just when his young imagination was all aflame with the idea of flight. Naturally, he did not have anything like a balloon. He did have a kite, and there was this ferocious old tom in the cobbler's shop, a great, vicious rat killer. One night he cornered the beast and forced him into a cage. He tied the cage to the kite along with a lantern. He let the offshore winds blow it to a thousand feet and lashed it a post to let it sway in the wind. Ran around town, he did, looking at it from every angle and admiring his feat. When he finally pulled it down, the tom was a shrunk furry bundle. The mean had been scared clean out of him."[9]

When they arrived at the Ordnance Bureau, the doorkeeper opened the double doors for them as a clerk ran up the iron stairs to tell Ripley the President was here. Ripley barely looked up from his pen to reply, "He knows where he can find me."

The clerk had barely disappeared when Lincoln and Sharpe entered Ripley's office. Sharpe was getting used to Lincoln's disdain for ceremony. Ripley rose from his desk. "Good morning, Mr. President."

"Good morning, Colonel." Lincoln introduced Sharpe. "I wanted him to meet you, Colonel, because he has my entire confidence and will be monitoring the development of advanced weapons in other countries, especially breech-loading and repeating weapons. We have to know what possible enemies are up to. I understand the Prussians are quite happy with their new needle gun."[10] Ripley radiated hostility despite that play on words of being needled entirely escaped him.

"I'm sure the Prussians will regret the decision, Mr. President, just as we would had we bought large numbers of these new-fangled gimcracks."

Lincoln smiled. "You mean the new-fangled gimcracks I keep telling you to order and that don't get ordered. Colonel Berdan has renewed his request for Spencers after Gettysburg. What have you done about it?"

Ripley mumbled something about suppliers unable to meet contracts. "They are faulty weapons, too great an expense, and an interruption of standardized production. Also, they showed no noticeable improvement on the battlefield."

Sharpe jumped in here, "I take it then you were at Chancellorsville and Gettysburg, sir. You must have some firsthand knowledge to sustain that statement."

"No, sir, but on good authority, I have heard that . . ."

"Well, I was on both fields, sir, and your 'good authority' is nothing of the sort. At Chancellorsville, Berdan's men taught the Stonewall Brigade about the meaning of the word 'retreat.' At Little Top on the field at Gettysburg, barely one hundred sharpshooters did the duty of a full regiment and carpeted its rocky slopes with the bodies of Hood's Texas Brigade. The sharpshooters alone delayed Longstreet's attack on the Peach Orchard by a vital forty minutes. I interviewed one of the sharpshooters who was captured in the fight and escaped. He said, 'It is impossible for me to describe the slaughter we had made in the ranks. In all my past service it beat all I had ever seen for the number engaged and for short a time. They were piled in heaps and across each other.' That forty minutes saved the day, Colonel."[11]

Ripley was squirming. He would not give up, though, and countered, "Even if we issued the entire Army of the Potomac with Sharps, we could never supply the ammunition to feed it. The expense would be enormous."

"That conclusion might seem sound for someone who lives in an office," Sharpe paused to emphasize his next sentence, "and for someone who has not heard the whistle of bullets." Ripley flushed. He may have been a military bureaucrat, but he knew a soldier's insult when he heard it. Lincoln recalled someone's definition of a gentleman as someone who never unknowingly gives offense.

Sharpe continued, "Consider, Colonel, that if the entire Army of the Potomac had been issued with the Sharps before Gettysburg, Lee would never have escaped." Lincoln grew suddenly intent. "We would have shot him completely to pieces. Nothing would have remained to escape across the Potomac. With Lee destroyed, the rebellion would have lost its main prop and soon collapsed. I think it worth the trouble of supplying sufficient ammunition for results like that. After all, we are not talking about a sustained effort of years. How many battles do you think we would have to fight with a seven-to-one firepower advantage over the enemy?

"And it is a completely one-sided advantage. The rebels have no capacity whatsoever to match us with such weapons or ammunition. They must rely upon the British for Enfields, and even the British cannot supply them with breech-loading weapons of the quality and number we are now capable of producing."[12]

BALTIMORE AND OHIO RAILROAD STATION, WASHINGTON, D.C., 12:30 PM, AUGUST 8, 1863

The carriage drew up to the main entrance of the train station just north of Capitol Hill and two men got out. They had been deep in conversation all the way from the British embassy. "I cannot tell you, Hancock, how useful this visit has been to me." From under the large front portico, an ordinary-looking man was paying attention to the two.

"I am glad to have been of service. Perhaps you will have more luck than I had in convincing someone at home of the importance of what is going on here. Lord knows, my reports to the Admiralty seem to drop like a stone in a well. The ambassador does not seem much interested in these 'strictly military affairs,' as he calls them. I don't believe that I'm saying this, Wolseley, but hopefully, it might have some effect going through Army channels."

Wolseley appreciated the twinge in Hancock's thoroughly Royal Navy nature. "Rest assured that I will be writing to important people at home. General Grant has an open mind and will find all of this of great interest. Now he has the ear of the government." He meant Hope Grant, of course, the most capable of the British generals and his patron, not the American Ulysses S. Grant, then much in the news.

As they continued their conversation on a vacant part of the train platform, Hancock commented that Wolseley was lucky to be taking the train directly through New York to Canada to enjoy the cool summer.

Wolseley paused. "No, I think I will take a detour through Maine. After all, the good governor has praised the railroad network to the heavens. The least I can do is examine it. I expect the weather there is as pleasant as in Canada. And I hear Portland is a scenic stop. Its harbor forts are as much recommended to the visitor by the governor as well. Good-bye, Hancock."[13]

As he settled into his seat, the ordinary-looking man took a seat nearby.

WAR DEPARTMENT, WASHINGTON, D.C., 12:50 PM, AUGUST 8, 1863

Charles Dana cursed as he read the just deciphered telegram from Colonel Carrington in Indianapolis. "Damn! And double damn! This is a real loss." He gazed out of the window at Seventeenth Street and saw Lincoln's carriage waiting in front of the Ordnance Bureau across the street.

Dana ran from the building to meet Lincoln and Sharpe as they emerged through the Winder Building's double doors. "Mr. President!" Heads on the street turned. A crowd surrounded Lincoln before he reached the carriage. The swarms of contractors and office seekers who were converging on Lincoln like a free lunch engulfed the single detective attending him. Dana plunged into the crowd and with Sharpe's help was able to push Lincoln back to the carriage and mount a rear guard as he climbed in. The driver cracked the whip, and they escaped with all the alacrity of so many of Lincoln's generals when pursued by Lee and Jackson.

"Why, Dana, I might have made my escape without a pitched battle if you hadn't been so all-fired excited to get my attention."

"Stidger is dead. I just received the telegram from Colonel Carrington saying they had identified another body at the site of the looted arms warehouse in Indianapolis. It was Stidger, shot right through the belly and his face stomped in."

Lincoln turned to Sharpe. "Well, Sharpe, it looks like you have your first problem."[14]

As they rode back to the White House, Lincoln smiled and said, "And now I'm giving you your second problem. Get me my balloons back."[15]

WASHINGTON NAVY YARD, WASHINGTON, D.C., 2:15 PM, AUGUST 8, 1863

Lamson opened the package delivered by courier from the Navy Department. There was a note from Fox on top. "Lamson, I thought you would find these reports on the rams useful. They have been supplied through the State Department from our consul in Liverpool, Thomas Dudley. These documents are to be considered private and confidential. You will find a secure place to store them." Lamson took the documents to an office in the superintendent's headquarters where he could be alone and began to read.

The two rams were contracted for construction by James Dunwoody Bulloch, the chief Confederate agent in Great Britain, the man responsible for building the CSS *Alabama* and the other Confederate raiders. Their builder was the firm of Laird Brothers; they were financed through the offices of the Fraser, Trenholm & Company, the trading company that handled all financial matters for the Confederacy in Europe and was itself a provider of considerable credit. Fraser, Trenholm & Company could afford it. They owned a fleet of fifty blockade-runners that did a large part in keeping the Confederacy alive and charged a half percent fee for its banking services. Bulloch had constructed an elaborate cover story to prove that the ships had been ordered by French interests and were to be sold to Egypt as the *El Toussan* and *El Monassir*. The rams were being constructed at the Birkenhead Ironworks, opposite Liverpool on the Mersey River, at a cost of ninety-three thousand pounds.

The two ships were referred to as Numbers 294 and 295. The CSS *Alabama's* number had been 292. The intended names were the CSS *North Carolina* and the CSS *Mississippi*. Lamson paused at this point. Like all sailors he was a bit superstitious about ships and the sea. As long as these ships had simply been referred to by the faceless name of "rams" they had not truly been real. Now that he read the names each would bear, he sensed the individuality and power that was growing in each ship. They became as real as his *Nansemond* and the other decks he had trod. Now they were alive.

He devoured the details of their construction. At 1,850 tons they were almost twice the size of the U.S. *Passaic* class monitors. The most striking feature was that they were modeled on the turreted monitors. They were on the cutting edge, with two turrets, one on the bow and the other amidships. Only the USS *Roanoke*, recently assigned to the defense of Hampton Roads with the North Atlantic Blockading Squadron, had double turrets. Each of the ram turrets was armed with twin 9-inch Armstrong rifles that could fire a 250-pound projectile. The most remarkable weapon, and the one that seized the imagination, was the 7-foot solid iron ram affixed to the prow.[16]

Each turret was wrapped in 10 inches of armor. The hull was teak over iron to a depth of 5.5 inches of wood. Overlaying that were 4.5 inches of iron armor plate on the hull and 3.5 inches on the prow. The deck was designed to ride only 6 inches above the water when fully loaded. The ships' dimensions were 224.5 feet in length by 42.5 in the beam. The draught was 16 feet and maximum speed was ten knots. Each would have a crew of 150 and enough stores for three months at sea.[17]

Lamson sat back in the chair to think. He would not like to go up against such a ship when it was fully armed and prepared for war even with the converted *Gettysburg*, which was less than half the size of the rams and unarmored. His only advantage would be speed; the rams could not outrun him. Luckily, his mission would confront the rams as they departed British waters when they were completely unarmed and with only enough crew to get them to their destination. He expected that, if they were anything like the American monitors, they would not handle well in open water, much less in rough seas.

Lamson rocked his chair back, his hand behind his head. One of the rams, the hull of the *North Carolina*, had already been launched and floated across the Mersey for outfitting at Liverpool's Albert Dock. It was a race for time, and he wondered if the hands at the Washington

Navy Yard could work faster than those at the Albert Dock. The Yard men had to work much faster to give him the time he needed to cross the sea and find out what was happening at Liverpool. Unforgiving time was making his odds an extreme long shot. He thought to himself, Long shot, hell; these odds would be a long shot with a limb in between.

OFFICES OF FRASER, TRENHOLM & COMPANY, LIVERPOOL, ENGLAND, 7:36 PM, AUGUST 8, 1863

Very careful planning was what James Bulloch excelled at. He had slipped the sharks out of British ports that were savaging Union commerce on the high seas — famous ships all – the CSS *Florida*, *Shenandoah*, and above all *Alabama*.

He had so far avoided every snare set by the Yankees to cripple his shipbuilding, but they were getting better all the time. He was sitting across from George Trenholm, the director of Fraser, Trenholm & Company. The company's connections within the British government had been critical in providing the initial introductions to Bulloch that had allowed him to operate with what amounted to an almost official blind eye. And when a blind eye did not suffice, sympathetic officials and judges could be depended upon to interpret claims or direct rulings in the Confederacy's favor.

Such was the case when Ambassador Adams had pressured the British government to seize the *Alexandra*, another of Bulloch's commerce raiders that was about to slip British waters. It had taken the threat that the U.S. Congress was willing to pass a privateering bill in retaliation to convince Russell to seize the ship. Bulloch immediately saw that the seizure was challenged in court. The judge instructed the jury that it should return a verdict for the defendants if it thought there was no intent to arm the ship in British waters. It took the jury moments to decide accordingly. Not only had the ship escaped, the British government had been discouraged from any precipitous action on the status of the two rams abuilding on the Mersey.

Such sympathy had been the reason the *Alabama* had escaped as well, but it did not come from the bench. In July 1862, U.S. Consul Dudley had amassed such evidence of the Confederate ownership of the *Enrica*, the *Alabama's* cover name, and its imminent escape that British barrister Sir Robert Collier was able to write a series of damning opinions that should have provoked immediate attention at the Foreign Office. At this point, Russell's undersecretary at the Foreign Office, Austin David Layard, member of Parliament (MP), intervened to delay action. Russell agreed with the Treasury's recommendation that the letters be submitted to the Law Officers of the Crown. Layard sent them to the senior Law Officer, who he knew had suffered a mental breakdown and was going mad. They languished for five days at his home before being forwarded. A new letter with even more damning evidence from Collier arrived, and Layard cleverly forwarded it to the office of the next senior Law Officer on a Saturday, when his office was closed, instead of to his home.

In the meantime, Layard warned Bulloch through another party that the ship could not safely remain at its berth for another forty-eight hours. Bulloch acted quickly and boldly. Any departure of a ship from Liverpool Harbor required the notification and permission of the Crown's collector of customs. There was one exception, and Bulloch sailed the *Enrica* right through it. A newly built ship on its trial run was exempt from this requirement. Under that pretext, the ship left Liverpool with the owner of Laird Brothers and his little daughter on board along with a large party of guests to provide the cover. Once out of the harbor, Bulloch announced that he intended to put the ship through night sailing trials and sent the guests ashore by an accompanying tug. He directed the captain to meet him at Moelfre Bay down the coast the next day. The order to seize the *Enrica* arrived the very day that Bulloch took to sea. He had made it by the skin of his teeth.[18]

The returned tug was to pick up a good part of the intended crew, but the women attached to the seamen had refused to let their men go without the customary first month's advance pay. This commotion attracted the interest of a customs official, who elicited from the crowd that they were on the way to join the "gunboat." The customs officer mailed a report and sent the tug on its way, and this was a full day after the order to seize the *Enrica* had arrived in Liverpool.

The episode had not put Bulloch off his plans but made him even more aware of how tenuous his position was. His very success in unleashing increasing pain on the United States had only served to increase the danger for him. Adams and Dudley had redoubled their efforts this time to ensure the rams never left British waters. Although a secretive man, Bulloch had shared much with his paymaster, George Trenholm. There was little that Trenholm had not done to further Bulloch's mission, and he was ready to do even more at this crisis. Not only did his sympathies lay with the Confederacy, his firm had paid out almost two hundred thousand pounds to finance the rams. Bulloch had concealed one subterfuge within another. Initially he had personally contracted with Laird Brothers for the two rams with no reference or connection to the Confederacy. When American pressure over the rams mounted, Bulloch further clouded their ownership by selling them nominally to the French shipbuilder Bravay and Company — with the advice and assistance of a Queen's counsel no less. Bravay, in turn, made a secret deal to resell the ships to Bulloch for a commission. Laird Brothers did everything to assist in this deception.

Now Trenholm was getting nervous and wanted reassurance from Bulloch. "We cannot expect a jury to pull another rabbit out of a hat on the excuse that these ships are not meant for war. For God's sake, John, these things are monitors with double turrets. Even the most sympathetic jury that can be found wouldn't have the face to say these are not warships."

"George, do not worry. It won't come to that."

"I tell you if it does, all of Europe, not to mention the Americans, will see it as an openly belligerent act. My God, that could trigger a war."

"Now would that truly be a bad thing if we take a broad view, George? The Union is crushed by the British Empire. It would serve everyone's interests, would it not? The South achieves its independence. Your country removes the greatest rival on the horizon and makes and secures the alliance of a grateful Confederacy that will keep any Union thoughts of revenge under control. Britain will have access to the Southern market unhindered by tariffs that have previously only suited Northern business interests. The future profits for Fraser, Trenholm & Company would be enormous. Think about it, George."

Trenholm did and decidedly did not like the thought. "Listen to me, John. It is not that most people in this country who matter, including those in government, would not like to see these things accomplished. And they would not shrink from war if there were no other choice. What they do mind is being manipulated by foreigners into it. We are a perverse people in that regard."

Bulloch realized he had touched far too soft a spot and sought to deflect Trenholm's distress. "I said not to worry, George. It will never come to that. My government would only wish the assistance of Great Britain if it were the result of great deliberation on a matter of imperial policy."

Trenholm was still nervous. "But there is still great danger. Dudley's men are sniffing around all the time. We cannot expect Russell to forever claim the mounting evidence Dudley digs up is only hearsay."

"Now George, I think Russell's basic sympathies for the Confederacy and his desire to see the bloodshed stopped will encourage him to see all evidence as hearsay unless it comes in written with the finger of God himself."

"Don't blaspheme, John. I'm afraid that damn Yankee is actually close to finding divine evidence."

"We still have our friend in the Foreign Office. Let us just hope that the rams are ready for their sea trials before Russell is forced to act."[19]

MILITARY TELEGRAPH OFFICE, WAR DEPARTMENT, WASHINGTON, D.C., 2:36 PM, AUGUST 8, 1863

Sharpe sent an urgent telegram to John Babcock, his deputy in the Army of the Potomac. He was to send Sergeant Cline to Washington immediately.

Lincoln may have given him the charter to put order into the intelligence operations of the government, but Sharpe knew that he would have to win the goodwill of powerful cabinet officers if he were to have any chance of success. Seward would be no problem. A fellow New Yorker and friend of the family, he would see Sharpe's appointment as the advancement of a protégé. He was also practical enough to see the effects of a central control. Sharpe paused to think for a moment as to what he would call his new office. Secret Service had already been given a bad name by Allan Pinkerton and McClellan and had become even more odious under Stanton's private henchman, Lafayette Baker. Sharpe turned over various alternatives in his mind, to include the name of his bureau in the Army of the Potomac — the Bureau of Military Information (BMI). But his new office would have more than military interests and be encompassing all the government's interests in intelligence. Nothing seemed to fit.

The first step was to find allies in the War Department. He did not consider Ripley as he had burned his bridges with him about as dramatically as Cortés had done in Mexico. Besides, if Ripley did not have the look of a man whose days were numbered, Sharpe was no judge of things.

He found Dana in his office late that afternoon and broached his plans to him. Dana was a shrewd man and listened intently. He had assumed many of the duties of intelligence at the War Department, but they were secondary duties, and he had not the time to give them the proper organization and attention they deserved. It was after seven when they finally finished brainstorming the new organization. Dana said as

he got up to put on his coat, "Well, Sharpe, what will you call this cen-
tralized intelligence agency of yours?"

"Hell if I know. Nothing comes."

"How about the Federal Bureau of Information?"

"Sounds too much like law enforcement. The parts are all there;
it's just a matter of putting them together."

On their way to dinner it struck him and he snapped his fingers.
"That's it, Dana, the Central Information Bureau! Just enough of a name
to be functional without attracting too much intention."[20]

"There, that's settled. Now for some airy business." Sharpe handed
a clerk another telegram to send. It was addressed to Professor Thaddaeus
Lowe, Valley Forge, Pennsylvania, and read:

> RETURN IMMEDIATELY WASHINGTON TO COMMAND
> NEW BALLOON CORPS STOP COLONEL'S COMMISSION
> AWAITS STOP REPORT TO ME STOP GEORGE SHARPE,
> BVT BRIG GENERAL, CHIEF, CENTRAL INFORMATION
> BUREAU STOP.[21]

LAFAYETTE SQUARE, WASHINGTON, D.C.,
10:05 AM, AUGUST 10, 1863

Sergeant Cline caught the train near Army headquarters and was in Washington the next day. He reported to Sharpe's home on Lafayette Square.
Cline was a hard man to surprise, but the Colonel had his head spinning
as he laid out the problem and the sergeant's role in solving it. First Cline
found himself transferred to Sharpe's new organization. Next he had a
transportation voucher for the night train to Indianapolis and was armed
with a letter of introduction to meet with Colonel Carrington. Sharpe felt
that Carrington needed someone to replace Stidger, an actor who could
command the stage. He had Lincoln's verbal orders to take the strongest
measures to scotch the Copperheads. Stidger's death was proof of that.
The need for action was immediate.

At the same time Sharpe had to organize and staff his bureau. He
was starting from scratch. The effort it had taken to create the intelligence organization for the Army of the Potomac shrank in comparison to
this. His first act was to acquire a competent deputy, and he asked for the
assignment of civilian James L. McPhail, the provost for Maryland. From
his Baltimore headquarters, McPhail had quickly gathered the strings of
espionage directed at Richmond. He had eagerly shared everything he

learned with Sharpe, a rare characteristic in the intelligence business. Sharpe was a frequent visitor to Baltimore to coordinate and exchange information. It was apparent that McPhail was the rare professional in a sea of amateurs. McPhail had come down to Washington the day that he received the summons of a War Department telegram.

Sharpe, for want of office space and the time to look for it in a crowded city, had started shop in his own rented home on Lafayette Square. A few carefully selected military clerks had taken over the front parlor as an office. He took McPhail into the library and shut the sliding doors. "Jim, we have the labors of Hercules before us. This has never been tried before—a single national intelligence effort."

"When do we start?"

"You already have by being here. You are my deputy, and I am going to work you near to death."

McPhail grinned.

"This is how I see the President's intent—to bring order to all these separate teams that are pulling each in its own direction, and this is where he is quite clear, he wants someone who will present him the equivalent of a thoroughly researched lawyer's brief on any particular subject. He said Gettysburg taught him how dangerous it was that everybody seemed to have a finger in the pie when it came to finding out what General Lee was up to, including himself. Neither he nor Stanton had the time to do this well. He was also aware that in only the most haphazard manner, if at all, does one Union Army learn anything of use from another army.

"In practical terms, this is how I see our job. We must be the clear-inghouse for all intelligence on the rebels. I do not mean to take over the staff work of the armies in the field, but they will provide us what they learn so we can build an overall picture to inform the President and Secretary Stanton. The President told me his inclination was to set up a separate agency that would report only to him, but he thought it not worth the fireworks from Stanton. He told me, 'You need Stanton as an ally, not an enemy.' For that reason I cannot touch Lafayette Baker's National Detective Police. Baker and his NDP are Stanton's pets."

McPhail said, "I wouldn't touch it with a ten-foot pole, George. Baker and his crew are a stench in the nostrils of honest men. Stanton protects them because they are his willing tools in any dirty thing he wants done."

Sharpe was emphatic. "If we took over Baker's crew, that stench would infect us as well. I mean the Bureau to be within the law, Jim. I shudder to think of how Baker has trampled on the law to abuse just about anyone he wants without writ or judge to stop him. I am a practical man, and in crisis I believe that the old adage 'Never let your conscience stop you from doing what's right' is sometimes necessary. The President himself has skirted the constitutionality of some of his actions, but they have been forced on him by necessity to protect the Constitution itself from destruction. That is the real world, not the ivory tower of civil libertarians who would see the Constitution burn up in front of their eyes rather than accommodate it to the fact that the roof is on fire. We shall stand on the right side of the law, but we will also follow Mr. Lincoln's policy of 'bending it here and there' where necessary.[22]

"Baker trumpets how well he has cleaned up rebel spies in Washington, but you know as well as I do, they continue to flourish here. What Baker excels at is shaking down merchants who supply the South."

McPhail commented, "Well, we will need our own organization to counter the enemy's espionage. How will you get around Baker?"

"Simple," Sharpe said. "I have an independent budget thanks to the President. Don't ask me where he gets it. We shall just set up our own organization to catch spies. Quietly. Let Baker make all the noise he wants to about catching Belle Boyd.[23] We will work rings around him. But watch him close, Jim; he's a dangerous man."[24]

Their attention at that moment was drawn to the noise of the doors sliding open and the young soldier standing there. He was one of the studious young men clerking diligently in the outer office. In the two days since Sharpe had acquired the services of Cpl. Michael Wilmoth, the young Hoosier had shown a remarkable talent for order-of-battle analysis. He had already committed Lee's order of battle to memory. "Sir, Professor Lowe is here."[25]

"Show him in." Almost immediately the tall, lanky form of Thaddeus Lowe appeared. "Professor!" Sharpe exclaimed and rushed over to shake his hand. "Thank God, you've come. Here, let me introduce you to Jim McPhail." The two shook hands as Sharpe waved them to sit. He sketched for McPhail's benefit the travesty of Lowe's treatment and the disappearance of the Balloon Corps. Lowe's strong jaw tightened in the retelling. He was the foremost aeronaut in the United States, a gifted scientist, and a man of great energy who had the will and ability to get things done, none of which had been proof against military martinets.[26]

"I tell you, George," Lowe said, "that the only reason I have come is as a favor to you." He looked at McPhail. "Colonel Sharpe was one of the few men I met who appreciated the value of my balloons. It was a pleasure to work with him, and I would have been a damn sight happier had I worked for him, instead of that officious. . . ." His voiced trailed off.

Wilmoth had appeared again and handed Sharpe a folder. Sharpe said, "And we're going to do things right this time." He drew a finely printed parchment out of the folder and handed it to Lowe. "Long overdue, it's your commission as colonel, signed personally by Lincoln and countersigned by Stanton." He drew another paper from the folder. "And here are your orders assigning you as chief of the Balloon Corps. You are in charge of all the U.S. government's efforts at aeronautics. And you work directly for me."

Before Lowe could reply, Sharpe went on, "Professor, you have no greater admirer than I. Your contribution during the Chancellorsville campaign made Gen. John Sedgwick's victory at Marye's Heights possible. I was with Hooker as he received your stream of reports within minutes of your dispatching them by telegraph from your balloons all the way down the Rapphannock at Fredericksburg."

Lowe's excitement had risen to the point where it seemed he needed a tether, like his balloons, to keep him grounded. "When do I start, General?"[27]

6.

"Roll, Alabama, Roll!"

It was a grand sight, sailing up the Mersey River with the great entrepôt of Liverpool to larboard and the smaller shipyards of Birkenhead to starboard. Lamson allowed the crew to line the decks to enjoy the sight. It was exciting, and he tried not to let it go to his head that not even a month ago he had been chasing down this very ship he now commanded. Then she was a swift blockade-runner; now she was the USS *Gettysburg*, and her fleetness was in the service of the United States Navy.

Fox had pulled out all the stops to convert her in record time; the Navy Yard made it top priority, and the crews had worked in round-the-clock shifts to strengthen her hull and decks to take the huge soda bottle–shaped Dahlgren guns. Her belly had been filled with all the ammunition and other naval accoutrements of war as well as the stores and the best of hard anthracite coal to see her on her way. Lamson had requested and received his old crew from the *Nansemond,* plus the pick of seamen then in Washington and Baltimore. The voyage across the Atlantic was blessed with good weather, and the *Gettysburg*'s fine engines sped her in record time. Gunnery practice and battle drills had filled the days and made them short.

Lamson was thankful that the breaks had all gone his way; he was also worried that they had all gone his way. He wondered if he had he used up all his good luck on the way to England. He was normally a young man who acted on the belief that you made your own luck through working hard, knowing your job, and being bold. If anything, his success had come as a result of boldly bending luck to his will. But he also knew her to be a fickle goddess, apt to burst a boiler at a critical moment as to throw a laurel in your path. Overlaying this premonition were his confidential orders—"At all costs you will ensure that the rams do not escape." At all costs. . . .[1]

The English pilot who was enjoying himself, pointing out the details of the great port, temporarily distracted his thoughts. The city was unique among great ports in having a system of enclosed docks. Liverpool was the child of the North American trade and an immigrant gateway as well. It was unlike London or New York, where the steady flow and depth of the Thames and Hudson allowed their docks to line the rivers. The city was so close to the Irish Sea that the tidal Mersey, which had a difference of thirty-three feet between high and low tide, would have left ships beached on her mudflats at low tide. Strong winds, a swift current, and twenty thousand acres of shifting sandbanks contributed to the necessity of building Liverpool's enclosed docks, where ships could be kept permanently afloat in deep water.

The pilot began pointing out the individual docks as they passed, each filled with masts, and connected by Wapping Dock, which allowed ships to move within most of the dock system without having to exit and reenter the system through the river. Lamson's ears pricked up when the pilot pointed out Albert Dock, where his quarry was in the last stages of fitting out. The pilot was explaining that the Albert Dock was used for only the most valuable cargoes, such as brandy, and that its seven and a half acres was surrounded by bonded, fire- and theft-proof warehouses of brick and iron. The docks were less than twenty years old but already becoming too small. Built for sailing ships, its entrance was too small for the new side-wheelers and difficult for the large, screw-propeller ships.[2]

"Captain!" Lamson turned to see Lieutenant Porter touching the brim of his cap. "The Royal Navy is coming down the river."

"Prepare to present full honors, Mr. Porter."

The crewmen who had been lounging by the railing were sent into a bustle of action by the executive officer's shouted commands. In less than a minute the men had gone from a gaggle to neat lines on deck. As the first British ship came even with *Gettysburg*, Porter shouted, "Present arms!" The sailors' hands shot to their caps, and the Marines presented arms. A keen eye would have noticed that the Spencer rifles they carried had no fittings for bayonets.

The first British ship was the wood screw frigate HMS *Liverpool*, dwarfing *Gettysburg* at two thousand six hundred and fifty-six tons.[3]

She was two hundred and thirty-five feet in length and fifty feet in the beam, not even three years old but already obsolete, some might say, in this new age of iron. She carried the standard armament of the Royal Navy. Pride of place was given to the breech-loading 110-pounder Armstrong gun, issued widely to the fleet in 1861; eight 8-inch rifles; four 70-pounders; eight 40-pounders; and eighteen 32-pounders.[4] The Royal Navy had been so impressed with the Army's tests of the Armstrong breech-loader that it had ordered almost two thousand guns of sizes that the manufacturer had not even designed, and later accepted them without trials. *Liverpool* was followed by the much smaller *Albacore* class wood screw gunboat HMS *Goshawk* with four guns. As the stern of *Goshawk* passed, Porter's commands sent the crew back to work to prepare for docking.[5]

Aboard the British frigate, there was no perceptible change in the normal activities of the crew as it passed *Gettysburg*. The officers on the bridge ostentatiously looked the other way as if the American honors were their due and not worth their notice.

Liverpool did not neglect the minimum customary honors that were owed to any warship of a recognized state. The British naval jack was dipped in salute. The U.S. Navy never returned such customary European honors on the principle that the Stars and Stripes bowed to no other flag. It was an irritation among other navies, especially where an irritation with the Americans was preferred.

When Porter dismissed the crew after *Goshawk* passed, there was a notable mutter as the men broke ranks. The snub had not gone unnoticed.[6]

Attention soon shifted to the marvel of the enclosed docking system, fascinating everyone from captain to cabin boy. The pilot directed them through Queen's Basin and from there down a short channel into King's Dock. Lamson was pleased at how well *Gettysburg* handled in such tight places.

No sooner had they docked than a civilian gentleman left his waiting carriage to wait for the gangplank to be lowered. As soon as it touched the stone pier, he dashed across it and said to the guard, "Permission to come aboard. I must speak to the captain immediately."

Lamson shouted from the bridge, "Permission granted. Mr. Henderson, show our visitor to the bridge." The man who climbed to the bridge was middle aged with a well-trimmed, graying beard and the serious look of New England about him. He exuded an alert competence.

He extended his hand introduced himself. "Good day, Captain. I am Thomas Haines Dudley, United States Consul in Liverpool. We had word that you had arrived and would be docking here this morning. We must speak privately."

Once they were in Lamson's private cabin, Dudley came right down to business. "Captain, I have been informed of your instructions; you have arrived not a moment too soon. I am convinced that the quarry has wind of Ambassador Adams's presentations of evidence to the Foreign Office proving that the rams have been built for the Confederacy. Not a moment to lose, not a single moment, sir. They moved Number 294 across to the Albert Dock last week and fitted the two turrets on the 28th and 29th. Half of Liverpool was there to see the biggest cranes in the port lift those great cylinders. They've been working feverishly ever since to rush her to completion."[7]

Lamson had looked forward to meeting the man who had sent such detailed reports on the rams, tracking their every stage of construction. He obviously had the trust of Seward and Fox. More important, he had the trust of Lincoln. Fox had explained that it was Dudley's timely and critical support at the 1860 Republican convention that had secured Lincoln's nomination. As a reward he had been offered the consulships in either Yokohama or Liverpool. Dudley had chosen the latter to be near expert medical care for a chronic illness. Whatever the illness was, it was not apparent in his urgent attitude now.

"Ambassador Adams had instructed me to inform you to report to him immediately upon your arrival. There is a train for London leaving this afternoon. I took the liberty of buying your ticket. I will escort you through your registration with the Custom House here and then see you off at the station.

"You must not lose a minute, literally a minute. As the warship of a belligerent, British law allows the *Gettysburg* only a forty-eight-hour stay in any British port to water and victual. That forty-eight hours begins when your papers are filed at the Custom House. You must get to London, see Adams, and take the next train back here. You will have just enough time. Thank God the British trains are so fast and dependable. They've built their tracks and grades with such care that there is almost never a derailment or delay. Unfortunately, that is something we cannot say at home." Dudley did not wait for Lamson to comment but stood up and said, "Let's go!"

Along the way to the Custom House, they were stopped in traffic by the open windows of a grog shop. The words of an enthusiastically rendered drinking song were clear.

When the Alabama's keel was laid,
Roll, Alabama, roll!
It was in the city of Birkenhead.
Roll, Alabama, roll!
They called her Number 292,
Roll, Alabama, roll!
In honor of the merchants of Liverpool.
Roll, Alabama, roll,
Roooooooll, Alabama, roll, Alabama, rooooooll
Roooooooll, Alabama, roll, Alabama, roll!

The carriage lurched forward as the traffic began to move. They could hear one last verse as they sped away.

To the western isles they made her run,
Roll, Alabama, roll!
To be fitted out with shot and gun.
Roll, Alabama, roll![8]

Dudley ground his teeth. "Even in song, the popular sentiment of this country favors the rebels. They *should* be singing her praises; after all, her crew is made up, almost to the man, of former Royal Navy sailors. This country might as well be at war with us.

"No, Captain, I must correct myself. If they are war with us, it is only with their little finger. We must keep them from using both fists. I have been here over two years now, and I am aware of the industrial might of this country. No one will come well out of such a fight."[9]

ALBERT DOCK, LIVERPOOL, ENGLAND, 2:35 PM, SEPTEMBER 1, 1863
Bulloch prowled the dock as if his presence would speed the already desperate pace the Laird Brothers' work crews were setting. The arrival of the *Gettysburg* in Liverpool, now docked barely a quarter mile away, had driven him from his normal behind-the-scenes station. His friends at the Custom House had reported immediately on Lamson's presentation of his papers and keyed on the fact that he had stated his ship was to

replace the purpose-built sloop, USS *Kearsarge*, as the single American warship on the U.S. Navy's English Channel Station. He had mentioned casually that every purpose-built warship was needed in American waters to close the noose tighter on Charleston and Wilmington. That only momentarily reassured Bulloch. He would feel better when *Gettysburg* actually left for the Channel Station, and given British rules on belligerents, that should be in two short days.[10]

Anything that was not absolutely essential to get the ship simply seaworthy enough to escape the harbor and cross the sea to the Azores had been abandoned. Bulloch had arranged for the last work to be completed in those islands before the guns and stores were fitted. He could feel the minutes slipping away as if they were grains of sand in his own life's hourglass. This time he had avoided the last-minute commotion with the *Alabama's* crew. The men that would take her out of the harbor were a skeleton crew, only enough men to run her trials at sea if anyone looked closely. The rest of the crew had already been quietly paid in advance and sent due west to wait in Moelfre Bay off Anglesey in Wales.

Bulloch's presence had not escaped notice of Dudley's horde of agents who buzzed around the Albert Dock. Not a bolt or mouse could enter or exit the dock without being noticed. John Laird had paid a gang of local toughs to clear them off, but Dudley had paid even more for a bigger gang. Club-wielding bobbies had more than once had to break up the street battles. It was no wonder that Bulloch was feeling besieged. He felt that he held the last hope of the Confederacy here in Albert Dock. The Confederate armies had suffered major defeats at Gettysburg and Vicksburg, and he realized it was only a matter of time before they wasted away. The South was consuming itself while the resources of the North only grew. The rams had to live up to their fearsome reputation in order to break the blockade and let new life flow into the Confederacy. The rams would then be free to trail the Confederate Navy's coat up the entire Yankee coast all the way to Canada and back, destroying the North's shipping and savaging their ports. He had no doubts because he had no more hopes but these. There was nothing he would not do to see that they lived.

Those hopes had flared when the Laird officer in charge of outfitting *North Carolina*—and that was what Bulloch called her now that her mighty turrets had been fitted—reported that the ship would be ready for sea trials on September 4.[11]

FOREIGN MINISTRY, LONDON, 3:14 PM, SEPTEMBER 1, 1863

Lord John Russell sat in his office deep in thought as he realized that the diplomatic ground was shifting beneath him. His undersecretary, Layard, sat silently, waiting for him to speak.

The twin Union victories that summer at Gettysburg and Vicksburg had a dramatic and sobering effect on the pro-Confederate British establishment. Ambassador Adams had written his son, Charles Francis Adams, Jr., who was serving with the 5th Massachusetts Cavalry, that the news had filled the London salons with "tears of anger mixed with grief."[12]

Adams's relentless pressure was supported by a flurry of affidavits and intelligence on the Confederate provenance of the rams. Its cumulative weight was having an effect, albeit a very reluctant one on Russell. In August, while on vacation in Scotland, Adams had informed the Duke of Argyll, the Secretary of State for War, that the French consul in Liverpool had denied that the rams were being built for the French. On his return he passed that information to Russell as well.

The British ambassador in Paris confirmed that Adams was telling the truth. Inquiries to Egypt also revealed that the previous ruler had ordered two ironclads from Bravay, but his successor had canceled the order in 1862. Despite this information, Russell responded in a letter dated September 1.

> Her Majesty's government are advised that the information contained in the depositions is in a great measure mere hearsay evidence and generally is not such as to show the intent or purpose necessary to make the building or fitting out of these vessels illegal under the Foreign Enlistment Act . . . Her Majesty's government are advised that they cannot interfere in any way with these vessels.[13]

Yet on the same day that letter was written, Russell was convinced by Adams's efforts that where there was all that smoke, there was probably a good fire. The message did not indicate that change of mind because Russell and the Crown's legal authorities had become fixated on the letter of a badly written law, the Foreign Enlistment Act. It had been suggested in the cabinet that this recognizably flawed legislation be amended, but even that drew opposition from those determined not to give the appearance of succumbing to American pressure.

That change of mind made Layard decidedly uncomfortable. His friend Bulloch had begged for any indication that the government was about to act. Now it seemed that the manifest need to take action was gathering momentum.

Russell put the issue squarely, "Layard, so much suspicion attaches to the ironclad vessels at Birkenhead that they ought not to be allowed to go out of Liverpool until the suspicion about them is cleared up."

"Then, do you still want to send Adams this letter?"

"Yes, indeed, but I will not give him the satisfaction of our taking precipitous action. I will not act until the Law Officers have supported such action." He believed that they would, but pride forbade him keeping Adams abreast of changing perceptions.[14]

By now, both governments were seriously talking past each other. Inexplicably, that letter was not delivered with any dispatch. Adams, however, would take the letter at face value in the absence of clarification from Russell.

AMERICAN EMBASSY, LONDON, 11:50 PM, SEPTEMBER 1, 1863

The cab from the station dropped Lamson at the embassy barely before midnight. He rapped at the door with the brass knocker until a young man in rumpled clothes appeared with a lamp. He seemed unhappy at being awakened.

Lamson introduced himself. The young man yawned. "You are expected. Come in." He introduced himself as Henry Adams, the ambassador's son and private secretary. "Wait here. I will let the ambassador know you have arrived." He disappeared upstairs, leaving Lamson standing in the dark.

Lamson sized up the young man in a glance in the way that a fighting man does other men. He was not impressed. There was something soft in Henry Adams, something that would give if leaned on.

While Lamson waited, he was turning over in his mind everything Dudley had told him and how that information would affect his mission and what the ambassador would have to say to him.

Eventually the light reappeared at the head of the stairs followed by young Adams, lamp in hand. "The ambassador will see you shortly. Please, make yourself comfortable in the parlor here." He motioned into the dark with the lamp and led Lamson into a room furnished with New England simplicity but quality. Lighting another lamp, he asked if he should rouse the servants to put on some tea. Lamson declined. He discovered to his dismay that young Adams had the gift of small talk to a great degree and, even more, could carry on without much of a response. The content was certainly consistent—Henry's travails in getting introduced into British society. He prattled on in tones of enervated boredom, aping a cultivated English accent that Lamson found more than annoying.

Bored is he? thought Lamson. I've got a cure for that—holystoning a deck soaks up a lot of boredom.

Not more than ten minutes later, the ambassador mercifully entered. Charles Francis Adams, U.S. ambassador to Great Britain, was an American institution. His position was practically an inherited office. His grandfather, John Adams, and his father, John Quincy Adams, had both preceded him to represent the United States. He himself had served as his father's private secretary, as his father had served his grandfather. Lamson considered Henry Adams and thought to himself that the tradition had no future. The Adams line seemed to have watered down considerably in this latest generation, but that was not true for the father. Charles Adams was all Massachusetts—obdurate, stoic, outwardly cool, duty driven, and humorless. He was a spare old man, balding with a thin remnant of white hair driven to the edge of his scalp. A carefully trimmed white beard ran under his chin. His greatest talent was the ability to relentlessly represent the interests of the United States to the British government with great force against a gale of slights, insults, and hostile acts. He was ever at Lord Russell's heels with another remonstration or argument.

Unfortunately, he failed to detect the true character of the senior members in the British Ministry. Russell had completely deceived him for two years. Unbeknownst to Adams, he had previously been the leading force in attempting to organize joint British, French, and Russian intervention to stop the war, which would have secured the South its independence. Russell firmly believed that a reunited United States would pose a long-term threat to British world hegemony and so British interests should be on the side of a dismembered Union. Palmerston, whom Adams blamed for the government's hostility to the Union, had actually been a check on Russell's rush in 1862 to force a negotiated peace on the North and South.

Charles Adams greeted Lamson politely but to the point. He made no small talk. Henry's talent in that regard must have been inherited from the female line. Undoubtedly the lack of the convivial nature of diplomacy was a hindrance to his role as minister, but he did not seem to care. He paused only a moment to appraise Lamson.

"I have already been informed of your mission by Secretary Seward. Since he stated that your arrival would be cut very fine, I took the liberty as well of informing Captain Winslow of the *Kearsarge*, which is lying off Vlissingen (Flushing) in the Netherlands, in case you did not arrive in time."

"Sir, I believe that the Navy Department was to inform *Kearsarge* as well." Lamson was not going to plan on being assisted by the *Kearsarge*, the one thousand and thirty-one–ton, eight-gun sloop cruising the U.S. Navy's Channel Station. All well and good if she appeared, but he must act as if that would not happen. Besides, Winslow would rank him if the ships met and garner all the glory.

Adams came to the point. "Dudley has briefed you on the situation with the rams in Liverpool. His daily reports indicate that they are nearing completion. I have submitted to Lord Russell the most damning proofs of Confederate complicity in the building of these ships.

"You see what we are up against. Palmerston had tied Russell's hands completely. There is not a single important instance in which the British government has not interpreted these issues in the favor of the Confederacy. I will take you into the strictest confidence, since your actions may well have to be guided by this information. Secretary Seward has instructed me to inform Her Majesty's government that the United States has no choice but to issue letters of marque and will pursue Confederate vessels into neutral ports that 'become harbors for these pirates.'[15]

"Moreover, there are strong elements within the British ministry that desire a war be initiated by the United States. That will be the signal for the European dismemberment of the United States. Louis Napoleon only awaits Britain's lead. Their only break, and it has its limits, is Russia, which has consistently offered its advice and goodwill and its diplomatic support. We are not entirely alone in Europe."

It was clear to Lamson what the stakes were. The British government was about to connive at the escape of the rams. If they were not intercepted, the United States would have no other choice than to go to war.

For the first time, Henry Adams spoke. "You forget the Germans, Father. Don't forget the Prussian king coldly refused to receive a Confederate agent or allow any of his officials to have anything to do with him. And I can hardly believe the Prussian prime minister, Otto von Bismarck, would see any advantage in supporting France in such a war, when it is France, and Austria, of course, that stands in the way of German unification, the chief strategic objective of the Prussian Kingdom."

His speech was another surprise for Lamson. The fop could think. He must have learned something in the last two years. Lamson was slightly impressed.

The ambassador turned to Lamson. "My son has shown you why I am sending him with you."

"Father!"

"He will be . . . as a political and diplomatic observer and adviser. You will be facing one of the most difficult and complex situations ever to confront an American naval officer. I have no doubt of your abilities as a naval officer, but this situation would daunt a man more than twice your years and experience."

The ambassador turned to his son. "Henry, pack quickly."[16]

USS *GETTYSBURG*, KING'S DOCK, LIVERPOOL, ENGLAND, 8:35 AM, SEPTEMBER 3, 1863

Lamson and Porter were waiting for their guest to join them. They turned when they heard footsteps but only the cabin boy approached. "Well, where is he, Tom?"

"Sir," the boy touched his knuckles to his cap diffidently, "I knocked and knocked on his cabin door and explained that the captain wanted him on bridge."

"Yes?"

"And, sir, he just yelled at me and told me to go away." The boy was scandalized that even a guest aboard the ship should treat the captain's request so. "Three times I tried, sir, and I even opened the door a bit to peak in and tell him, but . . ."

"Yes?"

"He threw his chamber pot at me, Captain!"

Lamson stifled a laugh. Porter bit his lip and turned away. "Carry on, Tom." The boy fled. "It seems, Mr. Porter, that our guest finds life at sea not to his taste." They both laughed, looking out at the placid surface of King's Dock. Lamson's opinion of Henry Adams had reverted to his original impression on their early morning train ride to Liverpool. He did not know that a man could whine without interruption for so long. The complaints only let up when Adams turned to name-dropping in his obsession with English "society." He had even found fault with his accommodations aboard ship. The USS *Gettysburg*'s origins as a mail packet had left her with a number of comfortable cabins, not all of which succumbed to the ship's conversion for war. The best, of course, was the captain's, but the executive officer's was still handsome, and he had graciously given it up for the representative of the ambassador.

"Mr. Porter, I'm afraid this mission is beyond poor Tom's diplomatic ability. Please, see what you can do with our guest. Mr. Dudley will be here shortly."

The consul arrived only moments after Porter escorted a very unhappy Adams into the captain's cabin. He winked at Lamson as Adams threw himself into a chair and asked when breakfast would be served. "Why, Mr. Adams, the officers have eaten already. My cabin boy notified you in plenty of time. I believe your answer was, 'Bugger off.' An English endearment, isn't it?"

Adams groaned.

"But there will be coffee for our meeting with Mr. Dudley."

"No tea?"

The consul was prompt. He was surprised to see Adams and raised an eyebrow when Lamson noted the ambassador had sent him as an official observer and adviser. Dudley obviously knew young Adams and had no higher opinion of him than Lamson had. Adams just sat there glum faced. Dudley tactfully changed the subject as the coffee was being served. "Coffee! Wonderful." Dudley exclaimed. "I have become so tired of tea. You can tell when an American has been here too long. He becomes a tea drinker."

Adams rolled his eyes.

"Well, to business, Captain," Dudley said as he put down his cup. "My agents report round-the-clock work on the *North Carolina*. The work crews are happy for the extra pay and the fat bonus promised by Laird. Bulloch himself haunts the ship as if his presence will speed its completion. He's scared that the ambassador has put so much pressure on the British government that even his friends in high places will not be able to save him. Their only chance to escape is to try the same ploy as they did with the *Alabama* and pretend that they are going out only for a trial run. I would not believe that would work twice if I did not know how blindness suddenly afflicts British officials where the rebels are concerned.

"He is also very afraid of you, Captain. My agents tell me his men have been asking about you everywhere."

"Well, Mr. Dudley, I am sent here to provoke just that reaction from him."

"But, Captain," Dudley barely stopped himself from calling Lamson a young man, "fear must be carefully applied to be useful. Too much fear will make him become too watchful and circumspect. Too little fear and he may just become careless enough to make mistakes."

"That is just what I intend to do, sir, calm the man enough so that he takes an eye off the weather gauge. Our forty-eight hours in port are just about up; I have notified the Custom House that we shall be departing on the afternoon tide. Our pilot shall be here shortly. I shall wait beyond the three-mile limit. But I shall have only a small chance to catch him unless I receive word from you of his departure. Can you do that?"

"Yes, I will have a dispatch boat ready to receive a signal the moment *North Carolina* leaves Albert Dock."[17]

FOREIGN MINISTRY, LONDON, 10:38 PM, SEPTEMBER 3, 1863

Russell was reading Layard's account of his discussion with Solicitor General Roundell Palmer of the day before. Palmer had suggested that the Liverpool Custom House detain the ships temporarily while proof was gathered of their ultimate destination. Russell immediately telegraphed Layard, "I quite agree in the course suggested by Roundell Palmer. I have made up my mind that the vessels ought to be stopped in order to test the law and prevent a great scandal." He then ordered Layard to write to the Treasury to advise that the vessels be prevented from leaving the port of Liverpool till satisfactory evidence had been given of their destination. Layard waited until late that afternoon to write to the Treasury, ensuring that the letter would not be delivered until the following day.

Before he did that, he had slipped away for a few moments. As he returned to write the letter, an anonymous party was sending a telegram to Bulloch. It read: "Flee! There is no more time."

USS *GETTYSBURG*, OFF LIVERPOOL IN THE IRISH SEA, LATE AFTERNOON, SEPTEMBER 3, 1863

To Lamson's distress, *Liverpool* had followed *Gettysburg* out of port the day before and had pointedly followed her as she attempted to prowl across the Mersey's mouth. The Royal Navy did not appreciate such an overtly predatory statement so close to the lion's den and was making that known.

"Mr. Porter, set a course for Dublin. We have to put distance between us to make him think we've departed these waters. Dudley has not notified us of *North Carolina's* escape. If they have not left now, they can hardly leave at night if they are to maintain the pretense of sea trials. We shall return in the morning to catch her if she comes out."[18]

CSS *NORTH CAROLINA*, MERSEY RIVER, ON THE MORNING TIDE, SEPTEMBER 4, 1863

Bulloch felt the power of the engines through the deck as *North Carolina* followed the tug out through the river's fast-running current into the Irish Sea. The tug was the normal accompaniment for a trial run in case the ship had to be helped back into the harbor. His bags were stored in the captain's cabin. It had not been hard to conclude that should he succeed in slipping the ram out of British waters, he would surely have outworn his welcome in that country. He was not thinking of that now. They would soon cross out of British territorial waters and be beyond the reach of British law. There was not a hint of alarm, no fast harbor craft speeding after to overtake him. It was a normal morning tide on the swift Mersey.

There was the excitement of knowing that it would be his command. The *Alabama* had been originally promised to him, but his value in building ships for the young Confederate Navy was deemed more important. As a man more dedicated to the success of his country than his own glory, he had not complained.

There was only momentary relief when the ram passed out of British jurisdiction because he knew that was not the end of his problems. He still had his crew to pick up in Moelfre Bay, and that would put him right back in British waters. He would have to be quick about it.[19]

USS *GETTYSBURG*, IN THE IRISH SEA, EARLY MORNING, SEPTEMBER 4, 1863

"Damn that ship!" Lamson exclaimed. Yesterday he had had *Gettysburg* stretch her legs to lose *Liverpool* as night fell across the Irish Sea. He had thought to swing wide to the north and come down to resume his station off the Mersey's mouth in time for the *North Carolina* to come out on the morning tide, if she were coming. Unfortunately, the British frigate was across *Gettysburg's* path that morning as well. "That captain has brains, Mr. Porter. He's anticipated me and has turned up like the proverbial bad penny. Touché, Captain!" he said as he touched the brim of his cap in the direction of *Liverpool*.

He was more distressed than he let on. The Mersey's mouth was filled with ships leaving Liverpool on the morning tide. The frigate would ensure that he did not sail among them easily or at all.

The last ship out was a dispatch boat that made straight for *Gettysburg*. When it came up alongside, Lamson could see Dudley on deck. He shouted across, "She's flown on the early tide. Gone to Moelfre Bay off Anglesey Island to pick up her crew. Moelfre Bay!"[20]

7.

French Lick to Halifax

THE BOWLES FARM, FRENCH LICK, INDIANA, 8:23 AM, SEPTEMBER 3, 1863

The Confederate cavalry company trotted into William Bowles's farm-yard with a jaunty air. The commander saluted a Confederate major who stood on the porch with a delighted Bowles. The major said, "As I told you, Mr. Bowles, the Confederacy has not forgotten its friends."

"Wonderful, wonderful, Major Parker. Our people will be heartened to know that the revolution will have such fine support," Bowles replied.

The assorted Union deserters, escaped Confederate prisoners, and Copperhead toughs who made Bowles's farm their headquarters had filled the yard to enjoy the sight of their visitors. The only one not smiling was Big Jim Smoke, who stood in the back of the crowd cradling a shotgun in his arm. He didn't like it, not one bit.

"This feller Parker comes waltzing in a week ago," he thought suspiciously, with an altogether too merry young Irishman as an aide, to announce that he had been sent to pick up the pieces after Morgan had got himself and most of his brigade caught.

Sergeant Cline was playing the part of Major Parker coolly. He had worn Confederate gray so often and with such believability that it was second nature. He always enjoyed these performances, the mark of a consummate actor. His audiences never failed to appreciate his performance. His supporting actor, young Martin Hogan, played his part with Gaelic style.

Cline took off his hat with a chivalrous flourish to Bowles. It was the signal to the men from his 3rd Indiana Cavalry who were in disguise as well. Forty Colt revolvers whipped out of their holsters to point at Bowles's guests. The muzzle of Cline's pistol touched the wild white hair on the side of Bowles' head. "You, sir, are my prisoner. I arrest you in the name of the United States."

The troopers did not see Big Jim as he raised his shotgun and fired. It sprayed into the gray cavalry; two men fell and a blinded horse went screaming and kicking through the ranks. Everyone started shooting. Bowles snarled and pulled his own pistol, but Cline struck him across the face with his Colt, and he fell into the yard. Another man was on him, but Hogan shot him in the face. The rest of Bowles's men on the porch were soon down, too.[1]

The close-quarters gunfight had been as deadly as it was short. Despite Smoke's surprise, the troopers had had the drop on the Bowles's gang and shot them to pieces before many of them could fire back. The survivors had thrown up their arms or fled through the yard, pursued by the troopers not overly concerned to take prisoners. Big Jim's position in the back of the crowd had saved him from the hail of lead. He threw away his empty weapon and was the first to turn and run. When he heard a horse thundering behind him, he sidestepped to let the trooper ride past, drew his pistol, and shot the man in the back. The dead man slumped in the saddle as Big Jim caught up to the horse, pulled the body off in one powerful leap, and threw himself on the saddle. He spurred the horse across the nearby field and into the woods beyond.[2]

Looking about the bloody, corpse-strewn yard, Cline thought to himself that a lot had happened since he had reported to Sharpe last month in Washington.

BRITISH ARMY HEADQUARTERS, MONTREAL, CANADA, 10:20 AM, SEPTEMBER 3, 1863

Wolseley read the letter from Captain Hancock with great interest. As they had suspected, their American dinner companion in Washington had not been a simple colonel of infantry.

> My sources report that Sharpe was the officer charged with intelligence matters in the Army of the Potomac. He has been promoted to Brigadier since our meeting and is in charge of a new organization, the Central Information Bureau. He has been introduced around the government in Washington by the President himself. We know little more than this.

It was not difficult to surmise that Sharpe was carrying on his intelligence duties at a higher level. The extraordinary endorsement by Lincoln did more than indicate that Sharpe had the President's favor and backing. The chief of staff to whom Wolseley reported, Col. E. R. Wetherall, was highly regarded in the British Army. Wetherall justified that opinion when he quickly recognized Wolseley's abilities and gave him a wide-ranging planning charter. Wolseley himself was an experienced staff officer, despite his impressive combat record, and he was aware of the importance of intelligence. Unfortunately, those resources were meager in his staff. After the crisis of the Trent Affair had passed, Wolseley and the rest of the Trent reinforcements had settled down into what was considered, along with the Greek island of Corfu, to be the best posting in the British Army.

Wetherall's and Wolseley's posting to British North America had been no accident. The War Office did not have an overwhelming faith in the commander in chief, North America, Lt. Gen. Sir William Fenwick Williams, and had therefore provided him with a superlative staff during the Trent Affair. Williams was one of those Victorian generals of legend. During the Crimean War, he had been appointed as the British commissioner to the Turkish Army in Anatolia and had effectively commanded their Field Army in the heroic defense of Kars. His spirited defense, though it had ultimately ended in capitulation due to cold, cholera, and starvation, was a bright spot in Britain's conduct of the war, and Crown and country were eager to shower honors on him. In 1859, at the age of fifty-nine, he had been offered the comfortable and quiet post in British North America. It had become apparent that however gifted Williams had been in a closely confined siege operation, he did not have the grasp to handle a command that stretched across half a continent.[3]

Had the Trent Affair spiraled into war, it had been the intention of the War Office to replace Williams with another commander, most likely Maj. Gen. Hope Grant, Wolseley's commander and patron in the Sepoy Mutiny and punitive expedition to China. Wolseley took some comfort that whatever Williams's failure as a theater commander, the old man was combative and likely to approve a bold, aggressive defense planned by his subordinates.

The Army's decision that Williams should have a first-rate staff was not particularly paralleled by the choice of subordinate commanders in Wolseley's opinion. Maj. Gen. Sir Hastings Doyle, KCMG, commanded the British garrison in Halifax was well thought of, but he had reservations about Maj. Gen. Lord Frederick Paulet, a Coldstream Guardsman, who brought over the two guards battalions and was slated for a major command in wartime. It was another example of senior command reserved for the guards. Of the two officers designated for division command, Maj. Gen. Hon. James Lindsay was dependable, but Maj. Gen. George T. C. Napier was clearly incompetent. How Wolseley wished his mentor, Hope Grant, could have been sent over.

Wolseley's trip to Washington and his subsequent return to Canada through Portland convinced him to remedy the Army's inability to collect intelligence on the Americans. At the very least, it would be an excellent professional exercise for the staff. He sent agents to glean every bit of valuable information on the railroad network throughout Maine as well as detailed information on Portland and its defenses, particularly the harbor forts. Already he had obtained a comprehensive picture.

His new interest had shocked his staff out of their preoccupation with hunting, fishing, and the very pretty Canadian girls. Wolseley himself remembered a golden-haired girl in Kingston, Upper Canada, with Shakespeare's "war of red and white in her cheeks," but that was best put aside for now. They had to do some work for a change. They were a good lot and had done a remarkable job in December 1861 of distributing the arriving British reinforcements across Canada in the depths of a hard winter. Compared to the logistics debacle of the Crimean War, the staff had done wonders in making sure every man was properly equipped with cold-weather gear and transport, to include snowshoes, and with ample food and medical care. Almost eleven thousand troops had been spread out in small garrisons to reinforce the seven thousand regulars already stationed in the Canadas and the Maritimes.[4]

Wolseley realized that the entire regular garrison was smaller than any of Lee's three corps at Gettysburg and consisted of thirteen battalions of infantry, twelve batteries of field artillery, seven batteries of garrison artillery, three companies of Royal Engineers, and two battalions of military trains. These units would barely constitute two normal British divisions, numbering a little over nineteen thousand men in all, to include staff corps. They were all first rate.[5] The government had wanted the quality of the reinforcement to be taken into account in American diplomatic calculations, which was why the two guards battalions — the 1st Battalion, Grenadier Guards, and the 2nd Battalion Scots Fusilier Guards — were included. The legendary Rifle Brigade had also sent its 1st Battalion.

Most of the regiments had their share of North American battle honors. The oldest was the Grenadier Guards, which had been sent to Virginia in 1677 to put down Bacon's Rebellion.

British Army battalions, often referred to as imperial battalions to distinguish them from colonial units, were unparalleled fighting formations, known for their obstinacy in battle often to the point of suicide. They had a sense of themselves based on the regimental system that gave them a wonderful resilience and cohesiveness. Leavened with Crimean War, Great Mutiny, and China expedition veterans, they knew the bayonet end of their business better than another other army in the world.

"Battalion" was not necessarily synonymous with "regiment." A regiment was the permanent organization that was organized into the tactical formation of a battalion with ten companies. Most regiments had only one battalion, though there were a number of exceptions when there were two or more battalions. The guards regiments all had more than one battalion. Battalions usually numbered about 1,000 men on paper, but actual strength usually varied from 800 to 950.

British regiments were also famous for their unique personalities and were often known by their nicknames. The 1st Battalion, Grenadier Guards, were known as "the Dandies," no doubt from their parade functions in London and the fact that as all the guards, they were selected for height to make a grander appearance. More often nicknames were born in battle. The famous red coat of the British soldier was actually scarlet and a new and more practical tunic cut adopted as one of Crimean War reforms. Different facings distinguished the various regiments. Black trousers and a black shako completed his uniform. The only exception to scarlet was the rifle green and black of the rifle battalions. It was Richard Sharpe, hero of the 95th Rifles—later 1st Battalion, the Rifle Brigade—of whom Wolseley spoke in his dinner conversation with George H. Sharpe.

The British soldier was also armed with the superb .577 caliber muzzle-loading Enfield rifle of the 1853 pattern, only rivaled by the American Springfield rifle. Ironically, the Enfield rifle was produced on American machinery and according to the "American method" of mass production.[6]

The Royal Artillery had also taken the lead in introducing a breakthrough artillery piece. The field artillery batteries had come equipped with the new breech-loading Armstrong guns. However, the average gunner and his officer could not deal with such a fundamental change and complained of having to rewrite the venerable gun drill "because the gun loaded at the wrong end. In the bloom of the industrial age, the British artillery was not yet prepared for the maintenance of delicate machinery."[7]

The Trent Affair had also given some impetus to the creation of an effective Canadian militia. The Canadians shared the mother country's outrage over the Trent Affair, but many English-speaking Canadians had a deeper dislike for the United States than for the imperial smugness of the British. Many were the descendents of the one hundred thousand American Loyalists who either refused to live in the new republic or had been "encouraged" to emigrate after the Revolution. They also continued to describe Americans as unsophisticated braggarts, using the epithet they shared with the British—"Brother Jonathan."

The outbreak of the Civil War followed by the Trent Affair had resulted in an initial burst of enthusiasm for defense by the provincial Canadian authorities. The new Volunteer Militia was quickly recruited up to its authorized strength and divided into small, organized units that drilled together on a regular basis. By 1862, there were thirty-four troops of horse, twenty-seven artillery batteries, 182 companies of rifles, and five companies of engineers. A Sedentary Militia, which theoretically included every adult male between the ages of eighteen and sixty years old, was also available, but they were not drilled and did not have weapons.[8]

As Wolseley reviewed the situation, he found he could count on about ten thousand men in the Voluntary Militia from Lower Canada (Quebec) and about fifteen thousand from Upper Canada (Ontario). Several thousand more could be found in the Maritimes. The process of consolidating the many independent companies into battalions had begun.

Three Canadian militia infantry battalions were brigaded with one British battalion for wartime operations as well as for training. The British Army had also provided several hundred officers and noncommissioned officers (NCOs) to train the Canadians. Nevertheless, there was a limit to how much soldiering could be passed on in the short training periods the Canadian colonial government was willing to pay for.

BRITISH ARMY HEADQUARTERS, MONTREAL, CANADA, 2:00 PM, SEPTEMBER 3, 1863

That afternoon, Wolseley reviewed the strategic defense of British North America with General Williams, Colonel Wetherall, and the rest of the staff. He said, "We face the unique military problem of an immensely long border with no strategic depth behind it. The inhabited regions of Upper and Lower Canada are rarely more than fifty miles deep. At the same time, the British forces in Canada and the Maritimes would show clearly that all of our scattered regular forces do not amount to a single corps in General Lee's Army of Northern Virginia. Our Canadian militia has an effective strength of even less than that. Because of the necessity to defend key points, there is no possibility that these forces could ever be consolidated into a single, large field army."

Although Wolseley considered his regulars more than a match for veteran American troops if war came, he also knew that the unblooded Canadians would have to be used very carefully until they had become seasoned. "We face another problem: Canadian officials tend to lose all interest in defense matters when the immediate cost is waved about. The attitude seems to be that since they are part of the British Empire, the empire will damn well have to defend them. If I remember correctly, that is one reason Brother Jonathan refused to pay his fair share for the Crown's expenses in the Seven Years War. And we know where that attitude led.

"Case in point, gentlemen, let me read you this comment from George Brown's newspaper, the *Globe*: 'We cannot agree to the dogma that Canada should provide entirely for her defence when she is not the author of the quarrels against the consequences of which she is called to stand upon her guard.'[9]

"On a more positive note, I am glad that the Canadian Volunteers are as splendid men as can be wished for. They are, after all, blood of our blood, bone of our bone. Unfortunately, the provincial authorities have been rather feckless in the selection of their officers. Social standing seems to be the primary consideration. They may well have considered Cromwell's standards when he said, 'If you chose godly, honest men to be captains of horse, honest men will follow them.' So, gentlemen, a major task is to nurse along these provincial officers as best we can until they approach the quality of the men they lead." As only British officers were present, there were no objections to his characterizations. If anything, there was knowing laughter.[10]

Wolseley continued. "Luckily the authorities have authorized an increase to thirty-five thousand, but they have to be recruited, organized, and trained. The authorities have agreed to begin organizing the next wave of battalions, from number twenty-four to sixty, though this will depend on the Crown arming and equipping them. Most of the militia companies already exist to be consolidated into battalions, and we can expect about a dozen to be established this month. Seven will be from Lower Canada and five from Upper Canada. A majority of the first twenty-three battalions are from Lower Canada, but they consist mostly of Her Majesty's English-speaking subjects; Her Majesty's French are less inclined to serve, though they have contributed several fine battalions.

"But getting them in shape to fight will take time; an element the enemy always tries to deny us. So the question becomes, What form would an American war take? Upon that answer rests our ability to plan for the most effective use of imperial forces. The Americans won't wait; they are an aggressive and even precipitous people. In 1776 and 1812, they immediately attacked Canada upon the commencement of hostilities. We cannot rely simply on history repeating their mistakes in those attempts.

"The Army's 1861 war plan, devised during the Trent Affair, plainly took that history into account and worked on the premise that the best defense was a good offense. It had recommended a major landing to capture Portland and occupy the entire state of Maine as well. British-held Maine would then form a strategic shield for the otherwise vulnerable Lower Canada and the Maritimes. It had two vital advantages, gentlemen. First, we would gain complete control of the Grand Trunk Railway to secure British North America's internal line of communications. Second, by offensive action we would put the Americans' forces on the defensive, which otherwise would inevitably and immediately attack Canada.

"So far, so good. Then for some inexplicable reason, this political assessment was also included. I read it for your edification.

> The interests of Maine and Canada are identical. A strong party is believed to exist in Maine in favor of annexation to Canada; and no sympathy is there felt for the war which now desolates the U. States. It is more than probable that a conciliatory policy adopted towards Maine would, if it failed to secure its absolute co-operation, indispose it to use any vigorous efforts against us. The patriotism of Americans dwells peculiarly in their pockets; & the pocket of the good citizens of Maine would benefit largely by the expenditure and trade we should create in making Portland our base & their territory our line of communications with Canada.[11]

Wolseley snorted in disgust. "What utter claptrap. Written, no doubt by some gentleman in London who had never been to North

America much less Maine. I just hope someone in the American government is not making the same assessment of Canada."

His recent trip to Maine indicated that its people would do more than resent an occupation. He had not forgotten Sharpe's account of the stand of the 20th Maine at Gettysburg either, nor how proud the people of Maine were of him and the rest of their regiments.[12]

He was also aware that if American politicians were assuming that the people of British North America would gladly look on forcible incorporation into the United States, they were equally delusional. The French had come to the conclusion that they would lose their exclusiveness that British rule allowed if absorbed in the huge sea of the Union. The Irish Canadians who had settled there in numbers as a result of the Great Famine were loyal to their new home; those who had hated the Crown had found the States more congenial and moved south. And as usual, the Scots were a bulwark to the Crown.

Though inclined to let others pay for their defense in the event of war, the people of British North America would fight. The Canadians had not understood the British outrage when the militia bill that would have funded much of the Canadian military expansion had caused the MacDonald government to fall in 1862. For them, the bill had simply been the proximate cause of the fall of a government that was on its way out. The Crown had swallowed its anger and provided a two million–pound subsidy that had allowed Canadian military preparations to continue. The new government was happy to spend that money, buying one hundred thousand Enfield rifles, uniforms, and ammunition, and using it to pay for the consolidation of militia companies into new battalions.[13]

ROYAL NAVY BASE, HALIFAX, NOVA SCOTIA, 12:00 AM, SEPTEMBER 4, 1863

As they often did, the whale oil lamps burned late at the headquarters of the Royal Navy's base in Halifax. The commander of the Royal Navy's North American and West Indies Station, Rear Adm. Sir Alexander Milne, was known as the foremost administrator in the Royal Navy. The closest he had come to combat in his thirty-six years in the Navy was to escort British and French troop transports in the Crimean War, which he had done with an efficiency that was uncharacteristic of the war. He ran a taut organization and tolerated no slack work. He showed a genuine concern for the enlisted men of the station and made improvements to make their lot easier. Milne came from a Navy family; his father, Adm.

Sir David Milne, had distinguished himself against the French in the Napoleonic Wars and had been impressed with the American naval performance in the War of 1812. The impression had had an ominous cast. He concluded, "I most sincerely wish to see their naval power nipped in the bud, for if they ever get it to any extent they will give us trouble enough."[14] The son had inherited his father's ability, but his opinion of the Americans was more judicious. He would not over or underestimate them.

Milne's exacting nature was not a surprise to the officers of the station. Naval officers were used to hard work; they had to know their profession to the smallest degree, or their warships, the most complex technological and organizational structures of the era, would simply cease to function. British Army officers were not, as a rule, so keen, especially in the aristocratic preserve of the cavalry regiments — work was too much like trade. It took more abuse to stop the functioning of a British infantryman or horse than the complex machinery of a ship. The Army officer, all too often, thought he had done his duty by dying well.

The late-working officers were surprised by the amount of work necessary to prepare for the Army's assistant quartermaster general for British North America's visit to Admiral Milne. The admiral's flag lieutenant, Basil Hall, could have enlightened them on the purpose of that visit to guide their labors, but he considered it too confidential to be batted about the mess.[15]

Instead, he had discussed it with Milne at tea that afternoon. Milne was a direct man, saving Hall from endless guessing games. The admiral leaned back in his stuffed chair by the great upper glass windows of the headquarters that looked out over the harbor and its sea of masts. It was a grand sight, the material evidence that Britannia did indeed rule the waves. Milne knew that that was a nice sentiment, but as an organized man, he wanted to add the numbers.

"Hall," he said, "Wolseley has an uncommonly good head for an Army officer. I much appreciated his observations from Washington and his discussions with Captain Hancock. It is his opinion that the Americans and we are sailing right into another crisis, similar to the Trent Affair. I read the American newspapers closely, Hall. I wish Lord Russell did as well. I'm afraid we continue to act under a badly written law that only threatens to drag us into a war by the very provocations it tolerates.

"You were not with me in December 1861 when I prepared a plan to be employed if we had gone to war with the Americans then. The desire for war burned hot in London at the time. We would have crushed their Navy. Now I am not so certain. Their Navy has grown in size, ability, and with the number of monitors they have . . ." He did not finish the statement but stared out the window for a moment as he sipped his tea.

Milne turned back to the flag lieutenant and put down his tea. "I prepared a plan that would have driven their Navy and commerce off the sea, broken their blockade, and thrown a counterblockade across their own ports. But then, the gentlemen in Whitehall never answered my question of 'what next' if the Americans did not sue for peace immediately."

"Oh, surely that would not happen, sir," Hall replied. "What country could survive such a blow? The shock alone would bring them to their senses."

"Really, Hall? And how many times did we do just that to the French and still have to fight long, grinding wars of exhaustion?"

Hall hesitated.

"And the Americans are not the French by any means. They spring from our own blood, as rude and arrogant a people as so many of our countrymen prefer to see them. In our two wars with the Americans, may I remind you of the number of ship-to-ship actions we lost?"

Hall began to look unsettled at the analogy.

"Cheer up, Hall, it is my job to see things without illusion. It is yours to be my sounding board. Now let me tell you of the improvements I have in mind for the war plan."

Milne first reviewed the original plan. It was based on the strength of the North American and West Indies Station that currently had a compliment of forty-two ships (totaling 70,456 tons), 14,551 men, and 1,319 guns. Of this number, there were eight battleships or ships of the line and thirteen frigates and corvettes. Every ship was steam powered. All of Milne's ships, however, were purpose-built warships whereas most American warships were converted commercial ships of one sort or another and armed with lighter ordnance.[16]

Milne noted that the most common gun in the fleet was the old 32-pounder, outclassed by the new Dahlgren guns the Americans had been producing in great numbers. That brought him to the problem that had been gnawing at him for months now. In 1861, the rifled Armstrong gun in various calibers had been issued to the fleet. It was hailed as a technological innovation of profound importance with a 1.5-mile point-blank accuracy and a reach of 5 miles for the 32-pounder Armstrong, seven times better than the comparable muzzle-loader. It had solved the problem of the great stress in the powder chambers of old cast-iron guns by shrinking wrought iron spirals over a wrought iron barrel. Being a breech-loader, the Armstrong did not have to be run out, reducing the movement of the gun in action. It had proved in practice, however, to be a profound disappointment. For such an advanced concept, the Armstrong guns were useless against the armor on American monitors for which they had never been designed. There were technical deficiencies as well that made the guns unreliable. The gun carriages were too low and forced the crews to stoop to operate the gun. The breeching bolts in the ships' sides were unable to resist the recoil of the gun, which Milne said was "so exceedingly violent that the gun and carriage was lifted bodily from the deck and came in with a crash, enough to tear everything to pieces, and the men were obliged to retire from near the gun." The lead shell covering, which was meant to mold to the rifling grooves, sometimes "puffed out," making it impossible to load. The heat of the tropics in which the ships of the station rotated tended to deteriorate the rubber fuse washers and the tallow-filled lubricators.[17]

The biggest problem was the poorly designed vent piece that frequently blew out when the gun was fired. As one observer noted, "I believe it occurred more than once that the block [vent piece] found its way into the main top to the discomfort of the men there." Milne had been unhappy when the Royal Navy purchased one hundred of the 110-pounders without trials, even though the manufacturer had stated that he did not think them suitable for such large calibers and for use at sea. Milne had more reason for his dismay with the guns as their deficiencies manifested, believing them overcomplicated and prone to malfunction in quick firing. He pointedly noted, "Americans won't look at them." Even Lord Lyons had noted to Russell that Union authorities relied on the "simplicity and stolidity" of Dahlgren's guns and had no confidence in breech-loading weapons.[18]

Milne had kept by him the report of Capt. George Hancock of the *Immortalité*, who had toured American ordnance facilities and spoken extensively with Admiral Dahlgren. The report was already eighteen months old but that only added to his disquiet. Even then, the Americans were producing more than thirty of the Dahlgrens a week. Milne had complete confidence in Hancock's judgment, and when the captain characterized the American guns as the "most efficient weapons of the day," he took it very much to heart. Dahlgren had devised a method to avoid the great weakness of all guns, the manner in which the trunions, on which the gun pivoted, were mounted. The shorter American gun carriage allowed the guns to be fired at a greater elevation than comparable British guns. The guns' soda bottle shape also meant that their center of gravity was not so near the ship's outer wall and reduced the ship's rolling, especially in heavy weather. The muzzles also extended beyond the gun ports more than British guns, reducing the chance of igniting the wooden sides of the ship or, when on the upper deck, of setting fire to the rigging. That last danger was the subject of special complaints Milne had made to the Admiralty. Hancock also noticed that the Americans had cut a hole behind each gun up through which powder charges were passed, thus eliminating the frantic rushing up and down the main hatchways of men carrying powder charges.

With all this in mind, Milne was preparing a report to state that although the Armstrong guns were "admirably manufactured and of great precisions," they were "not suitable for service afloat." That conclusion was a constant worry for Milne. The Armstrong guns were a large proportion of the station's guns. He had decided to request that they should be replaced with more reliable muzzle-loaders with particular emphasis on the 68-pounder that British testing had indicated would penetrate the 4.5 inches of side armor of American ironclads at two hundred yards.[19]

The backbone of the fighting power of the station was its ships of the line with their three decks of guns, which seemed from another world, and indeed they were. Most were laid down more than twenty years before. They were typified by HMS *Nile*, Milne's flagship. She had been laid down in 1839 and converted to screw in 1854. In 1862 she had been up-gunned with sixteen Armstrong guns of various calibers, though she still carried sixty-two of the venerable muzzle-loading 32-pounders.[20]

Milne's war plan had three basic elements: to destroy any American fleet or ship that dared to oppose the Royal Navy; to blockade the Union coast from Cape Henry, Virginia, to Maine; and to conduct powerful raids against coastal targets. He also wanted to seize sites in the vicinity of Martha's Vineyard as coaling stations. Inherent in this plan was breaking the Union blockade of the South at Charleston and possibly Galveston. The First Lord of the Admiralty, the Duke of Somerset, had written him as the Trent Crisis mounted, "In the event of war I do not send from here any plan of operations as you have probably better means of judging what to do, but the first objective would probably be to open the blockade of the Southern ports and without directly co-operating with the Confederates, enable them to act and to receive supplies."[21]

Milne had also expressed a strong desire to control the Chesapeake Bay and make a descent on Washington itself, a tactic that the Royal Navy had used successfully in the War of 1812. An Admiralty report on the feasibility of attacking Northern ports concluded that the "intricacy of the channels and the strength of the forts made such attacks unfeasible." Except for his pet project to strike at Washington, Milne himself did not favor operations against ports despite an Admiralty assessment that control of New York Harbor would probably end the war. As Milne went over these points with Hall, he explained, "The object of the war can only be to cripple the enemy — that is, his trade and merchant and whaling fleets." He realized that Great Britain could never truly destroy the North. "No object would be gained if the ports alone are to be attacked, as modern views deprecate any damage to a town. If ships are fired upon in a port the town must suffer; therefore,the shipping cannot be fired upon. This actually reserves operations to vessels at sea."[22]

Hall countered that the Union had shown no such punctilious regard for civilian lives and private property in its bombardment of Charleston and other Southern coastal towns. Milne was clear on this point. "The usages of civilized nations do no permit such depredations any longer."

"But, Admiral, would not such a prohibition also prevent an attack on Washington?

Milne replied, "That will not be a problem. Once the river forts are suppressed, the city is at our mercy."

Hall could only look into his teacup at the rebuff.[23]

Milne glided over the issue and went on. "Seizing coaling stations at Martha's Vineyard is vital to maintaining a blockade of the North, but they do not have the advantage of fully functioning ports when the North Atlantic winters will limit communication with Halifax. Bermuda, our winter headquarters, and Nassau, are too far away to sustain a blockading fleet. For that reason, I believe we must support the Army's plan to capture Portland. Colonel Wolseley is correct in his conclusion that for the Army to wait to receive an American attack would be fatal. A rain of blows is the only thing that will keep the Americans from conquering Canada. I am reminded of something my father said back in 1817. 'We cannot keep Canada if the Americans declare war against us.'[24]

"We must also have a more southern base on the American shore. I was thinking of the American Navy's forward operating base at Port Royal, south of Charleston, which they have conveniently prepared. Wolseley recommended the four thousand–man garrison of Barbados as a landing force to occupy it once we seize it.

"Like the Army in Canada, we too in the Navy have our own vulnerabilities that are best defended with offensive operations. We have no dry docks able to handle our ships of the line. We have had to depend on the American naval yards for emergency repairs in the past. Although we have a ready supply of coal in Nova Scotia, the best coal must still be brought from Wales. You know, Hall, I have another worry. Our base in Bermuda is woefully defended. My recommendations to London have fallen on deaf ears."

Milne stood up and began to pace before the great windows. "We must plan for the long war, Hall, if our initial strike does not bring the Americans to their senses. I fear that if that first blow fails, we will only have roused these people to even greater efforts.

"What was feasible in 1861 is fraught with problems today. The strength of this station to undertake such an operation teeters, Hall, teeters on the jagged edge of adequacy. I cannot recommend to the Admiralty that it be attempted with the forces we have. If such an issue ever arises, I would insist on powerful reinforcement. We must have all four of our broadside ironclads and a good part of the Channel Squadron itself. We shall also require the naval siege train, the 'Great Armament,' that was assembled for the capture of Sebastopol."

He stopped pacing. "I think such a war will make us long for the French as enemies."[25]

GOVERNOR'S MANSION, INDIANAPOLIS, INDIANA, 12:20 PM, SEPTEMBER 4, 1863

Governor Oliver Morton was a happy man as he raised a glass of wine. "Gentlemen, I toast the good Sergeant Cline." Sharpe was happy to comply, as was Col. Henry Carrington, the officer detailed to be the Copperhead catcher in Indiana. Cline's raid on Bowles's farm and the recovery from his barns of all the Springfield rifles stolen the last month had been a signal success in a difficult and shadowy fight against disloyalty.

Sharpe had sent Cline immediately out from Washington to report to Colonel Carrington. A week later, several companies of Cline's old regiment, the 3rd Indiana Cavalry, had followed. Sharpe had secured their detail to his bureau for special operations. This regiment had what was called "personality." Unlike most Union cavalry regiments it had never had to go through long periods of training simply to learn how to ride; its volunteers were already accomplished horsemen and owned their own horses and equipment. Hooker had put them to good use when he commanded a division in an almost independent command on the Eastern Shore of Maryland earlier in the war. Always eager for intelligence, Hooker had called on the services of Lafayette Baker, who was glad to train the regiment in aspects of counterespionage. They responded with such enthusiasm that on one occasion they captured a Confederate sloop loading contraband supplies on the Chesapeake Bay, earning the title of "Hooker's Horse Marines."[26]

With a crack unit like the 3rd at his disposal, Colonel Carrington approved Cline's suggestion to clean out Bowles's nest. Now Bowles was safely in prison without the protection of habeas corpus, his band was dead or captured, and his farm no longer served as a locus of subversion. Morton was in a very good mood. Sharpe thought it a good time to hand him a letter from General Meade. He requested a promotion to captain for Cline. Morton read it and huffed. "Captain! He thinks I hand out captains' commissions like candy. Why, sir," he said with a slight twinkle in his eye, "those are scarce as hen's teeth." He paused, "But I have a surplus of commissions to major at hand. While Captain Cline is a pleasant alliteration, I think Major Cline would be far more useful to our cause."

Sharpe had every reason to be as positive as Morton. He had set up his bureau successfully. McPhail was in Washington, assembling a staff. He had secured the detail of his "Horse Marines" for very special operations, and he had personally attended to the lancing of a festering boil in a state important to Lincoln for the sustenance of the war effort.

On the train the next morning he let his thoughts range in a stream of consciousness, which he had come to learn could be most useful at finding new perspectives. The Washington Arsenal came to mind, that complex of weapons munitions and storehouses and assembly factories on the southern tip of Washington where the Potomac and Eastern Branch rivers met. He had been intrigued by Lincoln's references to the coffee mill gun, and a few inquiries had revealed that all fifty the President had encouraged McClellan to buy were there. He paid a visit and found them in a shed, all neatly lined up and oiled, and looking with their hoppers very much like the coffee mills that Lincoln had named them after.

He had put in a requisition for ten of them and had been turned down flat by Ripley. Sharpe had stormed into Ripley's office. The old man had actually lied to his face that there were no coffee mill guns stored at the Arsenal. "I was there three days ago and saw them with my own eyes!"

Caught in a bold-faced lie, Ripley blamed an administrative over-sight. Then finding another argument, he said, "But in any case, you are not authorized such weapons in your present capacity."

Sharpe tossed away any pretense at courtesy. "Listen to me, you lying old fraud, I have the authority of the President of the United States, and I will not hesitate to use it to make sure you are issuing rations on a Sioux reservation in Minnesota by next week." Ripley blinked and signed the authorization.

Sharpe issued them to his old regiment, the 120th NY, now safely a part of the garrison of Washington. He had raised this regiment in Ulster and Greene counties back home, and no colonel in the Army retained a more paternal concern. They had bled badly at Gettysburg but had earned a reputation for stubbornness. He was proud of them, but what was more useful at this time was that he knew they were reliable and returned his devotion. Though assigned officially to the garrison, they were considered to be at his disposal. He arranged for them to replace the military guard at the White House and to train with the coffee mill guns at one of the firing ranges. He could rely on their acting commander, Maj. John Tappen, to run a taut outfit. Tappen was a first-class fighting man and held the respect of the men. He and Sharpe had been company commanders together when they marched off to save the capital in the first days of the war in their old militia regiment, the 20th NY State Militia Regiment. It would take him a few more weeks to get the 20th swapped out with another regiment gone soft in the Washington forts. Sharpe was a man of strong and even sentimental loyalties, and these were strongest with the two regiments he had served with. In fact, when he raised the 120th, he deliberately chose that number to reflect the old 20th, even though that put the new regiment behind in seniority. Sharpe was a Hudson Valley man who trusted his Ulster and Greene County compatriots first and foremost.[27]

The train jolted and brought him back to the purpose of his visit in the West. There was far more to do. He had intended to visit Major Generals Grant and Rosecrans, who commanded the two major armies in the Western Theater; brief them on his organization; and set up the military intelligence staffs that he had created for the Army of the Potomac. Unforeseen events had intervened. Grant was in New Orleans, disabled by an accident in which the vicious horse he had been riding had fallen on him. Rosecrans was also unavailable. He was marching into battle.

BRIDGEPORT, ALABAMA, 7:00 PM, SEPTEMBER 4, 1863

The Union troops marched across the pontoon bridge over the Tennessee River in an endless river of faded blue. There was great confidence in all ranks as the Army of the Cumberland, which had chased its opponent, the Confederate Army of Tennessee, out of Alabama and into northern Georgia. The mercurial Maj. Gen. William Rosecrans—"Old Rosy" to his troops for his good nature and his Roman nose colored red by the bottle—had run the fight out of his opposition, the sour and dyspeptic Lt. Gen. Braxton Bragg, whose only aggressive characteristic was the intensity with which he avoided a decisive battle. Bragg had systematically alienated every senior Army officer with his relentlessly nasty and blame-placing personality. Rosecrans, who was the most popular officer in the Union Army, had already beaten Bragg at the battle of Stone's River in December 1862, a tonic to the North after the disastrous defeat at Freder-icksburg a few weeks before.

The campaign flowed onward to what everyone could sense was coming—the decisive battle. It was understandable that Rosecrans had not had time to consider a letter dated twelve days before from a major of the 21st Illinois, despite the strong endorsements of his brigade and division commanders. Maj. James E. Callaway had been mightily impressed with the effectiveness of the innovation of mounted infantry armed with the Spencer repeating rifle and requested permission to raise a regiment of mounted infantry in his native state. A bold, intelligent, and far-thinking young lawyer, Callaway was the type of man who was attracted to the potential and thrill of the cutting edge of change. He pressed on Rosecrans, "There are already several companies organized in the state of Illinois that are anxious to enter the service as cavalry or mounted infantry." He threw in his political connections with the state adjutant general who had "pledged all the assistance in his power."[28]

Callaway was striking while the iron was hot. Already the brigade of mounted infantry under Col. John Thomas Wilder had proven its worth in Rosecrans's brilliant Tullahoma Campaign that June. The brigade was the brainchild of Maj. Gen. Lovell H. Rousseau, one of Rosecrans's division commanders, who had arrived in Washington in February "all afire with zeal for mounted infantry." Rousseau had deep credit with Lincoln. He had been, according to the President, "our first active practical Military friend in Kentucky." Now Rousseau was telling Lincoln what he wanted and needed to hear—that only mounted infantry armed with repeaters could deal with the likes of the infamous Nathan Bedford Forrest. He said, "I propose to organize and use such a force to be furnished with Sharps rifles. If I do not make this pay at the end of three months from today, I will cheerfully relinquish the command."

Lincoln was impressed and wrote Rosecrans, authorizing the experiment. Rosecrans had been an early supporter of Rousseau's idea and had requested repeating rifles in February only to receive the usual tart and disingenuous reply from Ripley's ally as general in chief of the armies, Maj. Gen. Henry Halleck. "You are not the only general who is urgently calling for more cavalry and more cavalry arms. The supply is limited, and the demands of all cannot be satisfied. In regard to 're-volving rifles, superior arms,' &c., every one is issued the moment it is received." Halleck did not mention that the repeaters had not really been ordered at all.

Rosecrans was not one to wait on Ripley's shifty promises; he immediately authorized Colonel Wilder to impress mounts and transform his infantry into a mounted infantry brigade. Wilder was even less willing to rely on normal requisitions. He bought Spencers with money borrowed from Indiana home state bankers, and his eager men repaid the bankers in installments. The federal government later reimbursed them. It was an effective way to get around Ripley. The Spencers soon proved their worth, whipping a Confederate brigade at Hoover's Gap with the weight of their firepower. The enemy commander thought he was outnumbered five to one and suffered three to one losses. Thereafter, they were known as "Wilder's Lightning Brigade."[29]

Callaway was determined to catch some of that lightning for himself, but he would have to wait. The big fight was coming, and for him it would be an old-fashioned infantryman's brawl. The Army pressed on; it could smell the enemy's fear.

Tremors of despair spread in every direction from all ranks of the fleeing Army of Tennessee. They arrived in Richmond and from there to the headquarters of Robert E. Lee at Culpepper Court House in Northern Virginia. President Davis feared the worst. Yet he would not replace Bragg for whom he had a great and unaccountable regard. Something would have to be done to save Bragg from himself. As usual, in such moments of desperation, Davis turned to Robert E. Lee.

8.

Battle at Moelfre Bay

OFF THE MOUTH OF THE MERSEY RIVER, LIVERPOOL BAY, 8:22 AM, SEPTEMBER 4, 1863

Lamson had asked his chief engineer for every bit of speed the engines of the *Gettysburg* could generate. The word had spread through the crew that the ship was speeding west to pounce on their unsuspecting quarry. The black gangs sprang to their broad shovels with a will to feed the boilers with the good Welsh coal taken aboard at Liverpool. The fires burned hot as the sweat slicked off them in dark, greasy rivulets. Had they been galley rowers in ancient Greece, they themselves would have been the motive engines of their ship, their muscles fed with energy from bread dipped in olive oil. Now the hard coal of Wales replaced muscles to power the world.

Moelfre Bay was just short of forty-five nautical miles from the Mersey's mouth. Lamson could make it in three hours or a bit less. *Gettysburg* had taken off like an arrow, leaving *Liverpool* behind just as she was joined by *Goshawk*. As it was, Lamson had a barely fifteen-minute head start. The lookout shouted that the British ships were coming directly after them. Lamson could only conclude that they would try to snatch his prey from him. Fox had chosen *Gettysburg* for her speed, and that speed was the only advantage he had now. *Liverpool* could do between ten and twelve knots to *Gettysburg's* sixteen. That meant they would arrive at Moelfre Bay in about four hours. None of this would mean a damn if *North Carolina* had already transferred its crew and departed. In that case, he would be following her most likely course to the Azores. There are too many ifs, he thought.[1]

Two hours and fifty minutes later, the biggest "if" was answered as *Gettysburg* steamed into Moelfre Bay. The lookout had already reported a few ships in the bay, including a cluster near the shore. It did not take long for Lamson's glass to reveal that it was *North Carolina* and several lighters. He slammed the telescope glass shut. "Battle stations, Mr. Porter." Most of the men were already at their stations, as eager for this prize as the captain was.

It took the crew of the new Confederate ironclad longer to discover the fast steamer racing toward them. When they did, everyone stopped and stared. One of the officers ran up to James Bulloch. "Sir, she's the Yankee that was in King's Dock."

Bulloch was tight lipped while looking through his glass. "So she is. So she is. Well, don't just stand there. Get the men to the sheets. Tell the engineer to give me full speed."

"We'll never make it, sir. Look how fast she is approaching."

Bulloch turned on him, drawing a pistol. "Now, Mr. Wilson."[2]

It did not take long for the *Gettysburg*'s lookout to spot commotion on the decks of the ironclad. "She's seen us, Mr. Porter. Prepare to put a shot across her bow." Lamson had extended his telescope again; he was within range and could see men scurrying to bring sacks and boxes from the lighter tied up to the ironclad. Then the last of them jumped aboard a small craft that peeled away from *North Carolina* whose own smokestack was beginning to puff deep coils of black coal smoke. *Gettysburg* raced through the waves like a greyhound as her prey began to get under way. "Fire, when ready, Mr. Porter."

"Are you crazy?" The scream came from behind him. Lamson turned on his heel to see who would address the ship's captain with such blasphemy. It was Henry Adams with a look of horror on his face. "We are still in British waters. You cannot fire on them here."

"Fire!" The forward XI-inch pivot gun snapped back as the round shot flew across the leaden waters of the bay to splash only a few yards from *North Carolina*'s bow. She did not stop.

"Mr. Adams, I will not be addressed so on my own quarterdeck. Kindly go below." He turned to Mr. Porter and said, "Aim for their steering gear." Adams did not go below. He stayed on deck and gibbered something about British territorial waters. When they closed to eight hundred yards, the pivot gun captain shouted, "Fire!' The great bottle-shaped gun sprang back again with a roar. The first shell struck just behind the stern and went skipping off across the water. The next struck the stern. It penetrated the three-and-a-half-inch armor plate there and exploded inside, but the ironclad was building up a head of steam, attempting to get out to sea. *Gettysburg* closed to four hundred yards and sent a steady stream of XI-inch shells from all her guns that could bear into *North Carolina*. They smashed the steering, punched through the armored hull in several places to explode inside, and sent the foremast crashing over the side. The ram's armor was no protection against Admiral Dahlgren's guns at full charge. Her trial-run crew was not up to the pounding; nor was the rest of the men, who had been taken on only the hour before and were still unfamiliar with the ship. They huddled belowdecks. The engineer and his crew had shut down the engine.

"Oh, dear God. Lamson, do you realize what you've done?" Adams shouted.

"Indeed, I do, Mr. Adams. I have obeyed my orders to prevent this ship from escaping to become another *Alabama*. Those orders were further seconded by Mr. Seward, if I remember your father's statement. Now get below, or keep silent." Adams leaned against the railing and put his face in his hands. Porter signaled to a Marine to escort Adams below.[3]

On the ram, Bulloch recognized the inevitable as the *Gettysburg* closed. All his dreams and efforts had been smashed by the XI-inch Dahlgrens. There was at least one more thing he could do. He went below to his cabin and threw open his sea chest. He drew out the gray uniform of a Confederate States Navy officer and caressed its fine wool and gilt buttons before changing into it. Next, he drew from the chest a dress sword presented to him by George Trenholm. He looked himself over in the mirror and was satisfied. At least, I will command this ship at her last, he thought. There was one more item in the chest. He held it reverently to his chest, then tucked it under his arm, and climbed to the deck.[4]

He found it almost deserted. He climbed to the quarterdeck and found the halyard from which the British merchant colors flew. He hauled them down.

Lamson was barely a hundred yards away and shouted the command to cease firing. The men saw the British colors come down and raised a cheer. "Do you strike, sir?" Lamson shouted through a megaphone.

Bulloch bellowed across the water, "No! By God, sir, the Confederate States Ship *North Carolina* has not struck!" He hoisted the Confederate naval ensign to the top of its staff. Then he walked over to the rail and shook his fist, "Now, sir! Do your worst!"

Gettysburg's larboard battery thundered, sending three more shells through the ironclad's plate to explode inside the empty casemate. "Prepare to board!" Lamson shouted. Lamson was drawing his sword when Adams, who had broken away from his escort, grabbed his arm. "You dare, sir?" the captain asked as he pulled back his arm.

"Don't you see? Don't you see? We are saved!"

"What the hell do you mean, Mr. Adams?"

Henry Adams was beside himself with excitement. "When he raised that rebel rag, he removed the protection of British sovereignty from his ship. He became a belligerent, liable to be attacked at any time or place, and revealed that was his intention all the time."[5]

Lamson blinked. All well and good, but he had more to do now than think about the rights of belligerents as *Gettysburg* came alongside *North Carolina*. Grappling hooks flew over the narrowing space until the hulls ground against each other. Lamson, sword and pistol in hand, led the boarding party of Marines and sailors over the side. Other than the angry man on the captain's quarterdeck, the upper decks of the ship were empty save for a pool of blood or two. The men fanned out as Lamson led a party up to the quarterdeck. He approached Bulloch, who stood there gloriously alone.

Lamson holstered his pistol and touched his fingers to his cap brim. "You are my prisoner, sir."

Bulloch bowed slightly and returned the salute. "I see that the fortunes of war regretfully have made that so, Captain." He slowly drew his sword and handed it hilt first to Lamson. The Confederate colors fluttered down the halyard at the same time and fell at his feet.

Lamson turned to the ensign that had come aboard with him. "Mr. Henderson, escort Captain . . ." he looked at Bulloch and said, "I do not believe I know your name, Captain."

"The name is Bulloch, sir, Capt. James Dunwoody Bulloch, Confederate States Navy."[6]

"Mr. Henderson, escort Captain Bulloch to my cabin and see that he is comfortable. Ask Mr. Adams to join me here."

Adams found Lamson searching through papers in Bulloch's cabin. Lamson looked up. Any anger he may have felt for Adams's hysteria on deck had evaporated in the excitement of what he had found. "Look at these," he said and spread papers across the table. His purpose was everywhere; there was even preprinted official stationary for the CSS *North Carolina*.[7]

"I saw at least three things on the way here, Captain, that were stamped or carved with the ship's name. Proof! Russell wants endless proofs. We can start with sending him the ships' bell." Adams pulled up a chair and started to go over the papers, "I will be awhile, but I think these will nail the British to the wall."

Lamson left him to his work and went back on deck. The ironclad's crew had been brought up and was under guard. There were a half dozen wounded men being attended by their own surgeon and the *Gettysburg's*. Porter was examining the papers of the crew. "These papers confirm that almost every man here is a British subject. If they weren't all Royal Navy, I'd be much surprised."

"They're nothing but a liability, Mr. Porter. Put them in the ship's boats and let them row ashore, but winnow out any of Captain's Bulloch's Confederates. Have the engineer report to me as well. Tell him I want to know the condition of this ship's engines and whether she has the coal to get to an American port. We may put a prize crew in her yet. It would be grand, Mr. Porter, to not only take this enemy but take her home as well."

"Aye, sir, grand indeed."

"Waste no time, Mr. Porter. We don't have much before our British friends arrive. I want them to find this bay empty of us." Lamson allowed himself twenty minutes to inspect the casemated gun deck and one of the turrets. The gun deck was a shambles of smashed and splintered teak and twisted armor plates. He carefully examined the damage; the Navy would be eager to hear what the Dahlgren guns could do to the best British armor plate. The turret was even more interesting, being built on a different principle than Mr. Ericsson's central moving spindle. There was much to learn, but so little time. A Marine found him and said that Porter requested his presence on deck.

When Lamson joined him, Porter pointed east. "*Liverpool*, Captain, with *Goshawk* fifteen minutes behind. Faster than we thought."

"Get Mr. Adams back on board *Gettysburg*. Have the engineer report to me. We will not be taking this ship home as a prize. But I won't give her back so that they can hand her over to the Confederacy. We will sink her right here."

Liverpool slowed warily as she approached the two ships. Her captain noticed that there was no smoke coming from the ironclad but plenty rising from the American ship. She would be able to leap forward at a moment's notice. He also noticed that the American ship moved to keep herself between the ram and *Liverpool*. The wreckage of an engagement aboard the ironclad was also impossible to miss, as were the American colors. The captain was in a quandary for his orders did not cover such an eventuality. The day before he had been ordered to observe and follow the American ship as long as she was in British waters. This morning, *Goshawk* had brought the urgent new orders — to pursue and seize the escaped Laird Brothers ram.[8]

He ordered beat to quarters. *Gettysburg*'s gun crews stood their posts in silence as they watched the British guns run out. They knew that *Gettysburg*'s broadside had only four guns as opposed to the almost twenty British guns. The *Liverpool* was only wood, but *Gettysburg*'s iron hull was vulnerable as well and its side-wheels even more so.

A boat came over from *Liverpool*. The captain himself climbed the ladder to be met by hastily assembled Marines and a petty officer to pipe him aboard. He tipped his hat to the colors and stepped forward to meet Lamson. He bowed and then saluted. Lamson returned the courtesies. Capt. Rowley Lambert was about forty, spare as a beanpole, and affected all the Royal Navy's disdain for the upstart U.S. Navy. He was especially disdainful of the mere youth that said he was the captain of this warship.

For a moment he looked around at the huge soda bottle–shaped Dahlgrens. He knew their reputation as the finest smoothbores in the world. He also knew that his thirty-nine guns, even as old as they were, could shred *Gettysburg* before she could get off many shots. He refused Lamson's invitation to go below for a brandy and came to the point. "I must know the meaning of your presence in these waters and why you have attacked a British ship in British waters."

Lamson had been coached by Adams to say, "I have pursued and seized a belligerent ship that was attempting to escape to open sea, sir."

"What rubbish is that, sir? She is a British ship, built by Laird Brothers of Birkenhead and on her sea trials."

"That is true that she was built by Laird Brothers, but when we found her she was flying the colors of the Confederate States, which your own government has recognized as a belligerent." Lamson told the necessary lie. "And her captain was in Confederate uniform. His papers clearly state that she was the property of the so-called Confederate States of America. Why, sir, even the ship's bell was cast with words CSS *North Carolina*. She is my prize, and I intend to send her with a prize crew to an American port."

Lambert was having none of this. "This ironclad is a British ship as far as my orders are concerned, and her status will be determined by

British courts. You have committed a hostile act in British waters. I must demand the surrender of your vessel." He paused, "Or I will take you by force. You have fifteen minutes to strike, sir."

"When hell freezes over, sir. Now, be on your way."

Lambert's face turned red at the peremptory dismissal from the mere Yankee cub. Not even the boldest Frenchmen would have dared to snap his fingers in the lion's face like that. He turned on his heel and hastened down the side and into his boat, eager to make good his threat.

No sooner had his boat pushed off than *Gettysburg* sped forward, the wake tossing Lambert's boat about and giving the captain a good splash. The American ship maintained station on the opposite side of the ram. Lamson was careful to keep his vulnerable paddlewheel behind the ram's forward turret. It was a furious British captain who climbed up onto his quarterdeck. His disposition did not improve as he attempted to maneuver around the ram to get a good shot at the American ship that just continued to circle the other way. It was obvious the American captain was using the ram's unloaded freeboard of only six feet to mask the fire of the fifteen 8-inch rifles and 32-pounder smoothbore guns of *Liverpool*'s gun deck battery. That left his eight 40-pounder Armstrongs and the bruising 110-pounder Armstrong pivot gun on the main deck. The four Dahlgrens that could bear on the *Liverpool*'s main deck fired 135-pound projectiles for a broadside weight of 540 pounds. *Liverpool*'s nine main deck guns totaled only 430 pounds of projectile weight. In effect, by Lamson's maneuver, the smaller ship had a 26 percent advantage in broadside weight. Even that was deceptive because the Dahlgren projectiles were far more destructive.[9]

Lamson's cat and mouse game with *Liverpool* gave *Goshawk* time to come up and take up station on *Gettysburg*'s open flank, but her one 68-pounder, one 32-pounder, and two 20-pounders were vastly outmatched by the larger guns that the American ship could bring to bear.[10]

Lamson looked at his pocket watch as the last few minutes counted down. Behind him Adams said, "You must let him fire first; it is imperative that the British start this."

"Have no fear, Mr. Adams. But I do suggest that you get below. Pray, sir, do not make me waste a Marine to watch over you." Lamson could feel the tension settle over all three ships as the last seconds fell away. The men were steady at their posts, the Dahlgrens double-shotted. The command to fire echoed across the ram from the British ship. Instantly *Liverpool* was engulfed in smoke as her main deck battery fired.

Lamson felt the shock wave cross the ram and push him back like the shove of a giant, and instantly *Gettysburg*'s guns roared back.

Through the smoke, Lamson heard the shout of the gun captains as their crews leapt back into action. All the guns were still in action. The British were now firing at will. A bullet struck the railing where he stood. Adams was still on deck and came up to point at the Royal Marines firing their Enfields from the rigging at Lamson. "Look out!" he threw himself at Lamson, knocking him to the deck. In the next moment he cried out and fell over Lamson. Two Marines ran up to pull Adams off the captain, then took aim with their Spencer repeaters. One by one the British Marines dropped from the rigging.[11]

The fire from *Liverpool* slackened. A breeze blew the smoke away enough to reveal the carnage of splinters, dismounted guns, smashed carriages, and the dead and dying across her decks. *Goshawk* was an even worse shambles, now drifting away with fires starting. Lamson inspected his own ship and found that a shell had detonated inside the smokestack and left it like a colander. Another shell had gone through the top of the engine house, and a 110-pound shot had lodged in the sternpost. His casualties were few, but *Liverpool* was not going to play his game any longer. She came about to circle around the ram, but Lamson was faster and rounded that ship in time to send a shell from his pivot gun into her stern and watch it explode, spewing out wooden debris and a body. Lambert turned hard to starboard, circling back to open *Gettysburg* to his gun deck battery. His ship rocked as it fired in one well-timed volley. At the distance of barely three hundred yards, it struck *Gettysburg* a brutal blow. The port paddlewheel disintegrated, and the crew of one of the waist guns was swept away in a bloody wind. With only his larboard paddlewheel in operation, *Gettysburg* automatically turned in that direction. The ragged cheer from *Liverpool* was cut short when Lamson's remaining Dahlgrens poured their fire into the *Liverpool*'s gun deck. He could see shells exploding inside, but the British fire did not slacken.

What Lamson could not see was the scene around *Liverpool*'s Armstrong gun. When the gunner pulled the lanyard, the vent piece on the gun blew out and straight up like a bullet. The breech blew back at the same time. The crew stood stunned, their stares only broken by the red-coated body of a Royal Marine who fell from the rigging, bouncing over the smoking breech, brought down by the vent piece.[12]

The two ships were now paralleling each other, trading blows in an arc as *Gettysburg*'s stricken paddlewheel condemned it to steaming in

BATTLE AT MOELFRE BAY

a circle. The crews of both ships had no time to pay much attention to the ram, which had slowly been settling. Lamson's engineer had opened the sea cocks as planned when *Liverpool* approached. With only six feet of freeboard, the ram settled fast. The water rushed over her decks and into the open hatches. She went under, barely noticed by either ship.

The laws of naval warfare clearly allowed Lamson to strike his colors at this moment. He had accomplished his critical mission when the *North Carolina* slipped beneath the waters of Moelfre Bay, and his ship was hopelessly disabled in those same hostile waters. Yet Lamson was just plain bloody minded and would sooner drag *Liverpool* to the bottom with him before he quit.

Lambert knew he had won. The American ship was crippled and could not escape. It was only a matter of time. He must strike, but he didn't. Instead that ship continued to send those deadly XI-inch shells into *Liverpool*'s guts, turning his gun deck into an abattoir. "Strike, damn you, strike!" Lambert shouted in rage. The *Liverpool*'s crew was so focused on its death struggle with the enemy that another ship was able to approach without notice—until a shell struck the frigate's port battery. *Kearsarge* had arrived.

Capt. John Winslow had taken Adams's letter seriously. *Kearsarge* arrived at the Mersey's mouth an hour after *Liverpool* and *Goshawk* had departed after *Gettysburg*. Dudley, still in his dispatch boat, had informed Winslow, who followed the other ships pouring on the coal. He had heard the battle and seen the smoke in plenty of time to come to battle stations. With an American ship in battle with another ship, he did not trouble himself with the niceties of international maritime law, but came to the rescue of the flag.

Aboard *Gettysburg*, Lamson shouted to the gun crews that it was *Kearsarge*. A cheer went up as the British ship turned to meet its new opponent. *Kearsarge* had the element of surprise, but it was still a big frigate against a smaller American 1,550-ton *Mohican* class sloop of war. Lamson and his crew were now spectators as their ship carved a slowing arc away from the British ship. *Liverpool*'s 32-pounders had been no match for the Dahlgrens, but at the close range they had been fighting, they served more than well enough to hull *Gettysburg* in a dozen places. The hull's iron plates had not absorbed the shock of shot as a wooden ship could but had sprung their rivets along their seams. The ship's carpenter reported that she was taking water faster than the men could pump it out.

"Well, Mr. Porter, at least we don't have to strike. Now she dies well." He struck the railing with his fist. "Bring the wounded up and prepare to load them into the boats that have not been smashed. Keep the forward pivot crew at their gun. I want it to keep in action whenever it can bear." The ship's arc took it away from the duel between *Liverpool* and *Kearsarge*. Winslow was keeping his distance and using his superior mobility and guns to strike the larger wounded frigate with little chance of being struck in turn.

Gettysburg slowed as she took on more and more water, despite the heroic work of the men at the pumps and the carpenter's futile caulking of the sprung seams. There was a perceptible list. The pivot gun fired its last shot before the list depressed it too far to sight, and Lamson watched its shell strike *Liverpool* square amidships, knocking a four-foot hole. It exploded inside, spewing debris out the hole. Smoke began to pour from the hole with orange tongues of fire darting through. Ammunition was exploding inside the gun deck. Fire began to gush out the gun ports. *Gettysburg*'s crewmen on deck stopped, mesmerized by the death of the frigate. They watched men jump overboard as the fire ran up the rigging and poured up through the hatches.

The *Liverpool* seemed to heave amidships, her back arching, as a column of fire burst from her deck and shot upward. The shock wave pulsed out, followed by the deafening sound. The force of the explosion shuddered through the ship, and then blew outward. *Liverpool* simply disappeared in the blast of its own magazines. The sound was heard in Birkenhead and Liverpool sixty miles to the east, through the vales and valleys of northern Wales to the southwest, and west across the Irish Sea. That was only the functioning of physics. The political shock wave would surge around the world.

UNITED STATES EMBASSY, LONDON,
4:11 AM, SEPTEMBER 5, 1863

Charles Adams had spent a sleepless night. Russell's note of the first had reached him only yesterday afternoon. He wrote in his diary, "I clearly foresee that a collision must now come. The prospect is dark for poor America."[13] In the meantime, Russell had done nothing to tell him of the decision to seize the rams. Adams dressed and sat at his desk to compose the most difficult letter of his life. He summed up the failures of the British government to stop the depredations originating from its shores and then delivered the ultimatum that Lincoln had ordered him to put before

Russell and the cabinet. On his own initiative, he spelled it out with a final sentence of his own, "It would be superfluous in me to point out to your lordship that this is war."[14]

A few minutes after dispatching the note, John Bright was announced. Adams saw him immediately. One of America's few friends in Parliament was always welcome, but the early hour indicated some crisis. Members of Parliament kept late hours, for the House met long into the night, but most were sound asleep by this hour. Bright was alert and visibly agitated, in contrast to his somber Quaker clothes.

"Mr. Adams, I must hear from you how this calamity has happened. The House sits at noon. Terrible rumors are spreading all over London. I must be able to speak with some knowledge of events."

"Mr. Bright, I am at a loss. To what calamity do you refer?"

Bright stared at him for a brief moment, incredulous. Then he said, "Do you mean to tell me you do not know of yesterday's late afternoon's battle in Moelfre Bay?"

"I know nothing of this."

Bright sat down as if the weight of the world had crashed down on his shoulders. "I have been informed by a most reliable source that two British ships and two American ships fought a naval battle yesterday over one of the rams that had escaped to Moelfre Bay. There has been terrible loss of British life. HMS *Liverpool* and *Goshawk* went down with almost six hundred men."

The stunned look on Adams's face was proof that the ambassador had not yet heard of the battle. "It must have been the *Gettysburg*. She was here to intercept the rams if they should escape as the *Alabama* did with the connivance of certain officials."

"Mr. Adams, the entire issue of the rams and the *Alabama* will drop by the wayside compared to a British warship sunk in British waters. When this knowledge becomes public, there will be such a cry for war that no government could withstand it."

"Then I must call on Lord Russell to explain what I can."

"Too late, I fear, too late."[15]

When Adams attempted to leave for Whitehall an hour later, he had to brave a crowd that had already gathered outside the embassy. The police moved the crowd back, but they could not prevent a brick from being thrown at his vehicle.

Layard received Adams with great coldness and silence. Adams waited an hour in the anteroom before he was admitted to Russell's office, where Layard took a chair as well.

Russell wasted no time on pleasantries but waved Adams's note and demanded an explanation, "Indeed, sir, this means war."

Adams asked to be informed of what Lord Russell knew. Russell sketched the broad outlines of the battle, concluding, "The *Kearsarge*, at least, had the decency to rescue the seventy-three survivors, mostly from *Goshawk* and set them ashore at Amlwch on Angelsey. The *Kearsarge* was last seen steaming southeast. Every ship within reach has been dispatched to take or sink her."

"Lord Russell, I assure you that my government gave no orders to attack ships of the Royal Navy. The captain of the *Gettysburg* had orders to intercept the rams should they escape from Liverpool." He added emphasis to his next words, "as the *Alabama* did with the open connivance of members of your own government."

"By God, sir," roared Russell. Adams had not suspected that such emotion lurked in so small a man. It had as much effect as rain on New England granite. "Do you mean that you blame Her Majesty's government for what can only be described as an act of war?"

"Indeed, I do, Lord Russell," Adams said. "Your government has done everything in its power to wage war on my country short of firing directly upon us. The United States has been provoked beyond all measure and has responded as is the right of every nation — to pursue pirates into the ports or waters that shelter them."

"Her Majesty's government determined to stop the departure of the rams and issued the appropriate orders."

"And with evident great success. You may recall the stream of communications with which I begged you for months to take such action. How, sir, am I to believe that when I received your note only yesterday that stated most firmly that no evidence existed sufficient to invoke the Foreign Enlistment Act."

Russell shot Layard a reproachful look. "Regrettably, the note was written shortly before our decision and unaccountably delayed."

"Then, sir, why did you not inform me at the earliest moment that you intended to stop the rams from sailing?"

"We desired to gain the approval of the law officers of the Crown in such an important matter."

"Not good enough, Lord Russell, not good enough. Your private note that you were proceeding along these lines would have defused this situation at once. I could have sent word to *Gettysburg* to stand down. None of this would have happened had you heeded my government's remonstrations earlier."

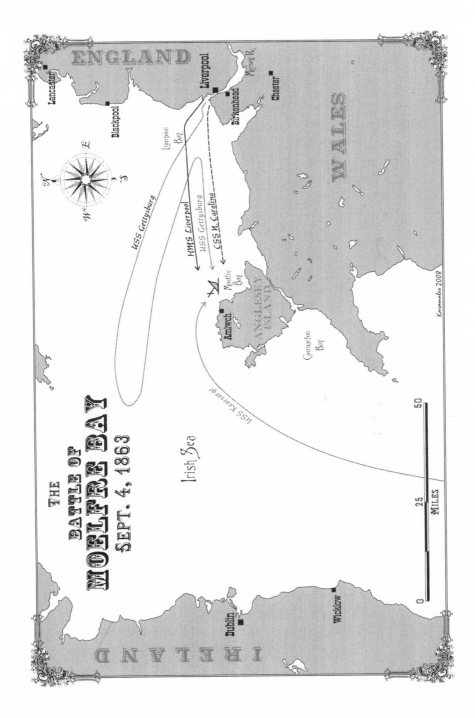

THE
BATTLE OF
MOELFRE BAY
SEPT. 4, 1863

ENGLAND

Lancaster
Blackpool
Liverpool
Birkenhead
Mersey R.
Chester

WALES

Liverpool Bay

USS Gettysburg
HMS Liverpool
USS Gettysburg
CSS N. Carolina

Moelfre Bay
Amlwch
ANGLESEY ISLAND

Caernarfon Bay

USS Kearsarge

Irish Sea

Dublin
Wicklow

IRELAND

Krismalas 2008

0   25   50
MILES

Having taken what he thought the moral high ground, Adams sought to be conciliatory. "Surely, Lord Russell, our governments can have the wisdom and patience to avoid war even at this late hour. These events can only be described as an accident, a terrible accident, but an accident all the same. A war would only multiply a thousand times the dead, and for what? An accident? Surely the fact that *Kearsarge* rescued all British seamen and set them ashore into the hands of British authorities and proper medical care indicates that no act of war was intended. I propose that a joint British-American commission be charged to examine this affair and report back to both governments. If that is not acceptable, I suggest a mediation by a disinterested state, such as Prussia."[16]

Russell intertwined his fingers as he said, "What is important, Mr. Adams, is that two British ships were attacked and sunk in British waters with the loss of six hundred British officers and men. I would expect your passport to be returned to you in short order. The cabinet meets in two hours."

A large crowd had gathered in front of Whitehall as news of the battle had spread throughout London. When it was revealed the American ambassador was meeting with Lord Russell, it became an angry mob. It took a strong detachment of mounted police to see Adams safely to the embassy.

He immediately began to pen a report to Seward of his interview with Russell and the events as he knew them. Before he dipped his pen in the inkwell, he paused for a moment to think of his son. "Henry, my boy. I sent you off hoping the experience would draw some strength out of you. And now you are gone with the *Gettysburg*. My boy, my poor boy . . . my poor country."[17]

USS *KEARSARGE*, RACING NORTH THROUGH THE IRISH SEA, 9:36 PM, SEPTEMBER 5, 1863

Winslow had not left the bridge since he had put the British prisoners and wounded ashore. He had sailed southeast until he was sure there was no pursuit and then doubled back to sail north through the Irish Sea. Lamson joined him, having spent much of the late afternoon and evening with his twenty-eight wounded men whom the *Kearsarge* had rescued. Winslow was smoking a pipe as he walked the deck while the stars were coming out to twinkle over the great, unhappy waves of the Irish Sea. He paused to think that St. Patrick had been brought over these waters from Britain as a slave to a band of Gaelic pirates.

Winslow was middle aged and had grown up with the Navy. If he had ever had the dash of Lamson, it had left him with his youth in the routine of decades of a peacetime navy. He was a solid man who knew his business and did not shrink from a fight. He had been "exiled" to the Channel Station after an impolite reference to the President in public. He was enjoying the momentary pleasure of considering how that would compare to his sloop sinking a British frigate. No U.S. naval officer in combat against the rebellion had sent such a ship to the bottom. Of course, he would give young Lamson all his due in beating the hell out of the frigate before *Kearsarge* came to the rescue.

Winslow thanked God that his own losses had been only one dead and twelve wounded. Eleven of Lamson's men had gone to the bottom with *Gettysburg*, and he had lost thirty-nine of ninety-six men. "How are your wounded, Captain?" he greeted Lamson, still according him the honorary title though he no longer had a ship and would revert to the permanent rank of lieutenant.[18]

"Doing well, thank you. Your surgeon is a man of rare talent, Captain. And you are a man of rare timing. I had determined to keep fighting until she went under rather than strike when the *Kearsarge* arrived out of nowhere."

"You can thank Ambassador Adams for that," Winslow puffed on his pipe and leaned over the side. "Speaking of the ambassador, how is his son doing?"

"The surgeon thinks he shall recover. He received a ball clean through the shoulder, courtesy of the Royal Marines. He will be able to dine out on it for the rest of his life. I owe him mine. He pushed me aside to take the ball aimed for me. I hadn't thought he had it in him."

Winslow tucked that away in his mind and turned to the matter at hand. "We shall be home in a week if we can avoid the entire damned Royal Navy, which I am sure is after us as we speak. There will be hell to pay, Captain. You realize that we have real naval war on us now, don't you? It's just not blockade duty or river gunboats or pounding away at forts, but a navy war with the greatest Navy in the world."

Lamson did not appear dismayed.

Winslow just shook his head and muttered to himself, "Hell to pay, hell to pay."[19]

9.

Pursuit Into the Upper Bay

NEW YORK HARBOR, NEW YORK, 12:35 PM, SEPTEMBER 11, 1863
Oslyabya is not a word that slips easily from the tongue of an English speaker. The crowds of New Yorkers that rushed to the docks to see the newly arrived Russian steam frigate of that name truly mangled it. None of them knew the ancient glory of its name, that of a monk who fought in the Russian shield wall at the battle of Kulikovo Fields in 1380, the first Russian victory over the dreaded Tatars, and their first step toward empire. None of that ancient symbolism mattered to the people who filled the docks where the frigate was tied up. It was the Russian Empire, the might it represented, and the friendship its presence meant that thrilled them.

It was fixed in the American mind that the only friend of the Union among the great powers of Europe was Russia. The arrival of this ship with the news that she was only the advance of a powerful squadron of the Baltic Fleet sped along the telegraph lines throughout the North. The timing of the *Olsyabya*'s arrival could not have been better. The twin victories of summer, Gettysburg and Vicksburg, had been so full of promise for a speedy collapse of the rebellion, but those expectations had petered out as the exhausted armies maneuvered to no effect throughout the late summer. Northern morale had sunk. It was on this tinder of faded hopes that news of the *Oslyabya*'s arrival fell like a spark.[1]

The North went wild with excitement. The press, desperate for good news, fed the public perception that the Russians had come to show support for the harried Union and that the natural alliance of Russia and America was soon to be officially cemented. Neither the U.S. government

An American cartoon of the 1860s depicting "Fair Union" beset by Copperhead vipers – antiwar Democrats.
Library of Congress

An American cartoon warning Britain not to interfere in the Civil War.
Library of Congress

Secretary of the Navy Gideon Welles left the details to his assistant secretary but never lost his nerve in a crisis.
National Archives

Assistant Secretary of the Navy Gustavus "Gus" Fox, an aggressive innovator who never hesitated to seize the main chance. Library of Congress

GENERAL GEORGE H. SHARPE

Brig. Gen. George H. Sharpe, Lincoln's protégé and the founder of American all-source intelligence. Author's Collection

Lt. Col. (shown here later as Lt. Gen.) Garnet J. Wolseley, the brilliant, one-eyed rising star of the British Army. Library of Congress

Dahlgren XI-inch and XV-inch muzzle-loading guns aboard the monitor USS Passaic. *Dahlgrens were the envy of the navies of the world.* Courtesy of Dover Publications

The British 110-pounder, breech-loading Armstrong gun, the most powerful gun in the Royal Navy, but fatally flawed. Author's Collection

Rear Adm. John A. Dahlgren, USN, the father of American naval ordnance, aboard the USS Pawnee *off Charleston in 1863.* National Archives

Col. Ulric Dahlgren, U.S. Volunteers, the twenty-one-year-old hero of Gettysburg and son of the admiral. Author's Collection

Lt. Roswell Hawke Lamson, USN , captain of the USS Gettysburg. Courtesy of Princeton University Library

The USS Gettysburg, *the fastest ship in the world, started life as a British blockade-runner only to be captured by Lieutenant Lamson, renamed, and given to him to command in a desperate mission.* Naval Historical Center

The sloop USS Kearsarge *was on station in the English Channel when the foresight of Ambassador Charles Francis Adams drew it into the Irish Sea.* Naval Historical Center

Adm. Sir Alexander Milne, RN, commander of the British North American and West Indies Squadron, who prepared the British naval war plan against the United States. Library of Congress

Forts overlooking the Verrazano Narrows leading into the Upper Bay of New York. Courtesy of U.S. Senate

Capt. George Bazalgette, Royal Marine Light Infantry, who planned fine English gardens and commanded desperate assaults. British Columbia Archives

Col. Joshua Lawrence Chamberlain, U.S. Volunteers, would fight his greatest battle on his native Maine soil. Library of Congress

Brig. Gen. Thomas Francis Meagher, U.S. Volunteers, former commander of the Irish Brigade, would lead the Irish again and the Germans into battle. Library of Congress

Passaic *class monitors and the USS* New Ironsides *line ahead at Charleston, the center of Admiral Dahlgren's battle line.* Library of Congress

The frigate HMS Black Prince, *of the* Warrior *class broadside ironclads, the Royal Navy's first armored iron ships and the largest warships in the world.*
Naval Historical Center

A Confederate mine of the type that lurked inside Charleston Harbor.
Courtesy of Dover Publications

nor the Russians did anything to dispel this notion, though their public statements confined themselves to traditional goodwill. It was too good for Northern morale and even better as an unspoken warning to Britain and France. The *New York Herald* editorialized:

> Should the Russian empire and the American republic form an offensive and defensive alliance they would necessarily preponderate and rule throughout the world. Our enemies should beware how they drive us to the cementing of a compact the existence of which would be the end of all opposing power and influence.[2]

The crowds that were welcomed aboard the Russian frigate as visitors found their expectations of the Russians realized. Almost every Russian officer could speak English well, the legacy of the fact that on-the-shore British naval officers, largely Scots, had officered much of the Russian Navy as it grew into a professional force in the eighteenth and early nineteenth centuries. The tall young women of New York, of English and German stock, were a bit taken aback, though, by the relatively short stature of most Russian officers.[3] A ball was immediately thrown for the ship's officers, who caused an unexpected reaction among the throngs of tall New York belles.

> Alas ! for the Russians. It is known, or should be, that these Slavic heroes are not the very largest of the human race—that they are small men in fact—and what is to become of small men in such a jam? Early in the night—indeed, very soon after the dance began—we saw several of them in the embrace of grand nebulous masses of muslin and crinoline, whisked hither and thither as if in terrible torment—their eyes aglare—their hair blown out—and all their persons expressive of the most desperate energy, doubtless in an endeavor to escape. What became of them we cannot tell.[4]

Another novelty was Protestant America's first encounter with the Orthodox Church in the form of *Oslyabya*'s chaplain, whom the press described as "an eminent theologian." The service aboard ship was reported with an open-mindedness rarely found for Roman Catholicism in America at that time.[5]

There was nothing about the Russians that did not find favor with the press and public alike. The dockyard pickpockets and thieves declared Russian sailors off-limits in a burst of patriotic fervor. The streetwalkers were even rumored to offer an occasional service gratis. "It is a noticeable fact that even the sharpers, who so fall foul of strangers, have kept themselves off these 'Roo-shans.'"[6]

It was in the midst of the excitement over the Russians that the Liverpool packet *Aurora* arrived on September 17. She was the first fast packet to race across the Atlantic since the battle of Moelfre Bay. Word of the battle spread throughout the city and was immediately wired to Washington. Eight hours later, the news was in Richmond as well.

The North went wild with excitement. The church bells rang from Maine to Wisconsin as they had for Vicksburg and Gettysburg. Pent-up anger at British connivance with the Confederacy exploded in cheers and adulation for the *Kearsarge* and *Gettysburg*, mixed with anxiety for the safety of Winslow's ship. The newspapers carried by *Aurora* trumpeted the fact that the entire Royal Navy had been set in pursuit of *Kearsarge*. In the South, the news spread just as fast, and the church bells would have rung with even greater joy had they not all already been melted down for cannon.[7]

THE WHITE HOUSE, 3:30 PM, SEPTEMBER 18, 1863

The mood in the White House shared none of the public's exuberance. Two days later, another ship arrived with Ambassador Adams's enciphered reports of the battle as well his dealings with Russell. The ship also carried the British papers. They all screamed for war.

Seward briefed Lincoln and the cabinet on the events of Moelfre Bay. He concluded, "The British have brought this upon themselves. They hid behind the Foreign Enlistment Act, a tissue of neutrality so pathetic that it made them the arsenal and storehouse of the rebellion. The entire attitude of the British government has been one of unremitting hostility. In demanding an unattainable level of proof that the rams, not to mention the other pirates built in British yards, were intended for use by the Confederacy, they hoped to hide behind a fiction of legality. I swear, Mr. President, that had Adams presented proof written with the finger of God Himself, the British would have referred it to a Lucifer in a powdered wig to rule upon its authenticity.

"Most outrageously, Adams informs me that after the battle, Russell claimed that they had decided to seize the rams. Yet, just as with

the *Alabama*, Laird Brothers and their rebel associates were forewarned
in time to attempt to slip the most completed ram out of Liverpool. It was
only because Dudley was able to warn *Gettysburg* was Lamson able to go
off in pursuit. As further proof of British collusion to help the ram escape, they dispatched *Liverpool* to protect her.

"Adams further informs me that it is unsafe for an American to be
recognized on the streets of London. The flag has been repeatedly torn
off the embassy's flagpole and burned. American merchants are making
preparations to flee to neutral European ports. The debates in the House
of Commons have been near hysterical in their demands for war. Most
ominously, Adams reports that there has been a frenzy of preparation in
both the Army and Navy."[8]

Lincoln's normally dark complexion took on a deeper shade as he
listened. His jaw was set. There was a glittering hardness to his brown
eyes. "Before the world we can rightly claim to have done everything
possible to avert these events. You all know that my policy has been
'one war at a time' and that at every turn we have sought reconciliation
and simple justice from the British. And what have we received in return? A thousand examples are at hand, but let me lay just one before
you. When Grant took Vicksburg, it was found that the thirty thousand
rebels were uniformly armed with the most modern British Enfield rifle.
Grant's men were armed with old flintlock muskets that been converted
to percussion and Belgian rifles more dangerous to their users than the
enemy. He ordered his regiments to exchange these weapons with the
captured Enfields. Does anyone believe that the Confederacy would not
have collapsed within a year had not the workshops of Britain kept them
supplied?[9]

"Some will argue that Moelfre Bay would never have happened
had we not sent that ship. What would have happened in that case is that
the rams would have been savaging our ports and breaking the blockade. That would have brought us to the same point but at great disadvantage."

He turned to Sharpe. It had not been lost on everyone else in the
room that the only uniformed officer in the meeting, other than the Army's
diffident general in chief, Maj. Gen. Henry Wager Halleck, was Lincoln's
new chief "spy." Even the formidable Stanton had not risen to give battle
over the man's independence of the secretary's grasp. That had been due
to Sharpe's realization that while he could afford enemies, he could not
have Stanton among them. He had made it clear that while he would

report directly to the President, he still considered himself part of the War Department and would keep Stanton fully informed. He also made it clear he would not be stepping on Lafayette Baker's toes. Let Stanton keep his thug for now, he thought. When Stanton had gone along, the rest of the cabinet had also fallen in line.

Lincoln's nod had been his cue. "Gentlemen, the President has asked me to report to you certain preparations the British have been making in Canada and the Maritimes." Sharpe went on to describe the information that had been gathered by the few agents he had been able to send into British North America over the last month. His network was too new and sparse to develop detailed information, but what they had found was disturbing. The tempo of raising and equipping the Canadian militia in British North America had picked up notably. The Canadian forces had also stepped up their training and often in conjunction with the imperial battalions, which were imparting to the Canadians some of their precision. His agents had also identified numerous British officers traveling in mufti on the American extension of the Grand Trunk Railroad, where they would make extended stops at every station on the routes. Most interesting was the number of officers who were coming to Portland. The number of port calls for Royal Navy ships had also increased.

Sharpe concluded with the latest reports that pointed to a sudden concentration of British and Canadian volunteer troops, ostensibly for training exercises in the region known as the Canadian "Peninsula," bounded by Lake Huron on the west, Lake Erie on the south, and Lake Ontario on the east. This area was the southernmost projection of Canada that wedged itself between Michigan in the west and New York in the east. There were two points between the lakes where the borders ran; one in the west opposite Detroit and another in the east opposite Buffalo. Every eye in the room was drawn to the map on the wall as Sharpe traced the concentrations. Each man could picture in his mind's eye the battle-grounds of the War of 1812, drawn with failure and danger. In this area, the U.S. Army had launched its ill-planned offensives only to be thrown back across the border and followed by British invasions, the most dangerous only stopped at Chippewa in 1814 by Winfield Scott. The memory of that train of disasters had not been lost on any American.[10]

When he finished there was a dead silence.

Seward spoke first. "There is no doubt that the British have planned a surprise attack on us. Russell's connivance to let the ram escape was only a part of this dastardly scheme. They have, no doubt, been planning this with the rebels for some time. Mr. President, war is upon us. We must act quickly to prepare."

Stanton spoke next. "There is not a moment to lose if we are not to wake up and see Detroit and Buffalo in British hands." He looked at Halleck. He was called "Old Brains" in the old prewar Army, where he had passed for that wonder of wonders, a military intellectual who actually wrote books on warfare. He certainly did not present a very martial appearance, a plump and bug-eyed man. As a field commander, he had been sound but overly cautious. With a subordinate like Grant to reap successes in his name, Halleck had found himself chosen as general in chief by a president desperate for sound military advice. That is what he got, but unfortunately that advice was not overly leavened with any boldness or willingness to take responsibility. Still, Halleck's strategic sense was sound and the necessary action obvious.

"I recommend that those two points be immediately reinforced with a division from Grant's Army and a division from Meade's Army. Although Rosecrans's Army of the Cumberland is closer, he is actively maneuvering to bring Bragg to battle, and I would not divert his forces and weaken him at such a moment."

Sharpe was worried, not about what he knew of British deployments but about what he did not know. The geography of his home state of New York fell like a template over his worries. The strong railway ran from Montreal to Albany and down the Hudson Valley to New York City. Halfway between Albany and the city was Kingston, his home town. It was a natural invasion route and one of historic importance. Burgoyne had tried it and come a cropper at Saratoga in 1777, just short of his objective of Albany. But then he had had to hack his way through a wilderness. Now the thick web of railroads and good surface roads knit the region together. Yet there was nothing like the studied activity of British forces in the Canadian Peninsula. That was very strange. He gave the British credit for common sense and more than that after his dinner with Wolseley. The absence of activity in that direction was immensely suspicious. The Grand Trunk led to Albany in one direction and to Montreal and Ottowa in the other. If Albany was about 135 miles from the Canadian border, Montreal was only thirty-five miles from the American border.

He raised the issue. Unfortunately, it was the vulnerability of Montreal not Albany that seemed to arouse the most interest. The discussion turned to the opportunity this presented. Stanton waved away the danger, his focus still on the Great Lakes. "The New York State Militia and home guards should be called up in any case. They should be able to delay any force the British could send across the border there." He glared at Sharpe, "As you've said yourself, Albany is 135 miles from the border. Buffalo and Detroit are right across the border."

Halleck came in on Stanton's side, to no one's surprise. "General Sharpe is correct to point out how vulnerable Montreal is. Here is an opportunity to strike at the heart of Canada. If we seize Montreal, we sever British communications and cut British North America in two. Remember, their settlements extend no more than fifty miles from the border. The XI and XII corps could be detached from the Army of the Potomac and deployed to Albany as a staging area." He glanced at Stanton for approval and saw the man's brow furrow. "But there is not the urgency that there is to defend the Great Lakes. There is no reason to rush up there now. We need to carefully plan this."

When Sharpe saw that Lincoln would support Stanton, he folded his tent.

The meeting dragged on into the night as the entire range of war preparations was discussed. Lincoln finally adjourned the meeting at two in the morning. All through the night, aides and secretaries had been filing in and out to carry messages to the various departments of the government, mostly war warning alerts to Army and department commanders, coastal forts, Navy bases and yards, and the blockading squadrons. As the meeting broke up, Lincoln quietly took Stanton by the arm and pulled him to the window. "I thank Providence we put Ripley out to pasture three weeks ago. We are going to need a lot of those 'new-fangled gimcracks' he hated so much. We should have Colonel Ramsey rummage about his old arsenal to see what Ripley hid away. We cannot afford to overlook any advantages. The full weight of their empire will be against us."[11]

"I've already done that. He reported to me yesterday that there were fifty of the coffee mill guns there in late August just before he took over the Ordnance Bureau from Ripley. Seems there are only forty of the coffee mill guns now." He looked over at Sharpe. "But two thousand Spencer repeaters have just been delivered."[12]

While they were speaking, Sharpe had taken Halleck aside. "May I make an impertinent suggestion, General?"

Halleck's protruding eyes stared briefly at him, disconcerting as ever. "Of course, General." Whatever else Halleck was, he was a military politician and had seen the favor Lincoln had bestowed on Sharpe, the only other uniformed officer who was a regular at cabinet meetings.

"I would suggest that a brigade at least might be usefully sent to Maine as well."

"But you reported no British concentrations against New England."

"Yes, I know, but prudence is a goddess who must be honored even by the boldest commander. I am worried about all the attention they have been paying to Maine."

Halleck realized he could have it both ways—play up to a presidential favorite and take out some strategic insurance. "Good suggestion. Yes, a brigade should be enough. I'll see to it tomorrow morning."

"One more thing, General. May I also suggest that all the Maine regiments be sent? Announce that only three regiments are going, but send them all—horse, foot, and artillery. The 20th Maine saved the Army at Little Round Top. It would help the President politically if we could send those heroes home for a while. Col. Joshua Chamberlain is very popular up there right now. They could even do some recruiting. God knows that Maine bled at Gettysburg."[13]

It was as good as done.

CHICKAMAUGA CREEK, TENNESSEE, 12:00 PM, SEPTEMBER 20, 1863

The Confederacy's mighty right arm had arrived on the battlefield of Chickamauga—"the Creek of Death" to those who fought there—on the second day of the fighting. Lt. Gen. James Longstreet was a big-bearded, burly man on a big horse, as befitted the man whom Lee called his "Old Warhorse." He commanded the First Corps of the Army of Northern Virginia, the strongest offensive organization in American history. Longstreet and two of his divisions had been rushed by rail to the aid of the defeat-haunted Braxton Bragg and his Army of Tennessee to save them from another thrashing by Maj. Gen. William Rosecrans's Army of the Cumberland. The first day of the battle had been fought without him. His troops were still detraining on that day and force marching to the field. Rosecrans had been warned by Sharpe to expect Longstreet's reinforcement. He had taken the news seriously, but the intelligence staff that Sharpe had installed was too new to catch wind of Longstreet's presence. Even had they been more experienced, Longstreet arrived with such speed that it would have taken a miracle for that news to have run ahead of him. In that light, Rosecrans thought he was lucky to finally force Bragg to fight before his reinforcements had arrived. He was in for a big surprise.[14]

Bragg's men felt Longstreet's presence immediately. One lieutenant remarked, "Longstreet is the boldest and bravest-looking man I ever saw. I don't think he would dodge if a shell were to burst under his chin."

As Longstreet coiled his corps for its strike, he was taken aback by the volume of fire that was coming from Wilder's Lightning Brigade almost a half mile away, and "thought for a moment that a fresh Federal corps had come crashing down on his left."[15]

Almost at once, his puncher's practiced eye observed the main chance opening up before him and seized it. A Union division pulled out of the line before its replacement was at hand. A wide gap yawned, and Longstreet threw the divisions of Hood and McLaws into it. The rebel yells that had flown over so many victorious fields in Virginia now echoed across the thickets and woods of Tennessee. Two Union divisions were driven back as Longstreet's men severed the Union battle line, and like a back-broke bull, that line collapsed. For the first time in the war, an experienced and valiant field army had been struck such a blow that it dissolved as Homer's "Godsent Panic seized them, comrade to blood-curdling rout," and sent the men in blue in flight toward the railroad hub of Chattanooga.[16]

Amid that rout was Maj. James Callaway. On the first day of the fighting, his brigade commander had relieved the incompetent commander of the 81st Indiana and put Callaway in his place. His presence on the demoralized unit was electric. He was truly charismatic—soldiers were drawn to him like iron filings to a magnet and his determination flowed out to them. All through the first day he led the newly emboldened Hoosiers of the 81st to become the fighting heart of their brigade. As other units fell under the enemy's sledgehammer blows, the 81st stuck it out and poured such fire into the attacking Confederates that their regiments melted away. Again on the second day, the concentrated fire of the 81st broke every attack.

> As soon as my battalion front was unmasked by the skirmishers we opened a terrible and deadly fire upon the advancing foe. The firing was continued with unabated fury on both sides, the enemy steadily advancing and our men determinedly resisting until but 3 men of the enemy's first line and about half of his second line were standing; their comrades apparently

had fallen in windrows and his farther progress seemed checked, perhaps, impossible.[17]

It was all for nothing. The flanking regiment, his own 21st Illinois, folded and broke. The Confederates were through and lapping around Callaway's men. He pulled out just before the whole regiment was captured. Callaway reformed his men and, with the brigade commander, gathered up every man they could to put back into the fight. They made stand after stand before falling back. At last, he wrote, "we then withdrew from the field quietly and sullenly with every regimental color and field piece of the brigade. . . ."[18]

Rosecrans and his corps commanders were swept away in the panic, all except Maj. Gen. George Thomas, who rallied his corps for the terrible rearguard defense of Snodgrass Hill. Again and again the Confederate waves struck the hill, each time seeming to crest it, but each time falling back in wreckage and ruin. Thomas held on and would not budge all that terrible day, earning himself the immortal title of the "Rock of Chickamauga." That honor would have meant nothing if Bragg had not obsessed about overwhelming Thomas instead of sending his army in pursuit. His corps commanders, Longstreet chief among them, begged him to pursue the enemy. They "produced a Confederate soldier who had been captured and then had escaped. He had seen the Federal disarray for himself and was brought before Bragg to testify that the enemy was indeed in full retreat. Bragg would not accept the man's story. 'Do you know what a retreat looks like?' he asked acidly. The soldier stared back and said, 'I ought to, General; I've been with you during your whole campaign.'"[19]

THE NORTH ATLANTIC, 11:20 AM, SEPTEMBER 21, 1863

Winslow's deception of sailing north through the Irish Sea and the Northern Channel to the North Atlantic had had its risks, and one of them had given *Kearsarge* away. While most of the pursuing British ships sent in pursuit followed his false start to the southeast through the St. George Channel, which connected the Irish Sea south to the Atlantic, he had been passed by a Liverpool steamer. *Kearsarge* had been flying false colors, the French tricolor, but the skipper of the steamer knew a Frenchman when he saw one. He also knew battle damage when he saw it. He stopped a few hours later at Stranraer, a ferry port in southwest Scotland, where the telegraph had brought the news of Moelfre Bay and ignited a firestorm of anger. From there, the captain's news sped south on the telegraph to London. Almost immediately upon receipt, the nearest Royal Navy warships were alerted and ordered in pursuit. Winslow had calculated that the northern route would encounter the fewest British warships; their bases were largely in the south and east of Britain. The odds were with him but luck was not. Coaling in Stranraer was the HMS *Undaunted*, a wood screw frigate of the same class as *Liverpool*. She was new, built in 1861; big at 4,020 tons; and fast, and she mounted fifty-one guns. Her captain did not wait for specific orders and put to sea at once. Captain and crew were out for blood.[20]

The captain shrewdly guessed that his prey would strike directly for New York, hoping to outrace news of the battle. He crowded on sail and ordered the engines at full speed. On September 12 he caught up with *Kearsarge*. When she was identified, the crew burst into cheers as the drums beat to quarters. Winslow's lookout had seen *Undaunted* almost at the same time. Battle stations were sounded. Lamson joined Winslow on the quarterdeck and extended his telescope.

"Looks just like *Liverpool*. And she is not blissfully ignorant of who we are. That ship is straining every plank to close with us."

Winslow lowered his own glass. "One British frigate is enough. It took the two of us and some luck to take *Liverpool*. I won't risk another fight with such a big ship."

Lamson felt a twinge of disappointment, but Winslow precluded any impertinent suggestions to stay and fight by slamming his telescope shut. "We are going to run away. The Navy will need this ship."

Running away was easier said than done. *Kearsarge*'s sails and engines gave it their all and began to lengthen the distance between them, but in a few hours it was apparent that the *Undaunted* was faster and would eventually close to within cannon shot. By September 15, *Undaunted*'s forward 110-pounder pivot gun fired its first shot, which fell well astern of *Kearsarge*. An hour later, her second shot struck only a hundred yards short. The next shell struck the sternpost and blew it to pieces.

Splinters from the impact blew out and up to fall on the quarterdeck. Winslow ordered the helmsman, "Hard about!" To his executive officer, Lt. Cdr. William Thornton, he said, "We will rake her, Mr. Thornton. Aim for her waterline. We must slow her down."

Excitement ran through the officers and gun crews of both ships as the *Kearsarge* turned. Hardly had the *Kearsarge* come round before the

Undaunted sheered, presented her starboard battery, and slowed her engines. At long range of about a mile, the British ship opened her full broadside, the shot cutting some of *Kearsarge*'s rigging and going over and alongside her. Immediately Winslow ordered more speed, but in less than two minutes *Undaunted* loaded and fired another broadside and followed it with a third but to little effect. *Kearsarge* was now within about nine hundred yards. So far, distance had prevented the rapid British broadsides from crippling the American.

"Fire!" *Kearsarge*'s starboard battery erupted. The XI-inch 5-second-fused shells crashed into *Undaunted*'s waterline to explode inside. The Marines manning the 28-pounder rifle dropped a shell onto *Undaunted*'s quarterdeck while the crew of the small Dahlgren howitzer spewed shrapnel on the main deck. *Kearsarge*'s guns were firing at will, pumping more shells into the enemy's waterline. Winslow sheered away, intending to break off the action and resume his course, but the *Undaunted* sent a powerful broadside into his ship. One of his 32-pounders was struck by two of the *Undaunted*'s 32-pound shot with a great resounding clang of metal on metal. A powder charge exploded in the crewman's hands, upending the gun and sending it spinning through the crew, reducing them to bloody rag dolls.

Kearsarge's engines throbbed as the ship found its running legs. *Undaunted* was slow to follow and gradually fell behind. Winslow could only assume his guns had done their work. He was right. The XI-inch Dahlgren shells had blown jagged holes in *Undaunted*'s hull. Water was pouring through and began filling the hold. Her carpenters swarmed to plug them with canvas and wooden braces. The Marine gunners had wounded *Undaunted* as well. Their shells on the enemy's quarterdeck had shattered the wheel and killed the captain. The ship's executive officer assumed command and threw every effort into saving the ship.[21]

Winslow breathed more easily as the enemy's sail grew smaller and smaller. His relief was premature. The *Undaunted* had barely been lost to sight when the wounded ship was overtaken by the main pursuit squadron consisting of the frigates HMS *Topaze* and *Dauntless* and sloops *Alert* and *Gannet*. *Undaunted* gave them *Kearsarge*'s course, and they leapt in pursuit. They were under the command of the senior captain, John Welbore Sunderland Spencer of the *Topaze*.

In two days the smoke from their funnels was visible from *Kearsarge*'s topsail. On the third day the ships were visible from the quarterdeck. On the fourth day it was clear that they had spread out to sweep the American into a closing net. Winslow drove his ship into a late summer storm that tossed it through heavy seas and driving rain. He changed course to the southeast as the storm moved in that direction. On the sixth day *Kearsarge* broke out of the storm into clear weather with none of his pursuers in sight. He resumed course for New York. On the eighth day four plumes of smoke again appeared behind him. This time the lookouts also spotted two plumes ahead of them. "I think company would be a good idea about now," Winslow muttered to himself. If they were British, it was unlikely they had heard of Moelfre Bay so far out; if they were not British, he might be able to hide among them or use them as a decoy. He needed one more break; they were only four days' sailing time from New York and the safety of its harbor forts. He did not think the invisible barrier of American maritime jurisdiction would stop them.

By the morning of the ninth day, September 21, the two ships ahead of him were seen to be flying the St. Andrew's cross, Russian naval colors. *Kearsarge* fired off a salute and hailed them. They were the Imperial Russian Navy screw frigates *Aleksandr Nevksy* and *Peresvet*. They were very impressive, large ships of a very American design, which was not surprising since Russia bought many ships from the United States and followed its shipbuilding advances. Large and well-armed, the 5,100-ton *Nevsky* carried fifty-one smoothbore guns, almost making her a ship of the line, and the *Peresvet* bore forty-four. All the guns in both ships were powerful 60-pounders, cast in Philadelphia, another sign of close Russo-American cooperation.[22]

Adm. Stefan Lisovsky flew his pennant aboard the *Nevsky*, the flagship of the Russian Navy. The Czar had not sent such a ship lightly. Lisovsky greeted Winslow enthusiastically and invited him aboard. His eagerness to see the Americans was flavored by his curiosity to find out how they had acquired the visible battle damage. Perhaps they had encountered the infamous *Alabama*. In any case, it would be a good way to begin his goodwill visit to the United States.

His curiosity spiked when he saw the young civilian with his arm in a sling being lowered into *Kearsarge*'s boat along with the captain's party. He gave orders to prepare a more comfortable hoist for the wounded man to save him the pain of climbing up the ship's ladder thrown over the side. As a special courtesy he was on the quarterdeck to receive his guests when they came aboard. When Winslow stepped aboard the boatswains' whistles piped and an honor guard of Russian naval infantry presented arms. Winslow saluted the flag and the admiral who returned the salute and extended his hand. Winslow introduced his party, and Lisovsky introduced his officers. The admiral was clearly interested in young Adams, not only as private secretary of the American ambassador to the Court of St. James, but as the grandson and great-grandson of presidents. He came as close to royalty as Lisovsky would find in America. Adams was still in pain from his injury but laid on the charm. Lamson was more reserved, but Lisovksy sized him up quickly as a formidable officer. Winslow was gratified that the entire conversation was held in English, but came quickly to the point. The British ships were closing with every minute.

There were gasps from the Russian officers as they listened to the account of Moelfre Bay and the sinking of two Royal Navy warships and the encounter with *Undaunted*. As shocking as the story was, the stock of the Americans had clearly soared. There was not a Russian naval officer who did not dream of avenging the Royal Navy's humiliation of the Russian Imperial Navy in the Crimean War.

Lisovsky was no less impressed, but he had other matters to consider. Lisovsky was a man of the world, and his life in the Russian Navy had exposed him to some of the seamier sides of that world. The Czar has chosen him for his sense of things beyond his naval duties. The enormity of the tale that Winslow unfolded stunned him. My God, he thought, I'm sailing into a war. His instructions had been clear: he was to take no part in the American Civil War on the part of the U.S. government, and he was to make no overt statement as to a Russo-American alliance directed against Britain and France. Such discussion was the duty of the Baron Stoeckel, the Czar's ambassador in Washington. While in the United States, Lisovsky was to be guided by Stoeckel's political instructions. However, and this was an enormous "however," Lisovsky bore sealed orders that he was to open should the United States be attacked by any foreign power or should such a power openly side with the Confederacy.[23]

Winslow was clearly in trouble. He was asking Lisovsky's help to avoid the British. The admiral knew that a misstep could drag Russia into the inevitable war Moelfre Bay would ignite. Yet he had speculated long and hard on his sealed orders and what they might be. He knew he was a pawn in the greatest game of all as Winslow said, "I beg your assistance, sir. They will overhaul me in less time than it will take for me to reach the safety of New York."

Adams added, "My government would consider your assistance to be the ultimate proof of his Imperial Majesty's regard for the United

States. I am fully acquainted with the correspondence between our governments. I have been present at my father's side when he and your ambassador in London have discussed the importance of a Russo-American common front in the face of British world hegemony. Your ambassador has stated in the clearest terms that those are the very objectives of his Imperial Majesty's government as well. And now, sir, may I observe that the cause of our common interest will be upon us shortly."

Winslow suggested that the Russians would help greatly by staying between *Kearsarge* and her pursuers. Lisovsky thought quickly and smiled, "I think we can do better than that, Captain. I propose that you sail with my ships. I will escort you into port, as, shall we say, an exercise of the first law of the sea—to aid those in distress." He gave a sidelong glance to *Kearsarge*. "Your gallant ship is obviously in danger of floundering from its wounds. We cannot leave you alone. His Imperial Majesty would never forgive me. Besides, my officers and I cannot wait to hear every detail of how you bearded the British lion in his own den."[24]

CHATHAM ARCH, INDIANAPOLIS, INDIANA, 8:37 PM, SEPTEMBER 22, 1863

Capt. John Hines thought about Col. George Grenfell's description of the man to whom he had just been introduced, Lt. Col. Pitt Rivers, late assistant quartermaster of the British garrison of Ireland: "a man of fierce temper, not untinged with violence, of considerable energy and enthusiasm, unsociable with his peers, a domestic tyrant and yet approachable to his labourers, a dominant and aloof father in the grand . . . manner, though possessing a dry sense of humor."[25]

Rivers was a man of complete self-assurance, as befitted an Englishman among lesser beings. He was about thirty-six and in his prime. As master of ordnance at an early age, he had been instrumental in the trials that led to the adoption of the Enfield rifle for the British Army. In the grand Victorian style, he was also a world-class archaeologist. He was above all a fighting man, brevetted and mentioned in dispatches for distinguished service in the Crimea. He had come over to Canada with the wave of reinforcements during the crisis of the Trent Affair in late 1861. Six months later he had been ordered to Ireland, his chief duty to ferret out the Fenian conspiracies. Those conspiracies spanned the Atlantic now and had drawn him back to North America. Wolseley had had "additional duties" for him, the cause of his presence in this modest hotel in this modest provincial city.

The only other man in the room was Col. George Grenfell St. Ledger, late of Her Majesty's Army and a soldier of fortune. Grenfell was the sort of antagonist a novelist would have portrayed—"At sixty-two years of age he was still an impressive figure of romance. Slightly under six feet, with light blue eyes and shoulder-length white hair setting off a face darkened by the sandstorms of the Sahara and the winds of the Mediterranean, he had the personal appearance of a Brian de Bois-Gilbert in *Ivanhoe*," as the Confederate cavalry general Basil Duke would say. An aristocratic black sheep, he had run off at an early age to join the French Chasseurs d'Afrique, fight against and then with the Moors against the French, scour Riffian pirates from the approaches to Gibralter, and join Garibaldi in his struggle for Italian independence. The lure of the American Civil War broke his only attempt at retired country life. Jefferson Davis had been glad to commission him a colonel and make him Bragg's inspector general.[26] With the Morgan fiasco still fresh, he had asked Grenfell for less conventional assistance. Grenfell had slipped through the Union states and into Canada, where he had made contact with Wolseley and laid Davis's proposals before him.

Wolseley had made the very clear point that Grenfell's proposals could not possibly be contemplated by Her Majesty's armed forces, but he was interested in a general, exploratory discussion of a completely unofficial kind. In the meantime, the news of Moelfre Bay and the Union disaster at Chickamauga had shifted the ground from under every party. It was a new game, with a new urgency redolent with opportunity.[27]

WAR DEPARTMENT, WASHINGTON, D.C., 9:05 AM, SEPTEMBER 24, 1863

Nothing but bad news was coming from Chattanooga and the trapped Army of the Cumberland. Stanton had sent Charles Dana there to be his eyes and ears, and Dana was sending back a stream of encrypted messages emphasizing the increasingly hopeless nature of the situation and the failure of its commander.

It was obvious to Stanton that Rosecrans needed reinforcements immediately. The XI Corps, especially, and the XII Corps of the Army of the Potomac could use a train ride now, he thought. The former was in especially bad odor among Meade's men. That relief force needed a man who could command an independent small army. It also needed a man who was burning with the desire to retrieve a failed reputation. The name of Maj. Gen. Joseph Hooker slipped into his mind. Hooker was on inactive status in New York. He was a superlative organizer and leader. No man was more suited by experience and ability to grasp this nettle. After Chancellorsville, he had much to prove.

Stanton consulted Lincoln, who assented, commenting, "I expect Joe now knows the difference between where his headquarters and his hindquarters go." The order went out that day. "Major General Hooker, U.S. Volunteers, will assume command of XI and XII Corps."[28]

NEW YORK HARBOR, 10:14 AM, SEPTEMBER 24,1863

Cannon fire echoed across the Verrazano Narrows between Staten Island and Brooklyn and up over the docks and streets of Manhatten Island. Word flew from mouth to mouth that the Confederate rams and the British were attacking New York. Work stopped as everyone in the great American metropolis rushed into the streets for news or climbed to the roofs to look into the harbor at the unfolding battle.

Admiral Lisovsky had assumed too much on the prudence of the British admiral in pursuit of the *Kearsarge* when he offered to escort her to New York. The Admiralty's orders were direct and ruthless—sink or capture the *Kearsarge*. "Pursue her to the ends of the earth and into any harbor in which she seeks refuge." With the zeal and intrepidity of a young Nelson, that officer had caught up with Winslow and Lisovsky only hours from the Hudson's mouth and immediately engaged when it became clear the Russians were trying to protect the American sloop. Lisovsky was surprised when the first British ranging shot plunged off the *Nevsky*'s larboard quarter, but he already has his crew at battle stations. Lisovsky wanted to avoid a decisive engagement and hold his ships in being as commerce raiders in case of war between Russia and Britain. Flee as he might, the British hung on his ships and *Kearsarge*, pursuing them with a hail of blows into the Hudson's broad mouth and up the river. The British captains had never seen their crews handle their guns with such speed and precision, and this was in a navy second to none in the smooth and deadly efficiency of its gun drills. It was only a matter of time before the Royal Navy inflicted another humiliation on the Czar's ships in desperation to take the *Kearsarge*.

Time was not on the Royal Navy's side this morning. The guns on Forts Tompkins and Richmond on Staten Island began to join the fight with scores of heavy guns. Every warship or gunboat of the U.S. Navy in the harbor rushed to get up steam. Adding to the din of gunfire was the ringing of the church bells in alarm throughout Staten Island, Brooklyn, Manhattan, and the Jersey shore.[29]

The British ships absorbed terrible punishment from the close-range fire of the forts without flinching in their pursuit. Passing through the Verrazano Narrows into the Upper Bay, the ships broke up into separate duels. The two British sloops drew the Russian frigates to give the HMS *Dauntless* and *Topaze* the opening to concentrate on the *Kearsarge*.[30]

Winslow was desperate. He faced two heavier ships with skilled and determined captains who were trying to position themselves on his starboard and larboard and crush him with the weight of their broadsides. Two of his 32-pounders were already out of action, and the shells and splinters had thinned out the rest of his crew. Lamson's men had rushed to replace every casualty, and their young captain had stepped in to replace the fallen executive officer. Smoke that the light breeze could barely move hung over the ships and was lit only by the tongues of flames that spit from the gun ports and main gun decks.

Lamson stalked the quarterdeck, encouraging the gun crews, his face sprayed and his coat drenched with blood from a man whose head was carried off next to him. His hat had flown off with a splinter. Yet he moved with the easy grace of a leopard, sure and calm, a cigar trailing from the corner of his mouth, his eye never missing an opportunity or a danger. "Handsomely done, boys! Lay it on! Lay it on!" A shot dissolved the gunner, and Lamson snatched the firing cord as it whipped through the air. He gave it a yank to fire the percussion cap to spark the charge in the barrel. The XI-inch roared and bucked, sending its shell to explode on *Dauntless*'s gun deck.

Kearsarge's crew was being savaged. How long could flesh and blood stand the pounding? Lamson glanced about and noticed a wounded man fight off an offer of help. "No, mate, stand to your post. Fight the ship!" He then crawled to a hatch to slide down the ladder. Two of the men at the XI-inch forward pivot had been sick with fever that morning, but they were manning the gun as if they had been the halest. More of *Gettysburg*'s crew, just below decks, was waiting to replace the fallen. He ran to the hatch and peered down into upturned expectant faces. "Mr. Henderson, take a gun crew to replace the Marines on the forecastle rifle. Tell the sergeant to report to me." Bullets slammed into the deck around him from the Royal Marines in *Dauntless*'s rigging.

Quarter Gunner Dempsey nudged another man in the direction of Lamson in the brief seconds of inaction between heaving their gun back along its lines before the gunner pulled the lanyard. "Did ya see? Did ya see? He don't flinch or notice at all."[31]

Topaze's captain concentrated the fire of his first division guns on *Kearsarge*'s quarterdeck, sweeping it clean of men and smashing the wheel. Another division directed its fire at the hull below the smokestack until a shot stabbed into the boilers. They exploded in a surge of superheated steam that spread scalding death into the black gang and engineers. *Kearsarge*'s screws spun to a halt. The ship was now barely drifting on the Hudson's current. It was enough. *Topaze* and *Dauntless* closed on either side. Captain Spencer was determined to walk on *Kearsarge*'s wrecked deck in triumph as soon as its captain struck. He wanted to do it with all of New York as witness.

Unknown to Spencer, he had already taken a good part of Albion's revenge. John Winslow was dead on his own quarterdeck, cut in two by a 32-pounder shot. The ship was drifting, engines dead, masts shot through or hanging shattered over the side. Its hull was riddled and taking water, its decks were a ruin, half its guns out of operation, and the dead and dying strewn across the wreckage. The two heavier British frigates were closing, their guns tearing the guts out the ship, and they were taking everything the surviving Dahlgrens could throw. The senior officer aboard *Kearsarge* was now Lamson. From *Dauntless* an officer called through a megaphone, "Do you strike, *Kearsarge*? Do you strike?"

"Fuck you, you Limey bastard!" a seaman shouted back, waving his fist. Lamson looked up to the quarterdeck and only then realized just the dead occupied it. "Do you strike, *Kearsarge*?" came again from *Dauntless*. If any man had the ability to take in a situation at a single glance and cut to the heart of it, it was Lamson. A glance at the *Topaze* saw the *Aleksandr Nevsky* cutting across the British frigate's bow and raking her with the larboard battery. She had come to join the fight after leaving the *Gannet* adrift and burning. The Marine sergeant, his head bandaged, reported to Lamson. "Sergeant, it's time for the Marines to be infantry. Use your Spencers to kill everyone on that deck."

Turning back to the *Dauntless*, he cupped his hands and bellowed, "Double canister! Double canister, sir! That is my answer!" He sensed what was coming next, could see with his mind's eye the *Dauntless*'s gun deck crews climbing the ladders to the decks armed with pikes, cutlasses, and pistols to board. "Prepare to repel borders!" he shouted again.

Dauntless lurched closer; the men massing on her deck were visible. Among the blue jackets and their pikes were the red coats of the

Royal Marines, their Enfields with fixed bayonets. Lamson's Marines rose from their concealment and fired their repeaters into the packed crowd as bodies pitched forward over the side or backward into the crowd. "Sergeant! The carronade!" Lamson grabbed him by the arm and pointed at the fat, blunt gun on the *Dauntless's* forecastle. This naval shotgun would sweep his deck with musket balls. The sergeant dropped the gunner with a single shot and then with a smooth cocking of the handle, he shot the next man who grabbed the lanyard. By then his men had dropped the rest of the gun crew.[32]

Dauntless was now a bare yard away, and the British were still massing on the side. The forward XI-incher swung on its pivot to point at a sharp angle down the side of the enemy ship. The British were flexing their legs to make the leap from their greater height as the ships closed that last yard when the gun captain yelled, "Fire!" The gun leapt back on its lines, spewing two large tins of small iron balls into the crowd. The ships ground against each other. The remaining members of *Gettysburg's* crew raced up the ladders to repel borders, but there was only silence from the British ship. They watched the blood pour out of the *Dauntless's* scuppers onto the *Kearsarge's* deck and then cascade out of the wreckage as the British ship drifted away, leaving a pink stain in the water.

From this moment, the *Kearsarge* became only a spectator to the last stage of what would be called "the Battle of the Upper Bay." The *Topaze* and the *Nevsky* continued to throw broadsides into each other, with the *Topaze* clearly getting the upper hand. The *Peresvet* was locked in a slugging match with the smaller but deadly *Alert*. Time had run out for the British. A swarm of harbor defense gunboats were steaming down the East River from the Brooklyn Navy Yard. Alone, none of them would be a match for any of the British ships. In a swarm they could hem a larger ship in and strike from any direction. The end was inevitable, especially since more powerful warships were also coming to their aid. The first of them was the *Oslyabya*, rushing to Lisosvky's aid.

Captain Spencer was no romantic; he knew when the game was up. He did take intense satisfaction to see the *Kearsarge* listing badly from the water rushing in through the colander that was her hull. She would go down and soon. His mission was all but accomplished. Now Spencer must save what he could. He signaled the *Alert* and *Dauntless* to break off action and steam for the Verrazano Narrows and escape. *Gannet* was adrift and in flames. *Dauntless* limped south escorted by *Alert*. Running the gauntlet of the forts at top speed *Topaze* and *Alert* made it through

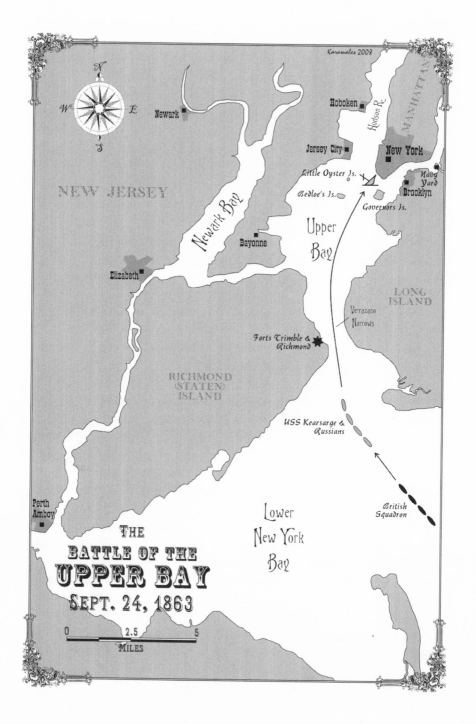

Karamales 2008

N

W   E

S

NEW JERSEY

Newark

Hoboken

Hudson R.

MANHATTAN

Jersey City

New York

Little Oyster Is.

Navy Yard

Bedloe's Is.

Brooklyn

Governors Is.

Newark Bay

Upper
Bay

Bayonne

Elizabeth

LONG
ISLAND

Verazano
Narrows

Forts Trimble &
Richmond

RICHMOND
(STATEN)
ISLAND

USS Kearsarge &
Russians

British
Squadron

Perth
Amboy

THE
BATTLE OF THE
UPPER BAY
SEPT. 24, 1863

Lower
New York
Bay

0   2.5   5
MILES

with heavy damage. *Dauntless's* slowness was her doom as the shot and shell from the forts hailed down on her. Slowed even more, she was caught by *Oslyabya* and the gunboats and pounded to pieces. She refused to strike and went down fighting.[33]

As Lamson watched the battle recede, the surviving engineer reported the damage below. The ship was taking water too fast. The pumps had been destroyed with the boilers. A gunboat came aside and asked if *Kearsarge* needed assistance. "I need a tow to the Navy Yard before I sink," he called over. It would be close. The ship was settling fast.[34]

BRITISH EMBASSY, WASHINGTON, D.C., 12:44 AM, SEPTEMBER 24, 1863

The Foreign Office special courier was rushed into the office of Ambassador Lord Lyons. He knew what news the courier brought, and it confirmed his worst fears. After Moelfre Bay, it could only be war. He imagined the news had spread immediately from the ship to the docks and must at this moment be flying through Washington.

Lyons called for his secretary and instructed him to personally request an interview with the Secretary of State. Then he carefully examined his instructions.

The halls of the State Department were crowded when Lyons entered just before two in the afternoon. The whispers that announced his identity silenced the crowd but did not quell their angry looks or the occasional hiss. Wretched manners, these Americans. He was ushered through open doors directly into Seward's office. Seward was facing the open window, hands clasped behind his back. He cut such a slight figure, but when he turned he seemed to grow from the anger in him.

Lyons did not betray his concern as he bowed. "Mr. Secretary, it is my sad duty to inform you that as of September 10 a state of war has existed between the British Empire and the United States of America." He went on to describe the justifications of Her Britannic Majesty's government for taking these much-provoked steps, reading from his instructions the precise language directed by the Foreign Office. When he had finished, he bowed once again and presented the declaration to Seward.[35]

"Lord Lyons, is it the custom of Her Majesty's government to attack before delivering its declaration of war? Even for Britain, that is a new and yet unfathomed perfidy."

"Attack, Mr. Secretary?"

"Lord Lyons, don't play games with me!"

"I assure you, sir, that I do not understand what you mean."

Seward's skinny face had flushed red. Lyons could not help thinking that with his shock of unruly white hair and great Roman nose, he
looked nothing more than a fighting cock ready to strike. "The telegraph
from New York has been on fire for the last two hours with news of a
great naval battle in New York Harbor. A British fleet pursued a U.S.
warship escorted by two Russian ships into the Upper Bay in a running
battle that rages as we speak."

Lyons blanched. He was aware from his instructions that a squadron had been sent in pursuit of *Kearsarge*, but not in his wildest imagination did he dream that they would hunt their prey into the heart of
America's greatest city, much less than it would happen before the formal declaration had been delivered. He could only keep an impassive
face and hand Seward his letters.

Seward snatched them from his hand. He spat on them, threw
them on the floor, and ground them into the carpet with his heel. Looking directly at Lyons, whose eyes had gone wide at the act, he said to his
aide, "Show this gentleman out the back door."[36]

RAILROAD STATION, NEW YORK CITY,
5:25 PM, SEPTEMBER 24, 1863

As soon as Lisovsky's ships docked at the Brooklyn Navy Yard they off-
loaded their wounded into the eager arms of ambulance crews. Mayor
George Opdyke immediately saw to the provision of a train to take
Lisovsky to Washington shortly after the admiral had broken the seal on
his orders, written in the hand of the Czar himself, and read them. The
progress to the station had been impeded by the huge crowds of cheering New Yorkers, hailing the savior of their city from British surprise
attack. As the police cleared the way to the station entrance, a police
captain ran up with a telegram and thrust it into the mayor's hand.

Opdyke's face turned white. He handed it to the admiral and stood
up to wave the crowd silent. "Good people of New York, I have just been
handed a telegram from the President of the United States." The buzz of
the crowd hushed in expectation. "I am informed that today, as the battle
raged in the Upper Bay, the British ambassador delivered a declaration
of war." He paused for the impact to sink in. The silence held, then burst
into a wave of anger from thousands of voices that grew into a howl of
incandescent rage.

The tracks were cleared for the train's run all the way to Washington. Ambassador Stoekel and a naval guard of honor were there to greet

it. The ambassador and he spoke quietly before the Russian party climbed into their waiting carriages with a cavalry escort to lead the way.
Crowds had gathered at the news of Lisovsky's approach and broke into wild applause as he sped to meet Lincoln and Seward.

They were immediately ushered into Lincoln's private study.
Stoekel had never seen two graver men than Lincoln and Seward. He
introduced Lisovsky, and after warm greetings, Lisovsky bowed and re-
cited the orders Czar Alexander had written him. "Your Excellency, my
Imperial Majesty has instructed me that in the event of an attack by a
foreign power, particularly Britain or France, upon the United States or
upon the recognition of the Southern Confederacy by either of those powers, I am to put my squadron at the disposal of Your Excellency. I have
three frigates now in New York. Two more corvettes and a clipper are
expected within a few days. I am also instructed to say that a squadron of
the Imperial Navy will shortly be arriving at the port of San Francisco
under the same orders. I am at your command, Your Excellency."[37]

Stoekel now spoke. "Mr. President, I am instructed by His Imperial Majesty under contingent orders that should the United States
be attacked by these powers, I am to confirm the admiral's orders and
state that upon notification of such an attack His Imperial Majesty will
declare war on the attacker. I am empowered to conclude a treaty of
alliance at once."[38]

10.

A Rain of Blows

FORT GORGES, PORTLAND HARBOR, MAINE,
2:00 AM, SEPTEMBER 30, 1863

The British sailors pulled slowly on their muffled oars through the fog. They had left the iron screw troopship HMS *Dromedary* some distance back. In the boats between the oarsmen sat Royal Marines, still and silent. In their blue greatcoats and shakos and with the Enfield rifles in their hands, they could easily be mistaken for American troops, especially in the thick fog.

A light, wan and struggling against the fog, appeared ahead. A clutch of guards, wrapped in their own greatcoats against the chill and huddling against a fire in an iron basket, could be made out under it. At last one cried out, "Who goes there?"

"Garrison relief," answered a voice in a good New England accent.

"Come in, then," answered the guard. Capt. George Bazalgette, the officer of Marines, sighed in quiet relief. They had surprise on their side. He silently thanked Providence that the worsening situation had snatched him out of the back-of-beyond station on San Juan Island on the Pacific coast south of Vancouver after the aborted confrontation between Britain and the United States dubbed "the Pig War." An assignment like this was bound to ensure that he was not remembered as the officer who almost fought in the Pig War.[1]

The plan had relied on the laxness of the Maine home guards who provided the garrison of the fort on rotation. The huge fort appeared as a shadowy mass in the fog. The officer had seen it before on a special visit he had made in mufti a week before. Build on a man-made island on Hog Island Ledge, it was a granite-built, six-sided fort with two tiers

158

of casemates, designed for 195 guns, at least half of which had been installed.[2]

The first boat came up to the stone pier. The guards looked on in curiosity as the officer stepped out followed by his men. Bazalgette's pistol appeared in the face of the sergeant of the guard as his men quickly overpowered the guards. More boats began unloading Marines. One of them carried a team of Army sappers who rushed along the stone pier to the thick iron-reinforced oak door of the main gate. They were planting their explosive charge when the small access door in the larger doors opened and an officer stepped out followed by the guard relief. The three sappers reacted quickly and bayoneted two of the guards. The officer, bolder and more quick witted than would be expected at two in the morning, pulled his pistol and shot two of the sappers. The third sapper killed the officer with a single cleaving blow of the engineer's heavy bayonet and bolted through the open door. Another shot came from within. Bazalgette came running, followed by the fifty men who had disembarked. He saw the open door. Another shot from within echoed. He jumped over the bodies and rushed through to find two dead men on the floor and the sapper struggling with a third. A Marine rushed past to plunge his bayonet into the guard. Other men unbolted the great gate doors and pushed back the leaves. The Marines poured in.

Bazalgette and the Army sappers had carefully studied the plans of the fort that had come his way courtesy of Lieutenant Colonel Wolseley. Armed with this knowledge, the Marines fanned out through the fort as more ships' boats unloaded the rest of the three hundred–man battalion assault force assembled from the ships of Admiral Milne's command at Halifax. The shots had started to rouse the garrison, but sleepy, inexperienced men on a foggy night were no match for Royal Marines. Men stumbling out of their barracks were shot down or bayoneted. The Marines stormed inside. In less than a half hour, Fort Gorges had fallen. In the morning the good people of Portland would see British colors flying from it as the Royal Navy entered the port in force. The greatest port in northern New England had all but fallen. The most careful intelligence had reported that the only troops in Portland were the home guard garrisons of the harbor forts. It would all be a matter of formalities.[3]

ST. JOHNS RAILROAD STATION, QUEBEC, CANADA, 2:00 AM, SEPTEMBER 30, 1863

For the last two days and nights, the Grand Trunk Railway in Canada had been filled with troop trains converging on Montreal, the nexus of the railway's connections with New York and New England. From the ancient site of royal France, the might of the British Empire was marshaling rapidly. Most of the forces that had been ostentatiously concentrating between Detroit and Buffalo entrained at night and sped east. The remainder, reinforced by the mobilization of the Sedentary Militia, had occupied the fortifications on the Canadian side. From Montreal the troop trains went south toward the New York and Vermont borders. Just south of St. Johns, the Grand Trunk Railway split to travel on both sides of Lake Champlain and then reunite south of the lake straight down to Albany. From there both Boston and New York City were a bare hundred miles away. Another force of regulars and Canadian Volunteers had concentrated east of Montreal at Sherbrooke along the Grand Trunk and struck southeast through the sleepy small towns of upper Vermont and Maine toward Portland.[4]

Wolseley walked the platform at the railroad station as the troop trains sped through south. Already the lead elements of the invasion of New York had crossed the border and seized the first American stations, brushing aside the militia units that had been called up a few days before and cutting the telegraph wires. With the railroad in British hands the invasion forces eschewed the roads and sped south by rail through the night. This time the red-coated regiments ensured that no one would be riding ahead to alert the country that the British were coming. Washington's eyes had been on Detroit and Buffalo, just as Wolseley had planned. The divisions they had sent north were defending borders the British had no intention of attacking. Militia and home guard units had been deemed sufficient for less threatened areas, the very places the British invasion force was pouring through as fast as their trains would take them. A few Maine regiments were to return home to recruit, he learned in the last week, but they would be dispersed across the state and of little military value.

There were any number of British generals and full colonels leading their men in the first invasion of the United States since 1813, but it was Lt. Col. Garnet Wolseley who had been the brain and energy behind the plan they were executing. Wrapped in his greatcoat against the deep chill of an early Canadian fall, he expounded to the eager clutch of staff officers around him. "We will strike Brother Jonathan so hard that it will drive any thought of attacking Canada right out of his head." It was exciting to be a part of the exercise of England's might against an upstart power, but in the presence of a true charismatic leader, the experience

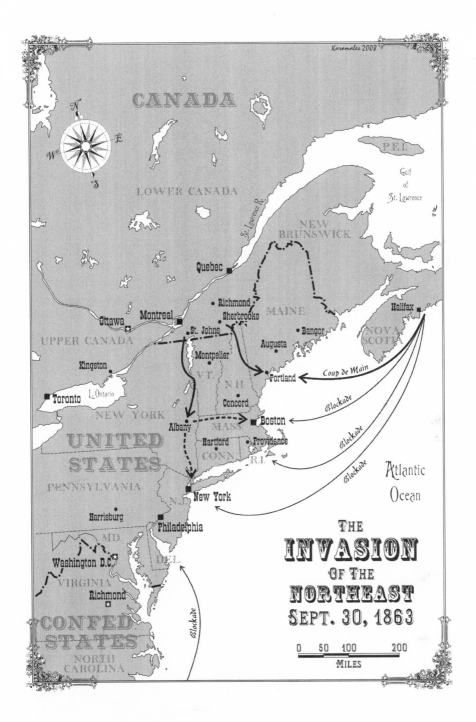

CANADA

LOWER CANADA

Quebec

Richmond
Sherbrooke

Montreal

Ottawa

St. Johns

UPPER CANADA

Montpelier

Kingston

L. Ontario

Toronto

NEW YORK

Albany

UNITED
STATES

PENNSYLVANIA

Harrisburg

Washington D.C.

VIRGINIA

Richmond

CONFED
STATES

NORTH
CAROLINA

NEW
BRUNSWICK

MAINE

Bangor

Augusta

Portland

N.H.

Concord

MASS

Boston

Hartford
CONN

Providence

R.I.

N.J.

Philadelphia

MD

DEL.

New York

NOVA
SCOTIA

Halifax

P.E.I.

Gulf
of
St. Lawrence

Coup de Main

Blockade

Blockade

Blockade

Atlantic
Ocean

Blockade

THE
INVASION
OF THE
NORTHEAST
SEPT. 30, 1863

0   50   100   200
MILES

Karamales 2008

was intoxicating. Wolseley went on, more to fill the time than to eluci-
date. All he could do now was to wait for the first reports of the execution of his plan to deliver such a blow that Union morale would crack
wide open.

He continued, "By seizing Albany and Portland we accomplish
four essential objectives. First, we are too weak to defend, so we must
attack. They cannot threaten Canada if they are threatened in their heart-
land. Second, by seizing Albany, the capital of New York, we disrupt the
richest and most powerful of their states and threaten their greatest port.
Third, by seizing Portland and the rest of Maine, we eliminate a geographical salient between Canada and the Maritimes, detach an entire
state from the Union, and add it as a buffer to the Maritimes. Fourth, at
the same time we acquire the use of another first-rate port south of over-
burdened Halifax from which the Royal Navy can base its blockade."[5]
He struck his fist into his open palm, letting the pop of cold leather on
leather punctuate his exposition. "Gentlemen, we are on the verge of the
greatest war to take place in our time. Mark me — it will dwarf the Crimea
and the Sepoy Mutiny. For those of you who think promotion slow, your
troubles are about to end.

"There's another thing, gentlemen. You will find man shooting is
the finest sport of all; there is a certain amount of infatuation about it,
that the more you kill the more you wish to kill."[6]

Privately he admitted that they would have "toughish work of it."
The Americans would not be an easy victory. They had too much experience after two and half years of war, and they were not shy about fighting vast, bloody battles.[7] That was why audacity had to be thrown in the
scales to redress British America's geographical vulnerability. Audacity,
yes, aided by indirection. The Americans must be so distracted by fires at
the back of the house that they would not be able to give full attention to
his breaking down their front door.

As to the front door, so audacious a plan could never have been
attempted if the invasion had been on foot and horse. It would take a
week of unopposed marching to reach either objective. The use of trains
in the offensive had never been tried before. Trains had been used to
rapidly move armies to their staging areas but never as the spearhead of
invasion itself. It was the only way to deliver a knockout punch. If the
element of surprise was maintained, a very big "if" indeed, then they
would seize both cities by the next day. If not, they would detrain where
necessary and press on by road. Maj. Gen. Lord Frederick Paulet had

been given command of the twenty thousand men of the two mixed British-Canadian divisions, designated the Albany Field Force, that would strike for New York's capital. The Guards Brigade was in the lead trains heading south to Albany. They had to be given pride of place in this operation. While the guards had burnished their battle honors in the Crimean War, they were not known for their dash or the quick thinking of their officers. Wolseley would have been happier with some of the scrappier line regiments with less social standing in the lead.

Those regiments were heading toward Portland.

CHATHAM ARCH, INDIANAPOLIS, INDIANA, 3:00 AM, SEPTEMBER 30, 1863

George Grenfell adjusted his cap in the mirror and took a moment to reflect how far he had come since he had set off for a life of adventure. His thoughts fled back to his days in the Moroccan Rif when the bloom of youth was on him. Now his hair was white, but he told himself, "Damned distinguished. Life's not done with me yet."

John Hines was not so reflective. The wiry, little man had already put on his uniform and not once glanced in the mirror. He was spinning the cylinder on his pistol to make sure its action was still smooth. He spared a glance to Grenfell. "I swear, sir, you look the dandy, but find the time to admire yourself when we don't have a fight to start."

Grenfell just smiled and ran his fingers under his fine, white mustache. "Now, Captain, you must allow yourself to savor a splendid moment. You never know when it will be your last."

"I'll do that when the war is over."

Grenfell did not reply that too many men never lived that long.

There was a knock on the door. They stopped still and glanced at each other and then toward the door. The last ten days had made them wary. That damned Major Cline and his band had dogged their heels far too closely. At times they despaired that their plan would disintegrate as Cline picked apart the pieces. Had he done so already? They had escaped him only by a hair on more than one occasion.

Another knock followed by a muffled, insistent voice. "We're ready." Hines relaxed. Even through the door, he recognized Jim Smoke's rasping voice. Hines let him in, and immediately the room filled with the big man's menace. "We're ready," he said again. "My men are all in place." Two hundred Copperheads were lying in wait around Camp Morton, the sprawling Confederate prisoner of war facility on what had been planned as Indianapolis's fair grounds before the war. Three thousand veteran soldiers of the Confederacy were sleeping inside, or so their guards thought. Word had come to them just hours before to be awake and alert this night. Not that the guards would have picked up anything out the ordinary. The experienced regiment that had been the camp's guard force had been transferred a week ago, their place taken by volunteer home guards. The new men were profoundly unaware of their duties.[8]

UNION STATION, PORTLAND, MAINE,
4:10 AM, SEPTEMBER 30, 1863

The city of Portland sits on a boot-shaped peninsula with the toe pointing northeast to the broad Casco Bay, sheltered from the Atlantic by a string of islands. Its harbor lay on the southern, or under side of the boot and made Portland one of the finest deep-water ports on the East Coast. The instep and big toe curled around Back Cove. The Fore River ran down the back of the foot and past the heel into the harbor. The town of some forty thousand souls occupied the peninsula from the toe to the heel. The Grand Trunk Railroad ran north to south down the western edge of the boot and curled east along the harbor to pass through the city's Union Station and then ran north to Canada again. Most Maine men remembered the cool green lushness of the city whose every street but the smallest was lined with stately chestnuts and maples, earning Portland the title of the "Forest City."

For the Maine men arriving from the Army of the Potomac, the station meant hot food and coffee on a chilly morning from the attentive ladies of the Sanitary Commission who maintained a permanent facility to attend to military personnel in transit. Portland was not on a main troop transit route and the facility was small, but the people of Portland had turned the entire train station into a reception center for their heroes home to rest and recruit back their strength. Since midnight the trains had been arriving, not with a few Maine regiments but with Maine's entire military contingent from the Army of the Potomac. Sharpe's suggestion had started the ball rolling, and that ball had rolled right over Major General Meade's loud protest to lose all his Maine regiments—3,241 men divided into one cavalry, ten infantry regiments, and three artillery batteries. Maine had taken 3,721 men into the battle of Gettysburg and lost 1,017. Since then hundreds of wounded and missing had returned to duty, but most of the regiments had been severely depleted even before Gettysburg. Had they been at full strength, the entire contingent would have numbered almost thirteen thousand men. It was an example of what wastage the Army had suffered in camp and in the field and of the failure to establish a regular replacement system (see appendix A).[9]

Thus the story that they were returning home to recruit was entirely plausible. As a cover story, the public announcement had indicated only three regiments were returning. The governor had only been informed of the true extent of the troop movement the day before. The ladies of the Sanitary Commission had had to scramble, but when the trains began to arrive, they were ready with tables piled high with food and enough hot coffee to float a monitor.

The trains had begun to arrive strangely enough about two hours before the Royal Marines had climbed into their boats to fall upon Fort Gorges. The train ride from Northern Virginia had been hurried, almost nonstop, but the men took the discomfort in stride as every uninterrupted mile took them closer to home. They had not bothered to ask why two brigade staffs had been attached to them, so intent were they for home. The gunners had brought their complete batteries to include horses, guns, limbers, and caissons as well as their supply and maintenance wagons. The cavalry had brought their horses as well. That raised questions, but they had been told there would be major parades in Portland, Augusta, and Bangor, and the idea of showing off to the local girls had disarmed any further curiosity. What no one bothered to note were the medical and supply units because they occupied the rearmost trains. It was an efficient logistical exercise, an area in which the Union excelled. It was also a clever strategic deception plan in operation. That was something the Union was now just beginning to excel at under the shadowy hand of Brigadier General Sharpe.[10]

Col. Joshua Lawrence Chamberlain, of Gettysburg reknown, had been instructed to accompany the Maine contingent and assume "administrative" control of five infantry regiments, including his old 20th Maine and a battery. The other five regiments and another battery had been similarly brigaded under another able Maine officer, Col. Ephraim Harper. Another battery and a cavalry regiment rounded out the Maine units (see appendix A).[11] Chamberlain and Harper had been briefed on their mission before leaving Washington along with Brig. Gen. Neal Dow. Known as a temperance fanatic, "the Napoleon of Temperance" was a brave man withal. People had not forgotten the heavy hand with which he had put down the Portland Rum Riot of 1855 during his time as mayor. Chamberlain and Harper winced when Halleck explained that in case of war, Dow would assume command of the "Maine Division" with the mission of defending the state and cutting the New Brunswick Road to sever communications between Canada and the Maritimes. Nobody liked Dow, which is not necessarily a requirement for success-ful command, but his constant emphasis on temperance was bound to alienate the troops. The men were aware that Dow had ordered his own 13th Maine to sign the temperance pledge. It was not something Cham-berlain would have tried with his own 20th Maine despite the men's affection for him.[12]

Since Little Round Top, Chamberlain had become something of a legend not only in the Army of the Potomac but also in Maine, where he was now the shining hero. That desperate bayonet charge downhill that had swept the 15th Alabama away had swept him up to glory. Com-mand of a brigade had followed, and he was among those few identified for stars in the future. A gifted college professor who had abandoned the classroom for the camp to serve his country in this great struggle for freedom, he had truly found himself in the Army. Inside that mild-man-nered bookworm was a fighting man whom other men rushed to follow. Campaigning had worked the softness of academe out of him and re-placed it with a lean, almost leopard-like presence. The sun had bleached his blond hair even fairer, and his drooping mustache set off his long face with its penetrating blue eyes. He was the natural warrior with an innate sense of Mars's three gifts of the art of war — "quick grasp, speed, and shock."

Word had spread of the arrival of the troops, and thousands of townspeople had left their warm beds to greet friends and relatives. Hundreds of lanterns were bouncing through the fog that drifted up from the harbor to gather around the station whose own lights were strug-gling with the wet, floating gloom. Inside the station, the men were fin-ishing their meals. Dow was conferring with Chamberlain and Harper when a familiar, whistling noise stopped every mouth. The shell crashed through the roof and exploded among the dining tables, scattering blue-clad bodies every which way and killing three Sanitation Commission ladies carrying coffee and doughnuts. More shells followed, turning the main hall into a shambles as the troops and civilians rushed for the exits, but they found no safety. More shells were falling into the crowd, which had turned into a terrified beast, screaming in fear.[13]

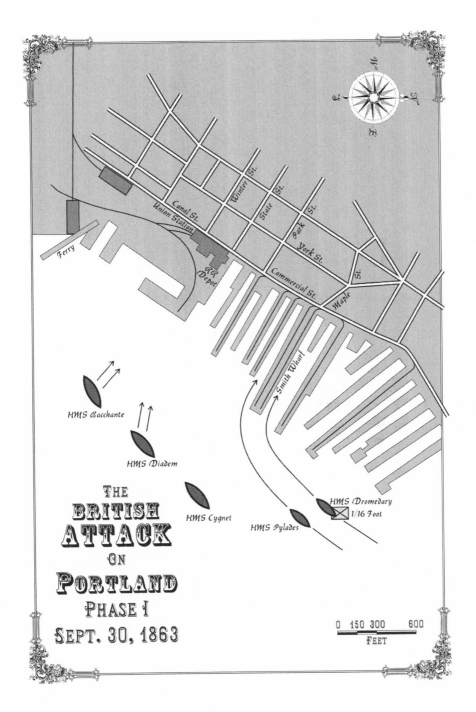

Winter St.

State St.

Park

York St.

Maple St.

Canal St.

Union Station

Commercial St.

Ferry

R.R.
Depot

Smith Wharf

HMS Bacchante

HMS Diadem

HMS Cygnet

HMS Pylades

HMS Dromedary
1/16 Foot

THE
BRITISH
ATTACK
ON
PORTLAND
PHASE 1
SEPT. 30, 1863

0   150 300   600
FEET

With Fort Gorges fallen, British ships had crept slowly into the harbor, drawn by the dull glow of light at the railroad station. His Copperhead informant had told the squadron commander aboard the frigate HMS *Bacchante* that the glow was the railroad station on the edge of the city. The officer ordered his shell guns to fire on the center of the glow. HMS *Diadem* followed with its own broadside battery. Here was an economic target important to the ability of the Americans to make war, he thought, disregarding Admiral Milne's instructions not to fire on coastal towns. For this he would be relieved, but not before his 8-inch shells piled the bodies of women and children up in the station and surrounding streets and gave the Americans an immortal battle cry — "Remember Maine!"

Temperance fanatic notwithstanding, Dow was quick witted and decisive in an emergency and ordered Harper to assemble and doubletime his regiments to the docks to repel any possible landing. If they were close enough to bombard Union Station that meant they had bypassed or seized the harbor forts. He instructed Chamberlain to hold his regiments in reserve and ensure that the trains were speedily unloaded to support combat. The gunners and the cavalry did not wait to be told; these were veteran troops and were already unloading their equipment and horses. The infantry regiments were equally in hand as soon as they had evacuated the now burning wooden station house. The smoke from that inferno mixed with the thick fog to wrap the city in a blur. The men of Harper's regiments moved easily through the streets of the city that was the hometown of many, their tread propelled by a deepening anger. Frightened night watchmen from the docks intercepted the columns and directed them to Smith's Wharf, where hundreds of the "Peacemakers" from the 1/16th Foot from the Halifax garrison were hustling down the gangplanks from the *Dromedary* onto its broad surface with its double rail lines. Wolseley's reconnaissance had picked the best landing spot. Light boat guns with their Royal Marine crews rolled down the gangways to clack with their iron wheels over the granite paving of the wharf. Boats from the bombarding ships carrying detachments of armed naval ratings clustered along the edge of the wharf, adding men in white and blue to the crimson mass moving down the wharf.

Lt. Col. Charles Langely, commanding the Peacemakers, was more than anxious after the Navy had started a bonfire whose dull red eye glowed even through this horrendous fog. The essence of a coup de main is stealth and silence, and now they had neither. He had hoped to be in control of the city as it woke to the morning and present its citizens with an accomplished fact that common sense would force them to accept. Now, thanks to the Navy, all would be chaos. He could not see but could hear the *Dromedary* pulling away from the wharf to pick up the Royal Marines at Ft. Gorges as a further reinforcement for Langely's command. "Thank God," he murmured to himself. "There are almost no troops in the town."[14]

There were only 112 men left in the 3rd Maine after it had watered the fields of Pennsylvania with its blood, but they double-timed up York Street as if they were the full thousand men that had left home two years ago. They turned right on Maple and crossed Commercial Street, which put them on the edge of the docks between Deakes and Brown's wharves. Even through the fog, the activity could be sensed and heard more than seen. The colonel stopped them only long enough to fix bayonets. The watchmen lifted their lanterns and pointed down the street to Smith's Wharf. Then he led them forward. Shots rent the fog; the colonel fell, but the 3rd Maine kept moving. Shouts in British English cut through the night. More shots came and more men pitched into the gutter. When a picket line emerged from the fog, too close to run, too few could survive the moving blue column that stabbed with bayonets and struck with rifle butts. The column broke onto the Smith's Wharf as the British firing line cut loose. The first blue ranks fell, but the rest broke into a run over the short space and closed with the Peacemakers before they could reload. Now it was man to man. The gunpowder and technological revolutions of the time disappeared as men fell into the ultimate savagery with bayonets and rifle butts, teeth and bare hands.

More companies of the 1/16th rushed into the fight as they clambered onto the wharf while the 4th and 5th Maine pushed in from the town. Soon the entire fog-blanketed wharf was a seething mass of fighting men with so little room that only pistols were of any use. There was no time or space to reload a rifle. Once fired, it became a spear.

There were no tougher professionals in that age than the British infantry, but even their toughness was no match for the veteran courage and rage of the Maine men, whose homes had been violated and their women and children murdered. The outnumbered redcoats were being pushed back down the wharf as bodies carpeted the planking or fell off the sides into the water. Lieutenant Colonel Langely's body was among them as it slipped beneath the murky harbor water. He would become a legend in the history of the regiment, likened to Horatio at the bridge. No

Army but that of the British can wring so much glory and inspiration from a death. With two bayonet men on either side, he had fought in the front rank with rifle and bayonet, prodigiously lethal in his own right. There was very little scope to command with men packed so tightly on a narrow front. At that moment, an example was all the command his men had needed. He had finally gone down in that blur of bayonets and crack of pistols as the Maine men shoved them back and back again.[15]

The rear American companies peeled off left and right to fire into the enemy on the wharf. They were joined by the 5th Maine Battery, which sent canister into the British and into the boats clustered at the end of the wharf. A British corvette, HMS *Pylades*, steamed up to fire into the struggling mass but killed as many of its men as the Americans it cut down. The battery turned its guns on the ship, sweeping the decks this time with case shot, killing the captain and helmsmen, and leaving its upper decks a splintered shambles.

The Peacemakers, mixed with naval ratings and Marines, were backed down the wharf, step by step, begrudging every bloody inch until the last of them were clustered at the end of the wharf as dawn began to burn off the last of the thinning fog. The corvette had drifted away, its engines now holed by a solid shot from the battery. Three hundred fifty-three were left of the nine hundred British who had set foot on the dock. Their backs to the water, the *Dromedary* gone, and their boats smashed, they fought on. Suddenly the fighting stopped. Both groups just stood there on the planking strewn with dead and dying men, mingled equally in Union blue and Her Majesty's crimson. Ten feet of silence separated the panting, blood- and sweat-soaked groups. The inner fires banked. An officer in blue stepped forward and demanded their surrender. A sergeant in red threw down his rifle, for there was not an officer on his feet; then the others followed. But the battle for Portland had only just begun.[16]

CAMP MORTON, INDIANAPOLIS, INDIANA, 4:15 AM, SEPTEMBER 30, 1863

Two hours before dawn when most of the guards at Camp Morton slept, the three thousand men inside the prisoners' barracks were awake. The word had gone out after midnight to rouse the men in silence. In the officers' section of the camp, John Hunt Morgan waited more intently than any of them. It was to him that Hines had sent word. He had shared it with only three of his officers, but at his command the camp had quietly stirred itself. He would have taken heart in these early hours suspended between night and day when courage is weakest if he had known that of the thousands of expectantly waiting men there was one who had clutched a camp-made battle flag, the square-shaped stars and bars, that he had painstakingly assembled from what bits and pieces of colored cloth had come his way. Such flags, "the damned red flags of rebellion," had quailed many a Northern heart in the past. This one was waiting to do so again.

A prisoner of war camp is designed to keep people inside; the eyes of the warders are focused inward and not outward. Of all the three hundred guards, only two had their eyes on the countryside outside the camp. They had not been under military discipline long and had not acquired a healthy fear of falling asleep at their posts. They did not notice the column of men shuffling along the empty road that led past the outskirts of Indianapolis to the camp. It was a great shame. They were missing an artful demonstration of military deception. A few men in Union blue rode at the head of the column of shabbily dressed men and a few more walked along the column with bayoneted rifles. At the rear rumbled six wagons.

Had the camp's guards been awake, they would have seen a detachment of new prisoners under guard. The column came to a halt in front of the gate. Their breath rose in little clouds in the chill air. Big Jim looked down and smiled like a wolf. The country boy guards were soundly in the arms of Orpheus. As Jim was shaking his head, two of the guards in the column brought two prisoners forward, wrapped in blankets. They too, for an incredulous moment, stared at the sleeping guards in the light of the single lamp hanging from the guard post. Grenfell snickered, "We really must commend the sergeant of the guard after this."

Smoke had dismounted. He walked over to the first guard and brought down his pistol butt on the first guard's head. As the man slumped to the ground, he struck the other. The man staggered back, awakened by the glancing blow, but Smoke was on him, striking again and again, the blood spattering the wall until he stood over the bludgeoned corpse and signaled the others forward with his dripping pistol. He stood aside as a team with a log came running up against the gate. The gate groaned with the impact. Another rush and the bar inside snapped. Grenfell and Hines rushed through, pistols in hand, their blankets flung aside, and their Confederate officer's gray and gold in full view. [17]

DANFORTH STATION, MAINE, 4:20ᴀᴍ, SEPTEMBER 30, 1863

The station manager at Danforth, the last station on the Grand Trunk before Portland, stopped the British trains by throwing the main switch. He had heard the cannon fire from the city and had seen the huge pyre of the burning railroad station. A dyed-in-the-wool Copperhead, the man had been part of the conspiracy to keep the railroad open straight to Portland. Now as the city burned and his countrymen died, he rushed to inform the British commander. His hatred for Lincoln had long ago passed beyond reason into a state of such self-sustaining bitterness that he would have his country strewn with corpses and ashes to see the man pulled down.

Maj. Gen. Sir Charles Ashe Windham, commanding the Portland Field Force, was not a man to take the word of a Yankee for anything. He would see for himself and climbed the station's observation tower to view the city with his glass. The man commanding the British ground assault on Portland was a man of wide experience and heroic reputation. He had led the assault on the Redan in the Crimean War and defended Cawnpore during the Sepoy Mutiny. Wolseley had come to know and admire him in Canada and said of him that "he was a man of the world, he had many charming qualities: was never hard upon others in word or deed, and always inclined to make allowances for human failings."[18]

He scanned the city carefully. His immediate impression was that the Navy had botched its end. What had promised to be a smooth coup de main was now a full-pitched battle. "Well," he muttered to his aide, "that's usually the way military plans go. No one's fault, just the way things go. Reminds me of a Russian military proverb I learned in the Crimea: 'The plan was smooth on paper, only they forgot the ravines.'"[19]

He could see the Navy's ships firing into the town. The main fort in the harbor also seemed to be firing into the town. At least the Navy had taken the fort. He quickly climbed down the spiral staircase and gave the order to dismount the trains. His lead brigade was built around the 62nd Foot with the Quebec-raised Canadian 50th Huntington Rangers, 51st Hemmingford Rangers, and 52nd Bedford militia battalions. Windham gave the command to force march the last few miles to the city.[20] He left his chief of staff to dispatch the artillery and the next two brigades built around the 17th and 63rd Foot. He was pleased to see the three Canadian battalions move out smartly and with little confusion. He knew that the 62nd Foot, "the Splashers," had shown them a good example in training. There were still many veterans from the Crimea in the ranks. Their nickname came from the battle of Carrickfergus in 1758 when they had run out of bullets and used their buttons for ammunition. Since then their buttons had been issued dented, or "splashed" (see appendix A). [21]

He had not gone a mile when Union cavalry pickets fired on his scouts. More cavalry came up to thicken the firing line and force him to deploy. His men's Enfields had the range of the enemy's breech-loading Sharps carbines, but the Americans could fire faster. He flanked them on both sides with Canadian companies, but the enemy cavalry mounted up and moved to the rear to throw a new skirmishing line up to repeat their delaying tactics. The men were behaving—smoothly and quickly, just as in training, despite the number of red-clad bodies littering their line of advance.

Windham had no illusions that the Americans would collapse at the first blow. It would take a rain of blows to beat them down, and he now knew that his men were up to it. He ordered them forward. They cheered him as they swept by.

CAMP MORTON, INDIANAPOLIS, INDIANA, 4:20 AM, SEPTEMBER 30, 1863

Major Cline had caught the scent of the plot to free the prisoners and followed it until it brought him to the outskirts of Indianapolis in the blackness of that same morning. Hines and Grenfell had barely broken into Camp Morton when Cline and his cavalry had thundered up the darkened road and right into the Copperheads trying to push through the shattered gate. They shot the horses drawing the wagons loaded with rifles and sabered and pistoled their way through the Copperhead column, which came apart like a bursting sack of corn, spilling into the ditches and across the darkened fields.

Cline was the first Union man through the gate. Before him the barracks were emptying of Confederate prisoners as two officers in gray ran toward them. Cline spurred on until he came alongside the officer with long white hair, waving his hat on his sword and holding a pistol. He fired down into his thick mane. The man tumbled head over heels into a heap. The first prisoner to reach him jumped for his pistol, which had fallen in the mud. Cline shot him too. His men were riding up now and firing into the mass of prisoners. The panicked men in front tried to get away only to be pushed forward by all those coming from the barracks.

The guards were spilling out of their quarters and shooting at the heaving throng. The other rebel officer, Captain Hines, tried to rally the prisoners as he strode before them with his pistol in hand. "Come on, boys! Charge and the place is ours. Charge!" He waved his arm and ran forward, followed by a mass of rock-throwing men keening the Confederate yell. The gallant line withered in the fire from Cline's men and the guards. Hines was the first to fall.[22]

SOUTH OF DANFORTH STATION, MAINE, 5:10 AM, SEPTEMBER 30, 1863

The commander of the 1st Maine Cavalry, immediately upon contact with the British, had sent an accurate and detailed report back to Chamberlain. In turn, Chamberlain sent it to Dow with his appraisal that the British column was the main thrust aimed at Portland. On his own authority he ordered the reserve artillery battery to accompany his brigade north to hold the peninsula against God knew how many British. The men were glad to step off now that they knew their purpose. They had waited in ranks in a state of high agitation as they heard the battle at the docks rage and watched the station burn. Chamberlain now passed to his colonels the word to march with a note of explanation that the enemy was approaching from the north. With his infantry, cavalry, and gunners, Chamberlain would have at hand just short of fifteen hundred men. He did not know that the enemy's advance brigade outnumbered him by 40 percent or that the follow-on force doubled that. He would be outnumbered more than three to one. He sensed that if he had any chance of holding the peninsula, he had to strike hard and fast and throw the enemy's lead force back on its heels. He kept his cavalry out as a screen to slow and divert the enemy's attention while he created a surprise.[23]

He reinforced the cavalry with one battery and the small 10th and 16th Maine. That temporarily held the British up. The British guns weren't up yet, and the shells from the Maine battery were tearing holes in their infantry. They may have been stopped, but they did not flinch and continued to return a heavy and accurate fire. Chamberlain stopped for a moment to admire them, but he had admired the 15th Alabama as well and had thrown them off Little Round Top. As he turned away, he was surprised to see the mayor ride up in his carriage. He waved and called out, "Colonel Chamberlain, Colonel Chamberlain." Behind him Chamberlain saw a hurried column of men in civilian clothes and old uniforms, sporting all sorts of firearms. "Colonel Chamberlain, I have brought you the city militia and volunteers. General Dow said I was to help you with our boys. What do you want them to do?"

The last thing Chamberlain wanted was militia in a fight with redcoats. In an open field fight, they were a liability, just as they had been in the Revolution and the War of 1812. They were good for something, though. "Dig! I want them to dig a fighting trench from the inlet on Back Cove across the peninsula to the Canal Basin by the Fore River, behind the creek that empties into the cove. Get every spade and shovel in the town but have them start now with their hands if they have to." Before riding off, he turned to a staff officer and said, "Captain, show them how it's done."[24]

Windham was not a man to waste time on a stalemate. He could see that the Americans had reinforced their cavalry with some infantry and strong battery, and together they had thrown up too strong a front to waste lives smashing through it when maneuver would drive them back. Again he peeled off companies of the 51st Hemmingford Rangers to circle around the American right flank. He was surprised that the obvious maneuver had not forced the Americans to pull back even as his flankers were about to slip around them.

Then he understood as a volley from a new battery burst over his main fighting line. To the east a wave of American infantry had crested a small rise and was heading for his own rear while a larger group hit his flanking companies. He was about to be trapped. He sent an aide galloping to the rear to hurry the rest of his command forward. It soon became clear that the advancing Americans numbered not more than five hundred men while the force blocking his rear was even smaller. He concluded that his opponent had played a bold hand, but it was a bad hand. It was time to call the bluff. In the back of his mind he was already regretting leaving his guns behind in his haste to reach his objective.

He sent off more aides with orders. The Hemmingford Rangers were to turn about and clear the Americans off the road in the rear, the 62nd Foot to wheel about to the left and strike the Americans coming on the flanks, and the remaining two Canadian battalions were to hold the front against the cavalry. Had they all been line British battalions it would have gone off without a hitch, but Windham expected too much of his green Canadians. So far they had done very well, but the body-shredding shell and case shot and the sight of their flankers being overrun had shaken them. Windham's coolness in the face of an enemy in his rear had the opposite reaction in his Canadian militia. They approached the line of troops in faded blue — the 17th Maine — with accelerating panic. With a single fluid motion the Americans took aim and fired, and the front

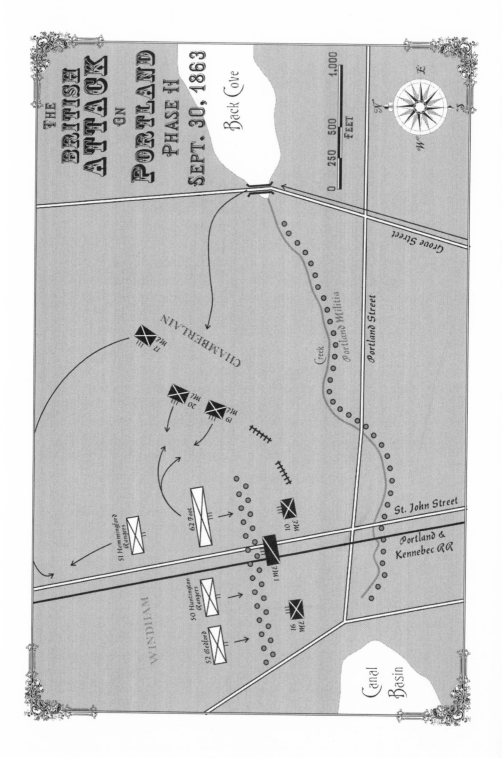

THE
BRITISH ATTACK
ON
PORTLAND
PHASE II
SEPT. 30, 1863

Back Cove

FEET

0   250 500   1,000

Grove Street

Portland Militia

Portland Street

Creek

CHAMBERLAIN

11 ME

20 ME   19 ME

62 Foot

51 Hemmingford Rangers

10 ME

1 ME

St. John Street

Portland & Kennebec RR

WINDHAM

50 Huntington Rangers

52 Bedford

16 ME

Canal Basin

Canadian ranks pitched forward or flew back. The Canadians received the command to aim just as shells burst overhead, whirling jagged metal through the ranks. They could manage only a ragged, ill-aimed volley. Again they heard the command, "Fire!" from their front. It was too brutal a baptism. They simply broke.

As the Canadians fled, the 62nd Foot and Chamberlain's two remaining regiments locked horns. The British battalion outnumbered the 19th and 20th Maine whose original strength had been wasted by hard fighting over the last year. The remaining core was veteran and hard. The little regiments were also seething at the sight of redcoats on Maine soil, especially having that morning had to help clear the dead and wounded civilians from the streets of Portland around the station. Chamberlain threw the guns of his two batteries into the scale by directing them to concentrate on the British with canister. The guns wheeled into line. The British made for a splendid target, moving in elegant precision across the field. The Maine men took time to admire their high style before twelve guns poured tin cans filled with lead balls into them. The two regiments fired next. The 62nd Foot staggered from the blow. Windham's aide flew from the saddle, and he himself felt a hammer strike him in the chest and throw him from his horse. He was dead when he struck the ground. The Splashers, with the amazing resilience of a British battalion, pulled themselves together and sent a volley into the Maine men, dropping dozens.

Chamberlain rode over to his old 20th Maine and found Major Ellis Spear, its new commander. "Ellis, give them the bayonet. The boys have got that one down, I think." He winked at Ellis, who grinned and then shouted the command, "Fix bayonets!" There was a rustle of clicks as the slim, blued blades were locked into place. "Follow me, boys!" The 19th Maine joined the charge. As the Maine men howled their charge, the 62nd got off another well-aimed volley.

Then they showed why British infantry had maintained such a reputation over the centuries. They charged. The crimson and blue lines collided in that great rarity in military history. Bayonet charges rarely resulted in melees. Either the attacker flinched at the sight of an unbroken enemy, or the defenders panicked and took to their heels. But now it was bayonet and rifle butt and pistol in a stabbing, clubbing mob. British bayonet battle drill was deadly as the men operated in wedges of threes. The best bayonet man was at the apex in the center while his companions supported him from the sides. The Maine men knew a thing or two about the bayonet as well, but this time they were not crossing blades with the exhausted and thirsty 15th Alabama.[25]

The commander of the cavalry screen saw his main chance when Chamberlain's men charged. He ordered his three hundred men to mount and charge the two remaining Canadian battalions on his front. They unraveled in the face of the oncoming mass of cavalry and fled to the rear. The 1st Maine Cavalry harried the terrified militiamen until the roadblock of the 17th Maine stopped the survivors. They surrendered.

By then, the Splashers and Maine men had pulled away from each other, dragging their wounded after them, and glared in silence as sweat-soaked chests heaved. The irresistible force had met the unmovable object. Chamberlain was clear sighted enough to realize that it was time to go. If the enemy's reinforcements he could see approaching were as tough as the shrunken redcoat band in front of him, his force would bleed to death on this field. Under the fire of his batteries, he ordered a careful retreat back to the Portland militia line. At least he could put the creek between him and the enemy. Chamberlain was the last man off the field. He paused long enough to throw a salute with his saber to the shrunken ranks of the Splashers before galloping off.[26]

He was surprised to see how much they had accomplished in the few hours he had bought. Fear and the need to do something physical had carved a serviceable trench over half a mile. The city had poured out its tools, and fear had supplied the will. His Maine veterans quickly jumped into the trenches and added their experience to the militia's energy. They had bought the time for the men of Portland to build the defenses to save their own city. These men now cheered as hundreds of enemy prisoners were prodded along past to be taken into Portland.

By the time the British and Canadian skirmishers gingerly approached, the trench system with its parapet would have earned passing marks from the Army of the Potomac's perfection-minded chief engineer himself. Chamberlain had mixed the militia with his own men to thicken the line and leave none of it without experienced men. He figured that his veterans would steady the militia and teach them what they could not have learned on their own. The day was too far gone for the British to assault the line, even if they'd had the energy left for such a hazard. Night fell. The First Battle of Portland was over.[27]

ALBANY, NEW YORK, 4:14 AM, OCTOBER 1, 1863
The Guards Brigade swept away the New York militia, which had gathered in the night, and marched into Albany eight hours after it crossed

the border. Copperhead employees of the rail companies had kept the railroad open straight to Albany. The government men of the Empire State had fled in their nightshirts, a rendition of events Lord Paulet was planning to dine out on for years to come. He had the honor to wipe away the stain of the 1777 failure and defeat of Gentleman Johnny Burgoyne at Saratoga on the very road to Albany. That city was in panic, but he was in no mood to keep order. He wasn't planning to stay long. Copperhead guides were taking parties of his men throughout the city to every site that supported the war effort: factories, foundries, warehouses, boats on the Hudson, and above all the Watervliet Arsenal. All were soon in flames. The fire and smoke fanned the panic of a fleeing populace. Paulet was glad to wave the fan himself if it would send out even more residents far and wide to spread tales of terror. He needed every advantage to multiply the power of his small force. Three more brigades were arriving as the city burned, giving Paulet more than ten thousand men. Canadian Volunteer Militia companies had been left as security at every station along the railroad back to Canada.

The reports of the British burning Albany ran ahead of the refugees and along the wires throughout the Union states. Coupled with the invasion of Maine and the initial report of the fall of Portland, the effect was stunning. New York City, the nation's great emporium and financial center, seemed to shut down with the British Army less than a hundred miles away up the Hudson. Boston was no less afraid. Both feared a simultaneous assault from the sea, all the more real after the Royal Navy's pursuit of *Kearsarge* into the Upper Bay itself. The wires to Washington burned with lurid tales of invasion as every governor with a northern border and every mayor within two hundred miles begged for massive reinforcements. This was worse than Lee's invasion of Pennsylvania in the summer for there was no Army of the Potomac nearby ready to dog the invader and bring him to battle.[28]

However, there were men of courage.

ROYAL NAVY DOCKYARD, IRELAND ISLAND, BERMUDA, 2:00 PM, OCTOBER 1, 1863

The entire ironclad strength of the Royal Navy — the HMS *Warrior, Black Prince, Defence,* and *Resistance* — steamed through the narrows of Ireland Island to the Royal Navy dockyard. The forts lining the thousand-yard passage fired their salutes to the iron might of the British race. At 9,200 and 6,100 tons the two pairs were the largest warships in the world and had come to reinforce Admiral Milne's North American and West Indies Station. They had not come alone. The Channel Squadron had been stripped in an unprecedented move to dispatch five ships of the line and fifteen frigates, sloops, and corvettes, not to mention the dozen or so support and supply ships. The British had not suddenly lost their ancient fear of unchecked French power in the English Channel that they would send Milne so much of its striking power. Intense discussions with Napoleon III had resulted in the simultaneous dispatch of strong French squadrons to Mexico at the same time.

The Royal Navy dockyards in Britain had worked miracles to prepare such a strong force. Instructions had gone out immediately after Moelfre Bay for the Navy to prepare for major operations. The order to depart had followed the dispatch of the declaration of war only by hours. Similar orders had gone to the Army at the same time. Now twenty thousand British troops were sailing behind the warships in a half dozen convoys. The garrisons of the British Isles, particularly Ireland, had been stripped to gather such an expeditionary force to reinforce British North America. Not a man from the large force in India was taken. The memory of the mutiny still oozed fear and caution. Haste had been the watchword. Britain must strike her crippling blows before the winter closed operations until spring. Another convoy was heading north from Barbados with four thousand men of the British West Indies garrison, primarily men of the black West Indian Regiment.

Milne's combined force now assembling at Bermuda was the strongest in sheer power that the Royal Navy had ever assembled. Many of these same wooden ships had only been converted to steam since the Crimean War. Moelfre Bay had imbued both officers and below decks with a righteous cause, though few bothered to consider that the Americans might describe the action as just desserts.[29]

PHILADELPHIA, PENNSYLVANIA, 2:20 PM, OCTOBER 1, 1863
The Western Union boy did not often come to this modest neighborhood and was surprised when the missus of the house actually gave him a nickel tip.

"Michael," she said in the lilt of Ireland as she came into the kitchen, "it's a telegram for you." Michael William McCarter took it in his left hand. The strength had not come back to his right arm. It was the wound he took at Fredericksburg charging up Marye's Heights with the Irish Brigade that had put his soldiering days behind him. He could use the arm, but its old strength was gone.

The telegram was addressed to Sgt. William McCarter. He opened it expectantly. MICHAEL STOP PUT ON THE BLUE STOP REPORT TO ME IN NEW YORK STOP MEAGHER. His eyes moistened. "Katie, he needs me again." Memories welled up of the man he considered a paragon of manly and martial virtues. The memories of Meagher's intemperance flitted over his mind as well and fell away, as McCarter saw him again on the fields of Antietam and Fredericksburg, always at the front in the thickest fire and framed by the regimental Green Flag of Ireland and the Stars and Stripes, or nursing the wounded in his own tent, wrapping them in his own blankets as he sat with them through the night. McCarter had come to know Meagher better than any other enlisted man and most of his officers. As a guard assigned to his tent, he had saved a besotted Meagher from falling into the fire. In gratitude, Meagher assigned him to his own headquarters and discovered his considerable administrative talents.[30] McCarter finally broke from the arms of memory to shout, "Woman of the house, shake the mothballs from my uniform!"

At that very moment, Meagher was standing in a wagon in the streets of New York, holding in thrall a crowd of thousands of his fellow Gaels. Many of them had taken part in the riots only a few months before, diehard Democrats who would not fight for the Union. All that was swept away when the Royal Navy had entered the Upper Bay and especially now that the redcoats had followed them to this new land, hovering to strike from barely a hundred miles up the Hudson Valley. Many had accepted the new land and worn the blue, but many had not and nursed the resentments of poverty. The British hammer had now forged ancient grievance to new affection for the land that sheltered them. Their ambivalence had burned away. They were ready to fight.[31]

11.

Treason, Frogs, and Ironclads

**THE WAR DEPARTMENT, WASHINGTON, D.C.,
11:50 PM, OCTOBER 1, 1863**

It was in times of unending crisis and disaster that Edwin McMasters Stanton became a truly great man. He remained a rock of confidence in a sea of troubles, and from his office a stream of telegrams sung over the wires, bringing order and marshaling the power of the federal government. Autocratic, vengeful, ruthless, relentless, and inexhaustibly energetic, he set about the task of defeating the invasion and preparing for the counterblow that would make the British pay dearly, unaware that a raging fire had been kindled in the Union rear.

If he took a moment for reflection, it was to lament the fact that he had been warned about Albany's vulnerability and to resent Sharpe for the warning. However, he was a man who could eat his revenge cold. He took some small satisfaction that Sharpe had been wrong about the threat from the Great Lakes; there was comfort in that everyone had been fooled there. Then again Sharpe's ploy to get the Maine regiments home under the cover of recruiting had obviously come as a painful surprise to the British and saved Portland, for the moment at least.

The problem at hand was to save New York and Boston from attack. New York, especially, was the economic and financial heart of the Union. At all costs it must be saved. The arrival of the rest of the Russian squadron and the strengthening of the harbor forts would relieve him of worry of another attack by sea and give him a free hand to deal with the British in Albany. Hooker's XI and XII Corps had entrained for their transfer to the relief of the Army of the Cumberland two days before. They would be turned around, and every other train would be sidelined to give them priority to New York City. Until then, they would have to rely on whatever forces were at hand to stop any British advance down the Hudson River Valley.[1]

A silver lining of the draft riots was that a number of regiments that had been sent to suppress them were still in the city. The city's remaining militia regiments were more experienced than would have been apparent. Many of them had served early in the war and had experienced men on their rolls. He ordered a call to all veterans not in the militia to reenlist and join the forces in the city. He was surprised to read in a telegram that Meagher had signed up more than ten thousand men from the Irish in one day, but they would not be ready in time to deal with this crisis. He did take time, though, to dictate to a clerk approval and praise of Meagher's actions and his appointment as a brevet major general with instructions to telegraph it immediately.

As if to prove the aphorism "It never rains but that it pours," one of the Union's major field armies had found itself trapped in Chattanooga whence it had fled after its defeat at Chickamauga. It was obvious Rosecrans was in a funk, or he would not have let that old woman Bragg finally get up the gumption to follow him much less put him under siege. And now the men were beginning to starve. If "Old Rosy" gave up at a time like this, then the entire line of the Ohio would fall. He could not pluck any more units from Meade's Army of the Potomac or Lee would be in Washington at the drop of a hat. The only other major source of troops was Grant's command, but much of that concentration had been nickel-and-dimed to tidy up a number of small problems Halleck's too orderly mind had obsessed about and to reinforce Maj. Gen. Nathaniel P. Banks for a Texas expedition that Lincoln favored.[2] Stanton would have immediately called Grant to the scene, but the man was barely able to move after his horse had fallen on him in New Orleans. Stanton knew his options were running thin.

That dilemma came down to a choice between New York and Chattanooga. The XI and XII Corps could not be in both places at once, and to send one to each crisis would do little good in either place. In the end, Lincoln made the decision—New York. Rosy would have to hang on and wait for Grant. That night Hooker received a telegram that appointed him to command the new Army of the Hudson. The corps would be diverted to New York immediately.

The lights burned late at the Navy Department as well. Gideon Welles may not have had Stanton's greatness in a crisis, but he was steady and a superb administrator. Backed up by a fighting assistant secretary, Gus Fox, he bent to his work. On his own, Fox had immediately dispatched ships to carry the news of war to the naval forces in Hampton Roads and the two blockading squadrons at Wilmington and Charleston.

In many ways the Navy faced a greater challenge than the Army did. Only a small part of the Army would or could be devoted to the British war. Most of it was locked in a struggle with the rebels and would have to remain so. Almost the entire Navy, save its riverine forces, would be going into harm's way. Britannia's mighty fist, its Royal Navy, would do everything in its power to bring the war home to America.

Already in Europe, American shipping was desperately sailing for neutral ports. Those that had not had the good sense to depart British ports after Moelfre Bay had already been seized. The Navy could do little to protect American commerce on the seas when it found strained to the breaking point to defend American harbors. Memories of the outrages perpetrated by the Royal Navy on the ports and coastal towns of the North sent a chill down the spine of every American. Those memories were also a spur to the naval service to see that they did not happen again. This time, the game was not so completely in the Royal Navy's favor. But the chancelleries of Europe would have given the U.S. Navy only the longest of odds.

Certainly the Quay d'Orsay did not. What Napoleon III would not dare to do on his own, he would be glad to do now that the British led the way. The French ambassador, Count Edouard-Henri Mercier, delivered the emperor's declaration of war the day after the British announcement, citing truly ludicrous justifications. Seward almost laughed in his face. Stanton and Welles could only count the addition of the French fleet and especially its large Army in Mexico to the order of battle of their country's enemies.

The Russian alliance, when it became known, would serve to complicate British-French plans wonderfully. Forces that would have gone to North America would have to be diverted to bottling up the Russians again in the Baltic and Black seas. But this time, the cat was out of the bag. The presence of two Russian squadrons in American ports was proof the Russians were not about to repeat the errors of the Crimean War. The strong Russian squadron in New York was a vital addition to the protection of the port. For good reason that night Welles wrote in his diary, "God bless the Russians."[3]

Towering over them was Lincoln, who rallied the English language in its majestic cadences drawn from the Bible and Shakespeare to the defense of the nation. Men are moved by words and define themselves by words. While his secretaries of war and the Navy organized the nation's defenses, Lincoln gathered and arrayed his words for battle. He addressed a joint session of Congress and asked for a declaration of war against the British Empire in terms that riveted every member, Republican and Democrat alike. It was not a long speech, but expressed with a simple dignity, its elemental truth and directness had the members soaring. His words bound up all the hopes of the American democracy as the foundation stone, not only of the progress of the American people, but of all mankind. It was a speech for the ages, and men who had been with Lincoln since the beginning said it bested even his speech at the Cooper Union in Boston when he was seeking the nomination, the speech that had thrilled and moved his skeptical Eastern audience to set his feet on the road to the presidency. His words sang over the wires throughout the North and by ship across the seas to Europe and the Americas.[4]

A copy rapidly found its way to the tent of Robert E. Lee, who gave it his complete attention. The news of the British invasion had sparked a general celebration of deliverance across the South, but in his tent Lee read Lincoln's speech. The man whose heart had broken in the choice between Virginia and the United States clutched the paper in his hand and wept.[5]

And well he might, for the Union people were tinder into which a match had been thrown. Doubts, demoralization, political differences were being consumed in the fire of an anger that had stirred them to their depths. A foreign invader on American soil, especially in a red coat, come to support the rebellion destroyed all restraint. The people were uncoiling their strength. Where the draft had failed to extract men, now volunteers flooded recruiting stations. New York State and the city, particularly, answered the call. It was not only the Irish who had done a volte-face. Patricians like Theodore Roosevelt, Sr., who had stood above the war and bought substitutes, now presented themselves for duty. Roosevelt organized a new brigade and commanded it through the rest of the war. His veterans remember that he came to the recruiting station with his little boy Teddy in tow.[6]

OFFICE OF THE CENTRAL INFORMATION BUREAU, LAFAYETTE PARK, WASHINGTON, D.C., 12:05 AM, OCTOBER 2, 1863

Sharpe's office was deluged with reports that overwhelmed his order-of-battle analysts, even the imperturbable, tireless Wilmoth. At least they had had a good understanding of the British forces before the war. The difficult part now was trying to identify where the different regiments were showing up and to put the operational puzzle together. The problem was that it was far too early in the game to get any results. They had only the wildest rumors from a few militiamen who had fled Albany, and their reports reeked more of hysteria than careful observation. Sharpe had to admit that they had absolutely no idea what was going on in Maine. There were rumors that the Guards Brigade was in Albany and that thirty thousand men were coming by train from Montreal. That latter tale was absurd; the British didn't have thirty thousand men in all of their North American possessions. Even with the Volunteer Militia, they couldn't put that many men together for one operation. It was not long before Wilmoth was pulling a few rabbits out of hats. While everyone had been focused on agent reports, he found some useful information in the British *Gentleman's Magazine* on the strength of the imperial battalions sent to Canada, specifically a complete order of battle of the Guards Brigade. Sharpe shook his head, laughing to himself at how often open sources trumped the most carefully held secrets.[7]

But Sharpe needed time, and he needed a commander on the scene who understood the value of intelligence. He had been immensely relieved to find out that Hooker was commanding the new Army of the Hudson. There was no better friend of military intelligence, and he and Sharpe had parted on good terms when the former had been relieved as commander of the Army of the Potomac. Hooker and Lowe had also been on the best of terms. For those reasons, Sharpe had sent a company of Lowe's Balloon Corps to support the new field army.

In the seven weeks since he had assumed control of his beloved Balloon Corps, Lowe had worked miracles. Luckily, there had been six superb silk balloons and their gas-generating equipment in storage in the Washington Arsenal. Six more had been recently delivered. With Sharpe's support, Lowe had reassembled the military personnel he had worked with before and the civilian aeronauts who had flown the balloons for him. The latter were now commissioned officers in the new Balloon Corps flush with money, equipment, and personnel. He had organized the corps into six companies built around pairs of balloons, with gas generators, crews, and support staffs. Two or more companies formed a battalion. Sharpe had been very clear that these companies could be attached to various field armies as were Signal Corps personnel, but their organization and support were in the hands of the Balloon Corps, which reported to him. Lowe's confidence was now unbounded that he had a resolute patron in Sharpe. It did not hurt that Sharpe had an even more resolute patron in Lincoln.[8]

Sharpe also plucked Capt. John McEntee from Major General Meade's staff with the Army of the Potomac. McEntee had been one of Sharpe's deputies when he ran the Army's Bureau of Military Information as well as a fellow native of Kingston. He would set up a similar bureau on Hooker's new staff. With him Sharpe sent an able lieutenant and a half dozen order-of-battle analysts, all recently pushed through the CIB's new school in Georgetown. The Signal Corps had howled when Sharpe had raided its own Georgetown "camp of instruction" for bright young men. He had an ulterior motive as well, to acquire trained signalmen and cipher clerks.[9]

Meade would loudly protest the loss of McEntee, but he was getting a lot of practice at that. Poor George Meade. His war after Gettysburg had been far from satisfying. Lee had led him in a fruitless dance of maneuver across Northern Virginia, running out the clock on the last of the year's campaigning season. Now his Army of the Potomac would suffer the death of a thousand cuts, supplying forces for the crises that were busting out all over the place. First the division from VI Corps had been sent to Buffalo, the three thousand Maine men had been detached, and then XI and XII Corps had been started north to Albany—a day late and a dollar short, to be sure, but still lost to Meade's command. Now the rest of John Sedgwick's VI Corps was heading north to save Portland. VI Corps was the core of the Army now after Gettysburg and Big John Sedgwick Meade's most reliable commander; his corps had been held in reserve and hardly engaged at all. Every other corps, except XII Corps, had been badly cut up and the finest combat commanders killed or wounded at Gettysburg. Reynolds of I Corps fell on the first day, Sickles of III Corps lost a leg on the second day, and the day after Hancock of II Corps had been wounded severely in the thigh. Meade would have to go on the defensive and hope he could find a position as good as Gettysburg's hills and ridges, for "Bobby Lee" could smell opportunity better than any man alive and would come sniffing right soon around his flanks.

Sharpe considered going up to New York himself to see that Hooker's intelligence operation was put in order and to organize his other collection assets more tightly, but the telegram from Major Cline had set him on edge. Even more had been the roundabout way it had come because every telegraph line to the Midwest had gone dead over the last two days. Cline's message was already almost four days old. If the Copperheads had succeeded in freeing the Confederate prisoners in Indianapolis, that could explain a lot, he thought.

It was worse than he realized. Washington had been isolated for the last two days from quick communication with the Midwest — as the Copperheads and their Confederate and British advisers had planned. The capital was already reeling from the British invasion of New York and Maine and had barely steadied itself through the examples of Lincoln, Stanton, and Welles. Had the capital known that Ohio, Indiana, and Illinois had been engulfed in revolt, panic might have overwhelmed even these men's courage.

Thousands of armed Copperheads had seemingly sprung from the earth, all too often led by Southern officers. Their agents in the telegraph offices and railroads had sabotaged communications thoroughly. Federal officials and Loyalists had been arrested, and more than a few had been killed. Larger numbers had swarmed soldiers guarding warehouses and railroads. Key railroads and river crossings had been seized. Worst of all had been the assault on the federal prisoner of war camps. Camp Douglas in Chicago, the largest of them all, had fallen. Seven thousand Confederate prisoners had been freed, armed, and organized in the heart of the largest and most important city of the Midwest. As Lincoln delivered his speech before Congress, unknown to Washington, the Stars and Bars flew over Chicago, snapping in the cold wind that howled down from Canada across broad Lake Michigan. It could have been far worse without men like Major Cline and Hooker's Horse Marines scotching the attack on Camp Morton.

THE BORDER CROSSING, BROWNSVILLE, TEXAS, 2:30 PM, OCTOBER 4, 1863

The French knew how to stage a military parade, and for their crossing of the border between Mexico and Texas at Brownsville they pulled out all the stops. To the light air of a cavalry march, Maj. Gen. François Achille Bazaine, commander of French forces in Mexico, led a regiment of Chasseurs d'Afrique across the border into Brownsville from Matamoros. The forced cheers of the sullen Mexicans in Matamoros were in contrast to the wild cheers of the Texans as the gaudy French Colonial Cavalry clattered through the streets.[10]

The French occupation of Mexico had arisen out of a French-British-Spanish intervention to collect debts owed to their nationals. When the British and Spanish left, the French stayed. Napoleon III had designs on the country now that the Monroe Doctrine had been suspended by the distraction of the Civil War. He was in the process of installing an Austrian duke as a figurehead emperor, backed up by fifty thousand French troops. Now this advance guard of twenty thousand troops was marching into Texas in their baggy red trousers, red caps, and dark blue coats. Their bayonets sparkled in the bright sun.[11]

Although the French jackal would not lead in this war, it would go where the British lion would not. The British had been faced with a conundrum in their decision to go to war with the Union, one they had mulled over as early as the Trent Affair two years before. Did war with the United States automatically mean recognition of and alliance with the Confederacy? Even then slavery had been so odious that the British had studiously decided to avoid any formal military cooperation, much less recognition and alliance. In two years slavery had not become any less odious, and the British had decided that they would separate the two issues officially. Napoleon had seen no necessity for such a distinction and followed his declaration of war with immediate recognition of the Confederacy, something he had not bothered to discuss with London. Lord Russell astutely understood that it would be impossible to come up with a formula on slavery "which the southerners would agree to, and the people of England approve of. The French Government are more free from the shackles of principle and of right and wrong on these matters . . . than we are."[12]

Napoleon was playing for different stakes and was well aware that should the Union triumph against the Confederacy, it would surely turn its wrath on the French presumption to carve out a colony in North America. A Union defeat then was the guarantee of a continued French free hand in Mexico. Jefferson Davis and the Confederate Congress were all too happy to confirm that guarantee as the price of recognition and alliance. They had to swallow hard because in January of that same year, Davis had to chastise severely the French consuls in Richmond and Galveston for, in the words of the Austrian ambassador in Washington, "imprudent ardor to foment a revolution in Texas against Mr. Jefferson Davis" in hopes of creating a buffer state under French protection. The French were being more than prudent. There had been enough evidence before the war of a decided Southern interest in annexing more of Mexico. That interest had not disappeared. Both sides had smiled and pretended that each would not immediately repudiate the agreement when the time was right.[13]

Bazaine was a product of colonial war. He had gained renown in fighting in North Africa, where he had become a colonel of the Foreign Legion, and as had Williams in Canada, he had gained fame in the Crimean War. In Mexico he had handled a division with great skill, defeating a Mexican army and compelling the surrender of Puebla in May, which opened the way to Mexico City for the French Expeditionary Army. This French general was nobody's fool; he could put the Union's political generals to shame. He was aware of France's ambitions in this region and made sure they supported his own. Much glory would accrue to the French general who liberated New Orleans.

He would not have to rely only on the troops he was bringing from Mexico. A strong French fleet was at this moment sailing toward Galveston to break the blockade and disembark strong reinforcements. The fleet then would support his attack on the first city of the South. The emperor had been known to say privately that his uncle's sale of that city and the immense territory it governed had been a colossal mistake. It had occurred to Bazaine that once the city was again in French hands, the emperor would be loath to give it up. The future was pregnant with such opportunities.[14]

SOUTH ATLANTIC BLOCKADING SQUADRON, CHARLESTON HARBOR, SOUTH CAROLINA, 11:00 AM, OCTOBER 5, 1863

Ever since his son had arrived with the ship that brought the news of war, Rear Adm. John Dahlgren had been looking over him in unguarded moments. He was searching to see if the gallant lad who had gone off to war early last year, still a teenager, still showed some spirit, or if losing a leg had also killed something in him. Lincoln had been a good friend in writing him of Ulric's recovery.[15] It had been an ongoing agony for the father to know that he had two sons hovering near death in Washington—Ullie wounded at Gettysburg and Charlie wracked with fever from Vicksburg. Dahlgren had written,

> The Sabbath arrives, and with it the brother who, wasted by the malaria and summer sun of the Mississippi Valley, had had just sufficient strength to crawl homeward for care and cure under his father's roof. Both are but wrecks of the active, care-free lads who went out from their home and offered their mite to the great cause. . . . In retrospect there is nothing to regret.[16]

He had known no more joy than seeing Ullie waving to him from the dispatch boat that had brought him to the flagship. In the next few hectic days his gaze would linger on Ullie as he hobbled on his crutches across the deck or struggled awkwardly to learn to walk with his new cork leg. Dahlgren's stern Swedish heritage kept him from showing the emotions that pulsed through him as he remembered the lithe, leopard-like grace of the splendid horseman and dancer who had swept away the heart of every girl in Washington. He could see that same intensity in Ullie that had made him excel at everything he had attempted. He was the same as his little boy, who would fall down and get right back up. The boy had mastered horses, dancing, and the saber. What was the cork leg then? Twenty years old and already a hero and a full colonel.

The day after he arrived, his father watched Ullie intently study-ing the gun drill of the crew, especially the Marines manning the 5.1-inch Dahlgren rifle on the spar deck. He remembered little Ullie at the Navy Yard, not yet ten years old, watching the gun drill his father had modi-fied for his new guns with just as much intensity. The sailors had thought him a lucky mascot and were glad to have him around. When his father was not around, they had let him help serve the gun in practice. Initially, the Marines had been nervous about having an Army colonel—a Navy captain equivalent—watching so closely, especially the admiral's son and a "peg leg" to boot, but he seemed to know his way around the guns as well as any man and better than some. After a while, the earnest and engaging young man became a favorite of the Marines.

It was only a glance here and there the admiral could spare. It had not been lost on him that he was most assuredly going to be the first American naval officer to command a full fleet action. Heretofore, the U.S. Navy's battle record had been mostly in single ship-to-ship combat or small contingents at most. Oliver Hazard Perry had come closest in 1813 on the Great Lakes, but what Dahlgren faced would dwarf that combat.

His South Atlantic Blockading Squadron numbered seventy-eight vessels but could not have resembled Admiral Milne's force assembled at Bermuda less. As the name of Dahlgren's force indicated, it was de-signed to blockade the shallow coasts and harbors of the South. Milne's command was designed to fight great fleet actions on the high seas. Of Dahlgren's almost four score ships, only four were traditional, wooden, purpose-built warships—one frigate and three sloops. Nine more ships were the new ironclads—the broadside ship *New Ironsides* and all eight of the *Passaic* class single-turreted monitors. There were another ten gun-boats. The rest were small screw or side-wheel steam ships, small sailing ships with mortars, or supply ships, and none were more than a thousand tons (see Appendix B). Secretary Welles had promised him four new monitors when they were completed within two months. Dahlgren concluded that it might as well be a year for all the good they would do him. He could smell war on the wind from Bermuda.[17]

Of all his ships, only twenty were off Charleston when he received the news of war with Britain on September 28. The rest of his ships were covering the numerous small islands, river mouths, and islets along the coasts of South Carolina and Georgia or were at the squadron's main forward operating base a hundred miles to the south at Port Royal.[18] A few small, fast ships prowled the waters from Bermuda and Nassau for blockade-runners.

Dahlgren immediately ordered the assembly of his squadron off Charleston. The repair crews at Port Royal were ordered to bend every effort to get the three *Passaic* class monitors there in the repair yard back to sea and on the way to Charleston. Welles had warned him that the British might make an attempt to break the blockade at Charleston or Wilmington. Dahlgren had no doubt it would be Charleston even if Wilmington was a more active and successful port for blockade-runners. The war had started here, and here is where the Navy kept its heavy punchers. He was ordered to give battle and under no circumstances abandon his station. It was obvious that he could not meet the Royal Navy in deep water. His slow monitors would be at the mercy of the faster-sailing British ships, and his purpose-built frigates and sloops and gunboats would be overwhelmed by the firepower of ships of the line. He concluded that the advantage would lie in forcing the British to operate in the shallows, where their deep-draft ships would be at a disadvantage. He must have warning that the British were coming, and to ensure that, he scattered his lighter, fast ships across the path the Royal Navy would have to take from Bermuda. He wondered what measures the commanders of the North Atlantic Blockading Squadron off Wilmington and the forces in Hampton Roads based at Norfolk would be taking.

Admiral Milne had given serious thought to those questions as well. Around him from the bridge of his flagship, HMS *Nile*, he could see the largest and infinitely more powerful fleet Britain had sent into battle since Trafalgar. The four huge ironclads surged ahead, the sharp spearhead of the fleet, followed by ten ships of the line and fifteen frigates, sloops, and corvettes. Behind them trailed a flotilla of supply ships. For their common objective along the South Carolina coast another squadron of four ships of the line and eight smaller ships had just departed the main force for its rendezvous with the transports carrying the four thousand men of the West Indian garrison of Barbados and the other islands.[19]

Milne was thinking several moves ahead, which is why his thoughts turned to the enemy's naval forces at Wilmington and Hampton Roads. Beyond them was the broad mouth of the Chesapeake, leading to the enemy's capital, which was captured and burned in a similar foray by his predecessors in 1814. To repeat the feat within forty-nine years would surely make the Americans choke on their insufferable pride. He would iron the smile right off their faces.

First he would have to deal with Dahlgren's force at Charleston. And of that force, he was fully apprised of its numbers, strengths, and weaknesses. Except for the monitors, Dahlgren had few ships that could match any of his, certainly not his ships of the line. Even the monitors, he thought, were overrated. His captains, on port visits to the Northern states and among their forces at sea, had heard the same complaints — monitor duty was unpopular, the conditions were brutal, and, of course, there was no opportunity for prize money, something the British naval officer could fully understand. But he did not underestimate John Dahlgren. The American's reputation stood very high in the Royal Navy for developing his remarkable series of guns. Already he was called the "father of American naval ordnance." Milne, however, chose to emphasize the fact that Dahlgren had had only eight years at sea and never commanded anything of this size or complexity. Even with the vaunted monitors he had not been able to subdue the defenses of Charleston Harbor. Fort Sumter, though beaten into a rubble pile, still stood defiant, as did the forts on the two opposing shores of the harbor.

WEST POINT FOUNDRY, COLD SPRING, NEW YORK, 9:20 AM, OCTOBER 5, 1863

The "deep-breathing furnaces, and the sullen, monotonous pulsations of trip hammers" of the great cannon West Point Foundry at Cold Spring, were much on their minds of two men. This greatest iron foundry in the world was producing hundreds of the U.S. Army's splendidly accurate Parrot rifled cannons a year and close to a million shells. As accurate as the British Armstrong but more reliable given its muzzle-loading design, this gun was an insurmountable advantage for the Union that the Confederates could only lag behind. They could only acquire such guns through capture or by importation of a very few British Whitworth rifled cannon, a poor substitute for Vulcan's workshop on the Hudson.[20]

Lincoln himself had toured the huge facility early in 1862, walking through the mud as delighted with the raw power of the technological wonder as any boy at the circus.

> Lincoln watched 100-pounder and 200-pounder Parrott rifles hurl their heavy shells thousands of yards through a gap in the highlands to the precipitous banks of "Crows Nest," while the deep clamor of gunfire echoed back from the hills like the roar of a great battle. Afterwards, he tramped delightedly about the plant, regardless of mud and rain. Raised a few inches from the ground on sleepers were bars of iron four inches square and sixty feet long, ready to be heated red-hot and coiled around mandrels by machinery. Near by, Lincoln saw these coiled bars welded by a great trip hammer, turned down, re-heated and shrunk onto guns — forming the bands which were the trademark of the Parrotts. His face felt the heat and dazzle of the foundry where the guns were cast. He looked on as they were bored, rifled, turned and polished. And in another building he watched workmen turn out Parrott shells, distinguished by the brass expanding ring for taking the rifle grooves. Before Lincoln left Cold Spring, he had had seen about all there was to see in the making of rifled cannon.

Three days after Lincoln left, the first batch of guns was shipped to Major General McClellan, who was fighting on the approaches to Richmond. But it was not the great pieces that Lincoln saw at the testing range that armed so many of the field batteries of the Union field armies. It was the 10- and 20-pounder medium and heavy field guns. The latter, posted on Little Round Top, had cut long, gory furrows through the ranks of the Virginians and North Carolinians who had marched to glory and slaughter in Pickett's Charge at Gettysburg. One shot alone brought down almost fifty men.[21]

This beating fiery heart of the Union war effort was much on the minds of two men as Albany's funeral pyre sent its smoke down the

Hudson River Valley. British raiding parties steaming down the Hudson or striking nearby cities were scorching the ability of the Union to make war. Barely ten miles to the north of Albany, Schenectady, a growing industrial city of ten thousand, was the first to feel the enemy's hand. British troops marched into the city to destroy the Schenectady Locomotive Works, which had already produced eighty-four superb locomotives for the federal government's war effort. Thirty miles south of Albany, the thriving river port of Hudson was the next target because of the Hudson Iron Company's ironworks. It was also the country's major inland refining and distribution center for whale oil. All it took was one overeager Canadian militiaman to throw a torch into one of the warehouses filled to the ceiling with refined oil. The fire exploded the building, sending flaming jets of whale oil through the air and flooding down streets. Its magnificent opera house was quickly wreathed in flames as the liquid fire licked up the walls. Soon the entire town was ablaze, and a huge pall of black, greasy smoke floated down the valley.[22]

Maj. Gen. Lord Paulet's orders, courtesy of Wolseley, had included a red-line paragraph to send a raiding party downriver, if practicable, to destroy the foundry at Cold Spring. With Watervliet Arsenal a gutted ruin, Paulet's appetite had been whetted. A guards' officer did not normally think in terms of destroying the enemy's industrial base, but he did often think of fame. And Wolseley had spent a great deal of time exciting Paulet's ambition by explaining how well this stroke would be received in England, where the idea of the world's greatest foundry being in America did not sit well at all.

The other man with the foundry on his mind was Lincoln. He vividly remembered the heat of the blast furnaces on his face and the smell of metal as it was cut and shaped by the great lathes and hammers. The place was as alive to him as a beating heart. He knew the Union could lose whole armies before it lost the foundry. He personally went to the War Department Telegraph Office and wired Hooker to protect it if he did nothing else.

Hooker did not need to be told twice. For all his defeat at Chancellorsville, Joseph Hooker was a remarkably good soldier. As a corps commander he had been one of the best the Union had produced. As an Army commander he had introduced innovative reforms that revitalized the Army of the Potomac and gave it the organization with which it had whipped Lee at Gettysburg. Hooker was that rare transformational man who could see the future and summon it to the present. He had been Sharpe's patron and the godfather of the first real professionalization of intelligence. Thus, he saw at an instant how vital the foundry was to the Union. The two corps that formed the striking power of his new Army of the Hudson would not arrive soon enough.

The aide had to fight his way through the crowds of Irishmen at Meagher's recruiting offices to present Hooker's instructions to report to him at once. Meagher was ushered immediately through the headquarters' hive of activity into Hooker's presence. The big, blond general rose and walked across the room, extending his hand to Meagher. "Tom, you don't know how glad I am to have a Third Corps man I trust here. Congratulations on the promotion and the recruiting. Are you trying to bring the old corps back up to strength all by yourself?"

"Yes, if it includes my old brigade. I must have the Irish Brigade. I must bring it back to life."

"Well, I doubt Lincoln will deny you anything with all the thousands you have recruited in so few days. But the President needs a bold man now, Tom, and I cannot think of a bolder man than 'Meagher of the Sword.' Come, let's look at the map." His finger touched down on Cold Spring just across the river from the U.S. Military Academy at West Point. "This is the situation, Tom. I have a direct presidential order to save the foundry. Without it, we would be hard pressed to stay in the fight. My two corps have not arrived, and neither has recovered from the Gettysburg bloodletting; together they might make one full-strength corps."[23]

He paused briefly, his thoughts running along a different path. "The Germans of XI Corps, you know, the 'Damned Dutch,' they ran at Chancellorsville and Gettysburg. Well, Tom, I ran at Chancellorsville, too, in a way. I ran away from command. I just lost faith in Joe Hooker. At least they had a better excuse. It's a rare soldier who will not flinch when his flank is turned, and the enemy is shooting you in the back." He looked out the window silently for a few moments, his thoughts lingering over that stricken field just over the Rappahannock in distant Virginia. His reverie broke, and his blue eyes were all business. "Well, Tom, both the Damned Dutch and I have a second chance."

Meagher's heart had been touched that his old commander would honor him with this confidence so straight from the heart. From his own heart, he said, "And well I should know it, General. I, who nearly swung on the Queen's gallows and was sent to rot in the desolation of western Australia, was rescued by America, which gave me back my life and my hope. This is the land of second chances, and third and fourth, and is always generous to those who don't quit. I am a living testament to that." He paused, "And so will you, General, you and the Damned Dutch."

Hooker half smiled to himself, buoyed by the Irishman's pluck. "Well, back to the point. I must keep the regiments I have in the city or the people will panic. The smoke from Albany has terrified them, and they did not need much after John Bull sailed into the Upper Bay ten days ago. How many veterans can you assemble among your recruits? Just veterans."

"At the very most, several hundred men I would trust with arms."

"Draw arms, equipment, and uniforms for them immediately. I will write out the order now and arrange for the transports to take you there. Secure the foundry until I can send a brigade up there. Leave tonight with the men you can ready. 'It is better to be at the right place with ten men than absent with ten thousand.' I always thought Tamerlane had a perfect sense of these things.[24]

"And Tom, think. If you are lucky, the redcoats will come."

HEADQUARTERS, ARMY OF NORTHERN VIRGINIA, ORANGE COURT HOUSE, VIRGINIA, 3:40 PM, OCTOBER 5, 1863

Robert E. Lee's style of military intelligence was old-fashioned in that like George Washington, he was his own intelligence chief. Over time, it was no match for Sharpe's superior organization and resources, but it worked when it had to. This was one of those times.

Gettysburg had sorely tried not only the strength of his Army but its faith in itself. Twinned with the loss of Vicksburg, the South had lost almost sixty thousand men in those few days in July. The progress of defeat had seemed inexorable until Providence had set the British and the Yankees at each other's throats. Now victory, so seemingly perched on the enemy's shoulder, was offering her laurels again to the Confederacy, and Lee had leapt to grab them.

His intelligence sources told him accurately of the reinforcements stripped from Meade's army and sent north to stem the British tide. That left Meade with barely sixty thousand men. Even with Longstreet's corps at Chattanooga, Lee numbered his troops at fifty-three thousand, near parity. Given that he had always been heavily outnumbered, parity was a sheer, undreamed of advantage. He marched.[25]

12.

Cold Spring and Crossing the Bar

COLD SPRING, NEW YORK, 2:02 PM, OCTOBER 6, 1863
Meagher had reached Cold Spring early that afternoon. Upriver, the smoke from burning boats and towns was hanging over the Hudson Valley. Major General Paulet had followed Wolseley's advice and ravaged his way south. At Albany and other river towns he had seized ships to carry raiding parties down the river to harry and panic the Americans. He had succeeded in sending waves of refugees from the river towns and farms south toward the city and into the countryside.[1]

Meagher and his scratch command of barely two hundred men had gone upriver in a commandeered steamboat past hordes of craft coming south, their decks filled with refugees. The captain had refused to take them until Meagher had stuck his pistol in the man's mouth and said, "I'm not joking, sir," as he cocked the piece. The captain suddenly gushed cooperation and hastened the transfer of Meagher's men aboard. A strange lot they were, too. Meagher had been lucky to find two hundred veterans among his horde of Irish volunteers. Half were from his old Irish Brigade, and most had been invalided out for wounds. There were too many limping legs and favored arms, but they were volunteers, and they wore their kit and handled their rifles as if it were second nature to them. He had seen more than one pair of eyes glow as man after man grasped the Springfield muskets fresh from the armory. Mc-Carter had arrived on the morning train. Meagher had promoted him sergeant major on the spot to pick the sergeants and corporals and whip them into the semblance of a unit in the few hours they had. Finding the uniforms had been impossible, all except the caps with the brass infantry bugle. The women had come to the rescue with red, white, and blue bunting armbands. That and the oath he administered would satisfy the laws of war that they were lawful combatants.[2]

At the last moment, as the men lined the railings while the crew threw off the lines and the ship began to edge away from the dock, a carriage clattered up the dock with a young woman carrying a green flag on a staff. It was Libby, Meagher's beautiful, young wife, her red hair bright around the edges of her bonnet. She alighted from the carriage and, carrying the flag, ran up to the ship. "Oh, Tom, Tom!" she cried out to the crowd on the railing. "Do not forget the flag, Tom!" It was the color of the 69th New York, one of the regiments of the Irish Brigade, and presented to him by the survivors when he had resigned. It had stood in the corner of his study ever since, ragged and stained with dust and blood, but its emerald green field and golden harp still were bright.

The men on the deck stirred at the sight, which was more than feminine gallantry but instantly evoked images of Ireland itself anthropomorphized in this young woman. Almost as if commanded by this goddess of myth, the ship edged back to the dock and the gangway was lowered. As it touched the dock, Meagher hurried down and took his wife into his arms. The kiss was long and passionate as the men cheered Meagher of the Sword and his goddess, lady of Erin. Then, flag in hand, he bounded up the gangway.[3]

The kiss was still sweet on his lips as the ship docked at Cold Spring and was challenged immediately by young men in cadet gray. The commandant of the U.S. Military Academy across the river had sent over a hundred of his cadets to guard the foundry under the command of one of their officer instructors. Meagher was pleased to see that that they had not wasted their time but had trundled a half dozen of the 10-pounder Parrot guns from the foundry down to defend the dock with the aid of many of the foundry's fourteen hundred workers. The officer had organized his cadets into gun teams, and they seemed to know their way around the pieces, which had been admirably hidden from direct view.[4]

Meagher barely had time to inspect the ad hoc defense when a cadet came racing down the street on long legs, his cap lost and blond hair whipping behind him, and clutching a telescope in his hand. He stopped in front of his officer and then recognized Meagher's major general's stars in a moment of confusion. He blurted out, "They're coming. I ran down from the church steeple, sir, where you stationed me to look. There's an armed boat with red-coated men aboard coming down the river."

Meagher asked, "How long, boy, before they get here?"

"Sir, twenty minutes at most."
In eighteen minutes the ship steamed up to the dock. Meagher
peered, half hidden, through a window next to the battery screened by a
wall of empty barrels. Two Armstrong field pieces were mounted on the
deck, which was crowded with several companies of British troops. He
was surprised to see with what confidence they came right up to the
dock, confidence borne of meeting little or no resistance as they fired
their way down the Hudson Valley. He was even more surprised to recognize the big men whose uniforms bore the facings of the Scots Fusilier
Guards. Others, not so uniformly robust and big, had different facings
and somehow did not move with the easy assurance of the guards. Canadian militia, no doubt. Canister would make no such distinction, but the
Queen would feel the loss of her own guardsmen more deeply than the
colonials would. Well, he thought, it was time the world's most famous
widow had something else to mourn.[5]

The ship bumped up against the dock. Shrill voices of the NCOs
echoed up the street as the men began double-timing down the gangplank. They began to fan out over the docks when Meagher gave the
command to fire. The barrels masking the guns were knocked over and
canister — tin cans filled with hundreds of bullet-sized lead balls — scythed
into the men rushing over the docks, crowding down the gangplank,
packing the decks, and clustering around the deck-mounted Armstrongs.
Rifle fire from his hidden riflemen cut down the men who had made it to
the street. The cadets leapt to the guns, as they had in their artillery training, to swab out the barrels and ram home new powder bags and canis-
ters. Again they fired.

"Cease fire!" Meagher shouted to give the smoke a chance to clear.
The ship was a charnel house, riddled and splintered, with its decks and
gangplank piled with the dead and wounded. The pilothouse was a wreck
as well. "Charge!" His Irishmen sprang from cover with a howl as he ran
down from the battery to join them and dashed across the dock to the
ship. The enemy had been so stunned that hardly a shot was fired as
Meagher's men climbed over the bodies on the gangplank to swarm over
the ship.[6]

USS *PHILADELPHIA*, INSIDE THE BAR, CHARLESTON HARBOR, SOUTH CAROLINA, 12:05 PM, OCTOBER 7, 1863

The USS *Flambeau* raced toward Charleston like a stormy petrel, the famous sea bird that races ahead of an ocean storm. She was one of the

picket ships that Admiral Dahlgren had thrown out to sea to warn of the British approach. Dahlgren dreaded this moment. His orders to maintain the blockade against any attempt to break it had presented him with a deadly dilemma. He dared not sally out of the bar to meet the British, yet to remain inside the bar would mean that he in turn would be blockaded. That would end in inevitable surrender as coal and supplies ran out. He had had the foresight to intercept every coal and supply ship bound for the main operating base at Port Royal and keep them with him off Charleston. He had ordered the evacuation of as much of the stores at Port Royal as possible. At the same time the repair crews were working around the clock. He needed every fighting ship at Charleston. Everything that could not be repaired or carried off was to be destroyed.

Dahlgren had another reason as well for not abandoning his station off Charleston — the eight thousand troops under the command of Major General Gilmore who had been reducing the harbor forts on Morris Island. There were also four thousand of the Army's troops garrisoning the Navy's forward operating base at Port Royal. The Navy would never survive the shame of abandoning the Army.

As if Dahlgren had not worries enough, the need to protect the Navy's most secret experiment also weighed heavily on his mind. He had been testing two small submersibles designed to remove underwater obstacles and to plant torpedoes (mines). These ungainly beasts could never be allowed to fall into British hands. He had orders to sink them if necessary in the deepest possible water. It occurred to him that the boats were not entirely liabilities. He had given much thought to the use of submersibles after having had the Navy's first submersible, the *Alligator*, repaired at the Navy Yard when he was superintendent, and he had requested the construction of several improved models. Now, more than a year later, he had been given delivery of two such boats for trials in the harbor of Charleston. He ordered that the submersible tender and the two boats accompany his flagship. His interest in submersibles had become even more acute two days earlier when the Confederate semi-submersible, CSS *David*, had attacked *New Ironsides* with a torpedo. The explosion had rocked the ship, which had been protected by its thick iron hull and armor casemate. Although the *David* had escaped, his men had fished two prisoners out of the water who had prematurely abandoned ship. They had detailed plans of the boat in their pockets.[7]

Only if the British came after him through the bar did he stand a chance of defeating them, Dahlgren thought. Even then, they only had to

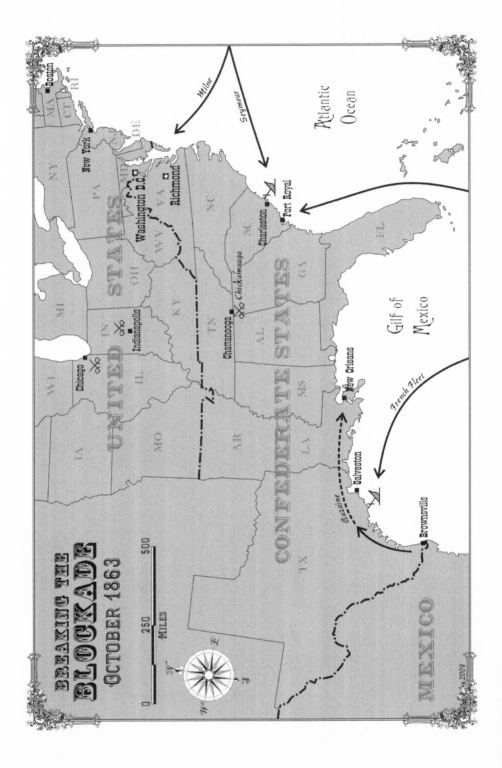

BREAKING THE BLOCKADE
OCTOBER 1863

MILES
0   250   500

MEXICO

UNITED STATES

CONFEDERATE STATES

Atlantic Ocean

Gulf of Mexico

Boston
New York
Chicago
Indianapolis
Washington D.C.
Richmond
Chattanooga
Chickamauga
Charleston
Port Royal
New Orleans
Galveston
Brownsville

Milne
Seymour
French Fleet
Bazaine

MA
CT
RI
NY
PA
MI
WI
IA
MO
IL
IN
OH
WV
VA
KY
TN
AR
NC
SC
GA
AL
MS
LA
TX
FL
DE

2002

retreat, stand off outside the bar, wait, and starve him out. Defeat would only be delayed. Only a decisive defeat of the British and their retreat could save him, and that, given the huge force Milne had assembled at Bermuda, was impossible. For a man whose Navy life had been a continuous quest for glory, the logic of this conclusion was bitter beyond belief. He could only redeem the coming disaster by following the order of Captain James Lawrence of the ill-fated USS *Chesapeake* in its battle with the HMS *Shannon* in 1813—"Fight her till she sinks!"[8]

Dahlgren knew that a large number of ships had arrived to reinforce Milne at Bermuda but not exactly how many and what types (see Appendix B). All he had to go on was a London *Times* article of July that listed the ships of the Channel Squadron.[9] That had arrived courtesy of Brigadier General Sharpe, someone Lincoln had mentioned in his letter as doing important work in organizing information about the rebels. Now it seemed the good general was throwing a wider net, something Dahlgren was thankful for. He desperately wished he knew how many and which of the huge Channel Fleet's four ironclad screw frigates Milne was sending against him. There wasn't an officer in the fleet who had not heard of the leviathans HMS *Warrior* and *Black Prince,* which were more than twice as large as his largest ship, the USS *New Ironsides.* The *Defence* class *Resistance* and *Defence* were both half again as large as the American ship.[10] Though she was considerably smaller, she packed a greater punch than the British ships. She was armed with sixteen guns, fourteen of which were XI-inch Dahlgrens and completely outclassed the armament of the British ships. The American gun carriages and recoil systems were also far more efficient than those of the British models. Her armor was *Warrior's* match as well. The British ships, however, had the speed advantage, able to move twice as fast as *New Ironsides's* puny six knots.

The combat experience of the *New Ironsides's* crew and those of the monitors would be a heavy weight in the scales of battle. Despite scores of hits from heavy Confederate ordnance, the *New Ironsides* emerged unscathed. The monitors' combat experience against the harbor forts of Charleston had led to the introduction of a sheet metal inner sheathing to the turrets to prevent injuries to the crew from exploding rivets propelled by shot striking the outer surface.

Their twenty-foot-diameter turrets, with ten inches of armor in one-inch molded plates, were invulnerable to any ship-mounted guns in the world. Their hull armor was five inches, a half inch thicker than the *New Ironsides* and *Warrior* class, but the low freeboard meant most of the hull would be under water. Deck armor was only an inch, thus requiring the expedient remedy of a layer of sandbags. Designs of the *Passaic* class had called for twin XV-inch Dahlgrens, but production lags forced them to substitute one XI-inch.[11] The turret was powered by its own small engine and could rotate 360 degrees in thirty seconds. Four iron beams in the deck served as slides for the gun carriages. "The slides would allow the guns to recoil a maximum of 6 feet, while the friction mechanisms could reduce the recoil to as little as two." The carriages rested on brass rollers, so that large crews were not needed to run the guns out. Oval-shaped, armored gun ports swung open to allow the guns to fire and then were shut as soon as the guns discharged. Because the guns were muzzle-loaders, the long rammers had to be manipulated through the open gun ports. At such times, the turret would be turned away from the enemy, loaded, then turned again toward the enemy, and re-aimed. [12]

This necessity was the greatest drag on the guns' speed of fire, a problem the broadside ironclad did not suffer. The XV-inch gun in the monitor's turret took an average of six minutes to fire, which could sometimes be reduced to a minimum of three. The XI-inch gun's speed was about half that average. The broadside-fired Dahlgrens were another story entirely. The IX-inch could be fired every forty seconds, and the XI-inch every 1.74 minutes for about an hour. Comparing monitor and broadside ships, it was a trade-off between invulnerability and rate of fire.[13]

There was no trade-off in punch. The XV-, XI-, and IX-inch Dahlgren shells with explosive charges weighed 350, 136, and 72.5 pounds, respectively. Their shot was even heavier, weighing in at 400, 169, and 80 pounds. The largest British shot, on the other hand, were the 110-pounder Armstrongs and the standard 68-pounder. Most British guns remained the venerable 32-pounders. Unlike the Armstrongs, the entire Dahlgren line was a byword in safety and reliability. The captain of the sloop the USS *Brooklyn* believed his IX-inchers to be well-nigh perfect and stated that "the men stand around them and fight them with as much confidence as they drink their grog." Unlike most British guns, the Dahlgrens had been designed to fire both shell and shot, giving them a powerful versatility. Because of the *Monitor-Virginia* standoff the year before, Dahlgren had rigorously tested his guns against armor plate. He found that they could easily stand to increase their powder charges by 50 to 100 percent in order to easily drive holes through iron plate and wood backing of thickness and composition similar to the British *Warrior* class — "4- to 4.5-inch thick iron faceplate, bolted to about twenty inches of wood,

sometimes with an inch-thick iron back plate, set up against a solid bank
of clay. In most cases, the Dahlgren shot penetrated clean through the
target and embedded itself deep into the clay bank, even with the target
angled steeply as fifteen degrees."[14]

The exploding shell was all the rage in naval ordnance, and no
gun delivered the destructive charge against wooden ships better than
the series of guns Dahlgren had devised. Against ironclads, the shells
were less effective. Dahlgren's guns were equally able to deliver solid
shot. Dahlgren had also taken to heart the error that had prevented the
original *Monitor*'s XI-inch Dahlgrens from punching holes right through
the CSS *Virginia*'s iron casemate. Navy policy had mandated that a powder charge only 50 percent of the maximum tested charge be used. Subsequent tests by Dahlgren showed that not only could his robust guns
fully stand the use of a 100 percent charge for long use but that they
would tear 5-inch armor apart. At the time, Dahlgren had been particularly incensed by the comment of the British First Lord of the Admiralty
that his guns were "idle against armor plate."

> During the Civil War two opposing schools of thought arose
> as to the best means of destroying armored warships. The "rack-
> ing" school held that projectiles should smash against the ship,
> distributing the force of the blow along the whole side and
> dislocating the armor. Once the armor had been shaken off,
> the vessel would be vulnerable to shell fire. The "punching"
> school held that the projectile should penetrate the armor, show-
> ering the ship's interior with deadly splinters in the process.
> . . . Dahlgren had concluded that racking was more effective
> against armored vessels than punching. Racking favored his
> low-velocity smoothbores over high-velocity rifled cannon.[15]

Dahlgren had had the satisfaction in June of seeing the monitor
USS *Weehawken* force the ironclad CSS *Atlanta* to strike its colors after
hitting it at three hundred yards with only a few XV-inch shot. One shot
alone dislodged the armor plate, sending a mass of iron and wooden
splinters into the casement battery, spilling all the shot in its racks, and
killing or wounding forty men.[16] The prize had been repaired at Port
Royal and was on the way to Philadelphia when Dahlgren intercepted
her. He asked for volunteers for a scratch crew and captain and found
himself with more than enough seamen and with a score of ambitious

lieutenants who could smell promotion in the air. Of them he chose Lt. B. J. Cromwell.[17]

As the *Philadelphia* was essentially unarmed, the admiral transferred his flag to the *New Ironsides*, from which he had commanded the previous attacks on Fort Sumter and the other harbor forts. His son, Ulric, had insisted on staying with the Navy rather than be sent ashore to join Gilmore's troops. "*New Ironsides* has been in action more than any ship of the squadron. Where else would I be, Papa?" he asked. He had already hit it off with the ship's captain, Stephen Clegg Rowan. An Irish immigrant, Rowan had joined the Navy in 1826 and fought "in the Seminole and Mexican Wars and had distinguished himself in the North Carolina sounds early in the Civil War." Under his command, the *New Ironsides* became the most feared of all Union ships to the defenders of Charleston.[18]

With *Flambeau*'s warning, a prearranged signal rocket from *New Ironsides* set the American squadron into motion. The lightest ships moved south to hug the shallow waters of the coast along Morris Island where the deeper draft British ships could not enter. These included eight steam gunboats, most of barely five hundred tons, and each armed with only a half dozen or so guns but sixteen of them Dahlgrens. He pulled his frigates and sloops inside the bar to join his ironclads.

The squadron had barely sorted out its formation when masts from at least a dozen ships dotted the horizon. Smoke plumes soon topped the masts as the engines were engaged. The inefficient engines gulped vast quantities of coal, and warships used sail as much as possible before switching to their engines for propulsion. Now that their objective was almost within sight, the British black gangs swung into work to stoke the fires that would give their ships that mobility and agility that sail could never match.

Finally, the last of the picket ships steamed through the bar to signal the flagship of the enemy's imminent approach. One by one the masts increased until fifteen and more could be counted. The captain of the picket ship came alongside to report that he had counted four ships of the line, the rest frigates and smaller ships. The captain shouted through his megaphone, "But leading them is the biggest ship I have ever seen in my life, Admiral. She's black from fore to aft. Must be the *Warrior*." There was a stir on Dahlgren's bridge among his staff, but the admiral's face did not show a flicker of change. Captain Rowan just smiled. He had fought his ship and had the utmost confidence in her and her crew in battle. He knew the *Warrior*'s captain, or for that matter, the captain of most Royal Navy ships at this time, could not say the same.

In fact, the picket ship's captain had been wrong. The great black ship he had seen was not the *Warrior* but her sister ship, the *Black Prince*, commanded by Capt. James Francis Ballard Wainwright. An able officer, Wainwright had commanded his ship for more than eighteen months and, as a mark of his ability, had served as second in command of the Channel Squadron.[19] The squadron sailing toward Charleston was only the smaller part of Milne's concentration at Bermuda. He shrewdly concluded that with the massing of the Royal Navys there was a clear indication that Charleston was its objective. The element of strategic surprise had never been realistic. He would have wagered to a certainty that the enemy knew the British were coming to Charleston. They already knew in Washington that the Royal Navy had seized Portland Harbor, though the town itself was still under siege. They were even more painfully aware that ships from Halifax were raiding the sea-lanes to New York and Boston. Their eyes were drawn north and south. It was toward the middle coast of the Atlantic seaboard that Milne was sailing with the bulk of his force—for Chesapeake Bay and the approaches to Washington and Baltimore. Admiral Cochrane had showed the way in 1814, inflicting great damage and even greater humiliation on the Americans by ravaging the shores of the great bay. Since they had seemed to have forgotten that lesson, he was determined to repeat it in such a forceful manner that it would linger and produce a national flinch whenever the thought of crossing the Royal Navy even occurred to them. Milne knew that the Union could never be physically destroyed, but it would give up the game if enough pain were inflicted. The second loss of their capital in less than fifty years would be a mighty weight dropped against the scales of their morale and will to fight.

He had wanted to trap the Americans inside the bar at Charleston and starve them out or destroy them when they came out to fight, but his plans had been countermanded by the Admiralty under intense pressure from the cabinet as well as the merchants of the great textile-manufacturing cities for immediate access to the millions of pounds of prime Southern cotton warehoused in Charleston. Factories were closing rapidly now in the second year of cotton starvation of Britain's mills. The government had also concluded that full employment was a prudent counter to any lingering sympathy for the Union among the mill workers. Beyond this was the cabinet's strategic calculation of the need to eliminate the Union's stranglehold on the South. He was ordered to immediately break the blockade by destroying the American South Atlantic Blockading Squadron. The strong squadron led by the *Black Prince* was more than enough to sweep away Dahlgren's little ships, overwhelm his frigate and sloops, and pound the monitors, admittedly at close range, into junk with their vastly superior weight of metal.

Milne had no choice. He would rely on his accurate long-range Armstrongs to do as much damage as they could before his ships closed with the Americans. The main effort would then be borne by the mainstay of the fleet, its 68-pounder gun. Milne had emphasized again and again to his captains who would go up against the American ironclads to close to within two hundred feet. The Admiralty reports indicated that only at that range would the 68-pounder be able to punch through American armor. It would be a matter of hard pounding at close range, something from which the Royal Navy had never shrunk.[20]

HMS *BLACK PRINCE*, OFF THE CHARLESTON BAR, SOUTH CAROLINA, 9:30 AM, OCTOBER 8, 1863

Rear Adm. Sir Michael Seymour, commanding the strike against Charleston, may have shared Milne's assurance that his force could make short work of the Americans inside the bar, but getting to grips with them was no easy matter. The normal prudence of a sailor and his experience in the blockade and bombardment of the main Russian naval base in the Baltic at Kronstadt during the Crimean War had confirmed to him the dangers of attacking through confined waters and into major estuaries. At the age of sixty-one and the son of an admiral, Seymour was about as experienced and competent a senior officer as the Royal Navy could produce. In the Kronstadt expedition, he had been second in command. After the war he had commanded the Royal Navy's East Indies Station and destroyed the Chinese fleet in June of 1857 during the Second Opium War and had taken Canton. The next year he had taken the forts on the Pei Ho River, forcing the Treaties of Tianjin on China. He was made Knight of the Bath the next year and sat as a member of Parliament for Devonport since 1859. When the Admiralty had sent Seymour out with the Channel Squadron reinforcement, Milne found him the natural and politic choice to command the Charleston expedition. Dahlgren would be facing a fighting man.

The Southern pilots Seymour had engaged at Bermuda had assured him that *Black Prince*, on which he kept his flag, and his other deep-draft ships of the line and frigates would be able at high tide to cross the bar off Charleston. The bar was a great ridge of mud pushed out to sea by the combined flow of the Ashley and Cooper rivers that swept around Charleston and emptied into the harbor, flowing around Fort Sumter before they met the sea. It was like a great undersea parapet behind which the Americans safely sheltered except when the tide ran in twice a day.

In the morning Seymour could see Dahlgren's ships across the bar. The large bulk of *New Ironsides* stood out in the middle of the American line. She was their toughest and largest ship, he had been informed, but less than half the size of *Black Prince*. Fore and aft of her floated four of the low-profile monitors, their black turrets more like bumps floating on the calm sea. In a parallel line behind them were the wooden warships, the frigates *Wabash* and *Powhatan*, and the three sloops, *Pawnee, Housatonic,* and *Canandaigua*. He was surprised to see so few ships — ten in all. There were supposed to be seven monitors, but the sharpest eye aloft could only count four: *Lehigh, Montauk, Nahant,* and *Catskill*. Seymour did not know that the remaining three monitors (*Patapsco, Weehawken,* and *Passaic*) had been sent to Port Royal for repairs.[21]

A few smaller ships hung in the distance to the south, hugging the shore off Morris Island. Seymour took these to be the support vessels of the American squadron trying to stay as far away from the action as possible. The small submersible tender with its two boats was not in evidence, hidden behind the American flagship as *Atlanta* hid behind the bulk of the *Wabash*.[22]

Seymour had to suppress a sense of elation that he had caught Dahlgren before he could concentrate his command. His Southern informants had provided detailed information on the strength and location of the almost eighty ships of the South Atlantic Blockading Squadron. Dahlgren's command numbered more than eight thousand men scattered in ships up and down the Georgia and South Carolina coasts and at Port Royal and a few other enclaves in offshore islands. Not more than twenty ships were actually at Charleston. Almost thirty were at Port Royal, under repair or coaling. The rest were spread up and down the coast.[23] What Seymour did not know was that Dahlgren had indeed been able to concentrate his sloops and frigates as well as the gunboats. The latter Seymour had mistaken for the support vehicles clinging to the shallow water of Stono Inlet off Morris Island. Their shallow drafts had allowed most to slip up the inlets and out of sight.[24]

Seymour's nineteen ships carried eight thousand men, or 13 percent of the strength of the Royal Navy, and mounted six hundred guns, the largest concentration of naval power the Royal Navy had committed to battle since Trafalgar. Seymour would have been even more encouraged had he known he outnumbered Dahlgren almost four to one in men. The American's crews numbered not even 2,200 men manning 114 guns, but 90 of these guns were Dahlgrens.[25]

The odds were with him, Seymour concluded. He paused to recite a passage from Thucydides. In the long days at sea as a midshipman, he had taken to heart the words of the Spartan king Archidamus II in the Peloponnesian War:

> In practice we always base our preparations against an enemy on the assumption that his plans are good. Indeed, it is right to rest our hope not on the belief in his blunders, but the soundness of our provisions. Nor ought we believe that there is much difference between man and man, but to think that superiority lies with him who is reared in the severest school.[26]

His thoughts drifted back to those golden days of his youth when ships were all powered by cooperation of God's wind and man's sail and did not trail a smudge of dirty coal smoke. He also summoned another comment memorized in his younger days, an American quote at that. It was from their Adm. Stephen Decatur on his observation of one of the first steam engines to power a ship: "Yes, it is the end of our business; hereafter any man who can boil a tea-kettle will be as good as the best of us."[27]

Seymour brought himself back to the present. He walked over the deck, put his hands on the sun-warmed railing, took a deep breath, and looked around at the wide expanse of sea and sky and the wide mouth of the Charleston Harbor entrance. He could take unalloyed pleasure that the weather would not be another adversary this day. Only the lightest breeze stirred the air in a cloudless sky, a perfect early October day. There was just enough wind to carry off the smoke.

If he had any qualms about the coming battle it was over the safety of HRH Albert, the nineteen-year-old son of the Queen (and second in line to the throne), a newly promoted lieutenant aboard the corvette HMS *Racoon*, on which he had been serving since January. It was a general consensus in the captains' cabins and crews' quarters of the fleet that Albert was a zealous and competent officer, but he was also had an angry and rude personality. He earned no love beneath decks, where they called him "the King of the Greeks." Just that year the Greeks, having disposed of their overbearing Bavarian royal line, had voted to make young Albert "King of the Hellenes." Victoria had not been amused. It was enough though that Britain's treaty obligations prevented a member of her royal family from ascending the Greek throne. The offer was politely declined.[28]

Dahlgren was also thanking the weather for its neutrality. A heavy sea would have been a greater danger to his monitors than the enemy would be. They were hard enough to handle in calm water without rough weather swamping their decks. It was lost on no one that the original *Monitor* had sunk in a storm. His monitors needed flat seas to steady their ungainly shape and allow the twin heavy Dahlgrens in their turrets clear aim. The admiral, like his British opposite, also had a young man to worry about—Ulric was all energy, pacing awkwardly with his new cork leg up and down the deck. Dahngren suggested a place of safety in the upcoming fight. "Ullie, I want you to be with me in the pilothouse."

Something flashed across Ulric's eyes, but he softened it into a smile. "It will be more exciting with the Marines, Papa. I will just get in the way in that tiny pilothouse, and I am familiar with the gun drill of the Marine gun crews. You of all people should know how well I can get around a Navy gun. How many times did I practice with them at the Navy Yard?"[29]

Dahlgren forced himself to tuck that worry away; the service was his life, and he owed it his complete attention. He had been in bad health for longer than a month now; it had deepened the lines of his already gaunt face. Now he summoned from the depths of will and duty every fiber of his ability for the supreme moment that was coming. Seymour was aware of Dahlgren's pioneering work in ordnance, but it was a general sort of awareness that did not seriously contemplate how much that expertise might weigh in the coming fight.

THE BATTERY, CHARLESTON, SOUTH CAROLINA, 3:05 PM, OCTOBER 8, 1863

It had not taken long for the word to spread through Charleston and its defenses that the British had arrived off the bar. The city emptied as people rushed down to the river and crowded the docks from the slave market all the way down to the Battery at the tip of the peninsula that held the city. The well connected found places in the balconies of the mansions that lined the Battery. From one of them, Gen. Pierre Gustave Toutant de Beauregard had given the order to fire on Fort Sumter almost two and half years ago. That was the event that had triggered this grinding war. The little Louisiana Creole dandy ostentatiously chose the same balcony to watch the distant battle, though little more than smoke would be visible at the five- to six-mile distance. Now many were quick to hope that they might witness the end of that war from the same vantage. With him was Capt. Duncan Ingraham, the commander of the Charleston Naval Station. To his immense chagrin, he had nowhere else to be. The two Confederate ironclads under his command, *Palmetto State* and *Chicora*, were idled by engine repairs. Had that not been the case, nothing on this earth would have kept him from joining the upcoming battle.[30]

The war had just about ruined Charleston. Hardly a blockade-runner got through Dahlgren's ships anymore. The warehouses along the docks were crammed to the rafters with bales of cotton. The white brick warehouse at the end of East Ager Dock just south of the battery alone held thousands of bales of unrealized wealth as the paint peeled from its walls. Once the leading port for the export of the South's "white gold," Charleston's economic life was near death; it was now plain shabby and its dwindling population increasingly threadbare and pinched.

It had become an article of faith among the people of Charleston that the mere arrival of the Royal Navy would practically usher in the Second Coming. They had pinned such hopes on foreign intervention to save them from Lincoln's remorselessness that hope became faith and faith a dream.

CROSSING THE CHARLESTON BAR, 4:55 PM, OCTOBER 8, 1863

Seymour crossed the bar on the afternoon tide just as Dahlgren expected. He came in two divisions line abreast. The first division was led by the *Black Prince* followed by ship of the line *Sans Pareil*; the big frigates *Mersey* and *Phaeton*; the corvettes *Racoon*, *Challenger*, and *Cadmus*; the sloop *Bulldog*; and the gunboat *Alacrity*. The armored frigate *Resistance*, captained by William Charles Chamberlain, led the second division, followed by ships of the line *St. George* and *Donegal*; the big frigates *Shannon*, *Ariadne*, and *Melpomene*; the corvette *Jason*; the sloops *Desperate* and *Barracouta*; and the gunboat *Algerine*.[31]

Just as Dahlgren expected, Seymour was determined to break the American line in the spirit of Nelson. Once the line was broken, his weight of fire could be used to overwhelm the American ships one by one. While the big ships broke the line in two columns, he would envelop the Americans as well with his sloops and corvettes. But what had worked so well for Horatio Nelson in 1805 against demoralized French and Spanish ships at Trafalgar was not as applicable in 1863 against experienced

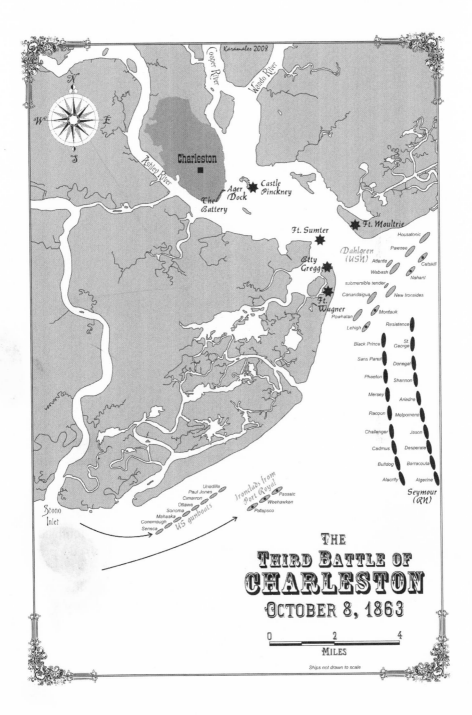

Karamales 2008

Cooper River

Wando River

Charleston

Ashley River

Ager Dock
Castle Pinckney
The Battery

Ft. Moultrie

Ft. Sumter

Housatonic

Dahlgren (USN)

Pawnee

Atlanta
Catskill
Batty Gregg
Wabash
Nahant
submersible tender
Canandaigua
New Ironsides

Ft. Wagner
Montauk
Powhatan

Lehigh
Resistance

Black Prince
St George

Sans Pareil
Donegal

Phaeton
Shannon

Mersey
Ariadne

Racoon
Melpomene

Challenger
Jason

Cadmus
Desperate

Bulldog
Barracouta

Alacrity
Algerine

Seymour (RN)

Unadilla
Paul Jones
Cimarron
Ottawa
Sonoma
Mehaska
Conemaugh
Seneca

Ironclads from Port Royal

Passaic
Weehawken
Patapsco

US gunboats

Stono Inlet

THE
THIRD BATTLE OF
CHARLESTON
OCTOBER 8, 1863

0   2   4

MILES

Ships not drawn to scale

American ships whose crews were as instinctively combative and jealous of victory as their British kin. It would be hard pounding then, and Seymour's ships had the great advantage in numbers and overall weight of metal.[32]

The Americans' ironclads in the first line were steaming slowly at a right angle to the approaching British; the monitors were lucky to do five knots. The two British columns were aiming to cut right through the American line. Seymour signaled to break the American line fore and aft of the *New Ironsides*. At two thousand yards the forward pivot Armstrongs on their lead ships opened an accurate fire, striking the *New Ironsides* and the turrets on several monitors. Seymour had directed that priority of fire to the ironclads. The excellence of British guns and gunnery were immediately evident. Unfortunately, they were completely without effect as their shot barely dented the American armor. Within minutes the vent piece from the *Black Prince*'s Armstrong blew out, silencing the gun.

As the range closed to eight hundred yards, the Dahlgrens opened up. The ironclads concentrated the fire of four XV-inch and twelve XI-inch Dahlgren guns on the *Black Prince* and *Resistance* in the lead. The *Wabash* and her sloops behind the ironclads fired over the decks of the low-slung monitors, with a broadside of another twenty-five IX-inch, one X-inch, and three XI-inch Dahlgrens as well as four 100- and 150-pounder Parrot rifles. The *Wabash* alone was a veritable spitfire. The huge frigate, at 4,650 tons, was larger than two of Seymour's three ships of the line. It carried one X-inch and forty-two IX-inch Dahlgrens, one 150-pounder and two 100-pounder Parrot rifles, as well as a smaller 30-pounder rifle and one 12-pounder gun howitzer. Despite her wooden body, the *Wabash* contained a significant part of Dahlgren's firepower that day.[33]

The storm of American shells converged on the two lead British ships in a visible stream of black dots against the blue sky. Months of practice in bombarding the forts in Charleston Harbor had honed a precision accuracy in the ironclad gun crews.

Black Prince staggered under the hail of 350- and 136-pound shells; her bow and forecastle disintegrated. The casemate armor that protected the gun decks did not extend around the bow or stern. The shells had ripped and torn her metal hull plates down to the water line, and she began to drink in the sea in great gulps as her powerful engines sped her forward toward *New Ironsides*. But watertight compartments, one of her design innovations, limited the amount of water gushing through the smashed bow that would have otherwise flooded the entire ship.

Seymour's flagship was about to experience the layered gunnery Dahlgren had instructed his captains to employ. As *Black Prince* and *Resistance* closed the distance with the enemy line, the American ships switched to solid shot to bear on the armored sides of the British ship. The large shot converged on both sides of the British ships. From within the 8-inch armored pilothouse on the *New Ironsides*, Admiral Dahlgren watched the huge shot arc over the sea or skip across the waves to ensure a crippling hull strike. It was the *Atlanta* all over again. The low-velocity Dahlgren shot ruptured the armor plates, detaching three-foot sections of the armor's teak backing and inner metal skin in showers of wooden splinters and metal shards that wiped out whole gun sections. The concussion sent the shot flying from their racks within the casement. Here the design innovations of the *Warrior* class came to *Black Prince*'s aid. Her gun deck had been designed as a series of compartments with armored 4.5-inch bulkheads between them, limiting the damage done by each shot to single compartments.[34]

By the time *Black Prince* broke the American line astern of *New Ironsides*, a third of her guns were out of action. The crews of the rest had not lost their nerve and fired accurately as she passed the American ship's stern. The Royal Navy believed its 68-pounders were the only ordnance it had that would shatter armor plate but at no more than two hundred yards. *Black Prince* halved that distance, firing its starboard battery almost point-blank into *New Ironsides*, each surviving gun firing as it bore. The *New Ironside*'s unarmored stern crumpled under the impact, its rudder shot to pieces. But even at a hundred yards, the British shot just bounced off *New Ironsides*'s armored casemate. A subtle advantage to the American ship was its seventeen-degree outward slopping hull, which presented an angled instead of a flat surface to the British shot. Its armor had been forged rather than rolled, giving it even more strength than the usual plating. Coupled with the strength of the casemate, the angle deflected the British hits with wild, deep, echoing clangs. The monitor *Catskill* swung its turret to follow *Black Prince* and fired both of its guns into the larboard battery as the enemy passed, wrecking another fighting section.

At almost the same time, *Resistance* cut across *New Ironside*'s bow, raking the latter as her guns bore. She then passed *Wabash* and fired into her stern. *Resistance* had suffered almost as much as *Black Prince* in its race to close with the enemy, and its crew now worked like men possessed to even the score. The fighting spirit of the island race was never keener as they worked the guns.

Attempting to follow *Resistance* through the American line was *St. George*. Her wooden bow and forecastle simply disintegrated from the explosive power of the shells converging on it. Shells spread havoc down the quarterdeck, turning it into an abattoir of blood and shattered bodies, its captain dead and wheel shattered. In a moment this venerable ship of the line, with its three gun decks counting 120 pieces of ordnance, had been stunned. But she plunged on, her screws spinning and pulling to starboard in the absence of the wheel's control. Her gun crews hauled away the dead and wounded and fought the fires that seemed to have ignited everywhere. The ship was now pulling unintentionally parallel to the American line, and for the first time she could fire back. The crews rushed to their larboard guns and fired as they bore. Her guns were accurate at this range, and the British gun crews, oblivious to the carnage on the quarterdeck, fought like demons, their famed gun drill taking charge, their motions fluid and powerful like the piston arms of powerful steam engine. Yet their skill and courage were wasted as the shot just bounced off the ironclads whose turrets had reversed to reload.[35]

Inside the turrets, the gunners felt the continuous concussive effect as a heavy vibrating hum. The turrets on the monitors *Catskill* and *Nahant* rotated back to fire at close range into *St. George*. Behind them, *Wabash*'s heavy Dahlgren battery added its fire. *St. George* seemed to fly apart in clouds of wooden splinters under the impact, huge holes smashed into her sides, her masts crashing down over the sides. *Wasbash*'s broadside battery kept the fire hot as the monitors rotated their turrets to reload. One by one, then by whole sections, *St. George*'s guns fell silent amid their dead and dying crews, blood washing the decks. As her engines took her out of the fight, she was more a floating wreck than a fighting ship.

Black Prince now turned slowly hard to starboard to bring it broadside to broadside with the crippled American falling out of line. The *Warrior* class ship was especially difficult to steer with any precision given its small rudder, and the American ship had time to prepare for the next round. The little submersible tender was barely able to steam away from *New Ironsides*, its submersible boats nowhere in sight. Following *Black Prince*, ship of the line *Sans Pareil* also turned to starboard to sandwich *New Ironsides* and pound her to pieces between them. The American ship was now dead in the water as the battle split into two parts. The monitors ahead of Dahlgren's flagship steamed on, engaging HMS *Donegal* and its following frigates, which were steaming into the same pulverizing hail of shells that had wrecked *St. George*.

From behind *Wabash*, the ram *Atlanta* emerged to swing wide and come in against the British 2nd Division line. She bypassed HMS *Donegal*, which was engaging the American line to aim squarely at HMS *Shannon*. This huge British frigate was the namesake of the ship that had taken the USS *Chesapeake* in 1813 and with its fifty-one guns approached the size of a small ship of the line. Her gunnery was as good as her renowned ancestor's, and she sent a stream of iron at the former Confederate ironclad that repeatedly struck her bow and sides. *Atlanta* steamed on, her smokestack shot away and her broadside guns useless at that angle of approach. Lieutenant Cromwell, barely used to the title of captain, was intent on closing with the enemy and put his reliance in the ironclad's spar torpedo. The gunpowder-filled torpedo extended beyond the prow just under water, its barbed point invisible in the muddy water around the bar. *Shannon*'s broadside of fifteen 8-inch shell guns and ten 32-pounders poured their fire into the oncoming ram, but they burst or bounced off her plate.[36] The frigate had only one gun, a 68-pounder that could hope to defeat even *Atlanta*'s inferior armor, and it had only one shot as it closed the last hundred yards. It was a direct hit that that knocked the top off the pilothouse and killed the young captain. It was too late for *Shannon*, however; *Atlanta* itself now was the weapon. She crashed into *Shannon*, driving the spar torpedo point deep through the ship's copper bottom and pushing the ship out of line.

Atlanta's engineer ordered engines reversed, but the spar torpedo was sunk too deeply into *Shannon*, and the underpowered Confederate engines did not have the strength to pull it free. The torpedo man hesitated; his orders had been to connect the battery that would send the current into the explosive after the ship had disengaged. *Shannon*'s guns were firing at top speed at the immobilized ironclad. *Atlanta*'s bow gun was dismounted by a direct hit through its gun port. Now HMS *Ariadne* came up alongside to pound her with her broadside. Her expert gunners sent 68-pounder shot through *Atlanta*'s single broadside gun port, dismounting the gun and savaging the crew. The third frigate, *Melpomene*, came up as well to hammer *Atlanta*'s stern. The patches in her armor failed as shot penetrated the casemate, killing the torpedo man and wounding the engineer. The casemate was filled with smoke and screams as the armor plate rattled with shot and more shells exploded inside. The engineer crawled over to the torpedo man. Pushing the body off the battery, he made the connection. He fell back and counted — one, two, three — then the underwater force of the explosion surged back through *Atlanta*,

pushing her back. *Shannon* shrieked as if in pain as the explosion ruptured her engine and broke her keel. An enormous hole sucked in the
ocean. Almost immediately she started to list. She died fast, slipping beneath the water in minutes.[37]

Many a man paused to stare at *Shannon*'s death. HRH Albert was
not one of them. If anything his sharp tongue lashed the gawkers back to
their duties aboard HMS *Racoon* as it led the smaller ships of the first
division in the envelopment of the American right. His captain was so
intent on the last ships in the American line that he did not notice the
flotilla hugging the coast to the south. He had no idea the initiative had
slipped from his fingers until an XV-inch shell landed amidships. The
lookout that should have seen them was flung into the sea as the mast he
was atop flew apart in a cloud of splinters. Another huge shell and then
another arced toward the corvettes. Against wooden ships, Dahlgren's
shells smashed their way into the gun decks before exploding with such
force to create shambles and a butcher's yard.

Albert scanned the shore but could see only the faintest shapes
close to the water. He scampered up the rigging to give height to his
glasses. "By God," he muttered to himself, "more of those damned monitors." They were the three monitors whose repairs had been rushed forward at Port Royal, and they were slowly moving toward the corvettes.
The second monitor shell to strike *Racoon* stove a great hole in her hull.
The third killed the captain and sent Albert in a bloody heap on the shattered deck. Fires broke out to feed on the mass of new kindling, and the
ship began to list strongly. Strong hands lifted the prince down into a
boat. Despised or not, he was still Victoria's son, and *Racoon*'s tars would
not have it said they left her boy to die.[38]

On the other flank the British envelopment had run into Dahlgren's
swarm of gunboats, which were rapidly closing on the main fight. There
HMS *Resistance* had picked out USS *Wabash* for its duel as the largest
American ship after *New Ironsides*. The two were pounding away at only
fifty yards, the side of each ship spitting tongues of fire. *Resistance*'s heavy
nineteen-gun broadside battery had a target it was designed for, a traditional wooden warship. Her gun crews were rapid and accurate. Big
chunks of *Wabash*'s side and deck were smashed, but her own broadside
battery of seven XI-inch Dahlgrens and a 150-pounder Parrot gun were
just as destructive to the armored hull of the enemy. So close were the
ships that *Wabash*'s shot was breaking through the ruptured armor and
followed by a shell to explode inside the gun deck.

In effect they had canceled each other out, but the fighting would go on until they had reduced each other to wrecks. Meanwhile, the American sloops *Pawnee* and *Housatonic* closely engaged *Resistance*'s other side. Her gun crews had been so winnowed that there were few to man the guns on that side as the sloops concentrated on holing her below the water line. Shot after shot had so dislodged and torn the armor plates and shattered the teak behind them that water began to fill compartment after compartment.

The center of the battle swirled around the two armored flagships as *Black Prince* finally came alongside *New Ironsides* again. Seymour had seen the shot bounce off *New Ironsides* and was determined to lay himself alongside, where his gunners could fire through the enemy's gun ports. *Black Prince*'s Captain knew his business and was getting everything from his ship and crew that they had to give. It was bruising and bloody work, for the American captain also knew his job. Wainwright would have to earn this victory the hard way.

Nevertheless, Wainwright knew he had the advantage. As damaged as his flagship was she still had complete maneuverability while the *Ironsides* was dead in the water. Huge projectiles sailed back and forth between the two ships, smashing through plate and wooden backing as *Black Prince* steamed past slowly, so close as to sometimes grind its casemate against the American's. At this distance, *New Ironsides*'s gun crews switched to shell, set at point-blank range with all three lead fuse settings torn off. They not only tore through the armor and backing but ignited the splintered wood as well. Here and there guns went silent as the crews rushed to fight the fires. *Black Prince* was answering slowly to the helm with her flooded bow acting as a dead weight. Turning about, Wainwright was engaged by the sloops *Canandaigua* and *Powhatan* but, he shook off their fire to reengage *New Ironsides*.

Admiral Seymour would have her. And in his single-mindedness, he tried to step into Wainwright's shoes and forgot the rest of his squadron. He had wounded *New Ironsides*, and now he was in for the kill. His spirit would have soared if he knew how close he was. His 68-pounders had battered *New Ironsides*'s pilothouse so severely that a chunk of metal had detached from the inner wall and struck Dahlgren a great gash in the thigh, sending him crashing into the bulkhead in a spray of blood. Rowan was first at his side to staunch the bleeding. It was a nasty wound. The deck pooled with the old man's bright blood. When at last it ebbed, Dahlgren lay ashen on the deck. Rowan ordered him carried below, but the older man gasped as three seamen lifted him. His hand clutched at the captain's coat. "Rowan, keep pounding. We can stand it longer than they can. Pound 'em. My guns won't let you down."[39]

On the spar deck Ulric Dahlgren was with the Marines manning one of those very guns—a 5.1-inch Dahlgren rifle. He had applauded the accuracy of the men with that piece and had been as admiring, albeit more ruefully, of the accuracy of the British Armstrong gunners on *Black Prince*'s own spar deck.[40] Their guns stopped one by one, whether hit or not, and the Dahlgren muzzle-loading rifle continued firing. Ulric had unconsciously hobbled up to take the place of a crewman felled by a splinter. By then the men had no time to spare for the bizarre scene of a one-legged Army colonel feeding the guns just like a tar. The gold eagles on his shoulder straps were more than incongruous. They attracted the fire of Royal Marine riflemen. The deck splintered around him, and rounds pinged off the gun. Another man fell to writhe on the deck. All the Marines aboard, not manning guns, had been issued the Spencers Admiral Dahlgren had so presciently ordered. Their volume of fire quickly dropped the enemy's Marines from the rigging and forced those on deck under cover.[41]

By now Captain Wainwright had brought *Black Prince* alongside *New Ironsides* again. Young Dahlgren saw an officer through the smoke shout through a megaphone, "Do you strike?"

Ulric hobbled to the side, his cap blown off and his blond hair streaked with powder. He cupped his hands and replied as the son of an admiral, "The Navy never strikes!" His Marines cheered. He looked back at them and winked, then turned to shout across the water again, "And neither does the U.S. Army!" Amazingly, the Marines cheered again, delighted with his pluck, Army or no Army. The gunner fired to punctuate their approval.[42]

Aboard *Black Prince*, the officer was blown off his feet, his clothes shredded and his megaphone sailing over the other side of the ship. He got up and staggered to report back to Seymour in his armored conning tower. The admiral looked at the man's glassy eyes and singed and torn uniform, and asked, "Well?"

"They said the U.S. Army refuses to strike, sir."

Seymour blinked and said, "What did you say?"

"They said the U.S. Army refuses to strike, sir." Then he fell over.[43]

Before Seymour could try to make sense of this, his flag captain, Arthur Cochrane, interrupted with the damage report from *Black Prince*'s captain.[44] It drained away much of his confidence. More than half his guns were silenced. The armored casemate was torn and rent the entire length of the ship. The men were fighting fires in a half dozen places. The upper decks had been swept with exploding shells until it was a shambles. The American sloops were steaming back forth, pounding the exposed side of the ship and forcing it to fight in two directions.

For Seymour, the whole battle had telescoped into the struggle between these two ships. Whoever triumphed would win the entire battle. It all rested on that. "Put her alongside, muzzle to muzzle, and we shall fight it out, Captain. Be prepared to board," he told Wainwright. The cry went out to assemble boarding parties. Seymour did not flinch as the two ships lurched into each other with a grinding squeal of metal on metal that would have frightened hell. The gun crews had been so worked up to the fighting that they barely took note of the eerie noise that echoed through the gun decks.

The only thing that kept the guns in action was *New Ironsides*'s seventeen-degree outward slant of her hull. Otherwise, the opposing hull would have shut the gun ports and the guns would have been unable to be run out. Locked in death's embrace, the two ships fired and fired — the British gunners now had open gun ports, small as they were, to sight through only yards away — gutting each other and smashing the opposing gun decks until only a handful of guns functioned on either side. For the British boarding parties waiting expectantly for the impact, the noise went straight through them, their hearts pounding in the few still seconds before the order to board was given. "Board!" They raced to the side and threw their grapples to snag the enemy. A few made it over the yawning gap made by the American hull's slant, but the boarding parties were stopped at the sides, unable to leap across so wide a space. Massed on the side they made too good a target for the U.S. Marine sharpshooters. Concentrated fire into the tight groups of sailors and Marines dropped a score and drove the rest under cover.[45]

Inadvertently *New Ironsides*'s gunners solved the stalemate by shooting through *Black Prince*'s mizzenmast. It screamed as it splintered, then with a groan fell over the side and onto the Americans' deck. Ulric instantly saw it as a bridge. He scrambled to the mast, pulled himself up by the strength of his arms and good leg, then forced his leg under him to rise to a standing position. He did not dash over the mast; rather, he hobbled almost crablike, dragging and swinging his cork leg after him. Yet the young man who had danced across the dance floors of

Washington with such grace summoned every last bit of that coordination and control to pick his way across that rounded, splintered, and rope-twisted mast. If he had been able to pay attention he would not have been able to tell which group of men was more incredulous at the sight — the British manning the stern Armstrong pivot gun or his own Marine gun crew. Finally reaching the enemy's side, he let himself down onto his good leg and sagged from the impact. He was on the deck of *Black Prince*. He barely had time to look up and see the gleam of a bayonet with a red coat behind it rushing toward him.

Oblivious to the drama on the surface, the admiral's two small submersibles had waited for just this moment for *Black Prince* to close. Their torpedoes bulged at the end of long spars. Finding the ship through the glass ports in the light filtering down from the cloudless sky, they made gentle contact with the iron hull with the strong magnet on the end of the torpedo. Once the torpedoes were locked onto the hull they backed off, unraveling the electric wires that connected with batteries inside the boats. Before the wires went completely taut, the circuits were closed.

Ulric had barely drawn himself up. The Royal Marine's bayonet was plunging toward his chest when the deck heaved, throwing him onto one of the Armstrongs. The gun crew had been thrown off their feet as well and were just getting up when the deck heaved again. An awful groaning came from deep within the ship.

Installed low in *Black Prince*, her engines had survived the hard pounding as her gang stoked the forty furnaces feeding the ten boilers that generated the steam for its 5,210-horsepower engines. But the torpedoes had struck where the Dahlgrens could not reach, bending the shaft and rupturing some of the furnaces. Burning coal, white-hot ash, and clinker spewed out among the stokers, who screamed out their last moments in hell. Water rushed in through the torn hull, flooding the engine rooms as the guns above continued to fight. When the seawater reached the boilers, they began to explode.[46]

The ship's death agony was not yet apparent to the men on deck getting to their feet. The tars were game and came for Ulric again. He had drawn his Navy Colt and dropped the first two men. A third struck him a numbing blow on the shoulder with a rammer; the pistol fell from his hand. The tar drew back to brain him, but he went down under the rush of men in blue coats. Ulric's own Marines had followed him over the mast armed with cutlasses and pikes from the ready racks. He was pulled to his feet by strong arms.

On the bridge, Captain Wainwright was desperately trying to reach the engine room through the metal voice pipes and the mechanical telegraph connected to it. The shrieks at the end of the voice pipe told him the worst. Everyone in the conning tower had been frozen listening to the death below. The shudders that pulsed up through the deck from the exploding boilers jarred everyone back to life. Wainwright knew his ship was lost. He found Seymour had slumped into his chair. "Admiral, *Black Prince* is mortally wounded. She can do no more. I must save the men who are left." Seymour's jaw set in a vise as the ship groaned in its death throes; he could only nod.

Wainwright left the conning tower to personally haul down the colors, an act he would not delegate to a man of lower rank. He made his way through the shambles on the spar deck. He could feel the ship beginning to settle under him as it listed to larboard. The smoke from the guns and a dozen fires on the deck hid the stern in its wispy black arms. He made out a group on the stern around the pivot gun and was about to order them to abandon ship, when the breeze quickened to part the smoke. They were not his men.

The officer among them was a young, fair man, leaning against the gun. A man raised a pistol to shoot, but the officer knocked it up to discharge in the air. The officer straightened up and touched the muzzle of his own pistol to his forehead in salute. "Colonel Dahlgren, United States Army, sir."

Wainwright was a hard man to fluster, and even this scene could not break through the iron presence of a naval officer. He touched the brim of his cap, "Captain Wainwright, commanding Her Majesty's Ship *Black Prince*, sir."

As the deck began to cant even more, Dahlgren coolly asked, "Do you strike, sir?"

"Damnation, sir. I do."

SOUTH AGER DOCK, CHARLESTON, SOUTH CAROLINA, 7:32 PM, OCTOBER 8, 1863

For more than two hours the crowds massed along the battery and the Charleston docks had been barely able to control their excitement. They could not actually see the battle six miles away beyond Fort Sumter and Morris Island, but they could hear the continuous rumble of the guns and see the pall of smoke. It was more than just gunpowder smoke. The funeral pyres of great wooden ships go straight up into the heavens. Signals from Fort Sumter added little.

That changed as the signal officer at Beauregard's side read the waving flags from his telescope. His voice shaking he said, "Sumter reports a huge British warship is sailing into the harbor." That could only mean that the British had won the naval battle. The arrival of the ship was the act in international law that would declare the hated blockade broken. Those on the crowded balcony spontaneously shouted in triumph. Word was shouted down to the street and spread with electric speed. The crowds erupted in near hysterical cheering, with rebel yells keening over the water. Beauregard announced that he would personally welcome the ship at the Ager Dock, and he bounded down the stairs, his staff running after. He shouted an order to have the Army Band meet him there.

Charleston's cheering crowds were the last thing on the mind of the captain of the *Resistance*. With most of his guns out action, a third of his crew dead or wounded, and his hull filling with water from the ruptured waterline armor, Chamberlain knew he had three bad choices. He could continue to fight his few guns and go under, he could try to make it to Bermuda and go down in less than ten miles, or he could break off action and take his ship into Charleston and probably go under before he reached a pier. If he was lucky, he could run it aground or dock it where it could be saved. Seeing *Black Prince* strike instantly decided his mind. His engines were still game; the water had not reached them yet. There was a good chance he could make the five miles to the city. The *Housatonic* pursued but sheered off when she came under the fire of the Confederate harbor forts.

As he approached Fort Sumter, he could see the cheering garrison lining its rubbled walls, and a tug emerged from around the masked side of the island and chugged toward the *Resistance*, blowing frantically on its whistle. Thank God, Chamberlain thought. The *Resistance* would need all the help it could get. She was slowing down; the water filling the hull was a drag on the engines. The tug kept blowing its whistle, and Chamberlain could see figures on the deck waving their arms frantically.

Resistance was finally within hailing distance of the tug when she hit the mine. The ship shuddered. Chamberlain could hear the scream of twisting and snapping hull plates from within the depths of the ship. Still the engines thundered to keep *Resistance* moving. He shouted into the speaking tube to the chief engineer who reported that the engine compartment was secure but that the water was quickly rising to the level of the boilers. He could not guarantee how much longer he would dare leave the black gang in the stokehold. "Give me everything you have got, then get the men out." He turned to one of his officers. "Start getting the wounded up on deck. I don't want them down there if we founder and sink."

The tug carefully made its way alongside. Its master paled at the buckled and gouged armor plate and the shredded upper deck. He read the ship's name and shouted up, "God bless you, *Resistance*! Can I be of assistance? You must beware of the mines. Let me guide you in."

Chamberlain bit his lip at the warning that had come only minutes too late. He yelled over the side, "Yes, thank you, sir. I have severe damage below the water line and am taking water fast. We will throw you a line." The little tug's engine exceeded its safety limits as the line went taut, trying to help pull the six thousand–ton warship. Thick black smoke gushed from its funnel.

On South Ager Dock, Ingraham's telescope had been to his eye for ten minutes. He said to Beauregard, "There's something wrong, General. Very wrong. I think the ship is in great distress. It entered our minefield and then stopped and has now taken a line from our tug. I fear it has struck one of our mines."

Beauregard felt his elation wilt under the implications of that statement. He could only watch over the next painful half hour as the great black ship slowly approached the dock, plainly getting lower and lower in the water. Its battle damage was easily apparent even to the crowds on the dock. A pained silence hung over them. As the ship inched closer, someone in authority had the presence of mind to order room for the dockhands to secure the lines that would be thrown down to them. Soldiers pushed through the press to form an honor guard. More came to line up behind Beauregard and Ingraham and to make a way for the dozen black dockhands.

At last she edged up to the dock, a great wounded beast, her naval ensign still whipping in the breeze. Everyone saw the marks of her struggle. Her magnificent figurehead, a neoclassical carving of a savage warrior with busy dark head and beard, was gouged and splintered. The silence of the crowd melted away in a rising mutter. Then the band struck up "God Save the Queen," the honor guard came to attention and presented arms, and the people started to cheer their long-prayed-for and gallant ally. The lines were thrown from *Resistance*.

Chamberlain missed the honors. He was below, personally ensuring that no wounded man had been left behind and that the engine spaces and stokehold had been emptied of his crew. The water was coming up around him as he stood on the ladder above the stokehold.

His engineer grabbed him by the collar and heaved him up. "There's no one else, sir. She's dying, and you don't need to die with her."

Chamberlain gave one last look as the water bubbled and swirled up the ladder around his feet before leaving. They had barely emerged on deck when the ship gave its death cry, a deep groan swallowed by the sucking noise of rushing water. The crowd went deathly silent again at the ship's death rattle. Then, in the sight of God and Charleston, the *Resistance* went down.[47]

To be continued . . .

APPENDIX A

Order of Battle of the Armies at the First Battle of Portland
September 30, 1863

PORTLAND FIELD FORCE (BRITISH)
Commander: Maj. Gen. Sir Charles Ashe Windham
    Headquarters and Staff: 75

1st Division (8,100)
    1st Quebec Brigade
        1/62nd Foot
        50th Huntington Rangers
        51st Hemmingford Rangers
        52nd Bedford Battalion (Bn)
        A Battery, 8th Brigade (Field)
    2nd Sherbrooke Brigade
        1/17th Foot
        53rd Sherbrooke Bn
        54th Richmond Bn
        55th Megantic Bn
        1st Battery, 10th Brigade
    3rd Niagara Brigade
        1/63rd Foot
        56th Prescott Bn
        57th Peterborough Bn
        58th Compton Bn
        6th Battery, 10th Brigade

Artillery Reserve (500)
        4th and 5th, Batteries, 10th Brigade
        2 batteries, Canadian artillery

Engineer Battalion (350)
        18th Co., Royal Engineers
        Co. Canadian Vol. Militia Engineers

Military Train (1,065)
        3rd Battalion, Military Train (315)
        Canadian Military Train (500)
        Canadian Train Guards (250)
            5 companies Canadian Militia Infantry

Royal Navy Landing Force
        Royal Marine Light Infantry Bn (350)
        1/16 Foot (850)

Total: 11,290

Guns: 42

THE MAINE DIVISION (AMERICAN)
Commander: Brig. Gen. Neal Dow
        Staff: 7

1st Brigade (Col. Joshua L. Chamberlain) (1,360)
        Staff: 5
        10th Maine
        16th Maine
        17th Maine
        19th Maine
        20th Maine
        Maine Light 2nd Battery

2nd Brigade (Col. Ephraim Harper) (1,423)
        Staff: 7
        3rd Maine
        4th Maine
        5th Maine
        6th Maine
        7th Maine
        Maine Light 5th Battery

1st Maine Cavalry (370)
Maine Light 6th Battery (81)

Division Train (350)[1]

Portland City Militia (2,500)

Harbor Fort Home Guard Garrisons (600)
        Fort Gorges (400)
        Fort Preble   (200)

Maine Division Total: 6,691[2]
Field Guns: 18

APPENDIX B

Order of Battle of the Fleets at the Third Battle of Charleston
October 8, 1863

BRITISH ROYAL NAVY'S CHARLESTON SQUADRON (ADMIRAL SEYMOUR)

First Division
1. IF *Black Prince*
2. SL *Sans Pareil*
3. Fr *Phaeton*
4. Fr *Mersey*
5. Cv *Racoon*
6. Cv *Challenger*
7. Cv *Cadmus*
8. Sl *Bulldog*
9. Gb *Alacrity*

Second Divison
10. IF *Resistance*
11. SL *St. George*
12. SL *Donegal*
13. Fr *Shannon*
14. Fr *Ariadne*
15. Fr *Melpomene*
16. Cv *Jason*
17. Sl *Desperate*
18. Sl *Barracouta*
19. Gv *Algerine*

U.S. NAVY'S SOUTH ATLANTIC BLOCKADING SQUADRON (ADMIRAL DAHLGREN)*

Charleston Battle Line
a. IM *Lehigh*
b. IM *Montauk*
c. IF *New Ironsides*
d. IM *Nahant*
e. IM *Catskill*
f. Fr *Powhatan*
g. Sl *Canandaigua*
h. Submersible tender
i. Fr *Wabash*
j. IR *Atlanta*
k. Sl *Pawnee*
l. Sl *Housatonic*

Port Royal Contingent
m. IM *Patapsco*
n. IM *Weehawken*
o. IM *Passaic*
p. IM *Chippewa*
q. IM *Nipsic*

Gunboat Flotilla in Stono Inlet
r. Gb *Seneca*
s. Gb *Conemaugh*
t. Gb *Mahaska*
u. Gb *Sonoma*
v. Gb *Ottawa*
w. Gb *Cimarron*
x. Gb *Paul Jones*
y. Gb *Unadilla*

Key:
IF	Ironclad frigate
IM	Ironclad monitor
IR	Ironclad ram
SL	Ship of the line
Fr	Frigate
Cv	Corvette
Sl	Sloop
Gb	Gunboat
Gv	Gun vessel

* The eighth ship of the *Passaic* class, the USS *Sangamon*, was at Newport News during this battle.

NOTES

CLARIFICATIONS

Although this tale is an alternate history, it is its own complete reality. As such, it would have created its own literature and records reflected in the endnotes, which normally would be found in a history. Endnotes are the sources of additional information of interest that are not part of the narrative. The use of alternate history endnotes, of course, pose a risk to the unwary reader who may make strenuous efforts to acquire a new and fascinating source such as Alfred Thayer Mahan, *Crossing the T at Charleston: Dahlgren and the Revolution in Naval Tactics* (New York: The Neale Publishing Co., 1895), p. 163.

To avoid an epidemic of frustrating and futile searches, these "alternate" endnotes that reflect the path not taken are indicated by an asterisk after the number. The reader is asked to enjoy these embellishments of a time that exists only in this telling.

INTRODUCTION

1. Samuel Johnson, "Thoughts on the Late Transactions Respecting Falkland Islands" (1771), *Political Writings*, vol. 10, 365–66, cited in Geoffrey Parker, *The Grand Strategy of Phillip II* (New Haven, CT: Yale University Press, 1998), 293.
2. Dean B. Mahin, *One War at a Time: The International Dimensions of the American Civil War* (Washington, DC: Brassey's, Inc., 1999), 150.
3. Burton J. Hendrick, *Statesmen of the Lost Cause: Jefferson Davis and His Cabinet* (New York, 1939), 278.
4. Mahin, *One War at a Time*, ix.
5. Ephraim Douglass Adams, *Great Britain and the American Civil War*, vol. 2 (New York: Longmans, Green and Co., 1925), 144. Adams's most serious competitor in this regard is surely Adlai Stevenson and his remark at the United Nations during the Cuban Missile Crisis, that he was waiting for a reply from the Soviet ambassador "until hell freezes over."
6. Mahin, *One War at a Time*, 181.

CHAPTER ONE: COSSACKS, COPPERHEADS, AND CORSAIRS

1. Donald Dale Jackson, *Twenty Million Yankees: The Northern Home Front* (Alexandria, VA: Time-Life Books, 1985), 103–10.
2. *"The Sacrifice of Willie Washington: A Hero of the New York Draft Riots," *Leslie's Illustrated*, July 25, 1863.
3. Daniel Farber, *Lincoln's Constitution* (Chicago: University of Chicago Press, 2003), 118.
4. James D. Horan, *Confederate Agent: A Discovery in History* (New York: Fairfax Press, 1954), 26.
5. Horan, *Confederate Agent*, 29.
6. Rear Adm. M. Abramov and Capt. 2nd Rank M. Kozhevnikov, "To the Shores of North America," *Morskoi Sbornik* 3 (1989): 18–23.
7. Nikolai Andreyevich Rimsky-Korsakoff, *My Musical Life* (New York: Tudor Publishing, 1936), 43.
8. Michael Cavanaugh, *Memoirs of Gen. Thomas Francis Meagher, Comprising the Leading Events of His Career Chronologically Arranged* (Worcester, MA: 1892), 369, 370–71.
9. Don E. Fehrenbacher and Virginia Fehrenbacher, eds. *Recollected Words of Abraham Lincoln* (Stanford, CA: Stanford University Press, 1996), 39.
10. Letter from Lamson to his fiancée, April 30, 1863, cited in James M. McPherson and Patricia R. McPherson, *Lamson of the* Gettysburg: *The Civil War Letters of Lieutenant Roswell H. Lamson, U.S. Navy* (New York: Oxford University Press, 1997), 103.
11. McPherson and McPherson, *Lamson of the* Gettysburg, 103.
12. Secretary of the Navy Gideon Welles, letter to Lamson, May 4, 1863, *Official Records of the Union and Confederate Navies of the War of Rebellion* (hereafter *O.R. Navies*), series I, vol. 8 (Washington: Government Printing Office, 1889), 789–90.
13. McPherson and McPherson, *Lamson of the* Gettysburg, 147.
14. James Tertius deKay, *The Rebel Raiders: The Astonishing History of the Confederacy's Secret Navy* (New York: Ballantine Books, 2002), 169.
15. Ibid., 174. "Here comes the *Alabama*, the *Alabama* comes over the sea."

CHAPTER TWO: RUSSELL AND THE RAMS

1. The Civil War Museum in Charleston contains half a shell from a Whitworth described as being fired from a gun that was given as a gift from the London Chamber of Commerce—the author.
2. David Hepburn Milton, *Lincoln's Spymaster: Thomas Haines Dudley and the Liverpool Network* (Mechanicsburg, PA: Stackpole Books, 2003), 7.
3. William Howard Russell, *My Diary North and South* (New York: Alfred A. Knopf, 1988), 42.
4. Dean B. Mahin, *One War at a Time: The International Dimensions of the American Civil War* (Washington, DC: Brassey's, Inc., 1999), 177. These ships were armed with steel rams, hence the name.
5. Milton, *Lincoln's Spymaster*, 91.

6. Mahin, *One War at a Time*, 33.
7. Charles Sumner to Richard Cobden, April 26, 1863, in *The Selected Letters of Charles Sumner*, ed. Beverly W. Palmer (Boston: Northeastern University Press, 1990), vol. 2, 161.
8. *Edward Maitland, *Lincoln, Russell, and Emancipation* (New York: The Neale Publishing Co., 1900), 83.
9. Don E. Fehrenbacher and Virginia Fehrenbacher, eds., *Recollected Words of Abraham Lincoln* (Stanford, CA: Stanford University Press, 1996), 370.
10. Anthony Gross, ed., *The Wit and Wisdom of Abraham Lincoln: The Best Stories by and About America's Most Beloved President* (New York: Barnes & Noble, 1994), 149–50.
11. Fehrenbacher and Fehrenbacher, *Recollected Words of Abraham Lincoln*, 436.
12. Howard Jones, *Union in Peril: The Crisis Over British Intervention in the Civil War* (Chapel Hill: University of North Carolina Press, 1992), 182. Gladstone stated that the Southerners "have made an army; they are making, it appears, a navy; and they have made what is more than either—they have made a nation."
13. Mahin, *One War at a Time*, ix. The Trent Affair referred to the incident in December 1861 in which the commander of the USS *San Jacinto* had stopped a British mail packet, the *Trent*, off Havana and seized two Confederate commissioners intended as ambassadors to Great Britain and France. The manner of the seizure was a technical violation of international law. Britain, whose rise to empire employed just such measures, was outraged and threatened war. It also quickly developed a war plan to break the blockade, counterblockade the North, and invade Maine. The Russian Foreign Ministry, whose good offices the United States had come to rely on, strongly urged that the commissioners be returned. The seizure of the commissioners had been wildly popular in the North, but Lincoln knew that the United States could "fight only one war at a time." He ordered the release of the commissioners, who proceeded to Britain and France.
14. When the United States huddled along the eastern seaboard early in the nineteenth century, the area that would become Ohio, Indiana, Illinois, and Michigan was referred to as the Northwest. As the country's territory and settlement expanded westward, the current term of "Midwest" came into use.

CHAPTER THREE: GEORGE THE CONTRABAND AND ONE-EYED GARNET

1. *George H. Sharpe, *Conversations With Abraham Lincoln, 1863–1868* (Philadelphia: L. B. Lippincott, 1886), 22–25.
2. "Story by General Sharpe," *Weekly Leader* (Kingston, New York), June 14, 1902.
3. *George Morgan, "Jumping on the Freedom Train," *Freedman's Weekly*, April 5, 1882.

4. William B. Feis, *Grant's Secret Service: The Intelligence War From Belmont to Appomattox* (Lincoln: University of Nebraska Press, 2002), 260–61.

5. Frederick Douglass (1818–95) was an ex-slave and a leading abolitionist, editor, orator, author, statesman, and reformer.

6. *Sharpe, *Conversations With Abraham Lincoln,* 27.

7. Edwin C. Fishel, *The Secret War for the Union: The Untold Story of Military Intelligence in the Civil War* (Boston: Houghton Mifflin Company, 1996), 437–40.

8. *Morgan, "Jumping on the Freedom Train."

9. *William A. Coleridge, *Snakes in the Grass: Revolt in the Old Northwest* (Chicago: Michigan Avenue Press, 1912), 24.

10. Eleanor Ruggles, *Prince of Players: Edwin Booth* (New York: W. W. Norton & Company, 1953), 157.

11. Ibid., 157.

12. Raymond Lamont Brown, *Carnegie: The Richest Man in the World* (Stroud, UK: Sutton Publishing, 2005), 37, 53.

13. *Arthur G. Stone, *Andrew Carnegie and the Mobilization of a Nation* (Philadelphia: Freedom Publishers, 1917), 47.

14. *Alexander C. Rutledge, *Spymaster of the Republic: The Life of George H. Sharpe* (New York: Excelsior Press, 1934), 219.

15. Regis A. Courtemanche, *No Need of Glory: The British Navy in American Waters, 1860–1864* (Annapolis: Naval Institute Press, 1977), 33. The British embassy in Washington at this time did not have permanent naval or military attachés. Milne characterized Hancock as "an officer of discreet and sound judgment." J. J. Colledge, *Ships of the Royal Navy: The Complete Record of All Fighting Ships of the Royal Navy From the Fifteenth Century to the Present* (London: Greenhill Books, 2003), 165. The *Immortalité* was a new wood screw frigate built in 1859, measuring 251 by 56 feet.

16. Garnet Wolseley to Colonel McCade, August 13, 1899, Maurice Papers, cited in Joseph Lehmann, *The Model Major-General: A Biography of Field-Marshal Lord Wolseley* (Boston: Houghton Mifflin Company, 1964), 121.

17. James A. Rawley, ed., *The American Civil War: An English View – the Writings of Field Marshal Viscount Wolseley* (Mechanicsville, PA: Stackpole Books, 2002), 40.

18. Col. Richard Sharpe, 1777–1860.

19. Lehmann, *The Model Major-General,* 24.

20. Ibid., 24.

21. Colledge, *Ships of the Royal Navy,* 352.

22. *George H. Sharpe, "My Meeting With Wolseley," *New York Herald,* October 23, 1880. This entire meeting is based on Sharpe's recollection in this article he penned for the *Herald.* Wolseley mentions the meeting though not in as great detail in his book on the war. *Field Marshal Viscount Wolseley, *The Great War in North America* (London: Longmans, Green & Company, 1890), 92.

CHAPTER FOUR: GALLANTRY ON CRUTCHES

1. Anthony Gross, ed., *The Wit and Wisdom of Abraham Lincoln: The Best Stories by and About America's Most Beloved President* (New York: Barnes & Noble, 1994), 185.

2. Spencer Tucker, *Arming the Fleet: The U.S. Navy Ordnance in the Muzzle-Loading Era* (Annapolis, MD: Naval Institute Press, 1989), 204–5.

3. William H. Roberts, *Civil War Ironclads: The U.S. Navy and Industrial Mobilization* (Baltimore, MD: The John Hopkins University Press, 2002), 165.

4. Robert V. Bruce, *Lincoln and the Tools of War* (Indianapolis: The Bobbs-Merrill Company, Inc., 1956), 81.

5. J. B. McClure, ed., *Anecdotes & Stories of Abraham Lincoln* (Chicago: Rhodes & McClure, 1888), 182–83.

6. Jospeh Lehmann, *The Model Major-General: A Biography of Field-Marshal Lord Wolseley* (Boston: Houghton Mifflin Company, 1964), 117.

7. Angus Konstam, *Duel of the Ironclads: USS* Monitor *& CSS* Virginia *at Hampton Roads, 1862* (London: Osprey Publishing, 2003), 92–94.

8. "Early Ironclad Battleships of the Royal Navy" is an excellent, comprehensive site: www.colonialwargamers.org.uk/Miscellany/Warships/Ironclads/EironcladsRN.htm.

9. David Pam, *The Royal Small Arms Factory Enfield and Its Workers* (published by author, 1998), 50–55.

10. Regis A. Courtemanche, *No Need of Glory: The British Navy in American Wars, 1860–1864* (Annapolis, MD: Naval Institute Press, 1977), 56–60.

11. Rear-Admiral Dahlgren, *Memoir of Ulric Dahlgren* (Philadelphia: J. B. Lippincott & Co., 1872), 159–76. Edward G. Longacre, *The Cavalry at Gettysburg: A Tactical Study of Mounted Operations During the Civil War's Pivotal Campaign, June 9, 1863–July 14, 1863* (Lincoln: University of Nebraska Press, 1986), 208–10.

12. Dahlgren, *Memoir of Ulric Dahlgren*, 174–77.

13. William "Willie" Wallace Lincoln, December 21, 1850– February 20, 1862, died of typhoid in the White House.

14. *George H. Sharpe, *Conversations With Abraham Lincoln, 1863–1868* (Philadelphia: L. B. Lippincott, 1886), 30–35.

15. Dean B. Mahin, *One War at a Time: The International Dimensions of the Civil War* (Washington, DC: Brassey's, Inc., 1999), 104–5.

16. Harold Holzer, ed., *Lincoln as I Knew Him: Gossip, Tributes & Revelations From His Best Friends and Worst Enemies* (Chapel Hill, NC: Algonquin Books, 1999), 71.

17. Edwin C. Fishel, *The Secret War for the Union: The Untold Story of Military Intelligence in the Civil War* (Boston: Houghton Mifflin Company, 1996), 291.

18. *Sharpe, *Conversations With Abraham Lincoln,* 45–48. Sharpe's recollections, vouched by contemporaries as precise, are one of the great primary sources on Lincoln. From the first day he met Lincoln, Sharpe made it a habit to commit each day's conversations to paper in the shorthand he learned in law school.

19. *The War of the Rebellion: Official Records of the Union and Confederate Armies* (hereafter *OR*), series 3, vol. 1 (Washington, DC: Government Printing Office, 1899), 589–90.
20. Ibid., 591.
21. Ibid.
22. *George Hancock, *Memoirs of the American War* (London: Marchand & Biddle, 1879), 87–90.

CHAPTER FIVE: SERGEANT CLINE GETS A NEW JOB
1. Robert V. Bruce, *Lincoln and the Tools of War* (Indianapolis: The Bobbs-Merrill Company, Inc., 1956), 112.
2. Ibid., 23.
3. Ibid., 110–11.
4. The Spencer repeating rifle, designed by Christopher Spencer in 1860, was a manually operated, lever-action, repeating rifle fed from a seven-round tube magazine in the stock. It fired the revolutionary rimfire .52-caliber metal cartridge. The Blakeslee cartridge box contained up to ten tube magazines. The Spencer was noted for its simplicity of design, ease of manufacture, and reliability. It also used many interchangeable parts with the already more common Sharps Rifle and was the cheapest repeater on the market. Armed with a Spencer and ten full magazines, the rifleman could fire twenty to thirty aimed shots a minute compared to two to three with a muzzle-loading Springfield or Enfield rifle.
5. Bruce, *Lincoln and the Tools of War*, 114.
6. Ibid., 119.
7. J. B. McClure, ed., *Anecdotes & Stories of Abraham Lincoln* (Chicago: Rhodes & McClure Publishing Co., 1888), 162.
8. Charles M. Evans, *The War of the Aeronauts: A History of Ballooning During the Civil War* (Mechanicsburg, PA: Stackpole Books, 2002), 285–87.
9. Mary Hoeling, *Thaddeus Lowe: America's One-Man Air Corps* (New York: Julian Messner, Inc., 1958), 23–24.
10. *Encyclopædia Britannica*, 11th ed. (1910–11). The Dreyse needle gun (German *Zündnadelgewehr* or figuratively "needle-firing-rifle") was a military breech-loading rifle. Famous as the main Prussian infantry weapon it was adopted for service in 1848 as the *Dreyse Zündnadelgewehr*, or Prussian model 1848. Its name comes from its 0.5-inch needle-like firing pin, which passed through the cartridge case to impact a percussion cap at the bullet base. The Dreyse rifle was also the first breech-loading rifle to use a bolt action to open and close the chamber.
11. Bruce, *Lincoln and the Tools of War*, 257.
12. *George H. Sharpe, *Conversations With Abraham Lincoln, 1863–1868* (Philadelphia: J.B. Lippincott, 1886), 53–57.
13. *Arthur H. Trumbull, *Wolseley and the American War* (London: Constable & Company, 1915), 111.
14. *Sharpe, *Conversations With Abraham Lincoln*, 59–60.
15. *Ibid., 62–63.

16. http://www.canis-publ.demon.co.uk/sofw2/ships/scorpion.html.
17. http://www.civilwartalk.com/cwt_alt/resources/articles/acws/larid_rams.htm.
18. Dean B. Mahin, *One War at a Time: The International Dimensions of the American Civil War* (Washington, DC: Brassey's, Inc., 1999), 147–53.
19. *Edgar C. Withersbottom, *Lifeblood of the Confederacy: Fraser, Trenholm & Company's Support of the Southern Cause* (London: Collins, 1948), 322.
20. *Charles Dana, *At the Creation: A Memoir of George H. Shape* (Philadelphia: J. B. Lippincott, 1892), 112.
21. *Thaddaeus Lowe, *Army Aeronautics in the Great War* (New York: The Century Company, 1878), 33.
22. *Woodrow Wilson, *George H. Sharpe and the Constitution in Wartime: The Struggle Between Civil Liberties and Necessity* (New York: D. Appleton, 1904), 318.
23. Maria Isabella Boyd (1844–1900), better known as "Belle Boyd," was probably the most famous of the Confederacy's spies. She worked behind Union lines and was finally arrested by Baker in July 1862.
24. *James McPhail, *My Service in the Great War* (New York: Seldon & Company, 1888), 23. Much of the success of the CIB stemmed from the superb work of McPhail as its deputy and his unerring loyalty to Sharpe.
25. *Thomas Shervington, *The Life of Michael D. Wilmoth, Third Director of the Central Information Bureau* (New York: Neale Publishing Co., 1900), 67.
26. Evans, *War of the Aeronauts*, 264–87.
27. *Lowe, *Army Aeronautics in the Great War*, 52.

CHAPTER SIX: "ROLL, ALABAMA, ROLL!"

1. *H. Emerson Harper, *Voyage of Destiny: USS* Gettysburg *and the Beginning of the Great War* (New York: The Century Company, 1903), 42.
2. Trading Places: A History of Liverpool Docks, http://www.liverpool museums.org/uk/nof/docks/index2html.
3. J. J. Colledge, *Ships of the Royal Navy: The Complete Record of All Fighting Ships of the Royal Navy From the Fifteenth Century to the Present* (London: Greenhill Books, 2003), 11, 193. Tonnage is here expressed in terms of builder's measure (bm), a unit of measurement used until 1875 and perhaps dating from the fifteenth century, determined by calculating how many tuns (casks) of wine a ship could carry. After 1873 displacement tonnage was used. In the case of *Liverpool*, this was 3,919 tons.
4. In this period, smoothbore guns that fired shot were designated by the weight of the shot—e.g., 32-pounder—and rifled guns were designed by the diameter of their bore, e.g., 8-inch.
5. Colledge, *Ships of the Royal Navy*, 14, 142, 193. The ninety-eight *Albacore* class gunboats ordered in 1855 were armed with one 68-pounder, one 32-pounder, and two 20-pounder guns.
6. *John P. Eldridge, *A Marine Aboard the* Gettysburg (New York: The Century Company, 1888), 97.

7. David Hepburn Milton, *Lincoln's Spymaster: Thomas Haines Dudley and the Liverpool Network* (Mechanicsburg, PA: Stackpole Books, 2003), 91.

8. The Cumberland Three, *Songs of the Civil War*: "Number 292" (compact disk) (Los Angeles: Rhino Records, 1991).

9. *Roswell H. Lamson, *Into the Maelstrom: A Memoir of the Gettysburg* (New York: George H. Doran Company, 1876), 112.

10. *Harper, *Voyage of Destiny*, 56–57. Maintaining that the *Gettysburg* was to replace the *Kearsarge* was part of the deception plan Fox had included in his orders to Lamson. He had coordinated this strategy with Seward, who mentioned it in a dispatch to Ambassador Adams.

11. *James Bulloch, *The Fuse of War: The CSS North Carolina* (London: John Murray, 1875), 119.

12. Dean B. Mahin, *One War at a Time: The International Dimensions of the American Civil War* (Washington, DC: Brassey's, Inc., 1999), 178.

13. Ibid., 179.

14. *Austen David Layard, *Origins of the American War: View From the Foreign Office* (London: Holmes & Sons, Ltd., 1886), 229. Layard went to great lengths in this book to deflect any responsibility for the coming war from himself, Russell, and the Foreign Office.

15. B. D. Adams, *Great Britain and the American Civil War*, vol. 2 (New York: Longmans, Green & Company, 1925), 143.

16. *Lamson, *Into the Maelstrom*, 150–52. Despite these initial impressions, Lamson and Adams developed a lifelong friendship, proving that opposites do attract.

17. *Edward R. Little, ed., *The Diaries of Thomas Haines Dudley* (New York: The George Doran Company, 1911), 93–96. *Walter B. Eddings, *Seward, Adams, and Dudley: Diplomacy and Espionage Leading up to the Outbreak of War* (Chicago: The World Publishing Company, 1922), 186–88.

18. *Lamson, *Into the Maelstrom*, 150.

19. *Albert Meyer, *Brief Glory: James Bulloch and the Short Life of the CSS North Carolina* (Richmond: James River Press, 1932), 131.

20. *Lamson, *Into the Maelstrom*, 165.

CHAPTER SEVEN: FRENCH LICK TO HALIFAX

1. *Martin Hogan, *Hooker's Horse Marines: The Adventures of the 3rd Indiana Cavalry* (Boston: James P. McPhee Company, 1882), 121–23. Hogan would stay with the CIB after the war and eventually rise to become the Director of Special Operations in the Bureau, succeeding Cline after the latter's death in 1882.

2. *"The Copperhead Assassin: Big Jim Smoke," *Harper's Weekly*, April 18, 1864.

3. Kenneth Bourne, "British Preparations for War With the North, 1861–1862," *English Historical Review* 76, no. 301 (1961): 619.

4. The Canadas (Lower Canada and Upper Canada) refer to present-day Quebec and Ontario, respectively; the Maritimes refer to Nova Scotia,

New Brunswick, and Prince Edward Island. In 1840 the British Parliament passed the Act of Union (1840) that merged Upper and Lower Canada to form the Province of United Canada.

5. Bourne, "British Preparations," 615.

6. David Pam, *The Royal Small Arms Factory Enfield and Its Workers* (published by the author, 1998), 50–58. Between 1859 and 1864, the factory produced 365,779 rifled muskets of the 1853 pattern. Private British arms manufacturers quickly followed the mass-production model at Enfield.

7. "The Gun—Rifled Ordnance: Armstrong," Royal New Zealand Artillery Old Comrades' Association, http://riv.co.nz/rnza/hist/gun/rifled3.htm.

8. A British or Canadian cavalry troop numbered about forty men.

9. Desmond Morton, *A Military History of Canada* (Toronto: McClelland and Stewart Ltd., 1999), 87–88.

10. Peter G. Tsouras, ed., *The Greenhill Dictionary of Military Quotations* (London: Greenhill Books, 2000) p. 339. Cromwell made the statement in September 1643 in a letter to Sir William Springe.

11. Mark Grimsley, "Net Assessment During the Trent Affair," http://people.cohums.ohio-state.edu/grimsley1/h582/2001/trent.htm.

12. *William R. Plimpton, *Staff Notes: The Wolseley North American Staff Lectures, 1863* (Toronto: The Defence Staff, 1914), 23–32.

13. *Ian Alan Tomlinson, "The Crown Subsidy of 1862 and the Canadian Militia Expansion," *Imperial Defence Journal*, December 1912, 45.

14. Ian W. Toll, *Six Frigates: The Epic History of the Founding of the U.S. Navy* (New York: W. W. Norton & Company, 2006), 352.

15. Regis A. Courtemanche, *No Need for Glory: The British Navy in American Waters, 1860–1864* (Annapolis, MD: Naval Institute Press, 1977), 129.

16. Grimsley, "Net Assessment," 5–6. "In December 1861 the Royal Navy boasted of 339 ships (324,063 tons), 61,342 men, and 5,304 guns, augmented by a naval reserve that could have been readied for maritime duties. The United States Navy, by contrast, possessed only 264 vessels (218,016 tons), 22,000 men, and 2,557 guns. More importantly, the Union Navy had only a few ships capable of joining a line of battle; most of those 264 vessels were simply hastily-converted merchantmen pressed into blockade duty and mounting only a few guns each."

17. Courtemanche, *No Need for Glory*, 163–66.

18. Ibid., 164.

19. Ibid., 166.

20. J. J. Colledge, *Ships of the Royal Navy: The Complete Record of All Fighting Ships of the Royal Navy From the Fifteenth Century to the Present* (London: Greenhill Books, 2003), 188, 228, 284.

21. Courtemanche, *No Need for Glory*, 56.

22. Grimsley, "Net Assessment," 6.

23. *Basil Hall, *The Battles for North American Waters: Recollections of a Flag Lieutenant* (London: Collins, 1935, reprint of the private 1875 edition), 128–30.

24. Toll, *Six Frigates*, 459.
25. *Hall, *The Battles for North American Waters*, 132.
26. Edwin Fishel, *The Secret War for the Union: The Untold Story of Military Intelligence in the Civil War* (Boston: Houghton Mifflin Company, 1996), 84, 292.
27. C. Van Santvoord, *The One Hundred and Twentieth Regiment, New York State Volunteers: A Narrative of Its Services in the War for the Union* (Cornwallville, NY: Hope Farm Press, 1983), 235.
28. Callaway to Rosecrans, August 22, 1863, Military Record File of Lt. Col. James E. Callaway, National Archives.
29. Robert V. Bruce, *Lincoln and the Tools of War* (Indianapolis: The Bobbs-Merrill Company, Inc., 1956), 254–56.

CHAPTER EIGHT: BATTLE AT MOELFRE BAY
1. *H. Emerson Harper, *Voyage of Destiny: USS Gettysburg and the Beginning of the Great War* (New York: The Century Company, 1903), 158. *Henry Porter, *The Battle of Moelfre Bay* (New York: D. Appleton, 1868), 130.
2. *James Bulloch, *The Fuse of War: The CSS North Carolina* (London: John Murray, 1875), 142.
3. *Roswell Hawks Lamson, *Into the Maelstrom: A Memoir of the Gettysburg* (New York: George H. Doran Company, 1876), 105.
4. *Bulloch, *The Fuse of War*, 144.
5. *Henry Adams, "The Case for the *Gettysburg*," *New York Tribune*, September 19, 1863. The owner and editor of the *Tribune* was Horace Greeley, who encouraged Henry Adams to write what was to become the definitive defense of the actions of the *Gettysburg* in the seizure of the *North Carolina* in British waters. It was widely circulated in Europe, where its conclusions did much to sway opinion in favor of the United States. It was widely supported and praised by Russian Foreign Minister Gorchakov.
6. *Bulloch, *The Fuse of War*, 148. Bulloch would be later exchanged and arrive in Richmond aboard a British warship to a hero's welcome and parade. He would later command the first warship built with the full approval of the British government for the Confederacy, the CSS *Robert E. Lee*.
7. *Adams, "The Case for the *Gettysburg*." The papers were indeed a diplomatic goldmine, especially Bulloch's reference to a "private but most reliable source" in Whitehall. Unfortunately, the war swept ahead of the publication of these documents, but they did much to affect opinion in the rest of Europe and South America.
8. *Lamson, *Into the Maelstrom*, 127.
9. Robert J. Schneller, Jr., *A Quest for Glory: A Biography of Rear Admiral John A. Dahlgren* (Annapolis, MD: Naval Institute Press, 1996), 105.
10. J. J. Colledge, *Ships of the Royal Navy: The Complete Record of All Fighting Ships of the Royal Navy From the Fifteenth Century to the Present* (London: Greenhill Books, 2003), 14, 142.

11. *Jacob P. Eldridge, *A Marine Aboard the* Gettysburg (New York: The Century Company, 1888), 199.

12. Regis A. Courtemanche, *No Need of Glory: The British Navy in American Waters, 1860–1864* (Annapolis, MD: Naval Institute Press, 1977), 163.

13. *Charles Francis Adams, Jr., *The Life of Charles Francis Adams* (Boston, 1890), 342.

14. Adams to Russell, September 5, 1863, *Foreign Relations of the United States* ("Papers Relating to Foreign Affairs Accompanying the Annual Message of the President) (FR–63, vol. 1, 367.).

15. *Mary K. Doering, *John Bright: Member From America* (New York: Regency Press, 1975), 228. *Charles Francis Adams, letter to Charles Adams, Jr., September 15, 1863, in *The Papers and Correspondence of Charles Francis Adams* (Boston: Concord Press, 1892), 293.

16. *"Dreadful Battle at Moelfre Bay, Americans Attack, British Ships Lost, Suvivors Ashore," *North Wales Gazette*, September 5, 1863. This article cited several references of the consideration with which the survivors were treated by the crew of the *Kearsarge*, their immediate landing at a small Welsh port of Amlwch, and the prompt provision of medical care provided the wounded.

17. *Charles Francis Adams, letter to Charles Adams, Jr., 396–405. *Charles Francis Adams, "Report to the Secretary of State of the Actions of the USS *Gettysburg* and *Kearsarge*, September 4–5, 1863," *Congressional Record* 5 (1863): 472–505. *Austen David Layard, *Origins of the American War: View From the Foreign Office* (London: Holmes & Sons, Ltd, 1886), 257. There are such significant differences in the accounts of Adams and Layard that one wonders if they were attending the same meeting. Russell's report to the cabinet included only a summary of the conversation and omitted Adams's more pointed comments.

18. *Ralph W. Eddington, *Winslow of the* Kearsarge: *Hero of Moelfre Bay* (Annapolis, MD: Naval Academy Press, 1925), 232.

19. *Lamson, *Into the Maelstrom*, 183.

CHAPTER NINE: PURSUIT INTO THE UPPER BAY

1. "New Alliance Cemented," *New York Herald*, October 2, 1863; and "Our Russian Visitors," *New York Times*, October 11, 1863.

2. "The Russian Empire and the American Republic Against the Western European Powers," *New York Herald*, October 7, 1863.

3. "A Russian Fleet Coming Into Our Harbor," *New York Times*, September 24, 1863, 2; "Our Naval Visitors," *New York Times*, September 26, 1863, 2; "The Russian Ball," *New York Herald*, November 6, 1863, 10.

4. "The Russian Ball," *New York Herald*, November 6, 1863.

5. "The Russian Padre," *New York Times*, September 27, 1863, 5.

6. "The Russian Guests," *New York Times*, October 3, 1863, 2.

7. *"WAR! U.S. Victory in Naval Battle off Welsh Coast; British and American Ships Sunk," *New York Tribune*, September 17, 1863, 1.

8. *William H. Seward, *The Diplomacy of the Great War* (New York: E. P. Dodd & Company, 1872), 152.

9. Ulysses S. Grant, *Personal Memoirs of U. S. Grant, Selected Letters, 1839–1865* (New York: The Modern Library, 1990), 384–85. "At Vicksburg 31,600 prisoners were surrendered together with 172 cannon, about 60,000 muskets and a large amount of ammunition. The small-arms of the enemy were far superior to the bulk of ours. . . .The enemy had generally new arms, which had run the blockade and were of uniform caliber. After the surrender, I authorized all colonels whose regiments were armed with inferior muskets, to place them in the stack of captured arms and replace them with the latter."

10. *Michael D. Wilmoth, ed., *Reports of the Central Information Bureau During the Great War*, vol. 1 (Washington, DC: U.S. Government Printing Office, 1888), 35–37.

11. Robert V. Bruce, *Lincoln and the Tools of War* (Indianapolis: The Bobbs-Merrill Company, Inc., 1956), 264.

12. *Martin P. Anderson, "The Coffee Mill Gun in the Great War," *Harper's Weekly*, July 15, 1869, 2; Bruce, *Lincoln and the Tools of War,* 263. In August 1863, the Spencer Company reported that it had two thousand of its repeaters on hand for immediate delivery. Ripley had been sabotaging orders from Spencer but was retired at this time. The repeaters were immediately ordered and were on hand at the time of the cabinet meeting.

13. John W. Busey and David G. Martin, *Regimental Strengths and Losses at Gettysburg* (Hightstown, NJ: Longstreet House, 1994) 241–63. Maine's contingent in the Army of the Potomac suffered 27.9 percent casualties at Gettysburg.

14. *Telegram from Sharpe to Rosecrans, September 15, 1863, National Archives, M504 Unbound, Roll 303. It is one of the ironies of the war that Rosecrans had put such confidence in Sharpe's message but underestimated the time in which Longstreet would arrive. He thought he would fight and beat Bragg before "Old Pete" arrived.

15. Peter Cozzens, *This Terrible Sound: The Battle of Chickamauga* (Urbana: University of Illinois Press, 1992), 376, 393.

16. Homer, *The Iliad*, trans. Robert Fagles (New York: Viking Penguin, 1990), 9.1–8.

17. "Report of Maj. James E. Callaway, Twenty-First Illinois Infantry, Commanding Eighty-First Indiana Infantry," September 28, 1863, *The War of the Rebellion: A Compilation of the Official Records of the Union and Confederate Armies* (hereafter *OR*), vol. 30, part I (Washington, DC: U.S. Government Printing Office, 1890), 525.

18. Ibid., 526.

19. Jerry Korn and the Editors of Time-Life, *The Fight for Chattanooga: Chickamauga to Missionary Ridge* (Alexandria, VA: Time-Life, 1985), 72.

20. J. J. Colledge, *Ships of the Royal Navy: The Complete Record of All Fighting Ships of the Royal Navy From the Fifteenth Century to the Present* (London:

Greenhill Books, 2003), 338. *Undaunted* measured 250 by 52 feet and 4,020 tons compared to *Kearsarge* at 201 by 33 feet and 1,550 tons.

21. *"Sea Fight of the USS *Kearsarge* and HMS *Undaunted*," *New York Tribune*, September 17, 1863, 1.

22. Albert A. Woldman, *Lincoln and the Russians* (Cleveland: The World Publishing Company, 1952), 140. *Harper's Weekly*, September 17, 1863, 661–62.

23. Thomas L. Harris, *The Trent Affair* (1896), 208–10. *Stefan Lisovsky, "Voyage to America," *Morskoi Sbornik*, December 20, 1870, 37–38.

24. *Henry Adams, *The Russian Alliance in the Great War* (New York: The McClure Company, 1880), 132.

25. M. Bowden, *The Life and Archaeological Work of Lt. General Augustus Henry Lane Fox Pitt Rivers DCL FRS FSA* (Cambridge: Cambridge University Press, 1991), 7.

26. James D. Horan, *Confederate Agent* (New York: Fairfax Press, 1954) 107.

27. *Edgar L. Steinhalter, "The Davis-Grenfell-Wolseley Conspiracy," *Midwest Historical Journal*, vol. 87, 89–93.

28. *OR*, vol. 41, part 1 (Washington, DC: U.S. Government Printing Office, 1890), 151.

29. *Alfred Thayer Mahan, *Gunsmoke Across the Upper Bay: The Battle for New York* (Boston: Concord Press, 1890), 199–205. This volume was the first of five in which Thayer wrote the definitive accounts of the major naval battles of the Great War.

30. Colledge, *Ships of the Royal Navy*, 39, 328. The *Dauntless* was a small, older frigate launched in 1847 at 2,520 tons and measuring only 219 by 40 feet and armed with four 10-inch rifles, two 68-pounders, and eighteen 32-pounders. By contrast the *Topaze* was launched in 1858 at 3,915 tons and measured 235 by 50 feet and was initially armed with thirty 8-inch guns, one 68-pounder, and twenty 32-pounders. By this time, each ship was armed with at least one Armstrong gun.

31. *John L. Hunter, Kearsarge *Gunner: The Life of John W. Dempsey* (Cleveland, OH: Ohio River University Press, 1986), 89.

32. *Paul R. Catlett, *Winslow and Lamson: Saviors of New York* (Boston: A. M. Thayer and Company, 1890), 262–65.

33. *John Welbore Sunderland Spencer, *Pursuit of the* Kearsarge (London: Longmans, Green, Reader and Dyer, 1872), 297–305. This book was Spencer's public explanation of why he did not ensure the destruction of the *Kearsarge*. A court of inquiry charged him with "failing to do his utmost." He was tried by court-martial, but in the face of both public outcry and the Queen's disapproval of the proceedings, he was acquitted. He never held command again.

34. *Winslow Carter, *Battle of the Upper Bay* (New York: The Century Company, 1895), 216.

35. *Lyons to Russell, September 24, 1863, in William Delancey, *The Diplomacy of Lord Lyons*, vol. 2 (London: Sampson Low, 1913), 395.

36. *John W. Wilson, *William H. Seward in War and Peace* (New York: The McClure Company, 1892), 187.
37. *Cassius Clay, *Forging the Alliance: My Two Years in Russia* (Lexington: Blue Grass University Press, 1932 — reprint of the 1869 edition), 278. News of the battle, deemed a Russian naval victory over the British because of the sinking of *Dauntless* and *Gannet*, sent Russia wild with joy as the church bells rang from the Baltic to the Pacific. Revenge for the humiliations of the Crimean War seemed at hand. Ambassador Clay was cheered by throngs everywhere he went in St. Petersburg. Lisovsky was promoted and ennobled. For once the Russian Imperial Navy had put the Army, its immense sister service, in the shade.
38. *Andrei N. Medvedev, *The Russo-American Alliance in the World War* (St. Petersburg: Kronstadt Publishers, 1880), 136.

CHAPTER TEN: A RAIN OF BLOWS

1. Http://royalengineers.ca/Bazalgette.html. Bazalgette had fought with distinction in the Anglo-French punitive expedition against China in 1857, as had Wolseley. The family name was probably pronounced "Basiljet." The Pig War was the dispute that arose over San Juan Island between modern British Columbia and Washington State in 1859 that resulted in a military confrontation between Britain and the United States. An American shot a pig belonging to the Hudson Bay Company that was rooting in his garden on the island. The British threatened to arrest him, and the local Americans appealed for help to the Army, which sent a company of infantry commanded by Capt. George S. Pickett. The British sent three warships. Neither side would back down, and Pickett became a national hero. Cooler heads eventually prevailed to defuse the issue. The British built the "English Camp" on the island. Bazalgette commanded the Royal Marine Light Infantry Company in garrison. There was so little of a military nature to occupy him there that he designed and built a perfect replica of an English garden for his wife and children.
2. Angus Konstam, *American Civil War Fortifications (1): Coastal Brick and Stone Forts* (London: Osprey, 2003), 60.
3. *"Bazalgette Mentioned in Dispatches for Seizing Fort Gorges," *Halifax Gazette*, October 8, 1863. Halifax took great pride in the feat of its native son, who was born there while his father served as adjutant general of Nova Scotia.
4. *Field Marshal Viscount Wolseley, *First Blow: The British 1863 Campaign in North America* (London: Collins, reprint of 1901 edition), 101.
5. Kenneth Bourne, "British Preparations for War With the North, 1861–1862," *English Historical Review* 76, no. 301 (1961): 631.
6. Joseph Lehmann, *The Model Major-General: A Biography of Field-Marshal Lord Wolseley* (Boston: Houghton Mifflin Company, 1964), 30.
7. Bourne, "British Preparations for War," 631.

8. *William F. Clarkson, *The Life of a British Adventurer: George Grenfell* (New York: The McClure Company, 1904), 382. This account comes from the recollections of John Hines.

9. John W. Busey and David G. Martin, *Regimental Strengths and Losses at Gettysburg* (Hightstown, NJ: Longstreet House, 1994), 241–63. At Gettysburg, of 3,721 present for duty on 30 June, Maine lost 130 killed, 649 wounded, and 238 missing for a total of 1,017.

10. *John C. Miller, "The Initiative That Saved Portland," *North American Historical Review* 21, no. 24 (1922): 43.

11. *Quincy M. Adams, *The First Battle of Portland* (New York: Dodd, Meade, 1877), 45. Chamberlain: 10th, 16th, 17th, 19th, and 20th Maine Volunteer Infantry and Maine Light 2nd Battery; Harper: 3rd, 4th, 5th, 6th, and 7th Maine Volunteer Infantry and Maine Light 5th Battery. Reserve: 1st Maine Cavalry and Maine Light 6th Battery.

12. Dow was a Quaker, tanner, and lumber magnate. He was also an ardent abolitionist, women's suffragist and, most important, prohibitionist. As mayor of Portland in 1851 (and again in 1855) he passed the "Maine Law," the nation's first prohibition law. Twelve states followed suit with their own prohibition laws — basically using the same wording as Dow's — within a decade. The Volstead Act, which outlawed alcohol nationally in 1919, was also based on Dow's Maine Law.

13. *"Massacre in Portland: Slaughter of Women and Children at the Train Station," *New York Tribune*, October 1, 1863, 1.

14. Sylvanus Urban, *The Gentleman's Magazine and Historical Review* XIL (January–June 1862): 213.

15. *"Langely of the 16th Foot to Receive Posthumous VC," *Edinburgh Disptach*, March 5, 1863, 6.

16. *Joshua Lawrence Chamberlain, "The Fight for the Portland Docks," September 30, 1882, speech on the anniversary of the First Battle of Portland, given in Portland, *Portland Intelligencer*, October 1, 1882, 2.

17. *Arthur P. Valentine, "The Assault on Camp Morton," *Historical Review of Indiana* 23 (October 12, 1899): 112.

18. Field Marshal Viscount Wolseley, *The Story of a Soldier's Life* (Westminster: Archibald Constable & Co. Ltd., 1903), 322–23.

19. Peter G. Tsouras, ed., *The Greenhill Dictionary of Military Quotations* (London: Greenhill Books, 2000), 266.

20. *George Denison, *History of the Canadian Armed Forces* (Toronto: St. George's Press, 1890) 176. These Canadian battalions had only recently been independent companies but were formed into battalions in the months before the war and given intensive training with their British mentor battalion, the 62nd Foot. Long-range planning had not anticipated their formation before late 1866, but Wolseley's emphatic advocacy of their immediate activation was decisive in convincing Lieutenant General Williams to apply sufficient pressure on Canadian authorities to approve and even finance such a move. It was one of the few remarkable examples of civilian forethought on military matters in Canadian history.

21. "British Army Nicknames—AWI" at http://ageod.com. The 62nd was also known as "the Springers" from their service as light infantry in 1776 in the War of American Independence. Arthur Swinson, ed., A *Register of the Regiments and Corps of the British Army: The Ancestry of the Regiments and Corps of the Regular Establishment* (London: The Archive Press, 1972).

22. *Daring Raid on Camp Morton," *Indianapolis Star*, October 1, 1863. Jeremiah Wilkins, *Copperhead Rebellion: The Democrat Stab in the Back* (Chicago: Prairie State Press, 1870), 92. Of the force of 211 Copperheads, eighty-two were killed and fifty-seven were captured, of whom twenty-seven were wounded. Another thirty-two were captured in the days after the attack. Cline's only comment on the high proportion of Copperheads killed to wounded was that "it was not due to their courage." Of the prisoners in the camp, forty-seven were killed and 180 were wounded.

23. *Wilson Eaton, "The First Maine Cavalry at the First Battle of Portland," *Journal of the Historical Society of Maine* 12 (October 2, 1915): 42.

24. *Chamberlain, "The Fight for the Portland Docks."

25. *"Epic Charge of the Splashers Drives Americans From the Field," *London Intelligencer*, October 9, 1863, 1.

26. *Joshua Lawrence Chamberlain, "Honor to Honor," speech on Memorial Day 1880, Portland, Maine. Chamberlain never lost his admiration for the imperial infantry, and his evocative and chivalrous description of the bayonet fight was proudly incorporated by the 62nd Foot as part of its official history.

27. *Morris Atherton, *Chamberlain: Hero of Portland* (New York: C. L. Webster, 1885), 177.

28. *"Albany Burned to the Ground," *New York Tribune*, October 2, 1863, 1. "Thousand Flee Ahead as British Ravage Upstate," *New York Herald*, October 2, 1863, 1.

29. *Sir Rupert Jackson, "The British Forces in the Great War in North America," *Military Historical Review* 10 (1983): 27–30.

30. Kevin E. O'Brien, ed., *My Life in the Irish Brigade: The Civil War Memoirs of Private William McCarter, 116th Pennsylvania Infantry* (Campbell, CA: Savas Publishing Company, 1996), 70–71.

31. *"Meagher's Speech Draws Thousands to Enlist," *New York Tribune*, October 2, 1863, 2.

CHAPTER ELEVEN: TREASON, FROGS, AND IRONCLADS

1. *John R. Clinton, *Edwin Stanton and the Crisis of 1863* (New York: Van Nostrand, 1877), 45. Clinton makes the point that the closer the fighting or direct threat to Washington got, the more nervous and panicky Stanton became. A case in point was the threat of the CSS *Virginia* in April 1862 when Stanton was so distraught that he was going to block the navigation of the Potomac with a barrier of stones, an idea that Secretary of the Navy Welles put a stop to.

2. Peter Cozzens, *The Shipwreck of Their Hopes: The Battles for Chattanooga* (Urbana: The University of Illinois Press, 1994), 2.

3. Gideon Welles, *Diary of Gideon Welles: Secretary of the Navy Under Lincoln and Johnson* (Boston and New York: Houghton Mifflin Company, 1911), 443.

4. *Charles Dana, *Greatness in Crisis: Abraham Lincoln* (Philadelphia: D. Appleton, 1880), 93–95.

5. *William Taylor, *Lee and the Battle of Washington* (Richmond: Cavalier Press, 1885), 93.

6. *Theodore Roosevelt, Jr., ed., *The War Diary of Theodore Roosevelt* (New York: Charles L. Webster, 1890), 5. Roosevelt senior's war record and subsequent but brief political career left his sickly son in the father's shadow for the rest of his life.

7. *The Gentleman's Magazine and Historical Review* 12 (January–June 1862): 211–12. This issue listed the strength upon embarkation for Canada of the Grenadier Guards (874), the Scots Fusilier Guards (919), the names of the brigade staff, as well as the strength of the 2/16th Foot (901), the 18th Co. Royal Engineers (120), and a military train (317).

8. *Thaddeus Lowe, *Phoenix: The Rebirth of the Balloon Corps* (Boston: Houghton, Osgood, 1990), 37–40.

9. *Michael D. Wilmoth, *School of Intelligence: History of the CIB's Academy* (Washington, DC: U.S. Government Printing Office, 1896), 11. Wilmoth would stay with the CIB after the war. He rose quickly to become Director of Analysis, Dean of the CIB Academy, and eventually filled Sharpe's shoes, succeeding McEntee in 1886.

10. *"Our French Allies Arrive," *Brownsville Gazette*, October 5, 1863, 1. "God Bless the French!" *Austin Dispatch,* October 6, 1863, 1.

11. *Edwin Swinton, *Smiles and Lies: The Franco-Confederate Alliance in the Great* War (London: Ballard & White Co. Ltd., 1910), 89.

12. Dean B. Mahin, *One War at a Time: The International Dimensions of the American Civil War* (Washington, DC: Brassey's, Inc., 1999), 136.

13. Ibid., 223–24.

14. *Pierre de Lury, *Bazaine: The Duke of New Orleans* (New York: The Century Company, 1896), 47.

15. *Abraham Lincoln to Admiral Dahlgren, October 2, 1863, *The Correspondence of Admiral John A. Dahlgren* (Annapolis, MD: Naval Academy Press, 1888), 377. Dahlgren would always treasure this letter in which Lincoln gave an intimate and tender account of Ulric's condition and hopes for recovery.

16. Rear-Admiral Dahlgren, *Memoir of Ulric Dahlgren* (Philadelphia: J. B. Lippincott & Co., 1872), 178.

17. *OR Navies*, series 1, vol. 15 (Washington, DC: U.S. Government Printing Office, 1902), 26–27. These included the 2,592-ton double-turretted *Onondaga* (2 x XV-inch guns and 2 x 8-inch rifles), and two *Canonicus* class ships, the *Canonicus* and *Tecumseh* at 2,100 tons (2 x XV-inch guns), and the *Passaic* class *Sangamon* (one XI-inch and one XV-inch gun), which was at Newport News at the time.

18. *OR Navies*, xv–xvi, 7, 113–14.

19. *Jackie Fisher, "Adm. Milne's North American and West Indies Station in the Great War," *Journal of the Royal Navy* 24, no. 11 (December 1885): 50–52.

20. Benson J. Lossing, *The Hudson: From the Wilderness to the Sea* (New York: Virtue and Yorston, 1866).

21. Robert V. Bruce, *Lincoln and the Tools of War* (Indianapolis: The Bobbs-Merrill Company, Inc., 1956), 187–88.

22. *Hiram Van Renssalaer, *The Burning of Upstate New York: British Depredations and Atrocities in the Great War* (New York: Smith & Brenner, Inc., 1871), 107–9.

23. *OR*, series 1, vol. 31, part 1 (Washington, DC: U.S. Government Printing Office, 1890), 801. Hooker's command at this point comprised 15,897 men. Both XI and XII Corps had only two of their normal three divisions.

24. Peter G. Tsouras, ed., *The Greenhill Dictionary of Military Quotations* (London: Greenhill Books, 2000), 478.

25. *OR*, series 1, vol. 29, part 1 (Washington, DC: U.S. Government Printing Office, 1881), 226. At this time, Meade's Army of the Potomac consisted of the I, II, III, and V Corps. The XI and XII Corps had already been detached for service in the relief of Chattanooga and then diverted to form the Army of the Hudson. The VI Corps had been detached for the relief of Portland. Counting cavalry and artillery also sent, that left Meade with barely sixty thousand men.

CHAPTER TWELVE: COLD SPRING AND CROSSING THE BAR

1. *"Terrified Refugees Pour Into the City," *New York Tribune*, October 5, 1863, 1. In the few days since Albany had fallen, more than three hundred river craft had fled to the city loaded with refugees to join the thousands more who came by train or wagon. Mayor George Opdyke rallied the Tammany Hall organization to find accommodations for what was estimated as 120,000 people. He was quoted as saying that "upstate is pouring into the City."

2. *Michael R. Flannery, "Meagher's Defense of the Cold Spring Foundry," *Journal of the Great War* 42 (July 18, 1975): 22.

3. *"Goddess of Erin Sees Meagher Off at the Docks," *New York Herald*, October 7, 1863, 4. The story of Libby Meagher at the docks became one of the great legends of New York City. A statue in bronze exists today at the New York Harbor Authority headquarters showing Libby rushing forward with the flag.

4. *John R. Kennedy, *Meagher of the Sword* (New York: Charles B. Richardson, 1872), 173–76.

5. *Ibid., 180.

6. *Arthur C. Wallace, *The Hudson Valley Campaign of 1863* (New York: Wilson & Hurlow, 1949), 129. The enemy detachment consisted of the 3rd Company, Scotts Fusilier Guards, and the 1st Company of the 3rd Battalion Victoria Volunteer Rifles of Montreal.

7. Mark K. Ragan, *Union and Confederate Submarine Warfare in the Civil War* (New York: Da Capo Press, 1990), 134–37.

8. Ian W. Toll, *Six Frigates: The Epic History of the Founding of the U.S. Navy* (New York: W. W. Norton & Company, 2006), 414.

9. Often incorrectly referred to as the "Channel Fleet," the Channel Squadron became a permanent formation in 1858 whose primary mission was to defend the British Isles from the French Navy. London *Times*, April 13, 1858, citing the House of Commons' Naval Estimates of April 12.

10. London *Times*, July 8 and 31, 1863. The *Times* listed the following ships: the screw iron frigates HMS *Warrior, Black Prince, Resistance, Defence;* the screw ironclad (over wooden hull) frigate *Royal Oak;* and the wooden screw frigates *Emerald* and *Liverpool,* the latter of which had been sunk in the Battle of Moelfre Bay. J. J. Colledge, *Ships of the Royal Navy: The Complete Record of All Fighting Ships of the Royal Navy From the Fifteenth Century to the Present* (London: Greenhill Books, 2003), 51, 95, 272, 352. Armament of *Black Prince* consisted of ten Armstrong 110-pounders (7-inch), twenty-six 68-pounders, and four Armstrong 70-pounders. The armament of the *Resistance* consisted of seven Armstrong 110-pounders, ten 68-pounders, and two 32-pounders. The *Defence* was similarly armed.

11. Angus Konstam, *Duel of the Ironclads: USS* Monitor *& CSS* Virginia *at Hampton Roads, 1862* (London: Osprey, 2003), 93

12. James L. Nelson, *Reign of Iron: The Story of the First Battling Ironclads, the Monitor and the Merrimac* (New York: William Morrow, 2002), 173.

13. Eugene B. Canfield, "Civil War Ordnance," *Dictionary of American Fighting Ships,* vol. 3 (Washington, DC: Office of the Chief of Naval Operations, Naval History Division, 1968), 6, 12.

14. Vol. 2, Entry 99, Record Group 74, National Archives, cited in Robert J. Schneller, Jr. "'A State of War Is a Most Unfavorable Period for Experiments': John A. Dahlgren and U.S. Naval Ordnance Innovation During the American Civil War," (monograph) U.S. Naval Historical Center; John Dahlgren, "Report to the Navy Department," November 22, 1862, box 27, Library of Congress.

15. Robert J. Schneller, Jr., *A Quest for Glory: A Biography of Rear Admiral John A. Dahlgren* (Annapolis, MD: Naval Institute Press, 1996), 204, 226.

16. Robert M. Browning, Jr., *Success Is All That Was Expected: The South Atlantic Blockading Squadron During the Civil War* (Washington, DC: Potomac Books, 2002), 206.

17. Schneller, "'A State of War.'"

18. William H. Roberts, USS New Ironsides *in the Civil War* (Annapolis, MD: US Naval Institute Press, 1999), 70–71.

19. London *Times*, July 8, 1863. Wainwright's previous command was the HMS *Shannon,* which steamed in the Second Division.

20. *Nigel Haythorne, ed., *The Papers of Adm. Alexander Milne in the American War* (London: Albright & Midgely, 1922), 103–110.

21. Only the *Powhatan* was a side-wheel ship; the rest were all screw driven. *OR Navies,* series 1, vol. 16, *South Atlantic Blockading Squadron From October*

1, 1863 to September 30, 1864 (Washington, DC: U.S. Government Printing Office, 1902), 7.

22. *Alfred Thayer Mahan, *Crossing the T at Charleston: Dahlgren and the Revolution in Naval Tactics* (New York: The Neale Publishing Co., 1895), 163.

23. OR Navies, series 2, vol. 1 (Washington, DC: U.S. Government Printing Office, 1921), 7, 113–14.

24. *Mahan, *Crossing the T,* 166. These gunboats were the *Seneca, Conemaugh, Mahaska, Sonoma, Ottawa, Cimarron, Paul Jones,* and *Unadilla.* The gunboats *Chippewa* and *Nipsic,* Port Royal guardships, were accompanying the three monitors from there. They would add another sixteen IX-inch and nine XI-inch Dahlgren guns to the fight.

25. Both of the following sources cite the size of the crews by ship. Colledge, *Ships of the Royal Navy,* 51, 95, 272, 352; http://pdavis.nlMidVic Ships.php?page=1, or Ships of the Mid-Victorian Navy. This website offers a mass of detail, including the size of crews and names of captains. Paul H. Silverstone, *Civil War Navies 1855–1883* (New York: Routledge, 2006), 16.

26. Thucydides, trans. Richard Crawley, *The Peloponnesian War* (New York: Everyman's Class Library, 1914).

27. Alfred Thayer Mahan, *From Sail to Steam* (New York: Harper, 1907), cited in Peter G. Tsouras, ed., *The Book of Military Quotations* (St. Paul, MN: Zenith Press, 2005), 238.

28. "The Hellenic Crisis from the Point of View of Constitutional and International Law," *The American Journal of International Law* 11 (1917): 60–61.

29. *Ulric Dahlgren, ed., *The Letters of Rear-Admiral John A. Dahlgren* (Philadelphia: J. B. Lippincott, 1885), 335.

30. *Lafayette A. Rhett, *Beauregard and the Defense of Charleston* (Charleston: Charleston University Press, 1976), 256. It is a major controversy of the war how much effect the entry of Ingraham's two ironclads would have had on the outcome of this battle.

31. Colledge, *Ships of the Royal Navy,* 51, 95, 272, 352. The entry for each ship in this source lists the number and type of guns. http://www.pdavis.nl/ShowBiog/php?id+760. Chamberlain's previous command was HMS *Racoon* in the First Division.

32. *Julian Corbett, *The Battle of the Bar and Its Effect Upon Naval Strategy* (London: Wilson & Sons Ltd, 1896) p. 76.

33. OR Navies, series 2, vol. 1, 51, 104, 159, 172, 234. Silverstone, *Civil War Navies,* 16. The *Wabash* also had a crew of 640, almost 30 percent of Dahlgren's fighting line strength.

34. *Mahan, *Crossing the T at Charleston,* 172. Dahlgren's tactics at Charleston were the beginning of the era in naval history and tactics in which the ability to concentrate a superior weight of firepower on an enemy by sailing perpendicular to his advancing columns became paramount. Corbett, *The Battle of the Bar,* 83–87. The conclusions reached on this battle

by Mahan and Corbett were remarkably similar, and those hoping for a transatlantic duel between naval strategists were to be disappointed.

35. *Charles H. Moody, *Death of the HMS* St. George *and Death of an Era* (London: Baker & Windemeer, Ltd.), 176.
36. Colledge, *Ships of the Royal Navy*, 96.
37. *R. B. Casterbridge, "*Chesapeake* Avenged! The *Atlanta* versus the *Shannon*," *Journal of Naval History* 17 (June 23, 1963): 35.
38. *Andrew Cochrane, *Sailor of the Queen: The Life of HRH Alfred* (London: Gossett & Sons, Ltd., 1912), 141.
39. *Ulric Dahlgren, *Victory at Charleston: Admiral Dahlgren and the South Atlantic Blockading Squadron* (Boston: Appleton, 1880), 301–2. Dahlgren's account is unabashed hero worship of his father both as a naval commander and as a man.
40. Unidentified newspaper article entitled, "The Warrior," dated May 11, 1861, found in the Dahlgren Papers, Library of Congress.
41. *William R. Thomas, *With Colonel Dahlgren and the Marines: Adventures on the* New Ironsides *at the Battle of Charleston* (New York: The Century Company, 1888), 206.
42. *Ulric Dahlgren, New Ironsides *and* Black Prince: *Duel of the Titans* (New York: The Sheldon Company, 1879) p. 229.
43. *Wilfred C. Baimbridge, *HMS* Black Prince *at Charleston* (London: Tinsdale & Williams, 1892), 324.
44. London *Times*, July 8, 1863.
45. *Mahan, *Crossing the T at Charleston*, 240.
46. *Aaron C. Davis, *Sinking the* Black Prince: *First Victory of the Submersible Service* (Annapolis, MD: Naval Academy Press, 2004), 192.
47. *Duncan Ingraham, "The Loss of the *Resistance* in Charleston Harbor," *Historical Society of the South* 4 (January 1876): 83–85. Chance had it that the *Resistance* sank at Ager Dock, which had a depth of twenty-six feet. The ship's twenty-five-foot draft meant that the ship merely settled on the bottom and did not go under; its upper decks were still above water. Nevertheless, the *Resistance* was out of the war. http://www.colonialwargames.org.uk/Miscellany/Warships/Ironclads/EIroncladsRN.htm. The draft of the *Warrior* class (the *Warrior* and *Black Prince*) ships was twenty-six feet and that of the *Defence* class (the *Defence* and *Resistance*) twenty-five feet.

APPENDIX A
1. Personnel of the trains were not Maine troops but drawn from the logistics establishment of the Army of the Potomac.
2. John W. Busey and David G. Martin, *Regimental Strengths and Losses at Gettysburg* (Hightstown, NJ: Longstreet House, 1982), 241, 243, 246, 248, 251, 255, 259, 261, 262, 263. The strength of the Maine Division on arrival at Portland is calculated by subtracting Gettysburg losses and then allowing for 50 percent of losses to be returned to duty either through recovery of wounds or missing returning to the ranks.

ABOUT THE AUTHOR

A former U.S. Army officer, Peter G. Tsouras is an intelligence analyst, a military historian, and the author or editor of two dozen works of military history and alternate history, including *Gettysburg: An Alternate History*, *Dixie Victorious: An Alternate History of the Civil War*, *Disaster at D-Day: The Germans Defeat the Allies, June 1944*, and *Military Quotations from the Civil War: In the Words of the Commanders*. Many of his books have been selected by the History Book Club and the Military Book Club as primary selections and have been translated into numerous languages. A regular guest on the History Channel and similar venues in Britain and Canada, Mr. Tsouras is an analyst for the Defense Intelligence Agency and lives in Alexandria, Virginia.